CRITICAL ACCLAIM FOR
THOMAS WHARTON AND *SALAMANDER*

W9-CCO-083

BOOKS BY THOMAS WHARTON

Icefields (1995)
Salamander (2001)

SALAMANDER

T HOMAS WHARTON

WASHINGTON SQUARE PRESS
New York   London   Toronto   Sydney   Singapore

This book is a work of fiction. Names, characters, places and incidents are products of the author's imagination or are used fictitiously. Any resemblance to actual events or locales or persons, living or dead, is entirely coincidental.

A Washington Square Press Publication
1230 Avenue of the Americas, New York, NY 10020

Copyright © 2001 by Thomas Wharton

Published by arrangement with McClelland & Stewart Ltd.

Originally Published in 2001 in Canada by McClelland & Stewart Ltd.

ISBN: 0-7434-4415-9

First Washington Square Press trade paperback printing August 2002

10 9 8 7 6 5 4 3 2 1

WASHINGTON SQUARE PRESS and colophon are registered trademarks of Simon & Schuster, Inc.

For information regarding special discounts for bulk purchases, please contact
Simon & Schuster Special Sales at 1-800-456-6798
or business@simonandschuster.com

Cover design by Regine Starace;
front cover illustration by Rafal Olbinski

Printed in the U.S.A.

I restore life from death

– early printers' motto

SALAMANDER

1759

A burning scrap of paper drifts down out of the rain. A magic carpet on fire. It falls with a hiss to the wet stones of the street.

The colonel dismounts from his horse and stands holding the reins, his eyes raised to the sky. The light rain that began as he entered the town has drawn off. The grey clouds are shredding away to reveal patches of deep blue twilight. Wind moans from within the black hole that was once the building's entrance, like the sound from a shell held to the ear.

There is a flicker of candlelight deep within the shadows of the bombed-out ruins. There shouldn't be. Sheltering in such places has been forbidden by decree of the governor.

The colonel ties his horse to a nearby rail and climbs a ridge of fallen brick to enter the building. The smoke, the drifting ash tell him that the bomb struck quite recently. Only a few hours ago, if his judgement of these things is correct.

A wigwam of smouldering timbers fills the middle of the narrow main floor, and he has to walk along the wall to proceed any deeper into the shop, for a shop of some kind it seems to have been, stepping carefully over wet and treacherous wooden wreckage. He feels a drop of rain on his face and glances up to see luminous patches of cloud through a cross-hatching of scorched and amputated beams.

A bookshop. Three of four huge glass-fronted bookcases that once lined the long walls have been smashed open, the books they contained scattered about the room. The one case that remains standing now leans backward as if half-sunk into the wall, its glass panels gone but a few of the books still intact on its shelves. Along the side walls ancient stonework appears in the places where plaster has fallen loose.

Two men are browsing through the books that remain on the shelves. They glance at the colonel, take in his uniform, put down the books they were examining and hurry out with furtive backwards glances. Looting has become a hanging offense in the abandoned town.

In the waning light the colonel gazes in wonder at the bizarre volumes issued by destruction. Books without covers. Covers without books. Books still smouldering, books reduced to mounds of cold, wet ash. Shredded, riddled, and bisected books. Books with spines bent and snapped, one transfixed by a jagged black arrow of shrapnel. In one dark corner lies the multi-volume set of an outdated atlas, fused into a single charred mass. The gold lettering on the spines has somehow survived the fire and glows eerily from the shadows.

Why is the world so made, the colonel wonders, that whatever is damaged shines?

As he steps forward the colonel's foot strikes another volume, one without a cover. It lies splayed open, its uppermost pages lifting and falling with the gusts of evening wind. A huge grey moth, sealed in its unknowable moth self.

Further back, where the roof is still intact, he finds the source of the light he saw from the street. Candles everywhere, in brackets, in crevices and holes blasted through the masonry.

At the back of the shop, in the midst of the light, a young woman crouches amid a great heap of splintered wood, picking up and setting down one piece after another, as if searching for something. Above her on wires strung across the room large sheets of blank paper stir in the wind like ragged sails.

The colonel watches her from the shadows. She is dressed in a tradesman's clothes: worn shirt, breeches, a coarse green apron. Her pale russet hair is tied back: he can see the slender white column of her neck. A girl, really, who should not be alone in an exposed ruin like this, at night. He clears his throat.

Mademoiselle? Do not be alarmed. I am an officer.

She speaks without surprise, making it obvious she knew he was there watching her.

I saw you come in, she says, turning. Well, I saw your wig, anyway.

The colonel laughs, relieved. This may be someone, one of the few in this benighted land, that he can talk to. He steps forward, pleased with the smart sound his new boots make on what is left of the floorboards.

Everyone wonders, he says, how I manage to keep powdered and polished in the midst of a siege. The truth is, I have a truly dedicated barber. Neither cannon, nor musket, nor dreadful scalping knife cows his spirit.

The young woman tosses a jagged stick back on the pile, rises and turns to him, studies him with steady blue-green eyes that belie her youth. Her face and hair are streaked with dust. Her right wrist is bound in a strip of white cloth. Was she here when the bomb fell? For the first time in a long while the colonel finds himself awkwardly searching for words.

I was riding through the town on my way to meet with the Marquis. I saw lights and thought I should investigate. Did you know there were a couple of looters in the shop just now?

They weren't looters, she says. They're old customers. They stare in the window every night after I lock up.

He is vaguely disturbed at her casual response to everything. The bomb, the intruders, him. This encounter is not going quite as he anticipated.

My name is Colonel de Bougainville, he says, doffing his tricorn.

The name seems to have impressed her, he thinks. Or the rank. She looks at him more closely.

You wrote a book, she says.

I did indeed, but —

About the integral calculus.

This is a first, he thinks. He's known in this country for his military exploits, his friendship with the Iroquois, his conquests of the heart. He himself sometimes wonders who it was that wrote that forgotten book with his name on it.

It's true, he confesses. Don't tell me you've read it.

I had a copy here. It may still be in one piece, somewhere out in the shop. But I have read about the calculus. In volume seven of the Libraria Technicum, page two hundred and three.

You've memorized an entire encyclopedia of science?

No, just volume seven.

Remarkable. It must be terrible for you, what has happened to your father's shop.

This is my shop, she says.

Bougainville smiles warily. This would not be the first lunatic he has encountered since arriving in the colony. War can collapse wits as quickly as buildings.

Be that as it may, he says, you really should not be here alone.

I'm not, any more. You're here.

She speaks French very well, he notes. He cannot place the accent. There is something strange in her look, the pale, translucent gleam of her skin, but the girl is not mad. His instinct for people is certain on that point. And she is pretty enough. Riding through the wet streets his thoughts had been as bleak and cheerless as the charred, deserted houses on either hand. He weighs the matter and decides he will linger here, for a while, a diverting interlude before the heavy task of bringing the Marquis more bad news about the doings of the English.

The young woman wipes her charcoal-blackened hands on her apron, pulls a chair towards her, and stands beside it as if waiting for the colonel's permission to sit.

There couldn't have been a lot of business left here for you, Bougainville says. Most of the merchants have closed up and gone.

This is my home. I have nowhere else to go.

Bougainville unbuckles his swordbelt and hangs it from the back of a chair opposite the young woman's.

May I?

Please.

He lifts the wings of his blue velvet coat, seats himself, and she does likewise. Her next words are another salvo from an unexpected quarter.

Do you like to read, Colonel?

Certainly.

What?

He shrugs.

A little of everything, I suppose. I particularly enjoy narratives of travel. I confess I have an ambition, once this war is over, to visit far-away places. Perhaps even discover an unknown island or two. And you, mademoiselle? Do booksellers read their books?

I used to, she says. Now most of them will become fuel, I suppose.

Yes, it looks like it will be a cold winter, Bougainville says. I'm sure, being of the nobility, you're not accustomed to this kind of hardship.

That surprised her, he registers with satisfaction. Once again, his intuition proves itself.

One can tell these things, mademoiselle, he says. You are very self-possessed, it seems to me, for such a young woman. And alone, as you are here, amid all this destruction.

Do you think the siege will end soon, Colonel?

Alas, not even my barber, sagacious as he is, can answer that question.

The people I've talked to lately are very disheartened. They think it's only a matter of time before the English make a successful assault.

This is not a subject he wished to have brought up. Especially by a girl who doubtless knows nothing of the art of war.

Time, he says with a soft huff of derision. Yes, well, time is one thing the gallant Major-General Wolfe has very little of any more. His chances of turning this siege into a conquest are withering with the autumn leaves. Soon it will be winter, and if he doesn't withdraw his ships they'll be frozen and crushed in the river ice. The cliffs are his last hope, but as the Marquis said to me the other day, we need not suppose the enemy have wings. In the few places where we have not posted sentries, the heights are unassailable – even the farmers who live along them say so. They cannot be scaled, especially by troops hauling artillery.

Her eyes hold his for a long moment.

Not everyone believes that, she says. Some say that the English will take Quebec, and when they do the world will surely end.

And what do you reply to such superstitious nonsense?

I tell them that whatever happens a world will end. And another one will begin.

You're wise beyond your years, I see.

I've had good teachers.

From the darkening street outside drifts the far-off frantic barking of a dog. Bougainville remains still, not wishing to betray himself, but when the sound dies away at last he sees that his hand has reached for his sword hilt.

It's so quiet this evening, the young woman says. Isn't this just the kind of night they would make an assault?

Is she taunting me? he wonders, and decides that a jest would be the best response.

What irony that would be. I see, mademoiselle, that you have read a few novels. Or you did, until today.

There's one book the bombs didn't touch, she says.

Volume seven?

No, another book. One I haven't read yet. A book I'd like to read.

I'm intrigued, he says, feeling the chill night air on the back of his neck. He shivers, leans closer to the warm glow of the candles. Why don't you tell me about it, then, this ideal book. I'm curious to know what sort of a book you would like to read.

It could take all night, Colonel. I'm sure you have duties. . . .

Well, let us call this an interrogation, then, since I have found you here, a young woman, alone in what looks like an abandoned shop. With no proof that you are who you say you are.

She smiles.

Who did I say I was?

Bougainville takes a deep breath, eases back in his chair. This is getting better by the moment. The little ballet of swordpoints before the duel begins in earnest.

Come now. I doubt any book could take an entire night to describe.

The girl looks down, examines the palms of her hands.

It's not that simple. I would also have to tell you about the books that this book might be. And the books that it is not. It could go on forever, really.

The colonel draws his chair closer.

Begin, please, and let's see where we end up.

She closes her eyes.

Well, I think every reader imagines this book a different way. Mine is slightly larger than pocket-size. Narrower.

Her pale hands trace a shape in the gloom.

The cover is sealskin, dyed dark green, and the pages . . .

She brings her hands together until her palms and the tips of her fingers touch. Her eyes open.

The pages are very thin. Almost sheer, weightless. When I close the book it's like a beetle's wings folding back under its wingcase.

You do know some science. Pardon me. Go on. Tell me what happens when you open the book.

I can't read the words at first. The text is like a slender black door. This could be any book.

A treatise, Bougainville suggests. A history.

Or a novel, the girl says. I can open it anywhere, even to the last page, and find myself at the beginning of a story.

And where will you start this time?

The girl gazes slowly around the ruin of the shop.

This time . . . this time the book opens out into a marvellous castle, with paper walls and ceilings and floors that fold and collapse and slide at the touch of a finger. There are cardpaper wheels that revolve and change what you see. And panels that slide open to reveal hidden passageways to other pages. You can get lost there. . . .

And does this wondrous castle have a name?

It does. But you see? Already it is happening.

What is?

In order to tell you about the book, I have to tell you about the castle. But to tell you about the castle, I have to begin somewhere else.

And where would that be?

With a siege, like this one. And a battle.

THE CAGE OF MIRRORS

By nine-thirty the guns have been firing for over three hours, churning black smoke into a sky of pristine blue. The sun shines with a glassy, distant brilliance that heralds the turn towards autumn.

The year is 1717. The Christian armies, united under the leadership of Prince Eugene of Savoy, have met the Ottoman Turks outside the walls of Belgrade. An early-morning fog gave the besieging force the opportunity for a surprise attack.

Now the world is a crystal of perfect clarity, and on a hillock above the battlefield Prince Eugene paces, scribbles orders to be sent to his marshals in the field, peers through his spyglass, nods approvingly and writes another missive. He is a small, clerkish man whose first great struggle was to win over his own officers. At first they were scandalized by his unorthodox ideas about making war.

Precision is the key, he often reminds them. *The most important weapon you take into the field is your pocketwatch.*

He is the only commander to spurn the privileges of his exalted rank and pitch his tent with the common soldiers, sharing with them the noise and stench and bad food of an army encampment. The men love him and call him Papa.

At nine-thirty the faintest trace of a smile appears at the corners of the prince's mouth. He permits his valet to pour him a thumbnail measure of brandy in celebration of what has become a certainty. The Turks, routed at almost every point along the battle line, are going to lose. It may take a few more days to convince the inhabitants, still cowering behind the walls, of that fact. But the cross will once again rise above the minarets of Belgrade. Scarcely a single green-and-silver banner still flutters over what is fast becoming a field of slaughter.

Prince Eugene crosses himself and dispatches the waiting messengers with his final orders to the marshals now scattered far and wide across the battle line. A few more moves on the chessboard, and this engagement, as well as the crusade he has led for the past three years into Ottoman territory, should be over, praise be to God. With the taking back of Belgrade from the Turk the centuries of warring back and forth over the same rivers, forests, and mountains will at long last cease. Today the clock stops.

This was a war of time, Prince Eugene announces to his aides-de-camp. *Our clocks against their musty lunar almanacs. You can't run an efficient military engine by the phases of the moon.*

The aides-de-camp nod and murmur agreement. They have heard these phrases many times. Among them is a young man named Ludwig, the only son of Count Konstantin Ostrov, one of the Prince's veteran commanders.

Ludwig is seventeen. He has stayed all morning by the Prince's side, held in reserve while the senior adjutants are chosen for the honour of relaying Papa's orders. Ludwig has been fidgeting, barely reining in his desire to do something, anything, other than wait here with the Prince and his retinue on this distant knoll, which only a scattering of enemy cannonfire has reached all morning. When his turn at last arrives and the orders are signed, sealed, and tucked into the leather pouch at his side, he is off, galloping his sleek black mount down the hillside, over the trampled yellow grass, past the blood-spattered tents where doctors are sawing limbs off the shrieking wounded, between the slow columns of sullen reserve troops brought forward to fill the gaps in the dishevelled lines. He rides as if this is the whole world, the roar of the wind, the lunging flanks of the horse beneath him, the intoxication of his body's youth and animal vigour. He surprises himself with the thought that this feeling surging up in him is an absolute joy.

I am happy, he thinks, and laughs out loud.

He remembers the letter that arrived in camp a month ago, informing him and his father of the death of the Countess, his mother, in childbirth. For the first time since that day the cold ashes in his heart have stirred to life.

I have a sister, Ludwig reminds himself. *Someday, when she is old enough to understand, I will tell her about this moment.*

He was sent to find his father, but it is his father who finds him. Led here by the captain who saw the boy fall, the Count at first does not recognize his son. Ludwig is stretched out on the grass, hat missing, his head propped against the wheel of a smouldering gun carriage. His hands are resting loosely, palms upward, in his lap. This is how beggars slump against walls. Ludwig's head lolls to one side and his jaw hangs like an old man's, as if in a single morning he has aged thirty years.

The Count dismounts and kneels beside his son. Ludwig's eyes are closed, his face chalk-white. He sighs like a gently roused sleeper about to awaken.

The Count turns to the captain.

What happened?

The man sputters. He does not know. He saw the boy fall from his horse, he rushed over and carried him to the gun carriage. The Count searches his son's uniform for traces of blood, gently opens the wings of his gold-embroidered coat. The white shirt beneath is spotless. At the Count's touch, Ludwig opens his eyes.

Let's go home, Father, he says in the tone of a bored guest at a card party.

He draws in a long, drowsy breath, as though about to yawn. His head falls softly sideways against the axle of the carriage. The Count moves closer and looks into Ludwig's eyes.

Peace to his soul, the captain says, doffing his hat.

After a moment the Count draws his blood-crusted sabre and cuts the braided topknot, the Ostrov badge of warrior ancestry, from the head of his son. He rises shakily to his feet.

What killed him? he asks the captain, who lifts his blackened hands helplessly and lets them drop. *He just fell from his horse?*

Yes, Excellency. I saw him coming down the hill, then he slowed up and began searching this way and that, shading his eyes with his hand. Looking for you, I suppose. He was riding towards me when just like that he slid off the saddle and fell to the ground.

When?

I had scarcely rushed to his side and carried him here when I saw you riding by, Excellency.

The Count tucks the topknot into his belt. He gazes over the trampled ground, as if he might find the past few moments lying among the other litter of war.

Others are pausing now on their way back from the last expiring groans of the battle, to gawk, crane their necks, find out who has fallen here. There being a nobleman on hand, it must be somebody of importance. The Count glares around, his naked sabre held before him like an accusation, as if someone here knows the answer to this riddle and refuses to tell him. Young men do not just die.

Two officers on horseback canter past, pausing in their conversation to take in the scene with impassive faces. A grenadier follows soon after, leading another whose eyes are hidden by a dirty bandage, his outstretched hands shakily patting the air before him. In the distance three infantrymen have upended a gunpowder cask and are already playing cards.

The world will not stop.

The Count tosses his sabre to the earth. Tomorrow perhaps, or the next day, the Prince's army will breach the walls and take its vengeance for the deaths of comrades, family, ancestors. He will not be among them. He will honour his son's dying request and return home. He will mourn his wife. See his infant daughter. And devote himself at last to his long-abandoned dream.

The next morning he resigns his commission. Prince Eugene tearfully embraces his old comrade-in-arms.

My dear Konstantin, what will you do?

Puzzles, the Count says, placing his sword in the Prince's hands. *I will do puzzles.*

φ

After his son's death Count Ostrov retired to his ancestral castle, on a precipitous island of rock in the River Vah. This ancient stronghold had been built by his ancestors on the crumbling remains of a Roman fort in the same year that Constantinople fell to Mehmed the Conqueror and Gutenberg printed his first Bible.

As a boy growing up in this castle, the Count had loved puzzles.

Cryptograms, mathematical oddities, those new criss-cross word games known in his native land of Slovakia as *krizovka*, riddles and philosophical conundrums, optical illusions, and sleight-of-hand tricks: all beguiled him and, so the Count came to believe, each of these puzzles was related to the others by some hidden affinity, some universal pattern that he had not yet uncovered. Their solutions hinted at a vague shape, like the scattered place names on a mariner's chart that trace the edge of an unmapped continent. The philosophers of the age were asking why or how God, perfect Being, had created an imperfect world, a world which at the same time the new science was comparing to an intricate machine of uncertain purpose. Perhaps the answer to such questions could be found in these seemingly innocent diversions of the intellect. Was not the mind itself, the Count conjectured, a composite engine of messy animal imperfection and clockwork order?

Yet if there were a single solution to the infinite puzzlement of the world, the young Count Ostrov had been forced to abandon the search for it. In the tradition of his forefathers he had taken up the sabre and spent his life on horseback battling the encroaching Turks. At the time the thought did not occur to him that he might make some other choice. One of his ancestors, after all, was legendary for having decreed that when he died, his skin should be fashioned into a drum to call his descendants to arms. Another still led his men into battle after an exploding shell had blinded him.

Now the Count indulged himself in puzzles as he had never been able to in his youth.

He had *trompe l'oeil* doors and windows painted on walls. Filled rooms with unusual clocks and other marvellous trinkets and curiosities: refracting crystals and magic lanterns, miniature cranes and water wheels, ingenious traps for mice and other vermin. The few dinner guests who stopped at the castle over the years were required to solve riddles before they were allowed to eat.

We are little airy Creatures
All of different Voice and Features;
One of us in Glass is set,
One of us you'll find in Jet.
Another you may see in Tin,
And the fourth a Box within.
If the fifth you should pursue
It can never fly from you.

He hired servants who were what he called human riddles. Massive-jawed giants, dwarves, beings of indeterminate age or sex, boneless contortionists, and people with misshapen or extra limbs. Many of the menial tasks in and around the castle were, however, performed by ingenious mechanisms installed in the castle by inventors from all over Europe. Count Ostrov dreamed of a castle in which there would be no living servants at all, but despite many attempts he had not yet succeeded in having a machine fashioned that could prepare roasted larks just the way he liked them.

φ

Not long after the Peace of Passarowitz, the Count found his cherished seclusion threatened by another kind of invasion: that of the document men. The castle was besieged by government functionaries toting satchels bulging with documents, rolled-up maps under their arms, maps which they spread out on his huge oak desk to show him what the Imperial Survey Office and the Superintendency of Frontiers had jointly decided: the River Vah now formed the revised boundary between the Duchy of Transmoravian Bohemia and the Principality of Upper Hungary.

Like a vast bloodstain the empire had changed shape once again. And once again, as so many times before, the land of Slovakia, like a slaughtered ox, had been sliced up the middle.

In consequence, the document men told the Count, *although your forests, fields, and vineyards are all situated in Bohemia, this castle stands precisely on the border with Hungary, and thus falls into two administrative districts.*

Which means? the Count growled, stroking his moustache.

Which means that Your Excellency is now subject to the duties, excises, levies, and fiduciary responsibilities pertaining to both states.

Which means, the Count said, stabbing a finger at the dotted line that bisected his homeland, *every time a pheasant is killed and*

plucked at my back door, roasted in the kitchen, and carried out to me
on the front terrace, another coin will be plucked from my purse.

He argued that by their own logic, his castle did not in fact exist, *as an entire castle*, in either Bohemia or Hungary, and thus should be exempt from taxation altogether, and from any other meddling in his affairs, for that matter. The document men plunged into their law tomes and surfaced with an obscure ninety-year-old *lex terrae* stipulating that a fugitive could not be shot at by soldiers from either of two neighbouring nations as long as he stood precisely on the border. *For if he be wounded in a leg that stands in one realm*, the statute read, *some of the blood he sheds will of necessity flow from that part of him residing in the other, the which transfer of vital humour clearly falls under the Unlawful Conveyance of Spirituous Liquors Act*. Such a man, in other words, remained suspended in legal and political limbo for as long as he took not a single step in either direction. And so it appeared that by analogy the Count's argument for autonomy was viable. Yet the document men insisted that an exemption of this kind could only take effect in the improbable circumstance that there were no separate, self-contained rooms in the Castle Ostrov.

Just as the several parts of a man's body blend together seamlessly, they reasoned, *so your castle would have to be a space in which, for example, no one could say exactly where the gaming room ended and the chapel began*.

At that moment Count Ostrov had the great revelation of his life. Not only would he fill rooms with oddities and brain-teasers, he would transform the castle itself into a devious labyrinth, a riddle in three dimensions, a giant puzzle.

Nineteen years were devoted to this grand design. In the world beyond the castle, peace gave way once again to war.

The Turks retook Belgrade and were rumoured to be preparing for a march on Vienna, where the newly crowned empress Maria Theresa, young and inexperienced, was already under siege by Frederick of Prussia and his opportunistic allies. Armies tramped once again across Europe, cannonballs flew and villages burned, and during a brief lull in the conflagration the document men returned to inform the Count that the border had been renegotiated and moved, freeing him (at least until the next war) from the threat of dual taxation. He treated the document men to a sumptuous dinner for their trouble (complete with the obligatory riddles), dismissed them from his thoughts and went on with his project.

Dry goods, cookware, clothing, furniture were gathered from their respective niches and redistributed throughout the castle. Ancient walls were knocked down and centuries-old doors taken off their hinges. Fixtures were unfixed, immovables became movables. There were windows set into floors and ceilings, inaccessible doors halfway up walls, winding passageways that circled back upon themselves or led to seemingly impassable barriers of stone that would slide away with the touch of an ingeniously concealed catch. Then came the tables, chairs, and beds mounted on rails in the floor, the mezzanines that lowered themselves into subterranean crypts, the revolving salons on platforms filled with halves of chairs, divans and settees whose other halves would be found along farflung galleries amid a clutter of incompatible household objects.

The workings of the castle were made even more complex by the Count's insistence that although the rooms merged, there would be no such intermingling when it came to social classes. Once every hour through the night, the Count's bed, and that of his daughter, Irena, left their temporary chambers and roamed the castle on their iron rails, in the morning ending up where they began. Despite this nocturnal meandering, the Count saw to it that neither of them came near the areas reserved for the servants. For their part, the servants learned to remain as unobtrusive as possible when they went about their tasks. Their presence was a constant reminder to the Count that he had not yet succeeded in creating a castle capable of functioning on its own without constant human intervention. As they made their daily peregrinations, the servants would conceal themselves behind moving pieces of furniture, or take circuitous routes that kept them well away from where the Count and his infrequent guests were to be found. Eventually he hired a Venetian metallurgist who fashioned automatons to take over some of the castle's more repetitive chores, and to these creations he gave the Slovak name for peasant labourers. There was a *robotnik* that polished silverware, a *robotnik* that folded bedsheets, a *robotnik* that woke the Count every morning by playing his favourite folk melodies on the violin.

The intended result was that the castle seemed scarcely inhabited by human souls.

But the crowning achievement of the Count's great labour was undoubtedly the library. A Scottish inventor, at enormous expense, designed a system of hidden tracks, chains, and pulleys, driven by water and steam, to create a ceaseless migration of bookcases that without warning would sink into the walls or disappear behind sliding wooden panels. Others dropped through trapdoors in the ceiling or rose from concealed wells in the floors. The entire castle in effect became the library, and no private space was inviolable. A guest at the castle might be luxuriating in a perfumed bath, or lecherously pursuing a servant when, with a warble of unseen gears, a seemingly solid partition would slide back and a bookcase or a reading desk would trundle past, the Count himself often hobbling in its wake, consulting his watch, oblivious to anything but the timing and accuracy of the furniture's progress.

As volumes began to arrive in parcels, boxes, and crates, they were unpacked, inventoried, and given a first cursory examination by the Count's daughter, Irena.

φ

When Count Ostrov first returned from Prince Eugene's campaign, Irena was in the care of her nurses, and so she remained until the day the women came to him in terror to tell him that the child had fallen ill and was near death. He descended like a thundercloud on the nursery, scattered the women, and finally got to know his daughter.

Never one to place trust in doctors, the Count installed Irena in his own bed, consulted the few medical treatises in his possession, and set to work to cure the disease himself. He spent a sleepless week preparing herbal concoctions and force-feeding them to the child, who immediately threw most of them up all over the blankets. He had her shivering body swathed in reeking medicinal gauzes. She was steamed, plastered, and bled.

Irena recovered, but the legacy of the illness, or the cure, was a weakened spine that left her unable to hold herself upright. Without the support of a pillow or someone's arm she would collapse like a cloth doll. Eventually the Count had the girl fitted with a corset of steel bands, hammered into a poised, properly feminine shape by the castle blacksmith.

It was also at this time that the Count realized Irena was old enough to read and write, and so might be of some use to him in his never-ending work. One morning he had her brought to his study.

He handed her a small Bible.

Read some of that.

Yes, Father.

She opened the book and then looked up.

What shall I read?

What you find there.

He listened while she read from Deuteronomy, with quiet confidence, never once faltering. *The secret things belong unto the Lord our God: but those things which are revealed belong unto us and to our children for ever, that we may do all the words of this law. . . .* He stopped her after a few minutes and gestured to the quill, inkhorn, and paper that sat on his desk.

Now write it out.

She set the Bible down, picked up the quill, dipped it in ink and began to write. After a moment he noticed that she was not looking at the book.

You know the entire passage by heart.

Yes, Father.

You must have read it before.

No.

He tested her and found that she was telling the truth. And so Irena became the permanent replacement for the string of secretaries who had attempted to live up to the Count's expectations and had either been dismissed in a downpour of abuse or had seen such a moment coming and fled in the night.

A quiet, serious child, Irena had, not surprisingly, grown into a quiet, serious young woman. She did not greatly resemble her mother, the Count was relieved to see. The memory of the beautiful young woman to whom he had scarcely spoken during the long years of his campaigning tormented him. Irena had the same thick russet hair tinged with gold, but her eyes were sea-green rather than topaz, and her face, no matter how closely he scrutinized it while she wrote the letters he dictated, remained out of focus, difficult to see.

When she was seventeen, Irena accompanied her father on one of his infrequent visits to the Imperial Court. No matrimonial offers materialized, but at a grand ball an elderly Hungarian noblewoman took Irena aside and told her to be thankful for her unusual looks.

Ours is the sort of beauty that attracts unusual men, who are of course the only men worth knowing.

In his lucid moments the Count was aware that Irena's unmarried state had more to do with the quality of the young men who were dragged by their avaricious fathers to the castle in the hope of a hefty dowry. Not one of these potential husbands read anything other than the numbers on playing cards, and that, in Irena's eyes, was a fatal defect. They talked of hunting, horses, and war, and when these thin rivulets of conversation dried up, they talked not at all.

In the end, when it came to his only surviving child, the Count found himself powerless to enforce his will, and so Irena remained unmarried at the worrisome age of twenty-four.

She was rarely seen without a book in hand, and in the evenings the Count would often find her motionless near a lamp or a candle, stealing a quiet moment of reading before resuming her unending duties. *My little moth*, he whispered to her affectionately when he found her like this. *Always hovering near the light.*

As the library grew, Irena submitted her report on the

shipments of books to her father, who approved or rejected each item and then allowed Irena to arrange the chosen few on the shelves, according to his deliberately arcane bibliographic system.

Almost every day shipments of books arrived from near and far. While unpacking a crate sent from Boston, Irena discovered that one of the books had been hollowed out inside, and within, another smaller book lay nested. The outermost cover was engraved with a title.

A Conjectural Treatise on Political Economy.

Irena opened the cover of the inner book, and found within its cavity yet another book even smaller, and within it, another, and yet another within that, reminding her of the dolls-within-dolls crafted by the local village toymaker. The innermost volume, its soft leather cover slightly curled, rested snugly in her palm like a tiny seashell. Only with the aid of a magnifying glass was she able to decipher the single sentence which made up the entire content of the smallest book.

The great do devour the little.

Dutifully Irena took this object of ingenious trickery to her father.

It's a joke, a pun, a riddle, he cried. *But not even the hairsplitters from the Imperial Court would disqualify it as an actual, functioning book.*

Irena handed her father the printer's catalogue, where his other books, both finished and projected, were described.

A Book Impervious to Fire
Knives from Persia
Memoirs of the Sibyl at Cumae
A book of mirrors is in the works at this time . . .

The Count turned the pages with an impatient flick of his finger, his eyes darting up and down the neat columns of print.

My magnifying glass, quickly, the Count said.

On the last page of the *Conjectural Treatise* he discovered the microscopic publisher's imprint, under the device of a phoenix amid flames.

"Vitam Mortuo Reddo"
N. Flood, Printer and Bookseller
London

Write to this fellow, the Count ordered his daughter. *We must bring him here.*

φ

The river was as still as glass on the wintry night that Nicholas Flood approached the island. The castle, perched on its slick wet rock, seemed to ripple like a watery reflection in the heated air from the barge's brazier, so that it looked to Flood as though reflection and castle had changed places.

He felt his breast pocket, where he kept the letter Countess Irena had written to him, folded in a cream-coloured envelope with a seal of red wax bearing the impression of the Count's odd coat of arms, a ribbon twisted into a loose knot above two crossed swords.

Dusting the snow off his hat, Flood jumped from the deck of the barge and climbed the wide stairs to the portico, his ascent watched from both sides by a row of winged stone lions with the faces of women.

He looked back once at the Slovak boatmen already busy

unloading the crates of his equipment onto the pier. He had travelled with them for days up the placid Danube and then the foaming, sinuous Vah. Not knowing a word of their language, he had shared their leathery bread and thin, over-peppered cabbage soup, hummed along to the sad and lovely melodies they sang in the evenings. They had not been curious about his unmarked crates, and now hard at work ridding the barge of them, the men did not spare him a glance. By climbing these stairs he had vanished to another plane of existence.

The Countess Irena met him in front of the doors with what she told him was the traditional offering to favoured guests, a glass of *slivovice* and a kiss of welcome. The colourless plum liquor burned pleasantly as it slid into his belly, warming his chilled and weary body. But the brief touch of this young noblewoman's lips left his wind-scoured cheek throbbing with another sort of heat. Irena herself seemed undisturbed by this sudden intimacy, and calmly ordered the clustered servants to see to Flood's baggage. *That is how she kisses every guest*, he decided.

– How was your journey? she asked him in faltering English as they passed into the torchlit entrance hall. Their shadows rose above them into a loft of darkness.

– Uneventful, Flood answered. The way I like them.

He did not speak of the dreary voyage in the Count's strange ship, an antiquated argosy that had taken him circuitously by sea to the mouth of the Danube. It was less dangerous and less costly, the ship's captain had explained, to pass through the eye of the Ottoman Empire than to attempt an overland journey across the plague-stricken, robber-haunted roads of the continent. The Count, he also learned, was something of an inventor and had installed a system of steam-driven winches that controlled the braces and the halyards. This meant that only a skeleton crew was needed to man the ship, and so Flood spent most of the journey in solitude, feeling as though he were sailing alone to the end of the world.

– My father has shut down the castle's machinery for the night, Irena said.

She led Flood through a dark and tortuous passageway where votive candles glimmered from niches in the walls. Irena's blue silk gown rippled in the changeable light like water. They climbed a curving staircase which caused Flood to stumble. When he glanced down at his feet he saw the reason: the height and width of each stair was decreasing as they ascended.

They went along another tunnel of fitfully illuminated blackness. When Irena spoke next she turned to look at him, her pale aquamarine eyes reflecting the candlelight. She seemed to him like one of the flames taken human form.

– My father wishes you to be comfortable, she said. Be prepared, however, for a few surprises in the morning.

They had apparently arrived at his chamber, although he had not noticed a doorway and saw only a bed and the indistinct shapes of panelled walls.

– May you have a restful night, Irena said. She lit the torch in the sconce attached to one of the bedposts and left him.

Even after Flood had undressed and sunk with relief into the depths of his vast, chilly bed, he kept putting a hand to his cheek in amazement. Finally he sat up, dug her letter out of his pocket, unfolded it, and smoothed out its soft creases.

To Nicholas Flood, printer and bookseller, from the Countess Ostrova,

    Dear sir, It is with pleasure that I discharge the office

appointed to me by my father, in offering you the following terms of employment. . . .

He had answered her letter on an impulse. He hadn't needed to. His painstakingly crafted, expensive novelties sold well, leaving him with no desire to crank out the heaps of pamphlets, travelogues, and fat novels that a growing reading public clamoured for. Every year he sent a catalogue to the Frankfurt book fair, boasting of new wonders to come. Impossible books that he could not imagine creating. And yet somehow he always found a way to turn his mad ideas into actual books that could be held in the hand.

No, he hadn't needed to come. But here he was. Transported a thousand miles from home by a letter.

Who was she? he had wondered the day he first read her elegant greeting. To conjure up a Bohemian countess, he resorted to the little he knew of the nobility, a patchwork of fact and conjecture that had been sewn together more out of reading than experience. From the remembrance of some of his more salacious commissions he constructed a haughty duchess, a soft white body armoured in boned taffeta. A stabbing glance of disdain giving way to purrs of delight once blood had been drawn.

He folded the letter, tucked it back in its envelope, and blew out the candle.

Lying awake in the dark, Flood thought back to what she had said about the castle's machinery. He remembered the bizarre ship, with its wheezing steam pipes and squealing pulleys, and he guessed that something similar awaited him in the morning. Closing his eyes and squirming deeper into the bedclothes, he remembered with drowsy amusement how soundly he had slept on that voyage, lulled by the ever-present vibration of the machines. Before he left London he had consulted Bostridge's *New Orthographical Atlas* for the location of the River Vah and found it at last, after his finger had made a meandering peregrination over mountain ranges and through forests, *there*, an inky rivulet issuing from the remote Carpathians. The nearest large place name on the map, he had been delighted to see, was the city of Pressburg. This seemed a good omen, although the Count's ship, at his first glimpse of it on the Thames dockside, dampened his enthusiasm for the adventure and gave him his first doubts.

He closed his eyes, exhaustion plunging him swiftly towards sleep. Through the halls of his dreams stalked a red-haired young woman in a white shift. He followed her down a tunnel lined with sphinxes, while all around them some vast hidden engine rumbled and throbbed.

φ

He awoke to find his mattress shuddering beneath him. Fearing some calamity – an earthquake, a flood, a peasant revolt – he parted the heavy crimson curtains. His chamber, if there had indeed been one, had vanished and his bed was moving along a curving passageway into a spacious hall, gilded and corniced, lined on one side with deep window alcoves pouring ice-light. From a vaulted firmament of cloudscape and cherubs hung a chandelier, a bloated glass spider. A tall pier glass stood between each alcove, and in the sudden bedazzlement of reflected brilliance Flood did not at first see the elderly man in an old-fashioned campaign wig and hussar's

uniform, sitting at a table giving orders to a small group of liv-
eried servants. The old man glanced at Flood's bed arriving
and clapped his hands twice sharply.

The assembly broke up. Servants and their wavering mirror-
twins hurried towards one another and then all these moving
bodies, both real and reflected, vanished with a ripple as concealed doors silently opened and closed like the valves of some
giant undersea creature. The old man, alone now in the centre
of the great hall, beckoned to the printer, who still had not
emerged from his refuge behind the bedcurtains.

– Good morning, Mr. Flood. Welcome to Hrad Ostrovy. I
trust you slept well. No need to be alarmed. All is functioning
as it should. Come, join us for breakfast.

Flood ducked back behind the curtains, searched frantically, and then stuck his head out again.

– Your Excellency, I haven't got my clothes.

The Count raised a finger.

– Yes. Just a moment.

A panel in the ceiling above Flood's head slid open. A wicker
basket was winched down to him by unseen hands. He took the
basket off the hook from which it hung and found inside it his
clothing, discarded in a heap at the foot of the bed last night and
now cleaned, pressed, and perfumed. By the time he had hurriedly pulled on his shirt, waistcoat, breeches and stockings and
had climbed cautiously down from the bed, the Count was
hunched over the table, busily attacking his breakfast.

Irena had joined him, Flood was alarmed to see. And a man
somewhat older than himself, strikingly handsome, wearing
the skullcap and black cassock of a cleric, his long raven hair
tied back in a queue.

The Count greeted Flood this time with a hearty grunt and offered him a less opulent and noticeably shorter chair than his own.

– I gather you were still asleep when the shaving machine stopped by your bed. That would have been . . . six-forty-five, by my reckoning. You didn't hear the bell?

– The bell? I –

– You've met my daughter, the Count said.

– Good morning, Mr. Flood.

– And this is the Abbé de Saint-Foix, from Quebec.

– Of course, Flood said, startled, the name immediately familiar to him before he knew why. The writer of – *what was the book called?* He had never met anyone quite this famous, and all at once found himself red-faced and groping for words.

– All Europe, he tried, is talking about your novel – *how do you address an abbé?* – Monsieur.

The Abbé acknowledged the compliment with a smile and a barely perceptible nod of his head.

– Have you read the Abbé's book? the Count asked Flood.

– Not yet, Excellency.

– Well, I have. I never read made-up stories, as a rule. They are, to my palate, mere concoctions of spun sugar, but since the Abbé's *conte philosophique* speculates on ideas of interest to me, I made an exception.

The printer sat down, disoriented and still dazed with sleep. As he turned at the sound of his bed trundling slowly back down the way it had come, a wheeled tray laden with dishes rolled up beside him. Numbly he took a platter heaped with pig trotters, spiced eggs, and an assortment of braided, looped, and knotted pastries. The tray clattered out again.

Flood glanced cautiously at the Count, intent upon the pastry roll he was buttering. Conscious of the fact that he had not yet washed or shaved, the printer could not bring himself to look directly at Irena. Out of the corner of his eye he took in her primrose-coloured morning gown, the lace cuffs embroidered with tiny silver violets, her quilted white satin petticoat that flashed in the light as she reached across the table to pour her father some coffee. Catching sight of his dishevelled hair in the polished silver coffeepot, he thanked Providence that at least he was in clean clothes. Mumbling a quick grace over his food, he picked up a knife and fork and began to push things around on his plate, still too overwhelmed to dare plunging a utensil into anything.

He was so dazed he almost did not hear the Count asking him the same question Irena had asked the night before. He stammered a polite reply.

– And what did you think of my ship?

– It took some getting used to, Excellency.

– Did it? I confess that answer surprises me, coming from someone like yourself.

– It does?

– *Light am I*, the Count intoned, *yet strong enough to carry a man away. Small am I, yet within me multitudes sleep, waiting to be awakened. Silent am I, yet my words cross great distances and never falter.*

– A book, Flood said after a moment's thought.

– Not long ago, the Count said, brushing at the flakes of pastry lodged in his moustache, I purchased a library from a retired colonel in Boston. One of its volumes was a book of yours.

Another panel in the ceiling opened and a servant in red livery appeared on a descending platform, vigorously brushing a pair of knee-length riding boots. He caught Flood's eye and, with a lopsided grin that spoke of resignation in the face of madness, disappeared through a trapdoor in the floor.

The Count dug in a pocket of his dressing gown and pulled out the *Conjectural Treatise on Political Economy*.

— I'm sure you recognize this.

Flood nodded.

— One of my first commissions. For a philosophical society in Dublin.

— Well, somehow or other it found its way to New England. I would be willing to wager that your so-called philosophical society is in reality a revolutionary cabal. With chapters on both sides of the Atlantic.

— I would know nothing about that, Flood said. I print what I am asked to print. What people do with the books after they leave my shop is their own business.

He quickly bit into a bread roll, alarmed at the resentment that had slid into his voice.

— Of course, the Count said. What goes on in your nation's disgruntled colonies concerns me very little as well. To tell you the truth, I was surprised to learn that there are such things as libraries in the American wilderness. I had always thought it inhabited only by painted savages and woodsmen.

While he was speaking, the Count had been removing each nested volume, until the innermost book sat in his palm.

— *The great do devour the little.* Ingenious.

— Excellency, I am —

— Indeed you are, Mr. Flood. A clever man. My daughter will tell you of my delight when I first saw this.

Flood raised his eyes to Irena.

— We were both very impressed, Father.

– And now, said the Count, at last – he closed his hand slowly around the tiny book – you are here. And I will tell you why. I am building a library like no other. A library of one-of-a-kind volumes, oddities, editions consisting of a single, unique copy. But there is yet, in spite of all my efforts, one book that has always eluded me. Rather than continue to search in vain, however, I've decided to have it printed for me.

– You have the manuscript.

– No.

– Then there's the matter of obtaining copyright, I suppose.

The Count snorted.

– Copyright. That is most amusing. To whet your curiosity, let me say that the text of this book has never been attributed definitively to any known author. And in fact, I've never even set eyes on a manuscript. Intrigued?

– And mystified.

– Glad to hear it. I surmised from your work that you would be one to accept a challenge.

Flood bowed his head.

– Your generous offer has –

– Yes, yes, the Count said, scratching at his wig and stirring up a cloud of powder. I have an idea, a chimera, you might say, that I hope you will be able to help me with. The finished work will be my property, of course, although you will be allowed to imprint the colophon with your device. You will find I am not parsimonious with credit where it is due.

– Thank you, Excellency.

The Count returned to his breakfast. Irena lifted a porcelain sauce boat shaped like a Spanish galleon and poised it over Flood's cup.

– Chocolate?

– Please.

She poured him a full cup of the thick steaming liquid, and it occurred to him he had never had a cup of melted chocolate in his life. He took a trial sip. It was good. Very good. He took another, longer gulp, savouring, then looked up, met the Abbé's amused gaze, and set his cup down with a clunk.

– Nothing quite like it, the Abbé said. Hearing a voice as smooth as the dark ambrosia he had just tasted, Flood realized these were the first words he had heard the man speak.

– Did you know, the Abbé went on, that to the Aztecs chocolate was a sacred drink? They used to offer it to their most distinguished victims, the ones considered worthy of having their hearts torn from their chests to feed the gods.

Flood let out a nervous, barking laugh and quickly bit into a crescent-shaped pastry. *I will not make another sound at this table . . .*

– Here we don't show our guests such courtesies, Abbé, Irena said. They usually leave with their hearts intact.

– I confess I find that hard to believe, Countess.

Flood glanced back and forth at the two of them, aware of a world unknown to him, where wit and flattery flew like shuttlecocks. The Abbé set his knife and fork down in the middle of his plate and sat back, stroking his immaculately shaven chin. Apparently he hadn't been so unexpectedly awakened, and Flood wondered whether he was a guest or a permanent resident. The slightest of smiles hovered at the edges of his full-lipped mouth, the kind of careful almost-smile Flood had seen time and again on men of a certain distinction who desired the services of a skilled and discreet printer. *I'm here but I'm not really here.*

– My daughter is in charge of the books, the Count said

without looking up. She will explain to you how we have arranged everything.

– I will, Father, Irena said.

The Count's head shot up again.

– Assistants, he said through a mouthful of sausage. I expect, Mr. Flood, you'll require assistants for the project I have in mind.

– I most often work alone, Flood said. But I would certainly welcome any –

– I have just the fellows for the job, the Count said, stabbing his fork in Flood's direction. Wait until you see them.

Glancing into the passageway down which his bed had disappeared, Flood saw a horse being led by a groom. He looked at Irena, whose line of sight also must have included the apparition, but she was busy pouring her father another cup of coffee.

– I see, the Count said, that the brewing machine has finally stopped cranking out that godless Mahometan gruel.

– I made the coffee, Father, Irena said. We tried all morning to repair the faulty valve, but it needs a new –

The Count's wrinkled hand paddled the air.

– We will have a look at it later.

– If I may say so, Excellency, Flood ventured, I am more concerned about *where* I am to work. I would imagine I could be most productive if a room were set aside –

– Set aside? the count growled, sitting back in his chair and dabbing at his lips with a white silk napkin. A room *set aside*, the fellow says. Young man, have you any inkling – Has no one, my daughter or some other member of my household, explained to you the workings of this castle?

– I arrived quite late last night, and as yet no one has explained anything to me. In any case, a printing press must be bolted down to prevent jarring and shaking.

– Of course, the Count said, blinking. He tilted his head back and gulped down his coffee. Of course. I will have my head carpenter discuss the matter with you later today. I am sure we will be able to arrive at some kind of suitable compromise. In the meantime, my daughter will provide you with a basic plan of the castle, and the latest timetable, to help you navigate.

– I'll see to those now, Father, Irena said, rising and nodding to the Abbé and Flood in turn. She glided noiselessly away, her long gown concealing her feet so that she seemed to slide across the floor like one of the castle's mechanisms. There was something in her carriage, Flood noticed for the first time. An odd stiffness. . . . He followed her with his eyes until a deep, sonorous *bong*, more a felt vibration than a sound, jolted him back to his former circumspection. He glanced quickly at the Abbé, who was regarding him now with a slightly more corporeal smile. As the reverberations of the sound died away, one of the pier glasses slid upward and a wall, panelled and wainscotted, began to slide outward into the room. At the same moment, another pier glass on the other side of the room also opened and a second wall began sliding towards the first.

A movement from the Abbé drew Flood's attention back to the table.

– I will take my leave as well, Excellency, the Abbé said, rising and brushing at his black cassock.

– Off to work with you then, my handsome friend, the Count said over his shoulder. You cannot disappoint those fair readers who are no doubt panting in their corsets waiting for your next offering.

The Abbé bowed slightly and then turned to Flood.

– I hope we will have more opportunity for conversation.

Our nations may be rattling spears at one another, but that is no reason for us to do likewise.

– Of course not.

The Abbé nodded, bowed again to the Count, turned smartly on his heel, and walked between the moving walls, which came together behind him with a soft click.

– Time, the Count said, checking the gold watch that hung on a heavy chain around his neck. Give us time, Mr. Flood. You will come to appreciate what at the moment seems only utter chaos.

From somewhere unseen a clavier struck a trio of spindly opening chords, and then a lute, a horn, and a high, plaintive voice joined in. Flood, who had never cared for music, found the noise vaguely irritating. Another distraction within a distraction, like everything else in this castle.

– Now to the heart of the matter, the Count said, rubbing his hands together. One of the possible origins for the name of my people, Mr. Flood, is the word *slovo*; that is, the word *word*. Thus we Slovaks, one might say, are the People of the Word. But what irony that our national literature scarcely exists. The republic of letters has no ambassador from our country. Tell me, can you name an imperishable classic by a Slovak author?

– Well, I –

– Exactly. The Abbé asked me the other day to recommend a good Slovak novel, and I had to tell him there were none. Not just no *good* Slovak novels. No novels whatsoever. Almost everything we read, everything we say, everything we think, comes to us in someone else's language.

He sat back, fingering his white silk napkin. The ceiling above his head opened and with a groan of gears another wall began ponderously to descend. The Count sprang forward again so suddenly that Flood jerked backward before he could stop himself.

– Did we Slovaks utter the first word? No. Will we utter the last word? Not likely. Those glorious absolutes are reserved for the youngest and the oldest of nations. Consult any history book and where do you find us? We are a footnote people, briefly mentioned in vast tracts about others. All too often I glimpse our name in an index, I flip to the page and am informed that *such and such an event also affected the Slovaks and the What-have-yous.* Well, we are going to do something about that, you and I. When we are finished it will be possible to say that the Slovaks are truly the People of the Word.

The descending wall came to rest and immediately folded in the middle to form a corner. The immense hall Flood's bed had rolled into earlier had vanished, and they were now in a small rectangular room, into which bookshelves began to rise from the floor. The Count smoothed out his silk napkin on the tabletop. He folded it in half, then in half again, his eyes not for a moment leaving the printer's.

After several folds he held up a thick, compact white bundle.

– I want you, Mr. Flood, to create for me an infinite book.

– Infinite?

– *Nekonečný. Unendlich. Sans fin.* A book without end. Or beginning, for that matter.

The Count's wrist flicked and the folded napkin snapped open like a sail catching the wind.

– The way you go about it is up to you. My one stipulation is that you bring every ounce of your native wit, imagination, and cleverness to this undertaking. No pasteboard trickery, no feeble jokes. I have shelves of that kind of thing already. No, this is to be a book that truly reflects what I have accomplished here. A book that poses a riddle without answering it.

– I can't think how one could –

– Don't try to solve the problem right now. Infinity can't be pounced upon. It is like a walled town that must be observed from concealment, reconnoitred, mined carefully from beneath. You're a young man. You're still on friendly terms with time. For the moment, let's just get you settled in. You can work on other things to begin with, like your book of mirrors.

The Count pushed his empty plate away and leaned back in his chair, nodding his head in time to the music. After a while he turned back to Flood.

– This one is called Tancovala. *On she danced.* Crystalline, aren't they? From Vienna, but they do know the old songs of my land. Which proves that something worthwhile may arise now and again from the Royal Capital of Mud.

Flood opened his mouth to speak but said nothing. The Count's hawklike eyes fastened on his face.

– Long ago I thought I was creating this castle of riddles in order to outwit a handful of government lackeys and thus protect my purse. But lately I understand more clearly what I have really been doing.

He clicked open his pocketwatch, frowned at what it told him, and tucked it away again.

– This is not a castle, this is a system. The priests and the madmen make systems out of dreams. The writers, like our handsome Abbé there, make systems out of words. I have made this system, my system, out of stone and wood and metal and glass. And why? To what purpose? Push your chair back.

– Pardon me?

– Push your chair back, I say. Quickly now.

Flood did as he asked, and at the same moment the musicians abruptly ceased playing. At Flood's feet a narrow gap opened in the floor, a slot stretching across the floor of the room and bisecting it into two hemispheres. With a whirr of unseen machinery, a huge metal bar, an arrow, a room-length, Brobdingnagian clock hand rose out of the slot, sending Flood scrambling from his chair. When the barbed point had risen to his eye level, something subterranean and metallic went *clank* and the gigantic ictus stopped, wavering slightly.

– The planets, the Count began, leaning sideways to sight along the arrow's diagonal while glancing again at his watch. The planets, the starry firmament, the unfathomable abysses of darkness and time through which we plummet without knowing how or why, the entire universe, I have come to realize, is a vast, unbounded book of riddles. A book written in the elusive and unutterable language of God.

The Count snapped shut his watch.

– What I want is nothing more or less than my own personal edition.

φ

As Flood discovered, there were areas of the castle where one function appeared to predominate over others. The head carpenter, a curly-headed young Savoyard named Turini, directed him to his proposed workplace, a gallery circling the rim of a central cavity. The immense hole, as the carpenter explained, was originally excavated to allow the Count's engineers easier access to the main clockworks far below. As the complexity of the castle's design increased, this great cylindrical shaft had become a central rerouting point for bookcases and other furniture. As Flood watched, leaning over the balustrade, the cases far below him swivelled ponderously, changed direction, dropped or rose to other levels on their way through the castle. At times they passed over and through the gallery where he stood, as he learned when the carpenter pushed him abruptly to one side to avoid being run down by a glass-fronted map cabinet approaching from behind.

Down the middle of the gallery's long sweeping curve ran a sunken rail along which a metallic angel of death glided (counter-clockwise, Flood noted) with lance raised on high. Under Flood's direction, Turini pried loose the life-sized memento mori and replaced it with Flood's press and work table, mounted on a small platform attached to the sunken rail in the floor. The undercarriage glided along smoothly enough that vibrations would not be a problem, except on the stroke of the hour, when everything jarred to a halt. Turini ran a callused hand through his hair and suggested that when Flood heard the clockworks beneath him tensing to strike, he would have to cease work for the next few moments. An annoyance, certainly, but not an insurmountable obstacle.

– That's what His Excellency told me, the carpenter said, when I first came to work for him. No obstacle is insurmountable. So I've set my sights on Darka, the contortionist. She's deaf and dumb, it's true, but what a beauty.

Flood was allowed to keep his stacks of paper and casks of ink in one place, a cabinet he could reach by climbing down a ladder into the central shaft. In order to reach what he needed he soon found he had to plan his path carefully through the moving labyrinth of bookshelves.

Turini helped Flood assemble the press, a device he had never seen before, and praised its ingenious construction.

– Before there was a machine to make books, he mused, how did men get smart enough to invent one?

By early evening the uncrating, assembling, and arranging was complete, and Flood wiped his grimy hands on a cloth and stepped back to appraise, for what had to be the thousandth time, the ungainly instrument of his livelihood.

We are both out of place here. As if aware of its incongruous presence in such surroundings the ancient workhorse seemed to hunker down before him, a faithful beast of burden awaiting the next load it was to bear.

Not for the first time he marvelled at what an odd composite creature a printing press was. With its legs and its stout frame and its various handles and protrusions, it resembled at one and the same time a bed, a pulpit, and an arcane instrument of torture. The weathered wooden timbers had been scored, cracked, water-damaged under leaky roofs, set on fire (once on purpose, by an author given to drink who'd found a typographical error in his book), realigned and repaired again and again. It had been taken apart, hauled to new lodgings, and reassembled countless times before this latest epic remove. Its wood and metal parts had been scrubbed and polished every single day of its existence, and replaced only after all attempts at repair had failed. The longest-surviving timbers, from the time of his great-grandfather the Huguenot exile, had been worn to the rounded smoothness of driftwood. The inscription burned into the underside of the frame, *N LaFlotte 1663*, had almost disappeared.

In their games of pretend he and Meg had called the press the *chimera*. It was his word, gleaned from the books of fabulous stories he read to her at bedtime. As always she took everything he said as an article of faith. She truly believed the press was some kind of monster, and was afraid to go into the print shop. He remembered her sudden tears when he pretended he had been turned to stone by an evil spell. She had lost him.

The press had waited for him like this, he remembered, the day she died. She was eight years old. He was eleven, a child watching another child die. Before he began his apprenticeship in the print shop they had been constant companions. While his father worked late hours, he was the one who cooked her supper, put her to bed, and read to her from the Greek myths, La Fontaine's Fables, *The Thousand and One Nights*. They invented an imaginary kingdom in which everyday things blossomed with wonder. The rooms of the house were transformed into ogres' lairs and the mossy caves of sorcerers. Their father was the king, but his printing press stymied them for a long time. It seemed their father was both its master and its victim, and so the press could not quite be any one thing.

He and his father sat by her bedside day and night while the smallpox slowly consumed her, burning her to ash before their eyes. They washed the bleeding sores that covered her arms and legs, and finally her face. When she woke screaming from the fever nightmares he soothed her with her favourite stories. His efforts to comfort her at last became empty when she went blind.

He remembered most of all the smell of her dying. In the end she became a thing to him, the source of the graveyard stench that turned her sickroom into an antechamber of hell. He hated her for what she had become, what she had done to both of them.

On the last day she drifted in and out of delirium, shivering, babbling nonsense, and then thrashing awake, moaning that she was on fire. *Papa, please make it stop.* He ran through the shop to fetch cool water from the pump in the court, and each time he passed the press he was aware of its silent waiting presence, mutely abiding all.

They sat at her bedside through the night until her tortured breathing finally ebbed away. Still he remained kneeling beside her, exhausted, his heart worn as thin as paper. After some time he heard the creak of the press screw from the shop. He hadn't noticed when his father had left the bedroom, but he was gone, already back at work finishing his latest commission. After listening for a while to the sounds from the shop, he finally left Meg and went to join his father at the press.

The work went on. Every day since then, and here, too, in this castle that was like something he and Meg might have dreamed. Flood took a deep breath and tied on his apron.

There was a noise behind him and, thinking it was one of the bookcases, he stepped nimbly aside.

– I'm sorry if I startled you, the Countess said. Sometimes I forget what this place can do to newcomers.

He was glad to see her again, the only sane soul, it seemed, in this madhouse. He hoped she would linger and talk for a while, but she merely asked him if he was satisfied with the arrangements. He told her that he was, and then wondered why he had, since he most definitely was not. She said she would inform her father that all was well, and turned to leave.

– Once I've finished a book, Flood said quickly, stepping down from the press platform, all I will have to do is deposit it on one of the passing shelves.

Irena frowned.

– I'm afraid no one is allowed to add or remove anything from these bookcases, she said, without my father's approval.

– I had thought from what the Count said that you were in charge of the library.

– That is how it works in theory, she said with a smile. In fact, my father inspects everything that gets done here, even down to how many mice the cats are catching. Nothing escapes his notice for long.

– Does he ever sleep?

– He does. He says sleep has its uses too. Dreams give him some of his best ideas.

She turned to examine the press, and he knew somehow that there was more she wished to say. He wondered how he might encourage her to speak, and drew closer.

– Don't worry, Mr. Flood, I wasn't going to touch anything.

– I didn't think –

– I wondered, she said, if I might be allowed to watch you at work from time to time. I read a lot of books but I've never seen one being made.

As he quickly consented, the great clock struck the hour. Irena looked up, the eagerness fading from her eyes.

– I must go, she said, stepping away from the platform. I will return tomorrow.

– Wait, he said, suddenly remembering something that had been nagging at him all day. Now he hesitated, confounded by the delicacy of the question.

– Yes?

– I'm not. I don't. Could you tell me how to find my bed?

φ

The next morning she brought the assistants the Count had promised him.

One was from the Count's collection of human puzzles, a nine-year-old boy named Djinn, who had six fingers on each hand. Even discounting the extra digits, Djinn was the most exotic creature Flood had ever seen. Kinked African hair of a blond hue, coffee-coloured skin, almond-shaped eyes with blue irises. He could speak several languages, some from as far away as China, as well as Arabic, Spanish, and what Flood at first thought was Greek but turned out to be Gaelic. The Count had acquired the boy as a present from a Turkish envoy who visited the castle with a troupe of strolling actors. The Castle Ostrov, as the envoy had guessed, proved to be ideal for the performance of a play involving trapdoors, ghosts, and descending gods. The Count was most impressed, however, with this twelve-fingered boy who plucked a haunting melody on the lute at the play's close. The troupe reluctantly surrendered Djinn to the Count, at the envoy's insistence. The actors themselves had found him in the streets of Constantinople but guessed that he was from somewhere much farther away.

– My father, Irena explained, thought Djinn's fingers could be usefully applied to some aspect of printing.

The boy kept his gaze fixed on her, his mute despair palpable. She was going to leave him here.

The other assistant was an automaton of milky *blanc de Chine* porcelain and joints of bronze that, when wound with a key, nodded its head, moved its arms, and took a few halting steps. The automaton, clean-shaven and sporting an apple-bright spot of red enamel on each cheek, was dressed in the uniform of a cavalry officer. Kirshner, the Venetian metallurgist, had fashioned the inner workings and installed them in a porcelain body that had been cast at Meissen by the wizard Kaendler.

Ludwig, as Irena called the automaton, was originally designed only to march a few steps and brandish its sword. When her father saw what the machine's creator was capable of he had him add other functions, and now the automaton could dance a stiff minuet, write a few words with a quill pen, and drink a glass of wine. Ludwig's limited movements, the Count had thought, might be adaptable to some of the more mechanical press operations. Flood admitted his doubts.

– It can't respond to my commands.

As he spoke, a bell-like echo of his voice seemed to rattle around inside the automaton, reemerging at last in a buzzing string of words.

– *Can tress tomb man.*

Flood stepped back, startled.

– Someone's in there.

Irena shook her head.

– He repeats what you say, but he leaves parts out.

– *Reap you tea*, the automaton buzzed. *Eve arts out.*

Irena handed Flood a large brass key.

– The metallurgist was very clever. Certain sustained tones move sensitive weights inside Ludwig, so that you can make him do things by singing to him. Watch.

She leaned towards the automaton's ceramic ear and hummed a long, wavering note. With a click and a whirr Ludwig's arm rose, bending at the elbow, until the tips of his fingers touched his tricorn.

To Flood's surprise, Irena was the one who tinkered with Ludwig's machinery and adapted him for presswork. She returned in the afternoon with a case of watchmaker's instruments and an odd brass-plated paper-cutter that she set on his desk and connected to a treadle and a handwheel.

– We designed this, she said, to help you with all of the pages you'll be producing. You slide your paper in here, like so. These spools fold the sheet and then the blades cut it. And you can adjust the folding and cutting for an eight-, sixteen-, or thirty-two-page sheet.

– *We* designed this?

– My father and I.

She unscrewed a panel in the automaton's back and moved aside to let Flood see the secrets of Ludwig's design. With the tips of a tiny pair of jeweller's forceps she tapped a toothed copper cylinder ringed with thin disks. Patiently she showed him how a system of these disks, or cams, transferred the rotary motion of the clockwork to the rods and levers that controlled Ludwig's movements. Depending on which set of cams was put in place, Ludwig's routine could be altered. There were sets for eating, for swordplay, for dancing. By mixing and rearranging the cams, she explained, she was hoping to approximate the repetitive motions required in printing.

– Can I stop him myself? Flood asked. If he starts to get ahead of me, for example.

– You can hold his arm, yes, but I wouldn't prevent his motion for too long. He may be a machine, but he can be rather temperamental.

Flood asked her where she had learned such uncommon skills.

– I watched the man who put Ludwig together, she explained, and asked a lot of questions. My father and Ludwig's creator did not . . . get along. It occurred to me that, once Signore Kirshner had gone home to Venice, someone here would have to be able to repair these things.

They had drawn close together to examine Ludwig's inner

workings. In the silence after her last words Flood could hear Irena's breathing. He glanced at the boy, who was watching them with wide eyes.

– Before I got it, Flood said, what was it supposed to do?
– Live.

He detected something in the tone of her strange reply, and then it occurred to him how, in a kind of lifeless parody, the automaton resembled her.

– Ludwig was my brother's name, she said. I never met him, but my father tells me that this Ludwig is a good likeness.

That afternoon she told him the story of her brother's death at the Battle of Belgrade, and the Count's hope that he might resurrect something of his son in the form of a machine.

– That's why the Abbé de Saint-Foix is here, she said.

In the Abbé's novel, she explained, the notion was put forth by one of the characters that the human soul might be found in the hair and fingernails. It is well-known that both continue to grow after death, and this astounding fact could be attributed to a residue of the divine spark. She quoted the novel from memory, he was dismayed to see.

– *The spirit, in its longing to return to the spiritual realm, ceaselessly flows, like electricity, from the core of the body to the outer regions. The soul, in other words, might at certain times be lodged in a person's coiffure.*

– The idea, Irena said with a smile, has been very popular with fashionable ladies.

– And so has the Abbé, I've heard.

– My father, for his part, thinks the idea worth pursuing.

When she spoke of the Count, Flood noticed, her voice was softened with affectionate forbearance. She spoke of how her father had supplied the Abbé with her brother's topknot.

The faded hank of hair that the Count had cut from his son's head had been mortared into oily dust and mixed with an unguent to grease the joints of the porcelain soldier, in the hope that any glimmer of vitality remaining in the battlefield memento might be transferred to the machine.

– I take it the experiment has been a failure.

Instead of answering, Irena straightened the automaton's cocked hat and bent to kiss the boy on the forehead.

– Look after them, Mr. Flood.

When the adjustments were completed Ludwig could stand at the press much longer than Flood himself, inking the formes and tirelessly lowering and raising the platen, until his mainspring finally wound down and had to be cranked up again.

φ

The first problem: how might one bind a book without beginning or end? On his third day in the castle Flood paced alongside his moving press and drew up a list of the ways books can be held together:

- *with the hands*
- *with thread*
- *with hair*
- *with cloth*
- *with bone and animal sinews*
- *with wood*
- *with paste*
- *with other books*
- *with the teeth*
- *with hope*

And even if you could bind such a book, how might the contents be made truly infinite, having been given an enclosing frame? The Count likened infinity to a walled town, but to Flood's mind it was more like everything that lies outside a walled town. *If the text gets over that wall*, he wrote in his journal, *it spills right out of the book, doesn't it?*

When he was not consulting with the Count about the other volumes he wanted printed in the meantime, Flood compiled a tentative list of possibilities.

♦ *A cylinder of sheets of stiff cardpaper, rotating constantly around a central axle and throwing off infinitely repeated phrases, like the prayer wheels of the holy men of impenetrable Tibet. A reader can never decide that one particular page is the ending or the beginning. Note: this would be unlikely to satisfy the Count's definition of true infinitude.*

♦ *A book that is sealed shut, with the word* infinity *burned on its wooden front cover. The reader cannot read the book and thus is free to entertain an infinite number of conjectures about the contents. Problem: as above.*

♦ *Philosophical idea: For every actual numbered page of the book, there exist hypothetical not-pages that . . . exist . . . elsewhere?*
    No.

♦ *By some as yet undetermined application of the principles of chemistry on the composition of ink, the printed words are not fixed on the page, but can be rearranged at the reader's whim.*

An ashen rain was falling on the morning the Abbé de Saint-Foix came to see him. Thick runnels of water slimed the panes of the windows, dimming the interior of the castle in a glaucous undersea light. Flood was restless, frustrated by his lack of progress, and did not welcome the interruption of his mood.

– I see you've replaced Death, the Abbé said. He was punctual, but not well-liked.

He drifted up to the press platform with a studied nonchalance.

– The Count has asked me to see if I could be of any help.

The thought, bitter and unexpected, lanced across Flood's mind: *Your fraternity was no help when my ancestors were butchered on St. Bartholomew's Day.*

– By all means, he said, setting down the tray of type he was sorting. After all, the infinite would be more your area than mine.

– It depends, the Abbé said, on which infinite you mean.

He gestured to the window.

– How many drops fall, do you think, in a rain shower like this?

– Thousands, Flood said with a shrug. Millions. I have no idea.

– One wouldn't say, though, that the number must be infinite. Merely indefinite. Unknown. And yet for all the difference it makes to us, the number of drops might as well be infinite. We can never determine for certain that it isn't.

The Abbé plucked a piece of type from the case on Flood's table, examined it for a moment, and then dropped it back in its compartment.

– Then there is the useful infinite, Flood said.

– I see you know something of mathematics.

– A little. My father made it part of my training in typography. Geometry, some calculus.

– Where lovely paradoxes bloom like nightshade in the garden of the mind. My fellow Jesuit, Cavalieri, worked out a method for deriving the volume of a solid object by assuming that a cube, for example, is composed of an infinite number of infinitely thin planes.

The Abbé's eyes did not blink in unison, Flood noticed. The left lid lagged ever so slightly behind the right, a barely perceptible tic that nevertheless lent to his assured speech a faint suggestion of derangement.

– So, Flood said, if I could print a book with infinitely thin sheets of paper . . .

– Indeed, the Abbé said, seating himself in the embrasure of the window. But that is not quite what the Count has asked you for, I understand.

– No. He's left the form of the thing up to me. It's the content that matters to him. He wants a book that contains everything. A book without beginning or ending.

The Abbé's eyebrows rose.

– Ah, now, there is your content.

– What is?

– Time. You must get it all into your book.

– I don't understand.

– As St. Augustine said, *If you ask me what time is, I know. If I wish to explain it to you, I know not.*

– A riddle worthy of the Count. Just remove the word *time.*

– What if time is not what we imagine it to be? Not a smooth continuous absolute, the same for everyone.

– You mean something like the fact that right now it's night on the other side of the earth.

– Not exactly. Perhaps, like the gods of India, time has many faces.

The Abbé tapped idly on the windowpane.

– Perhaps everything really happens at once. What if time is like the rain? We make a path through it, and a few drops touch us and we call that our lives. But if one could slip between the droplets, or gather them all, like water in a well . . .

Flood rubbed the back of his neck.

– My head is starting to spin. I haven't had your schooling in these matters.

The Abbé turned away from the window and smiled.

– Which returns me to the thought of how I might assist you, he said. I have in mind certain volumes in the Count's library which may be of help. We will, of course, need the assistance of the Countess. A remarkable woman. She knows every book in the castle, I believe, by heart.

– Yours, too, Abbé.

– Does she? I almost wish you had not told me so, Mr. Flood. After all, self-possession is difficult enough to achieve in the presence of such a woman, don't you agree?

At the mention of Irena, the muddied pool in Flood's thoughts smoothed to a still mirror. He looked at the rivulets of water blindly seeking their way down the dirty windowpanes, and felt an ache of tenderness for the mute, persistent things of the world. He wanted to tell the Abbé that his brief summary was incomplete, that there was another infinity he had neglected to mention, but he knew the words for his intuition, if there were any, would elude him.

Irena met them among the shelves.

– Good morning, gentlemen, she said. Shall we begin?

Armed with the Abbé's suggestions and Irena's unerring knowledge of the library they prowled the shelves. Xenophanes and Aristotle. Giordano Bruno's *De l'infinito universo*. Newton's *Optics*. The *Orbis Sensalium Pictus* of Comenius. Ancient and recent treatises on alchemy, astrology, and the Abbé's favourite topic, time. The *Aenigmatum* of Abu Musa contained tantalizing hints, but the Count's copy of this extremely rare book contained a hidden clockwork mechanism that turned the thin metal pages at its own set pace. Flood found the attempt to copy intriguing passages left him with little more than broken quills and pinched fingertips.

As they searched, they wandered among the shelves, and as each of them stopped here and there to examine an enticing volume, they drew farther and farther apart, until they found themselves calling to one another from different levels. Flood made his way back down to the last place he had seen Irena vanish among the bookcases, but when he peered around a shelf he saw her with the Abbé, the two of them sharing a laugh. He backed quietly away and waited until they came looking for him.

At the end of the day Flood's work table was barricaded with a wall of books. He spent that night and the next three days reading, collating and taking notes, gathering and comparing the thoughts of poets, mathematicians, philosophers, and mystics, searching for ideas that might somehow be applied to the physical object known as a book, a finite sequence of words printed upon a finite number of sheets of paper. Invariably he found that what each of these authors had to say about infinity was both too much and not enough.

Hoping at least to organize his acquired material, he decided it was possible to divide his growing swarm of infinities into two main categories:

1) the same thing recurring endlessly;

2) almost the same thing, but not quite, recurring endlessly.

In an argosy of Hellenistic authors he found an amusing diatribe against the reading of novels.

Section XXVII:

♦ *Lassitude during public debates indicates the chronic reader of books full of lies, coincidences, and impossibilities.*

♦ *Some of these pernicious works have been known to bring on fits of sneezing, others cause blood to flow from the ears. Those which contain didactic passages may fill the lungs with mucosity and impair breathing.*

♦ *Inflammation of the eyes from protracted reading of such works may be alleviated by drinking slightly watered wine.*

♦ *Care should be taken of the books given to a pubescent female; if the breasts begin to swell to unusual fullness, reading should cease.*

♦ *These noxious books are often hastily bound with pastes derived from the boiling of animal hides. The inferiority of such bindings is usually matched by the worthlessness of the contents.*

♦ *Curiously, eunuchs do not read these books, nor do they go bald.*

He was intrigued by Sabbatai Donnolo's comparison of God to a book. If you could cradle this fearful volume in your hand, and were to open it anywhere, beginning, middle, or end, you would find that between any two pages there would be always a third, between any two words there would be always another, between any two letters would be an unheard, invisible letter, a doorway to the void known only to mystics, where reigns a silence so profound that the roar of the entire universe rushes to fill it.

Each morning Irena arrived, took away the books that he had sifted, and brought him new ones. When no one was about, Flood did some searching of his own, often turning up volumes that revealed the Count's weakness for puns and riddles. The *Little Treatise on the Teeth*, a disguised case for combs. A fat tome titled *Fuel for Enlightening Thought*, which turned out to be a solid block of cleverly painted pine.

Yet everything he read and examined, no matter how frivolous or profound, how elliptical or to the purpose, left the completion of his task as remote from the reach of his hands as the moon.

Well and good, he told himself, slamming shut another long-untouched volume that sent up a plume of fine dust. *I will carry on. I will go along with this, I will stay here and humour him, as the Abbé does, because it is profitable. And because in so doing I am honing my craft and thus not really taking advantage of anyone.*

And because of her.

– Irena Ostrova, Flood whispered to Ludwig later that day, and leaned close to catch the buzzing reply.

– Rain. Trove.

He turned to see Djinn watching him with his steady blue eyes.

He had more or less ignored the boy until now, but Djinn's extra digits, Flood quickly realized, would be of tremendous help in the laborious composing of type. The problem was that they would have only the bare rudiments of German in common to converse with. Having chosen to print in English to begin with, Flood would have to teach the boy to set type from manuscripts he could not read. It was not long, however, before Djinn had learned to fill and lock up a chase in half the time it took Flood himself.

He could be Mongol, Iroquois, from the Moon, the Count had said, *for all he can tell you of his earliest memories.* Which, when at last Flood was able to converse with the boy, amounted to little more than a hazily recollected glimpse of green hills beyond the flap of a tent, and in what seemed to be a memory from a slightly later time, his own feet, foreshortened in water, kicking lazily next to those of someone else, a girl who seemed to be a little older than he, since he was listening – but in what language he could not remember – as she instructed him to watch out for the biting turtles.

As the days passed he became familiar enough with the Count's system to be no longer startled by walls, floors, and people vanishing and popping up where they were not expected. He looked forward to every opportunity to see and talk with Irena, yet often found his attempts frustrated by the metamorphic nature of the castle. On his way to fetch ink or water for cleaning the type, he would glimpse the Countess at the other end of a corridor. Hastily, but with what he hoped was the appearance of nonchalance, he would head in her direction, only to have the corridor bifurcate in front of him so that Irena slipped away down one passage and he was sent stumbling into another. He would wander into an unfamiliar region of the castle from which a servant had to help him find his way back.

Often he leaned back from his work table to see the Count on a higher gallery, circling the central hollow of the castle and gazing down like a watchful hawk.

φ

7:00 a.m. Wake, get out of bed, wash at revolving basin, dress.

7:15 a.m. Pluck breakfast from cart while descending to mezzanine level to pick up fresh sheets for the day's work. From there leap onto passing shelf containing collected works of Leibniz and step off into the upper clock works. Duck immediately to avoid getting coat caught in gears.

7:25 a.m.   If clothing & self still intact, return to platform and commence work.

8:00 a.m. – 2:00 p.m. Work.

2:01 p.m.   Eat remainder of breakfast among moving shelves until north wall panel swivels open. Dash through, blocking panel with large book to provide quick route of escape. Climb stairs to observatory level and stand at oriel window.

2:15 p.m. Irena takes daily stroll along terrace with Abbé. (What do they talk about?) If she glances up, remember: smile, do not stare.

2:16 p.m. Return to work by circuitous route (must remember map next time) to avoid Count. Remove jammed book from wall panel to avoid suspicion.

2:30 p.m. – 7:00 p.m. Work.

7:01 p.m. Take refreshment and await invitation to dine with Count.

7:30 p.m. If no invitation forthcoming, return to work.

φ

Hurrying to keep pace with the huge moving bed, Flood handed the Count a single blank sheet.

– I've been working on the book of mirrors you asked about, he said. If I can make the paper reflective, the words will reproduce each other and thus repeat the text endlessly.

The old man, propped up on a bastion of pillows, a tasselled nightcap on his head, turned the paper over and over.

– An intriguing notion. Has it yielded a result?

– I'm still working on a gloss for the paper, he said. One that will reflect light yet hold ink. This stage has proved more difficult than I expected.

The Count thrust the sheet back at Flood.

– Try something else, he said as his bed rolled away. Toy around. See what you can do.

– There's another difficulty, Excellency, Flood said, trotting to keep up. I haven't replaced my type for quite some time. The faces are getting worn out, and it's beginning to show on the page.

– One wonders, Mr. Flood, if you take proper care of your tools.

Flood bit his lip.

– I've filed and polished, but the metal will take only so much of that. To speak plainly, I don't think my type is quite up to the task.

The Count pulled at the wings of his moustache.

– Then we'll get you some new type. There must be a foundry in Pressburg. Or more likely Vienna, since they can get all the lead they need by mining what passes for brains at court.

– The Countess told me about the metallurgist from Venice who created the automatons. Samuel Kirshner.

– Yes. The ingenious Jew. What of him?

– His foundry makes type as well. The Countess showed me some samples of his work –

– As I've found, it can be troublesome doing business with those people. They're always getting themselves hauled off by the Inquisition or driven out of town by angry mobs, and then where are you? Out of pocket. Or, as in Signore Kirshner's case, they make grand projections and fail to deliver. But you rate his type-work highly.

– The finest I've seen.

– Write to the man, then, if you must. Order what you need, or we'll bring him here again if we must.

Flood drafted a letter to Kirshner, outlining the nature of the problem and inviting the metallurgist to come in person. He was hoping to avoid it, but mention of the word *infinity* managed to find its way into his letter.

He returned to his platform and lived on it for three days, pacing to the edges while Djinn set type and the automaton printed, looking down into the rumbling chasm of bookcases like a sightseer gazing into the crater of Vesuvius. He neglected to shave, and slept under the press on a bolster, waking up to find food and drink at hand and hoping Irena had been the one to bring it. From time to time the Abbé, wandering by on his own mysterious peregrinations around the castle, would wave distantly to Flood on his platform as if to someone on a ship about to vanish over the horizon.

As she had asked to do, Irena came now and then to watch him work. He took her through the stages, starting with Djinn at the composing desk, turning a manuscript page into neat rows of type. As they watched Djinn's fingers dance over the compartments in the type case, he told her that each size of type had a name. The smallest, six-point type, was known as *nonpareil*. The sizes most commonly used in books were *long primer*, and *pica*.

– Although I prefer *small pica*. Or as its sometimes known, *philosophy*.

– *Small pica, or philosophy*, she said. It sounds like the title of a novel. With a girl heroine.

He showed her the various parts of the press and how they worked together.

– This sliding carriage is called the coffin. You crank the rounce and –

– I see, she said. The coffin slides under the stone slab –

– The platen –

– And slides back out again. I see now. That's why the inscription on your books. *Vitam mortuo reddo.* I wondered about it.

Flood nodded.

– *I restore life from death.* It was the motto of the family business long before I was born.

A stab of regret silenced him. He thought of the crude unvarnished box they had laid Meg to rest in. Though they worked side by side for countless hours, there were many days when he and his father said nothing at all to one another, unless it were to correct a fault or call for a brief halt. He looked back on that time in his life as a great silence.

A printer can be of service in many ways, his father once pronounced when he took a commission for a collection of bawdy ballads. *Sometimes by not printing.*

Books as novelties, as jokes. Books to gratify the whims of a lunatic nobleman, to win the admiration of his daughter. He saw his father, wiping his hands on his greasy apron and shaking his head in dismay. There was little doubt what he would have to say, were he still alive. *Reckless, reckless.*

At last Flood showed Irena his first finished trial piece: a scroll inspired by the Ostrov coat of arms. In order to make sense of the story, one had to unroll it entirely and join the ends into a loop, but with a twist, so that the paper seemed to have (or perhaps did have) only one side. For a text, he used an old legend he found in Zecchino's *Antiquities*, concerning the founding of Venice.

– There were two wealthy Roman families in Aquilea, he told Irena, who each had one child born to them on the same day, a boy and a girl. The children were wondrously beautiful, but the local sibyl warned that should they ever meet, they would instantly fall so deeply and irrevocably in love with one another that they would expire on the spot, their mortal bodies too frail to withstand such unearthly and absolute desire.

He paused, seeing Irena frown as she handled the unwieldy ribbon of paper.

– Go on, she said. I'm listening.

– The two families had a city constructed on the sandy islets in the lagoon. A city designed as an elaborate maze of walls, streets, and canals, something like this castle, if you will. The idea was to prevent the boy and girl from ever meeting. By the time they reached the age of sixteen, however, they had both heard rumours of each other's existence, and understood that the city was in fact their prison. So the boy and the girl escaped into the streets to find one another.

– The looping design, Flood went on, reflects their endless pursuit. The boy's story is printed on one side, the girl's on the other. But when the ends are joined, both follow the same single-sided story, so to speak, unaware that only if one of them stops moving will they be able to meet.

He waited for some comment from her, and when she handed the scroll back without speaking, he said,

– You don't think the Count will care for this?

She glanced up with a look of confusion, as if she had woken suddenly from a dream and still expected to see its landscape around her.

– It's very clever. I think you should show this to my father.

He did so that afternoon, despite his misgivings.

– Have you ever been to Venice? the Count asked, handing back the scroll.

– No.

– If you had, you likely wouldn't have chosen a romance for your text. The Queen of the Adriatic is toothless, senile, and smells bad. Still, this is a clever contrivance and I am not displeased. Persevere, Mr. Flood.

φ

Instead of persevering he stepped out for a breath of air and a leg-stretch on one of the parapets. He walked up and down, rubbing his hands together, glared at by gargoyles with long icicle noses, their gaping jaws dribbling water into an abyss of cornices, spires, slate roofs, and flying buttresses. He stood gazing out at the outside world that for days now he had virtually forgotten. How long had he been here? Today made it . . . eleven days. Only eleven days.

The river was frozen over but for a narrow scar of black water. The pines on the mountains were cloaked with snow, the ribbed white roof of the sky streaked with smoke rising from the village. From the forested hillsides came the sound of trees being cut, the axes striking the wood in an irregular tattoo that somehow soothed him. If not for that vaguely pleasing sound, the world would have seemed locked away in crystal.

Had anything ever changed in this valley? For all he could see or hear that revealed otherwise, it could be the year 1000. Or the year 1400, Gutenberg's invention of movable type still half a century away.

What would he be if he had lived then? A scribe, a monk, if he was fortunate. But more likely he would be down there in the forest with the timber-cutters, one of those who had likely never held so strange an object as a book in their callused, dumbfounded hands.

About the time this castle was built, according to the Count, the Mainz goldsmith had begun his cataclysmic innovations. And now, three hundred years later, the world was just beginning to drown in books. Like the magic wine cask in the old story, the press, once set flowing, could not be stopped by human power. Everyone, rich and poor, inquisitive or merely bored, was clamouring for things to read, and here he was, in this spellbound corner of the world, busily adding his own trickle of inked paper to the biblical deluge that was surely coming.

Someday books would even spill into this valley, and the people down there would scoop them up out of curiosity and drink, and learn the taste of knowledge, which always left one thirsty for more. And then that pleasantly distant sound of axes would grow much louder, as freshly sharpened blades started biting into the roots of this castle.

He heard a sound near him and peered around the corner of the parapet to see the Abbé de Saint-Foix, wrapped in a thick cloak, pacing and reading a letter. When Flood approached he glanced up as if emerging from a deep cavern.

– You're only in your shirtsleeves, Mr. Flood. Aren't you afraid to catch a chill?

– I thought winters in Quebec were a lot worse than this.

– They are. Why do you think I left?

For the first time, they shared a smile.

– I see that the Countess Irena takes quite an interest in your craft. If only I was staying on here. The three of us might have worked together on your impossible project. As it was in the beginning, is now, and ever shall be, Book without end, Amen.

– It sounds like you're planning to leave soon.

– I must. In any event I have found life inside this giant clock a little confining. I will be returning home, to Quebec, at least for a while. This letter informs me that my brother, Michel, has gone to his eternal reward.

– I am sorry.

– You needn't be, the Abbé said, meticulously folding the letter and tucking it into his cassock. He was brother to me only by accident of birth. Life under his rule, after our parents died, was rather like life here at the castle. Come to think of it, Mr. Flood, I have a story about my childhood that may be of use to you in your labours for the Count.

THE ABBÉ'S NARRATIVE

During Sunday Mass, wedged with his squirming brother and sisters between the sombre bastions of his parents, Ezequiel listened to the priest expound upon the eternity of bliss enjoyed by the righteous in heaven, or, more often, the eternity of torment awaiting sinners in hell. He would attempt to form a picture of it – *what would an eternity of bliss be like?* – since he never seriously contemplated the possibility that God would send him elsewhere, and in any case the priest already supplied a vivid description of the other place. He had much to say about what activities would be occupying the hours of the damned in hell, but he never went into similar detail about what the blessed would be doing with all the time at their disposal, other than singing the same hymns they sang here in church, only even more interminably.

What did it mean to say that for those in heaven, bliss would never end? How could that be? A thing only made you feel good because there was a time when you didn't have that thing, and so when you did, you could remember how much less enjoyable life had been not having it. Eternal bliss meant you were happy always and at every moment, without ever passing through a time when you were not happy. Every moment of that timeless time you would be aware that, yes, you were in heaven and this was bliss. Always. An unpassing passage of time, it seemed to him then, that might be like the long, dark winters of this land, like the fields of snow that stretched out endlessly beyond the walls of Quebec, perched on its rocky height above the silent white river.

His mind, like his delicate stomach the day his brother forced him to eat a scrap of the leathery cured meat favoured by *les coureurs de bois*, instinctively rejected the idea. That was no escape. It was mindless, the dream of slaves. He realized quite early how life in the colony was ruled by the clock. Each spring, when the ice broke up and he waited with everyone else for the arrival of the first ships from France, it occurred to him that time was their creator. Quebec did not believe in its own existence until those white sails were sighted on the horizon. Then the people around him, the pale ghosts of winter, would jerk to life like marionettes, pat one another on the back, drink toasts, observe that the ships were early this year, or late, or right on time, and place bets on just when the wind was likely to bring them into port.

Every year, the same performance.

He burned with the feverish desire to grasp time, hold it and cage it, so that he might find out what was left in its absence. He wanted not so much to escape his enemy as to subdue it. He became obsessed with numbers, and during Mass would keep a running tally of coughs and sneezes, or do sums with the rows of pearl buttons on his coat, in the hope that even such exercises in futility would use up a little more of that hated all-pervading element.

On that particular Sunday, he was attempting to count slowly enough that one tally of all the buttons from collar to skirts and back would last from the opening hymn to at least the profession of faith. But he swiftly tired of this old ritual and was left with things as they were, with himself as he was, stiff and itchy in his starched jabot, trying to ignore his older brother's finger jabbing him mercilessly in the ribs under cover of his folded arms. Far from a state of bliss.

All at once he felt the dim approach of something, a presence, first as the faintest trembling in the air. Then the wooden pew beneath him began to vibrate, like the grinding of the river ice as it broke up in the spring. He glanced furtively at his brother and sisters, his parents, the other members of the congregation. No one seemed to have noticed it. No one else but him even seemed to be breathing.

And then, descending towards him through the clouds of incense came a dark sphere, revolving and growing larger by the moment, the deep vibrato of its ponderous spin growing louder, pressing like a physical force against his eyes, drumming through his bones, roaring in his blood.

His adversary.

– Each instant, the Abbé said, gazing out across the wintry valley, and every insignificant thing it contained, like the counting of those buttons on my coat, all my moments of weakness and humiliation, my every movement and eyeblink and thought, every twitch and tremor and cough of each and every other soul in that church, in the colony, in the world, not only flowing into the next moment and the next incarnation of itself, but solidifying. Each instant, each button and jab and cough and thought accreting into this grey impenetrable mass. This was the universe, and the universe was only this, an iron prison I was helping to build with every breath. This was time.

The Abbé smiled.

– You look pale, Mr. Flood.

– For a child to see, or even to imagine, such a thing . . .

– Well, I assure you its terrors have faded somewhat in the intervening years. I've come to see it as a sign, if you will, that with such powers of fancy I was destined to be an author. But at the time, yes, it did make quite an impression.

It was then that he suffered his first bout of the recurring apoplexy that was to leave him unfit for any career but the church. A thunderclap to the brain that pitched him forward, the crown of his head colliding with the back of the pew in front of him. His body lying rigid, his mind aware of everything that was happening but unable to will a limb, a muscle, an eyelash to move, staring up at the vaulted ceiling of the church and into the indifferent gaze of an archangel, until he was at last lifted and carried out by his red-faced and puffing father, his weeping mother dabbing at his bleeding head with a handkerchief, his older brother, Michel, and his sisters trailing after, their eyes fixed on him in mingled fear and suspicion.

He was brought home and installed on the sofa. The doctor, who had followed the family from church, knelt to examine him, lifted his hand by the wrist and let it drop, poked the soles of his feet with a penknife, waved a lit taper in front of his unblinking eyes. When at last he ushered Ezequiel's parents out for a whispered consultation in the next room, his brother suddenly appeared and stood over him, his face as expressionless as the stone archangel's. Finally Michel leaned forward, placed a hand over Ezequiel's mouth and stuck two fingers up his nostrils.

His body began to scream silently for air. He closed his eyes, unable to bear Michel's impassive gaze, then opened them again when panic overpowered him. Finally, as his vision clouded over and he felt himself sinking into black flames, the hands went away. His lungs shrieked, flooding with air.

That evening, Ezequiel defied the doctor's sombre prognostications, got up off the sofa as if nothing unusual had taken place, and joined his astounded family at the supper table where they had been eating their soup in morose silence. Michel, eager to forestall any mention of his little prank, led everyone in a prayer of thanksgiving for his brother's recovery. It did not occur to Ezequiel to turn informer. Michel, like time itself, was a tribulation as inevitable and pointless to protest against as an illness or lessons in Latin.

And there was of course his secret refuge: the library. His father used the room only on those rare occasions when he wished to impress an important visitor from France. Most days the room remained locked up, and, ever since Ezequiel could remember, forbidden to the children. His brother's relentless persecution, however, had led him to steal the key from the steward's cupboard and shut himself up from time to time in the library, where one day he discovered the blank books.

Since all books were meant to be read, he assumed that these called for a particular kind of reading, one which he hadn't yet been taught. Perhaps these books, and not the tall glass cabinet filled with frosted decanters of red and black liquor, were the reason the room was forbidden. And so he read the books, one at a time, not starting a new one until he had worked his way through every page of the one before, each volume a compact Canada of perfect snow-white pages. He would touch the cool, creamy surface of the paper with his fingertips, his cheek, his lips. From the marbled endpapers rose the faintly intoxicating, hermetic smell of binding paste.

When he turned the pages they rattled softly, like far-off thunder.

The vision of time he had glimpsed that day in church still haunted his sleepless nights, but now he had something, a bulwark of books to seal himself in against it. Here and there among his treasures he found a printed volume. The sight of its neat blocks of text was distressing, as if a thorny hedge of words lay between him and the other book, the one he truly wished to read. The only ordinary printed book he treasured was his father's atlas of the world, in which the names of fabled places like London and Paris were neatly printed alongside tiny fairy-tale countries of blue and pink and green. Perhaps in one of those true places he might be something more than a figment of time.

When he was twelve, his parents died at sea, while making a crossing to France, and Michel was now officially the master of his brother's destiny that he has always considered himself to be. By then Ezequiel had come to understand that the blank books were not meant to be read, that they were in fact only part of the façade of gentility that was his father's life. Still, having read through more than half of them by this time, and looking forward to making his way through those that remained, he was crushed when Michel sold off the entire library, to finance the building of a gaming salon.

— For six years, the Abbé said, I endured the prison that my house, my city, had become under my brother's merciless and arbitrary dominion. Michel was now the lord of time. Of the cycles of the year, the epicycles of the months, the stations of the week. Every hour of my day and every minute of every hour circumscribed and entered in advance in his ledger. Every moment of idleness, unless it were his own at the gambling table or the brothel, ruthlessly punished. Finally, at the age of seventeen, when it seemed to me my life was already over, I was suddenly free. Michel had already had our sisters tucked safely away in convents and now he wanted me out of his sight, too. So I was sent to Paris, to the Jesuit College, to begin my studies for the priesthood.

There, he discovered Versailles. Or rather, like so many exiles before him, he was caught by it as if by gravity, and revolved in that glittering orbit like a grubby coin circling a collection plate. Before long, his greatest ambition was to become confessor to the true power in the realm, the king's mistress.

– Things did not turn out that way, Flood said.

– Fortunately, they did not. I soon discovered I was not cut out to be another painted lackey, scurrying to the palace every morning to witness the awesome spectacle of the royal toilet. Dukes standing at attendance with towels, while others vied for the honour of holding his chamber pot. The great achievement of Versailles, I saw, was to make time turn in a never-ending circle around the sun of ceremony. But it was a false eternity, an illusion inviting its own demise. I turned away from it, and began to write. And since one cannot expect people to read a book of blank pages, I wrote a novel.

While the Abbé was telling his story, light flakes of snow had begun to fall. The two men looked at one another, shivered and went inside, laughing and brushing the snow from their hair.

– You must have overcome your dislike of print, Flood said. You know so many of the Count's books so well.

– Of course, the Abbé said. Within every book there lies concealed a book of nothing. Don't you sense it when you read a page brimming with words? The vast gulf of emptiness beneath the frail net of letters. The ghostliness of the letters themselves. Giving a semblance of life to things and people who are really nothing. Nothing at all. No, it was the reading that mattered, I eventually understood, not whether the pages were blank or printed. The Mohammedans say that an hour of reading is one stolen from Paradise. To that perfect thought I can only add that an hour of writing gives one a foretaste of the other place.

– What are you working on now? Flood asked. To his surprise the Abbé's face darkened.

– Don't you know, Mr. Flood, that is the one question you must never ask a writer?

φ

Irena was always the first member of the household to awaken. Long before the servants had begun their daily circumnavigations she would open her eyes. The sun would not yet be up, and since she had never overcome a childhood fear of the dark she would quickly light a candle.

This morning, as always, her bed was back in its chamber, motionless for the moment, and in the stillness she could listen to the rest of the castle. All around her, the clock ticked. Far below, the boilers rumbled. All sounded as it should.

She rose in her shift, pulled on a morning gown, and hurried on bare feet through the corridors, to a tall oak cabinet set into a niche. Slipping a small brass key from her pocket, she stepped up into the niche, unlocked the cabinet, swung open its narrow doors, and gazed upon the tarnished silver of her mother's face.

When she was a little girl Irena had asked her father where *the poor Countess* was that the nurses often talked about in sad whispers. The Count told her that her mother had died bringing her into the world. On Irena's twelfth birthday he brought her to this cabinet and revealed his gift, the first of the automatons fashioned by the Venetian metallurgist: a mother of polished steel and brass. The creature shuddered to life, whirring like a startled pheasant, tilted forward, and spread its arms wide to take the girl into its embrace. Irena screamed, bolted in terror, and could not be made to go near the thing again, despite her father's command that she do so. Eventually the Count locked the automaton away and forgot about it, and only then, much later, did she come to the niche on her own, when no one else was there to see her. She opened the cabinet, closed her eyes, and allowed herself to be caught by these cold, metallic limbs.

Now it was a ritual for her, even though, after years of neglect, the automaton's inner workings had rusted and the arms no longer moved when the cabinet was opened. Irena said nothing to her father, not wanting him to know about her secret morning visitation.

She leaned forward and kissed the gleaming forehead, held the immobile hands in hers and felt the warmth of her own body flowing almost imperceptibly into the icy metal, until she could no longer tell where she began and the machine ended. She wondered why it was not possible for that warmth to bring a pink flush of life to cold metal, to light a spark in eyes of glass, as her father had tried to do with the replica of Ludwig. On mornings like this she would stay as long as she dared, listening to her own heart beat against the automaton's unyielding skin, until she heard the clanking of pots and dishes from far below as the cooks began their day.

And the printer. She closed her eyes and heard it, barely audible amid the clatter of the awaking castle, but there nonetheless, running on its own time, apart from her father's clocked and precise system. The creak of the press. She felt her heart quicken, and smiled. There was no hiding it from herself here. She would be seeing him soon, when she brought him more of the books he requested. She wondered why his scroll had disturbed her so much. Or perhaps it was his obvious pleasure at having created the thing. Just like her father when he posed a particularly difficult riddle.

— She is beautiful. The image of her daughter.

The Abbé stood just below the niche, his hands clasped behind his back.

— This is not my mother, Abbé Ezequiel.

— But I gather it was intended as a kind of surrogate.

Irena looked away.

— I see I've intruded upon your privacy, the Abbé said with a bow, and I will take my leave.

— No, said Irena, swinging shut the doors of the cabinet. You've reminded me I should be getting to work.

— Well, at the very least please forgive my crude attempt at flattery. When a man admires a woman, such trite phrases are woefully inappropriate, are they not?

— There was no harm done.

He bent his head.

— You are very gracious, Countess. May I tell you what I admire in you?

— This will be a more refined attempt at flattery, then?

The Abbé laughed.

— It is so refreshing, he said, to talk to someone like you. Do you know, you must be the only woman I've met in my travels who is capable of more than rehearsed coquetry.

– I doubt that. Perhaps you did not give those women enough time. To show you who they really were.

– Well, with you, may I say, very little time was needed. I saw enough right away to incline me to stay and learn more.

– I'm glad. But now I should be getting on with my chores . . .

The Abbé stepped forward.

– At the risk of offence, let me tell you, Countess, what it is I've learned. You are most pleasing to look upon, but vastly more important, you are the most intelligent woman I have ever met. If my awkward declaration offends, let me excuse myself by admitting that I would be more at ease with a woman whose mind did not continually surprise me. And yours does. Surprises and delights me, challenges me. I can only confess that you've crumbled all my defences.

Irena locked the cabinet doors. She turned to face the Abbé.

– It wasn't a planned attack, she said coldly. I've enjoyed the conversations we've had, certainly . . .

– That is precisely the point, the Abbé said. We've begun without the usual tedious moves and countermoves.

– Begun what?

– You and I, Countess, have the opportunity to be what few men and women dare to be in this painted, mercenary age.

– And what is that?

– Friends.

– We are that already, I had thought.

– True friends who speak candidly to one another, keeping nothing back. Baring their hearts.

– Abbé Ezequiel . . .

– Countess, I am speaking of feelings that rise above our differences in other matters. Believe me, I am well aware of your reservations concerning the ideas put forth in my novel.

– Tell me, then, do you believe your own theory of the soul?

– Were I not here, your father would find someone else to encourage him. Like the Englishman, for example. Perhaps you should ask Mr. Flood how long he plans to spend trying to print an infinite book.

– It is not my place.

– I agree. This is not your place at all.

He turned and walked to the nearest window.

– You belong out there, he said. In Paris, Vienna, Milan. Your place is among men and women who think and act and change the world, not here in this madhouse.

– That is not what I meant, Irena said.

– Then let me state more plainly what *I* meant, the Abbé said, facing her again. I have inherited my brother's estate in Quebec, and I must return there before the government or the Church tries to appropriate it. So as you see, I have no intention of further encouraging your father's dreams. On the contrary, I have dreams of my own. Dreams which can only become reality with your help.

– I don't understand.

The Abbé stepped up to Irena and took her hand.

– Countess, in the months I've spent here I have come to see that with you as my confidante, my intellectual sparring partner, my severest critic, I might accomplish a truly great work.

Gently, Irena slid her hand free of the Abbé's grip.

– Is this a declaration of your feelings, Abbé Ezequiel, or are you simply looking for an editor?

The Abbé frowned.

– I am thinking of a coupling of minds, yes. But I also dare to hope our concord would be ratified as often as possible with communion of a more physical nature.

– Abbé, you are a handsome man, and a fine writer. But as any reader will tell you, there's no accounting for taste.

The Abbé stepped back. Muscles pulsed in his jaw.

– This has nothing to do with taste, he said, his voice trembling. I am speaking of love. The divine madness.

Irena lowered her eyes.

– I am truly sorry, but if it is a divine madness, I do not share it.

The Abbé recovered himself, took a deep breath, and bowed.

– So it must be. To spare you any further embarrassment I will leave for Vienna this very afternoon.

– You tell me, Irena said, that you cherish honesty above all. I am only telling you what I think you already know. That this is not really about me.

She turned from him and locked the cabinet. The Abbé stared at her.

– You mean to imply, he said slowly, that my regard for you is feigned. Or perhaps you think that I offer you this chance for freedom out of pity.

Irena faced him, an angry flush darkening her pale features.

– Pity?

– A writer learns to be observant. I've watched you. The way you walk. The way you rise from a chair. I'm curious to know how old you were when the disease struck that crippled you.

Irena slipped the key back into her pocket. She stepped down from the niche.

– No, I don't think you pity me. I think you were looking to distract yourself from something else, something that you hoped I might help you forget, at least for a while.

– What a novel idea. Have you mentioned it to your friend the printer? I'm sure he will be impressed, as he always is, with your keen insights.

– I don't know what it is you really want, Abbé Ezequiel, but I sincerely hope you find it. You seem to me to be a very unhappy man.

φ

He closed one eye and peered with the other through the narrow glass panes. He could see her, sitting motionless at a table, writing. She was wearing spectacles. He had not known she wore spectacles.

His blunt fingers awkwardly plucked at the tiny latch and finally succeeded in opening the window. Carefully he reached in a hand and gently touched the little porcelain figurine.

He withdrew his hand and stepped back from the display case, marvelling and strangely saddened at the same time. The entire castle, in miniature, down to the last detail. There was even a crank at the base of the model for setting its walls and floors in motion.

He froze, suddenly aware that something around him had changed. He had been so absorbed in the miniature that he had forgotten the real thing, and in a moment he realized that the castle had *stopped*. The walls, the floors, the roving furniture frozen and silent. The stillness sent a tremor of dread through him, as though he had just been told someone had died.

He hurried to the edge of the gallery, fighting the urge to

call out and see if anyone was there to answer. On the level below him, Irena was kneeling on the bare floor of an aisle between two shelves, holding a large cloth-bound book, her gown spread around her like a cataract of pale blue silk. At first Flood imagined that she too, like the castle, had somehow come to a halt. Then her hand stirred, turned a page, came to rest again. The look on her face was one of guileless concentration.

As if her slight motion had started the castle working again, metallic banging and hammering began to drift up from the lower floors.

Irena glanced up, saw Flood leaning over the rim of the gallery and rose hastily to her feet.

– The fusee went out of alignment and threw everything off schedule, she said. The engineers have had to stop the entire works in order to get at the problem.

– Your father must be displeased.

– He is away, she said. On business in Pressburg.

– This quiet is unnerving, he said. I've become so accustomed to the constant noise.

– I think the silence is beautiful, Irena said, sliding the book back into place on the shelf and brushing at her gown. It's like the enchanted castle in the old stories.

She climbed up the ladder to where he stood.

– May I ask what you were reading?

– An old encyclopedia, she said. It's called the *Libraria Technicum*.

– I know it, Flood said. I worked for a while with the man who printed it. Synonym Wilkins, we called him. Did the Abbé recommend it?

– The Abbé has gone. He left last night, in the coach with my father.

– He told me he might not be staying much longer. I don't think he was happy with the . . . clocks.

– He didn't tell me so. I hope he will find the clocks more to his liking at his next destination.

– So what did you find in old Synonym's encyclopedia?

She told him she loved books from places she had never been. Reading the *Libraria Technicum* she believed she could hear, behind or within its dry, technical sentences, the bustle of the port of London, the cry of the gulls, the ever-present rattle of carriages through the busy streets. She had always wanted to know if her image of the City of the New was in any measure accurate. She had heard so many wonderful tales about London.

– The people of highest and lowest class mingling together in the streets, greeting one another without ceremony as fellow citizens.

He said that it was true everyone mingled in the streets, but it was not because of overflowing love for one's fellow man.

– It's the result of cramming so many people into such a small space.

Wasn't it true, though, she asked, that the city was full of surprises? It was said you could find anything there.

He told her that if she wanted to know what London was like, the castle would give her a good idea.

– People are always in motion there. No one stays in one place for long.

– Here the walls and ceilings and floors move, she said, and the people stand still.

He looked into her eyes and at that moment a truth that he should have seen right from the beginning became clear to him. The castle, the automatons, the clockworks, all of this was her father's system and functioned by his rules, but Irena had her own system, quietly running on its own inside the Count's. He was not sure why she had disabled the great clock, but felt a rush of hope that she had done it to bring about this encounter with him. Feeling the colour rising to his face, he turned to his press and saw that Ludwig had wound down at the bar.

— And you, Mr. Flood, she said. How do you feel about the clocks?

He hesitated, and was aware again of what seemed an unearthly stillness.

— I like them at the moment, he said.

By dinnertime the problem with the castle's machinery had not yet been resolved. The servants were thrown into confusion by the change in their routines, and so Irena herself saw to some of their tasks. Later that evening she brought fresh candles to replace the guttering stubs on Flood's work table. As she approached, a gust of air followed in her wake and overtook her, blowing out the flames and plunging the room into blackness.

— Wait a moment, he said.

She heard his chair scrape on the floorboards as he pushed it back. A moment later she saw a fuzzy patch of faint green light bobbing in the darkness, approaching her.

— What is that? she whispered.

His face swam closer to hers. The pale green glow came from a sheet held in his hand.

— I've coated the paper with a tincture that absorbs not only ink but light.

Now she could see his hands and his forehead as well, which also faintly luminesced.

– A book you can read in the dark, she said.

He held the paper to the dying spark of a candle and it crackled into sullen flame. She quickly relit the other candles and smiled over the bouquet of light she was handing him. As the paper burned up she saw through the green flames the image stamped upon it, melting and writhing. She asked him if he had chosen the phoenix as his symbol for just such moments.

– Salamander, Flood said.

– What?

– The creature is supposed to be a salamander.

The little dragon that dwells in fire, he explained, without being consumed, was a reassuring thought for people who work with paper. Originally he wanted a chimera, but the engraver he hired had gotten his mythological beasts confused.

– We have them in the castle, she said. The real sort of salamander, I mean. In the underground crypts, among the gears, where it's dark and damp.

– It sounds a lot like London. The sort of climate where printers thrive.

– If that's so, she asked, why did you leave?

He felt his face burn.

– I can't resist a challenge.

– We can move you to the crypts if you wish, she said with a smile.

She left him, and Flood went back to his platform. Instead of sleeping he worked fitfully through the night, dozing off and waking again with a start, until he suddenly found morning in full possession of the castle. Djinn appeared at his side, yawning and rubbing the sleep out of his eyes. Flood rose stiffly from his chair. His head swooped, and he had to clutch the table edge to keep from toppling over. When had he last eaten?

He patted the boy on the shoulder.

– Let's see if we can't find something for breakfast.

As they followed the smell of baking he went over his conversations with the Countess. Something had been nudged to life inside him. Something for which he did not yet have a name. He was in love with her, of course, but there was something else. Something more . . .

He and the boy finally tracked down a tray standing unattended near the kitchens, loaded with baked goods and coffee. They helped themselves, grinning at one another as they stuffed rolls into their apron pockets, and then sat together at the bottom of a curving staircase to eat their ill-gotten gains.

I like her, he thought. That was it. He looked at Djinn, sleepily chewing his buttered roll, and a laugh bubbled out of him. The boy glanced up quizzically.

– Good?

Djinn nodded.

– Yes, it's good, Flood said.

That morning, as the printing platform rolled past a row of narrow pier glasses, he caught sight of his grinning face, dyed to a bluish swarthiness with ink. The sheen of sweat on his brow. His neck and arms, muscled like a bullock-driver's from years of heaving the bar. His stained apron and holey stockings.

Look at yourself.

The days and months and years of apprenticing, the fluid dexterity he'd had to develop as he moved from one step in the process to another, the gallons of ink that he'd no doubt absorbed into his skin, all of it had turned him into a sinuous, oily creature best suited to the dank dungeon of a print shop. People came to him for what they needed, they bantered with him, exchanged jokes and gossip, politely ignored the reek of the urine he used to soften the leather ink bats overnight. He was a good listener. People had always confided in him, told him family stories. Secrets.

They would haggle amiably over the price until they saw he would not budge an inch, and then they left, with or without their commissions engaged but always with a smile, usually not to be seen again, unless he caught a glimpse of them frequenting some other printer's shop.

Unlike the handsome Abbé, he had never been pursued by any woman, let alone a continent of them. He was almost thirty, and the one amatory interlude that had embellished his life thus far had been with the woman who came into his shop early one morning and asked him what he sold besides books. As he began to run through the stock – *prints & mariners' charts; journals & pocketbooks; embroidered letter-pouches; bills of lading & shipping paper* – she slipped off one glove and ran a slender white finger along the surface of a ribboned stack of envelopes – *best gilt, black-edged, post & plain writing paper; sealing wax & wafers* – she unpinned her hat, shook her hair out, and began to tug at the strings of her bodice . . . *ink & ink powder . . . scissors & penknives . . . bookmarks & booksnakes*. . . . He never found out the woman's name or anything about her other than the obvious fact that her passion was aroused less by his charms than by stationery. He looked at his trade with new eyes after that day, aware of just how many solitary women frequented his shop. But after that one frantic encounter, half-clothed atop his desk amid spilling paper, life went on as before.

He was a printer's son, a printer's grandson and great-grandson. Despite the notoriety of his creations he was simply a tradesman. The wealthy were the only people who could afford his books, and yet he did not know them. He was appreciated best when unseen, like one of the cogs that moved the hands of the immense clock. Or the pumps and gears down in the crypts where Irena had said she'd seen salamanders.

He wound up Ludwig and got him started on a fresh batch of sheets. The printing platform appeared in another mirror, one with a flaw in the glass that caused his reflection to elongate and ripple slightly, as if he had turned to water.

It was as if she were still there before him. The air stirred faintly by the sweep of her gown as she turned. Her slender neck as she reached up to light the candelabra. He saw himself drawn towards a fountain of white flame. Crawling out of cold muck, his hands reaching into the light, to replenish himself in that fire.

— Salamander, he said in a louder voice.

— *Alam*, came the buzzing echo from Ludwig. Djinn's head shot up from his tray of type.

— *Alam*. Does that mean anything? Flood asked the boy. Djinn nodded. He had learned a little English by this time, but out of shyness or some other motive Flood could not discern, preferred to speak to the printer by way of his craft. His insect fingers scuttled across a tray of italic type and in a moment he handed over his composing stick. Flood spelled out the backwards English phrases.

alam is everything my lord. is all world.

Flood thrust the composing stick back into the boy's hand.

— I am not your lord, he said.

φ

Love is always a conspiracy against some part of the world. In the end, Flood could not doubt what had passed between the two of them the moment Irena looked into his eyes and he guessed that she herself had stopped the castle clock.

He would draw near the flame.

Setting aside the book of mirrors, he began work on a small octavo volume, the text an old sermon taken from his stock of waste sheets. The sectarian preacher in London who'd commissioned the work had fled the country, and so Flood had been forced to break up what he had already set in type and find another use for the already printed pages.

He inked the formes in a kind of delirium, laughing and humming to himself. He prayed the Count would not appear unannounced and see the idiot grin on his face. As he stitched the signatures together his hands shook.

When the secret book was printed and bound, the word *Desire* gold-tooled on its spine, he tucked it away with the seventeen-volume *Libraria Technicum*. In order to make his interloper fit on the shelf, he had to remove the seventh volume, *Helix–Longitude*, which he tucked away in the concealed compartment of his type-cabinet, the place he always kept dangerous manuscripts.

φ

In the morning the requested cases of new type arrived from Venice, along with a tarnished spoon, and a letter.

I've already been to the Count's giant orrery. The only reason I might be tempted to return would be to see the Countess again.

However, I will simply ask you to give her my good wishes.

I trust the cases of type are as ordered. The other enclosed item is my response to your comments about infinity. My father always used to say, The spoon tastes not the broth.

Regards,
S. Kirshner

φ

She stood beside him, her hands cupped together, waiting until he swam up out of his thoughts and became aware of her.

— I didn't hear you, he said, rising from his chair.

— I know, she said, nodding to the lines and angles he had been drawing. You were in the land of geometry. I found something down in the cellars. Something I think you'll like.

She lowered her hands to the desk and opened them. On her palm sat a small, shiny creature, like a frog but with a tail. Its S-shaped body a glossy black speckled with bright yellow spots. He realized he had never seen a real, living salamander.

— She's a beauty, he said. Or *is* it a she?

— I'm not sure. We have Linnaeus' *Systema Naturae*, but it wasn't much help.

— Oh, yes. The Swede who's invented categories for all living things.

Irena nodded, her eyes brightening with amusement.

— He suggests animals be classified on the basis of whether or not they have breasts.

In the silence that followed they both examined the creature intently.

– She led me a merry chase though, Irena finally said, stroking the salamander's back. They live among the steam engines and the gears, where the dungeons used to be.

– It's not moving, Flood said. Is it . . . ?

He extended a tentative finger. Before he could touch it the salamander writhed out of Irena's palm onto the desk and disappeared into a surf of loose paper.

– Where did it . . . ?

– There –

– Got you!

Flood's hand rose with a flourish. Between his thumb and forefinger was a short stub of yellow-and-black tail. He grimaced.

– I've dismembered the poor thing.

Irena shook her head.

– She'll grow herself a new tail. If you'd pulled off her leg she could grow that back, too.

– Not even the mythical salamander can do that.

– I read about it, in Pliny.

She closed her eyes.

– *An . . . insectivorous batrachian, that springs from some unknown Source, appearing during great Rains, or, according to ancient Authorities, arising from the Midst of the most ardent Flames. When seiz'd by their Enemies, these Creatures elude Capture by leaving a Leg or a Part of their Tail behind, the Missing Extremity soon replaced by the growth of another –*

She broke off as the salamander emerged. Flood gently scooped the creature up and returned it to Irena's hands.

– I should take her back where I found her.

There was a stutter of gears as the castle started into motion again, a hiss of steampipes venting, a long groan of metal against metal, and then silence. Irena leaned over the balustrade of the gallery and peered down into the depths.

– Has your father returned, Countess?

– I am expecting him any day.

– Do *you* ever leave here?

– My father trusts only me to maintain things in his absence. At least until the day he perfects his system.

They heard a muffled shout and saw, on the far side of a lower gallery, Turini the carpenter with his arms around Darka, the contortionist. She was trying to squirm free, her face flushed with delight.

– My father's dream, Irena said, is a completely self-regulating mechanism, like the spheres of the planets. He sees the castle, long after he and I are dead, without a living soul in it. Walls and floors and furniture making their transits in silence. Forever.

Flood argued that nothing in this world lasts forever. Metal rusts. Gears wear down. Wooden beams warp, rot, get gnawed by insects. And people never leave anything alone. They will always pry, and interfere, and try to improve, correct, or tear down what is supposedly finished and perfect. That was why printing was so difficult. The press was a nearly flawless invention, almost capable of working on its own, but it produced as much opposition and interference as it did pages.

She asked him why, if he believed that, he persisted in printing.

– My father liked to say that by multiplying the number of books in the world we multiply the number of readers. And with each new reader the ranks of the book-burners thin out a little more.

– Is that why you're here? she asked him. To escape the book-burners?

– I'm here because of a letter, he said. I wanted to find out who had written it.

She slowly turned away, cradling the salamander in her hands. He sat for a while after she had left, astounded at himself, and then craned his neck over the balustrade. He caught sight of her now and then as she made her way in a meandering spiral down into the depths of the castle.

He turned back to his drawings, took up his pen, and traced the curve of her movements.

A spiral.

He scribbled a set of numbers, took up his rule, and drew a rectangle. Inside the empty frame he inscribed a single character: φ

He thought back to his father's lessons. *Are you listening, Nicholas? The golden section. A proportion based on a ratio in which the lesser value is to the greater as the greater is to the sum. It can also be found in nature . . .*

In the spiral of a seashell, for instance, which is itself only a fragment of a greater spiral of increase. An infinite one.

Yes, Father. I remember now. Thank you.

φ

Having the entire library filed in her head, Irena knew she had never seen this little volume with *Desire* gold-tooled on the spine. It had to be a creation of Flood's, even though she had warned him not to place anything on the shelves without her father's permission. Perhaps he had thought to conceal his indiscretion by tucking it away here.

That night she took the book to bed with her and by candle-light skimmed through the sermon it contained.

> . . . these Earthly Promptings that come like thieves in the night and rob us of sweet Tranquillity and Reason. . . . Intimations in the Flesh of the Soul's one right Desire, for Communion with the Radiance of Eternal Truth. . . .

After several pages of this she shut the book, set it on the night table, and blew out the candles, disappointed. He had hidden the book where he did, she was sure, to let her know it was a message. But not the message she had expected. Was he warning both of them not to go any further?

She became aware of a faint illumination against her eyelids, and staring into the darkness saw a pale green glow along the book's fore-edge. She sat up and opened the book again. In the spaces between the lines of the sermon, repeated on page after page in unbroken cursive pica, she read her own name.

She was in bliss and torment at the same time. Unable to gather her thoughts, her first impulse was to hide this confession that lit up the curtains of her bed. As she reached down to tuck it under her mattress, the book slipped out of her hand and hit the floor with a terrible bang. Irena climbed from her bed, letting it trundle on without her while she crept back along the passage. The incriminating volume lay splayed open, bathing the walls and ceiling with its spectral glow.

Stooping quickly she picked up the book, wrapped it in her arms, and started off after her bed. Her mind and her feet were not pursuing the same course, and after a while she discovered she had managed to accomplish the unprecedented and lose her way. She stood still, listening, her bare feet chilled by the icy stone of the floor. Something was approaching, and soon she saw that it was her father's bed. He was not there, she knew, but still she backed slowly against the wall, holding her breath and hugging Flood's book tightly to her breast as the bed rumbled past and slowly vanished.

The next morning she kept *Desire* with her, concealed in the folds of her gown, breathless at the thought that she was leaving an unaccounted empty space on one of the shelves, a flaw in her father's system. Whenever she could steal an unobserved moment during her daily rounds, she opened the book and turned its pages, mouthing the bituminous phrases of the sermon with secret delight.

At the end of the day she returned the book to its place on the shelf, having decided upon her fate. Taking a ring of keys from her apron pocket, she unlocked a trapdoor in a remote passageway. Glancing around quickly to make sure she was unobserved, she climbed down a ladder into the dank underneath of the castle and in an instant was swallowed up by steam and darkness.

φ

In the evening she brought the printer coffee on a silver tray. As she passed Ludwig at his post beside the press she tickled his jutting porcelain chin. Djinn was dozing on a settee, wrapped in Flood's threadbare bombazine coat. He stirred as she went by and mumbled words in one of his half-remembered languages.

Irena set the tray on the work table at Flood's elbow. Beside the coffee decanter lay the small octavo volume of *Desire*.

Flood stared at the book without daring to look up into Irena's eyes.

– When the clock tells a quarter past three tonight, she finally managed to whisper, my bed will pass yours.

She turned and went back the way she had come. Flood sat, frozen, then reached out and put his hand on the cover of the book.

That night, as the striking of the great clock reverberated through the draughty halls of the castle, Flood, in shirt and breeches, leaped barefoot, like a pirate boarding a galley, from his moving bed to Irena's. He found her sitting at the head with her arms around her knees, eyes glittering. She was still dressed in her blue silk gown, but her long russet hair had been released from its pins and lace and spilled about her shoulders.

Just as he was about to move towards her, he stopped. Her face was contorting, her eyes squeezing shut, her mouth dropping open – Was she about to weep, or scream . . . ?

– Countess –

She sneezed. They looked at one another for a moment and then laughed.

– We've confused the dust, she said.

– Do you always wear your gown to bed? he asked, not daring yet to do anything else but speak.

– You don't know much about women's clothing, do you?

– No.

She leaned over to the side of the bed and blew out the candle.

– I dismissed my maid early. I need you to help me with all of this.

Shyness constrained them to take things methodically:

Laced modesty piece in the French style.
Damask stomacher stitched with silk rosettes.

Back-lacing jacket bodice.

Apron of printed Indian cotton.

Overskirt of cream silk embroidered with gold thread.

Watered-satin petticoat.

Quilted camlet under-petticoats (2).

– You have to do this every night?

– And every morning, in reverse.

Whalebone birdcage-style hoop.

Persian stays (also stiffened with whalebone).

Double-stitched pocket-ribband with perfume sachet.

Linen chemise *á l'Angloise*.

– There.

When she set aside the last garment he reached for her and his fingers touched cold metal.

– Go on, she said. That comes off too. I won't be needing it tonight.

φ

There was no time.

In the darkness they devoured one another, fell back into themselves, spent, and came together again.

– I want to see us.

She lit a candle. They looked, dazed, at their gleaming bodies. Together they were a new world.

He blew out the candle and they lay nestled against one another in the blackness. The bed rolled through the castle, stopped, moved on again.

She told him of her childhood illness, and how she had come to wear the cage. He told her about the sister he had lost.

– How old were you when she died?

– Eleven. But I remember it all so clearly, as if it only happened yesterday.

– Perhaps everything did, she said. The past is who we are.

φ

In the half-light before dawn he finally saw the cage, lying tenantless at the foot of the bed where he had cast it with her other clothing.

– I don't want to put this back on you, he said. Every day . . .

– I've gotten used to it over the years. It's part of me.

Flood's bed approached like a comet returning in its long revolution. She told him her father was expected home today. When they embraced one last time, he said it was strange, the way they had been drawn together. As if, like the Count's automatons, they had no choice.

– He's been working on machines, she said, that will one day replace both him and me. We've been waiting for the casings to come from Meissen.

– He already treats you like a machine. I want to take you away from here. We could go to Venice. Hide there, find a ship to take us to England.

She shook her head.

– Nicholas, I . . .

He rose and cautiously parted the curtains. His bed was almost abreast of hers.

– If he found out, what would he do?

Without answering, she kissed him. As he made ready to leap he dug in his pocket and handed her a small T-shaped piece of metal.

– It's a quoin key, he said. If something happens, leave it on my work table.

He was gone, leaving a faint glow of phosphorescence lingering on the sheets and on Irena's skin. She held her hands in front of her and watched the light vanish into them.

φ

At breakfast the Count placed a sealed letter on the table, propping it against the chocolate boat.

– I almost forgot, he said casually to Irena. The Abbé asked me to give you this.

– Thank you, Father.

The Count turned to Flood.

– I'm pleased you could join us, my friend. I so look forward to hearing what you have accomplished during my absence.

As he spoke, Irena slid the letter off the table and slipped it into her pocket.

– Ah, my dear, the Count said. I thought perhaps you might favour us with the contents. I find I already miss the Abbé's intelligent conversation.

He smiled at Flood's look of surprise.

– There are no secrets at this table, sir.

Irena carefully slit the letter open with her knife, unfolded the paper and read.

Countess,

Your kindness will always remain impressed upon my soul. I fear that pen and ink cannot express how attached you have become to my heart, as if with unbreakable bind- ings. I will always treasure the memory of our too-brief acquaintance, and I thank you for the undeserved respect and consideration you showed me from first to last. Believe me when I say that I hope someday to have the opportunity to repay it.

Yours with all due respect and esteem,
Saint-Foix

— Hm, said the Count, sipping his coffee. Surprisingly con- ventional, for a man of his talents. Although *bindings*, now, strikes me as somewhat original. *Bonds* is the more usual figure of speech, I believe.

He gave a wheezing laugh.

— It sounds, Mr. Flood, as if he's borrowing his metaphors from your trade.

φ

He had been aware for some time of a presence stalking the halls and galleries, someone or something that moved at the periphery of his vision, like a mirror-self glimpsed down a distant corridor, but which vanished whenever he turned to look directly at it. He felt its shadow like an invisible eclipse moving across the faces of his many clocks, causing tiny erran- cies in their usually flawless timekeeping.

At first he had blamed the disruption caused by the printer's activities. The nautical creaking of the press screw, the click-clack of type slugs dropping into place in the boy's composing stick, the flutter of sheets drying on cords, stirred by the cold draughts that found their way into the castle despite his best efforts: all these annoyances had disturbed the order of things, but he knew that this *other* presence was something more than mechanical. It was intangible, amorphous, and therefore a true threat. After his return he could not sleep, and rising in the night followed mysterious glowing handprints on walls, naked footprints on floors, tracks that swiftly faded and disappeared before he could arrive at their intended destination. He felt it in tiny, subtle shifts of mood and energy shown by his servants, the way one will be aware of an oncoming bout of influenza long before the actual symptoms occur. He saw it in the face of his daughter, who had begun to neglect her duties, an unprece-dented dereliction, and was often found staring dreamily at nothing, no longer even with a book in her hands to explain these lapses from her day's well-ordered round. At first he thought the presence of the handsome Abbé had distracted the females of the household. But now the suave Frenchman was gone and it was the awkward Englishman, he was forced to conclude, who had introduced an unknown, pernicious element into his smoothly running system, one which he was determined to track down and root out.

To that end he scrutinized everything done and everyone doing it more minutely than ever, eventually noticing that one of the bookcases seemed to be gliding with the merest suggestion of an imbalance, an infinitesimal disturbance in his grand design manifesting itself in the form of a slight wobble.

A brief search confirmed his suspicion: there was an empty

space on the lowest shelf. Missing was the seventh volume, *Helix–Longitude*, of a foreign encyclopedia that he had not consulted in many years. Only one person could be held responsible for this outrage. The Count's hands shook.

– Irena.

He tracked down her empty bed as it rolled along its accustomed route. He emptied out the night table, stripped away the sheets, tossed aside the pillow and found a paper neatly listing women's toiletries – *powder, pomade, scented soap, rosewater* – and their estimated cost, a list she was no doubt going to submit to him the next morning for his approval, as she did without fail every quarter. The list, belying its innocence, was tucked into a small octavo volume the Count had never seen before. Slowly, and then with increasing swiftness, he turned the pages, a tremor beginning in his hands and along the grey ridge of his chin.

– My moth, he muttered hoarsely. My little moth.

φ

On the fourth night that Flood leapt through the red velvet curtains of Irena's bed, he found the Count there with two of his huntsmen brandishing fowling guns.

– You neglected to consider how much I enjoy a good riddle, the Count said. He held up the book of *Desire* so that the pages faced Flood, who saw faint patches of rust on the paper and then realized it was Irena's name, visible here and there amid the straight black pews of the sermon.

– Your recipe for secret ink, the Count said as Flood was seized and carried off, stands in need of serious modification.

He was taken down into the clockworks, to a stone chamber with a huge toothed gear for a roof. Pungent steam rose from a grate in the floor.

There was a straw pallet against one wall and above it a narrow embrasure that let in a weak, nacreous light. He could hear water trickling somewhere. Once every hour the gear overhead creaked to life and with a dull clunk ratcheted around one tooth, splattering oily water into the cell.

The Count came to inspect the new arrangements, sliding open the door's spyhole to have a look at his prisoner.

– You can't do this, Flood said when he saw the old man's eyes fastened on him. I am not one of your subjects.

– If you were to consult the most recent surveyor's maps, the Count said, you would find that this castle does not exist. And now, neither do you.

Flood sank onto the straw pallet.

– At least let me have my press. I can still work on your book.

– I've changed my mind concerning that, I'm afraid. Books need readers, and when I am dead, there will be no one here to do any reading.

– Where is the Countess?

– Oh, I've brought her to see you, the Count said, stepping away from the spyhole. Since the two of you will never meet again, I thought it only fair that you should have the chance to say your goodbyes.

There was a rustle of silk and Irena's face appeared. She gazed into the cell, expressionless.

– Countess, Flood whispered, unable to move.

– She was not for you, the Count's voice said.

His long thin fingers spidered up to Irena's temples, sank

in like talons. With a click her face came away in his hands. All that remained were her eyes, two naked orbs in a hive of twitching, buzzing machinery.

The panel slid shut.

φ

He howled. Pounded the door, scraped at the walls until his fingers bled. Wept himself into exhausted sleep.

After a murky expanse of time he heard a sound overhead and a basket on a rope came down through the gear housing with his meal: a heel of loaf, a stone bottle of water, half of a stale meat pie. He left everything where it was and did the same when the basket came down the next day. The day after that, the basket failed to appear. When it finally descended again three days later he snatched at its contents greedily and from then on ate every last crumb.

φ

He set himself to ignore the sound of the gear before it drove him mad, until he realized that the mental effort needed would lead even more quickly to the same result.

He tormented himself with questions he could not answer. What did the Count mean by showing him that clockwork parody of her? Was she dead? Or had that *thing* been her all along? No. Another of his riddles. An insidious joke. She had to be alive. She was the only thing in this prison that was.

Horror-struck at the abyss beckoning his sanity, he set himself a daily regimen of imaginary printing. Unencumbered by the limitations of real paper and ink, the dumb recalcitrance of inanimate objects, he was free at last to dream a book unlike any other. In his head the calculations based on the golden section flew together in angelic concord. It all made sense now. The book would climb into being on the infinite spiral of the Fibonacci sequence. The frame, the container of the words, was the key.

The various stages of producing each sheet were parcelled out by the ratcheting of the gear. To make the work expand to fill the vague gulf of time before him, he went about it more slowly than he would have with a real press, setting and printing only one single sixteen-page forme every hour. As night fell and the cell sank into darkness, he would peel an invisible sheet from the type, blow on its intangible surface, hold it before his unseeing eyes to check the quality of his nonexistent impression.

In time his phantom presswork failed to distract him from his situation and he sank into a torpor out of which he would jolt awake in the dark, having sat heedlessly on his pallet through an entire day. He eventually decided that he was neglecting to imagine the text that was to fill his spectral pages. To his inner vision the impression was always clean, unblemished, his best work, but the matter remained utterly obscure, veiled from him as if he had lost the ability to read. He had always relied on his customers to supply him with the text that he would print and bind, but now, he realized with dismay, he would have to become author as well as printer.

No other possibility presented itself than that of beginning with Irena. He had already filled a book with her name. *This* book would contain everything else about her that he could remember, their first meeting and all that followed. He filled column after imaginary column with the timbre and nuances of her voice, with every word they had spoken to one another, with the changing colour of her eyes, the coolness of her hair streaming across his naked chest, her body, volcanic, supple, entwining with his, the scent and taste of her skin, until, remembering his last sight of her, on the far side of the gallery the morning of what was to have been their fourth night together, he was so overcome with despair that he left his work and curled up in a ball on his pallet, seeing and hearing nothing and hoping only for death.

To survive he would have to begin elsewhere. He recalled a passage he had found in one of the Count's books, a commentary on the tenth-century *System* of Al-Kindi, who postulated the causal influence of everything upon everything else. The entire cosmos, from the tiniest atomies to the vast silent spaces beyond the moon, formed a web of connectedness within the mind of God. From this astounding proposition the Arab philosopher conjectured that a complete knowledge of one single thing, *any* single thing, be it a chair, a feather, a raindrop, the merest trifle, will lead at last, through the web of relations, to an understanding of everything else. A radiant knowledge of All. The tiniest pebble under one's feet a mirror in which the entire Creation was invisibly reflected.

Casting about for an object to be the seed of a universe, he plucked a straw from his pallet and described to himself its length, shape, coloration, and texture. From there began a meticulous survey of the pallet from which he had taken the straw, followed by an inventory of every square inch of his roughly trapezoidal cell, each stone of the walls and every crack and crevice in the mortar between each stone, the mouse droppings he found each morning on the bare floor, the comings and goings of the rats and the many-legged vermin that nested in his pallet and that ate the mouse droppings, the tiny scraps of dry and scaling skin that would fall from him like snow whenever he scratched his burning limbs, the tremulous webs of light reflected from the water that ran beneath his cell, the reef of dirty ice that slowly formed on the embrasure when winter came and just as slowly thinned and wasted away the next spring.

His senses, their sphere of action limited, did not grow dull but rather began to sharpen on what little was available to them. In time the soft patter of a centipede's legs resounded for him like the tread of a column of marching men. He could watch the stones of the walls settle a little farther each day into one another as they sank slowly towards the river. Lying awake at night he smelled the blood moving under the surface of his skin, felt the tug of the rising moon in the glands of his neck and groin. One day, instead of printing, he sat on the floor and watched a spider build a web in the crook of his arm.

Everything was woven into his work.

He moved, inch by inch, through the halls of the castle and into the world.

φ

From time to time he heard the panel in the door slide open. He would not look to see who was observing him. He kept on with his printing. Let them wait. They would get their book when it was damned well ready.

Chewing his heel of loaf he bit into a rolled cylinder of paper. A note from Djinn. The backward message, once he had deciphered it, told him that the Count had gone with his men to a hunting *salash* in the mountains and that if they acted quickly Flood could be freed and spirited out of the castle that night. The printer sliced his finger on the edge of the paper and sent back a message scribbled in blood, asking Djinn to wait, if he would be so kind, until his work was finished.

φ

One spring the river rose through the grate in the floor. He climbed from his bed one morning into ankle-deep icy water.

The flood subsided after a few hours, but not before collapsing a section of the wall opposite the door. Behind the fallen stones stood a gnarled trunk of bare wet rock. The unhewn roots of the castle. When he put his ear to the crevices at dusk he could hear the squeak and flutter of bats waking.

φ

A pair of night herons nested for a season in a corner of the cell. Their luminous eyes followed his movements back and forth across the tiny space. After a while he ignored them, certain that they were mechanical toys belonging to the Count.

Time became spherical. Past events gathered around him like words in a book he could read as he pleased, in any order.

One day he stepped back from the press, wiped his brow, hung up his leather apron, and peered out the window of the shop. It was a cold winter morning in Lady Chapel Court. Snow was falling softly, silently, and the stones of the court had vanished under a covering of white. He wiped at the frost on the warped pane and saw a small figure in a red cloak. Meg, making snowballs. She looked up, saw him in the window, waved and shouted, although he could not hear the words. *Come out, Nicholas.*

He went to the door and opened it. The court, the snow, Meg had vanished. He turned back to the shop and he was in his cell.

From time to time he was visited by people he had known. His rivals in the printing trade. Papa Martin, the playing-card maker, one of his father's old friends.

And people he did not recognize. An elderly white-bearded man in a green cloak stood near him all one evening at his work.

– Do I know you? Flood finally asked.

The old man did not speak, but held up his large, powerful hands to reveal strange characters burned into his fingertips. Letters, Flood finally realized, of the Hebrew alphabet.

φ

He awoke one morning to find that the space where his imaginary press stood was taken up by the wooden skeleton of a real press. He approached the empty frame warily, wondering if by relentless mental exertion he had imagined part of it into existence. He spent the rest of the day collating sheets rather than give in to the temptation to touch the apparition and have it vanish into nothingness.

The next day the impression assembly – the screw, the bar, the platen – had joined the frame. He could no longer resist, and smiled as his hands slid into their old familiar grip around the well-worn contours of the bar. This, his hands told him, was *his* press, the old workhorse of the House of Flood and Son.

The following morning the carriage assembly was there: rounce, coffin, tympan and frisket, the ink bats hanging from their hook beside the ink block. He set a forme of imaginary type and was about to lock it into the coffin when he stopped, set the forme on the floor, and lowered his own face to the cold surface of the press stone. Like a rider greeting his mount he stroked the smooth, dark wood.

He slept fitfully that night, and was awakened at dawn by an unfamiliar sound. He sat up and peered into the corners of the cell, searching for the source.

A key, scratching like a mouse in the lock.

The heavy wooden door swung open with a faint squeal of hinges that told of the recent application of oil. A slender dark-skinned young man stepped warily into the cell, carrying a tray of type. He was followed by a girl of ten or eleven with pale russet hair, dressed in a boy's waistcoat and breeches. Her eyes in the stark light gleamed a watery aquamarine. The young man and the girl stared at Flood for a moment, then at each other. Finally the girl stepped forward.

– Greetings, Signore Flood, she said in English. My name is Pica. I am your daughter.

*S*ometimes the reader places her ear close to a book and hears a distant sighing of waves. In the crevice between the pages her fingers touch a wand of cold wet sand, studded with tiny fragments of iridescent shell. The ribbed and sloping paper itself seems to invite her.

She wades in cautiously, her naked feet moving like snails over the sharp stones.

THE BROKEN VIOLIN

After floating on the sea for days and days, she was washed ashore on an island where stood the palace of a beautiful but sad Queen. When the ladies-in-waiting opened the windows that morning, they saw the quaint little cask lying on the sand. *Your Highness*, they said, hoping to cheer her, *you should see the lovely little cask the waves have washed ashore.* The Queen ordered them to bring the cask to her, and when it was opened, out stepped the maiden, as radiant as the moon. *Where are you from*, the Queen asked her, *and why are you sailing the sea like that?*

She has wet the bed again. Above her, the winged face of Sister Beata hovers in the blackness.

- Filthy child. The third night in a row. Get up.

She must stand in the lavatory until dawn. Water trickles from stone spouts like gaping mouths. The unpassing night. Something scuttles over her bare foot. A rat, squirming itself into a crevice in the rotten masonry.

The young novice who patrols the rooms every night with a shaded lamp looks in on her once each hour, on Sister Beata's orders, to make sure she remains standing.

The novice whispers from the doorway.

— It's no wonder you wet your bed all the time. You were born at sea, they say. On a ship.

Before sunrise the girls in their nightdresses drift into the lavatory, glancing at her with sleepy curiosity. One of the older girls steps up to her.

— Hey. Pissalina. You've got funny skin. It's shiny, like a frog's.

Francesca is beautiful. Several times before this day she has caught Pica staring at her creamy skin, her long, lustrous black hair. Francesca is speaking to her, but her angry gaze burns through Pica to something else.

— Your mother named you Pica? The magpie. So are you a magpie, then, or a frog?

— I'm not . . .

– The Maestro had red hair like yours. He died the day you came to the Ospedale. Maybe you're the Maestro's little secret, and that's why he died. One look at you.

The girls laugh and turn away, tugging off their nightdresses. They chatter, shriek at the rats, shove each other under the waterspouts. Their shouts in the vaulted room slapping night awake. The bells of San Zaccaria sound the hour and voices rise in answer from the chapel:

*Venetus surge, sta in excelso, et vide jucunditatem
quae veniet tibi a Deo tuo . . .*

Your name is a typeface, he told the girl. Except you pronounce it pike-a.
– I say it peek-a.
She asked him if there was anything he needed.
– A bath. Please.
He would not leave his cell, and so Djinn repaired one of the Count's few useful contraptions, a tub that could fill itself with hot water from an adjoining boiler. Flood lay back in the scalding water, his armour of dirt dissolving. When he rose out of the bath and looked at the thick black film on the surface, he had the feeling he had left someone behind.
Djinn fetched a barber from the village who sheared off Flood's matted nest of beard and trimmed his tangled mane. It had been getting so long, he told the girl, that it was starting to dip in the ink block.

She showed him the T-shaped piece of metal she had always had, carried around her neck on a ribbon.

– I couldn't find anything in the castle to fit it.

– That's a quoin key, he told her. For keeping a forme of type locked tight in a chase.

He studied her. She was here to learn the craft, he decided. That was why she had brought the quoin key. He scrabbled in his typecase and took up a lowercase letter *a*.

– On the bottom are the feet and the groove. On the body is the nick, here, and the pin mark. At the top, the shoulder, the neck. And lastly, the letter itself. The face.

He looked up. She was gazing around the cell, not listening.

– Who was your mother? he asked

– The Countess, she said.

She returned to his cell in the evening, bringing him a supper of bread and beet soup. When she set the tray on the press stone, he stepped up close to her, reached out, and touched her face.

– You're cold. Porcelain?

She backed away.

– No, signore. It's cold up here. That's why I thought you might like some hot food.

– How old are you?

– Eleven. Or twelve. I'm not sure.

– Those are boy's clothes you're wearing.

– I ruined my own clothes getting across to the island. Djinn gave me some of his.

– You . . . swam here? Why didn't you take the ferry?

– It was full of people.

– People coming here?

She looked away as if embarrassed.

– To see the castle, she said. They pay to see . . .

– The freaks, he said. And the madman.

He looked up at the gear in the ceiling, its teeth rusted to stumps. The machinery had been silent for so long.

– She's dead, isn't she?

– No, the girl said fiercely. I don't know where she is. No one does.

A grey, gusty morning, the torn sky sending down a few stray pinpricks of icy rain. This is the hour they take the air in the walled corte, *watched by the novices, older girls who had been accomplices until their heads were shaved and their bodies swathed in black. The younger girls are not supposed to speak to anyone who comes to the gates, but men stop there often, to watch them and sometimes call them over to talk. When this happens, the novices turn away and say nothing.*

She cannot remember ever having been outside the Ospedale. The map of Venice in her head has been constructed of rumour, stories, vague scraps of knowledge that might possibly be clues to the world outside, like the sign set into the wall threatening parents with dire consequences should they try to pass their own children off as orphans.

Most of the girls will become the wives of merchants and tradesmen. Sometimes the nuns decide that a girl should be married to God and become one of them. And there are a few girls who one day are just gone, and no one says anything. Francesca is sure they are sold like slaves to rich men.

Pica catches sight of a shard of blue glass lying on the cobbles. She halts, wondering how it got here, how it escaped the sweeping-woman's broom. She stoops swiftly, plucks the bit of glass from the ground, slips it into her apron pocket. Later she will hide it with her other treasures, in the secret hollow in the wall beside her bed.

She hears a sound and quickly straightens up. A red-faced old woman in a frayed cloak is watching her through the bars of the gate. The midwife who brought her to the foundling home. They have met at the gates before. The old woman tells her stories.

– I wanted to see how you were getting on, mouse.

– I'm well, thank you.

– You look thin. Are those stingy old women feeding you enough?

– Yes. I don't eat sometimes.

– Why not?

– I put the food in my pockets for later, but I forget about it and it goes stale. The girls say that's why I was named Pica. *(She will dare a question she has never asked.)* Did my mother name me?

The midwife heaves a deep sigh and Pica catches the faint vinous reek of her breath. She loves the smell, like the wine they sip at Mass from the gold chalice. The old woman's stories, breathed to her on this dark incense, hold the same mystery as the words the priest intones over their bowed heads on Sunday.

– The poor dear was so weak, all she could do was whisper. *She's so small*, she said, and then, *Pica. Call her Pica.* I'd never heard such a name for a girl, and I wanted to ask and make sure, but they hurried me out of the room with you squealing in my arms.

– Does my mother send you here to see me?

– No, child. That was the last time I saw her.

– Why did she give me up?

– Oh, mouse, she didn't. They took her away. They broke her heart.

– Who?

Tears glitter in the midwife's bloodshot eyes. She strokes Pica's cold hands through the bars.

– You're so tall, mouse. And so pretty. Just like the princess in the stories you used to like. You won't be caged in there much longer, that's for certain. There'll soon be rich young men stopping here instead of foolish old women.

– They say I was born on a ship.

The midwife sobs, exhaling another sacramental gust.

— She had a hard time of it, poor thing. You were not going to come out, I thought, and then when you did you were all black and curled up and I thought, *The little tadpole is already finished before she's hardly begun.* Then you gave a slippery little kick in my hands and started bawling. . . .

— This was on a ship.

— Oh, mouse, I swore —

— Tell me, please.

The midwife glances around, and Pica is startled to see fear in her eyes, fear of someone or something other than the nuns. Finally she moves closer to Pica and speaks in a hurried whisper.

— It was the oddest thing I've ever seen. High at the ends, like castle towers, and made up of different sorts of planks, as if it had been knocked together from a hundred shipwrecks. Steam billowing out of the portholes, and all these frightening rumblings and other noises too. I got a good long look, you see, because they rowed me to it. The ship was anchored in the lagoon, out past the Lido.

— Here in Venice?

– Yes. I thought it was strange they wouldn't just bring your mother to the lying-in hospital, and then when they hauled up the side, all of a sudden I thought, *The plague.* I was sure that's why they were bringing me out in secret, and I started blubbering and carrying on. Then the man in black sticks a gold coin under my nose and says, *You see this? This is all you need concern yourself with.* He takes me in to the locked room where your mother is already well along, and the last thing he says to me is, *You will not speak a word to her. She is not to know where we are.* That was when I knew the poor girl was their prisoner –

Sister Beata appears on the steps of the Ospedale, glaring at the midwife, who moves away from the gate.

– Now you'll be in for a hard time of it, mouse. I'm sorry.

– I don't care. Just come back again, please.

They were leaving the castle. The coach was already waiting on the ferry.

He sat in the entrance hall on a chair with the velvet torn from its back, while Pica, Djinn, and the boatmen went back and forth with the baggage. He was not strong enough yet to help, and the sight of the unroofed sky filled him with dread. They had only convinced him to leave his cell by telling him he could bring along his press and the rest of his printing equipment.

He gazed around the draughty shell of the castle. Sliding walls hung crookedly, arrested forever in their unfinished paths. A winding staircase ended in mid-air. The remaining bookshelves stood motionless, some toppled, their shelves plundered. Pica had told him that when the Count died, the servants ran off with almost everything that might be of value.

She had found what was left of the automaton of her mother just inside the doors of the castle. The glass eyes had been removed, the russet wig torn away, one of the arms broken off. At first she had insisted on bringing the thing with her when they left. Ludwig, after all, had been crated up with the rest of Flood's printing tools and sent downriver on a barge. But at the last moment, she decided to leave the automaton where it was, propped up against the door, a ring of keys in its one remaining hand, as if she wanted something to be there to greet her should she ever return.

The man from the Imperial Court who had been hovering around all morning finally had Pica look over his heap of documents. From what Flood understood, she had to sign away to the state all the Count's land, to pay his immense debts. What remained of his possessions was hers.

Like me, Flood thought.

She had told him a little about herself, but he had found it difficult to follow the thread of her story. She would break off unexpectedly, wind time back and forth, carry on somewhere else without telling him how they had got there.

And where they were going . . .

From the rumours Pica had gathered at the Ospedale she described the strange vessel to Djinn and he had nodded in recognition. Turini, the carpenter, lived now on the Count's ship with his wife the contortionist and their two children, identical twins. They made their living as acrobats, giving performances up and down the Danube. He had written to them, Flood gathered, let them know the daughter of the Countess wished to see the ship.

A very old ship, Pica had described it. *With strange machines on it that give off steam.*

Only now did Flood realize that this had to be the same doubtful vessel that had brought him from London all those years ago.

– Signore?

He looked up to see Pica beside him, her hand hovering just above his shoulder. Djinn stood at the doors, watching him as he always had, with guarded curiosity.

– We must go now, Pica said quietly. This place doesn't belong to me any more.

An orchestra and choir of thirty-three girls in white linen robes, playing and singing Salve Regina. *The concertmaster claps his hands once to call a halt and the music collapses with a dying wheeze. The concertmaster points an accusing finger at Pica, who lowers the violin from her shoulder.*

– As the immortal Horace wrote, *Lament, friend, among the chairs of your lady pupils.* You are running ahead of the rest of us, child.

– I'm sorry, signore. Francesca dal Contralto stepped on my foot.

– She's lying, signore. I did not.

The concertmaster rubs his temples.

— How on earth did the Maestro endure this for twenty years? I sincerely doubt he wrote this piece with the intention of having it sound like an overwound watch. The truth is, child, you are always ahead. Am I to believe that someone is perpetually treading on your foot? No. It is clear you cannot keep time, and so you are excused.

The violin lies at her feet. She scratches at the burning red patches on her arms. Her furious nails climb to her neck, are caught by a thin ribbon, which she tugs out of her bodice. She holds up the strange key, examines it for the thousandth time.

Two tiny letters are engraved on the haft:

N F

Today is visiting day. All afternoon the flustered nuns come and go. One by one girls are called out to the visiting chamber, where ladies in hooded cloaks and men in masks are gathered expectantly on the other side of a long wirework grille, like customers in a shop.

Sister Beata appears at the door to look for Francesca, who has gone missing. Pica holds up the key.

— This was my mother's.

— I have told you all I know, and all I wish to know. You would do well to follow my example.

– The old woman said she didn't die.

Sister Beata scowls.

– That midwife is a drunkard and a fool. *(She sighs and shakes her head.)* My child, my child, be content with your lot. Never forget how fortunate you are to have been accepted here, where so many care for you, for your welfare. You can never make yourself legitimate, but in this place, with God's help, you may make amends for your birth.

Sister Beata sweeps angrily from the room and after a moment Francesca crawls out from under a bed. She always hides on visiting day. She hates the men who come to look at her and tell her how lovely she is growing to be, and that if they are kind to her she is sure to be kind to them.
   She creeps catlike to the doorway, listens, then turns to Pica.

– Don't believe anything that old witch says. Go on, ask them who your father was. I dare you. They'll tell you he's dead too. It means one of them, your mother or father, was titled and the other one wasn't.

– You mean like a lord or –

– I've heard stories. From the girls who've left. They say your grandfather is a Hungarian prince, or something like that, who lives in a castle on an island. That key of yours probably came from there. Things like that always happen in the books. Your grandfather must have had you brought here, when he found out that his darling son or daughter . . . you know . . .

Pica waits wide-eyed for her to finish. Francesca snorts.

— No, you don't know. Here, read this. *(She hands Pica a tiny book bound in red cloth, its fore-edge grimy with much handling)* There's a scene in here that will explain what your parents did to make you.

— I'm not finished the last book you gave me.

— Take it anyways. You're better at hiding things, magpie. If Sister Beata catches me with another novel I'm done for.

She crouches in an alcove just off the refectory, holding the book to the light of a single wall taper. Since she first began reading Francesca's forbidden novels she has memorized paths through the Ospedale that avoid the undeviating routes of the nuns.

. . . her shining Eyes swam in a Sea of Languor, her Cheeks glowed anew like Embers, her Bosom heav'd more quick: a sweet Confusion reigned in every Part. The transported Lover snatch'd her to his burning Breast, printed unnumbered Kisses on her Lips, then held her off to feast his Eyes on her yielding Charms; — Beauties which till then he knew but in Idea. His eager Hands were Seconds to his Sight, and travell'd over all —; while

she, in gentle Sighs and faltering Accents, confessed she
received a Pleasure not inferior to that she gave ...

She hears a sound and shuts the book. Two of the younger
nuns glide past, whispering to one another, wrapped in their
own conspiracy. She has heard that some of them were shut
away here for the same crime as her mother's. That was what
Francesca called it: a crime. That was why she was a prisoner
on the ship. Pica tries to imagine her mother and father in the
scene she has just been reading. Two people without faces. They
burned for one another, as Francesca's books always say.

She came from that fire.

Distracted by a flicker of light, she turns to the candle.
The flame, slender and faintly wavering, looks to her like a
fragile living thing, weaving, searching. Slowly she reaches out
and touches a hand to the flame.

Everything was moving too quickly. One day they were in
Vienna, the next Pressburg, and two days after that Buda,
where Turini and his family awaited them. Each day of their
journey began with the trial of stepping outside the inn they
had put up at the night before and facing the limitless world.
He was almost left behind several times, lingering in rooms and
courtyards long after it was time to carry on, bewildered by the
swiftness with which things were happening and desiring, like a
child, to flee from what he could not control.

In the cities, crowds swept through the streets like flocks
of startled pigeons. Didn't they see how fast they were going,
that they were bound to smash headlong –? After eleven years
in a small trapezoidal room he needed the world to conform

to that maddening, essential shape. He walked with his hands stretched out in front of him like a blind man, anticipating walls and corners. He shrank into his cloak as they sped along in the coach, unable to bear the sight of the road rising, falling, curving away ahead of them and behind them with such reckless freedom.

The world, *things*, seemed to be carved of exquisite crystal, every facet, every sensation brilliant, miraculous. The sight of cobwebs jewelled with dew in a dead tree at dawn. The reek of wet straw wafting from a distant farm. The whack of a hod carrier's missile of spit against a gatepost. It was not long before Pica stopped letting him pay the coach drivers and porters, since he would give them most of the money in his purse, enchanted by the dull clink of coins falling into an open palm.

In the coach Pica had begun reading to him from her little collection of books, and he realized eventually that she was trying to keep his wandering mind occupied. She read from Ovid's *Metamorphoses*, *Gulliver's Travels*, and the seventh volume of the *Libraria Technicum*, which Flood had found where he had concealed it eleven years before. He had told her it was a favourite of her mother's, but before he gave it to her he proceeded to name its parts. *Fore-edge. Joint. Rib.*

– Before I teach you to print a book, you should take one apart and put it back together.

– Not this one, she said, tugging the seventh volume out of his hands.

– Only when you unbind books, piece by piece, do you truly learn to love them.

After that she would not let the book out of her sight. Now she read to him from it cautiously, repeating words until she was sure of them.

Inoculation: From earliest Times the Women of remote Circassia have communicated the Small-pox to their Children, by making an Incision in the Arm and putting into it a Pustule taken from the infected Body of another Child. . . .

He asked her to read that entry again and she looked up from the book.

– Djinn says my mother was very sick when she was a girl, she said. Was it smallpox?

– I don't think so.

She flipped back and forth in the book, settled on another entry.

Huguenots: French Protestants, fleeing Persecution and Slaughter, who have found Refuge in more tolerant Nations, such as England, Holland, and the American Colonies. Many are skilled Craftsmen and Artisans, working in such Trades as Watchmaking, Weaving, Printing. . . .

– That's us, Flood said.

The girl looked up from the book.

– Us?

– You are Huguenot, on my side.

She took this in, then read the rest of the entry in silence. When she was finished she closed the book.

– Tell me about us, she said.

Now that he was not speaking about his craft, his words came haltingly. He told her that his great-grandfather had come to London in the last century and set up a print shop. He had changed his name when he discovered that the English were not quite as tolerant as he had been told.

– Your mother liked to read about London, he said.

She flipped through the book and found the entry. She read it out loud, then after a while fell silent so that he glanced at her and saw that she had returned to the beginning of the volume. She was reading the whole work through, every word, from time to time marking passages with scraps of newspaper she collected as they travelled. She lay the strips of paper carefully onto the pages, the way a priest might mark his place in a Bible.

– A man came to see me once, she said. He spoke French.

She has never been called to the visiting chamber, and so when Sister Beata appears at the door with the summons, she is too shocked to move.

She is already dressed in her best clothes. All the girls must wear their finest on visiting day, and so all she need do is follow obediently and keep her eyes on the floor. But she cannot move. Her heart is hammering and a cold sweat has broken out on her forehead. She wonders if she is about to be sick.

Her name is hissed again from the doorway and she moves at last, following the hem of Sister Beata's habit to the audience chamber, scarcely daring to breathe. She has been drilled in the proper etiquette: she stands beside her chair, eyes on the floor, waiting for the invitation to sit. It comes, in a man's voice. On the verge of fainting she obeys, and then at last raises her eyes to the grille.

A tall, thin man stands there, dressed in a priest's black cassock, a pair of black gloves and a mask in his hands. He looks her over in unreadable silence for a long moment and then speaks, his voice soft and yet cold underneath.

– Signorina, I bring you greetings from your grandfather. As he heard I was on my way through Venice, he asked me to stop and visit you. He wishes me to send word to him that you are happy and in good health, which I trust you are.

– Yes, signore, she says, as she has been taught. I am grateful to be here. Thank you.

He has spoken, and she has replied, in French. He seems pleased to hear how well she speaks the language.

– You like to read, I'm told.

– Yes, signore. Very much.

– So do I.

The stranger toys with the mask and gloves in his hands, his eyes never leaving her.

– Good. I'm glad to hear that all is well. Then . . . it would appear that I have fulfilled my commission.

The stranger tugs on his gloves. Pica glances at Sister Beata, who is just turning away to fetch the next girl. She leans forward and clutches the grille.

– Excuse me, signore. Please. My grandfather . . . who is he?

The stranger frowns, as all adults do when she asks the wrong questions, but Pica is certain she sees something else in the dark eyes that watch her so carefully: a glint of amusement like the glimmer of a distant star.

– I am sorry, signorina, but I am not at liberty to divulge that information. Your grandfather, let me say, is a man who prefers the posing of riddles over their solutions. However, I have no doubt that you will be enlightened in due time.

The stranger is already turning away when the midwife's words come back to her.

The man in black.

He held up the raw potato she had bought from a roadside peddler and peeled to share with him.

– Pretend this is a piece of copper.

In his other hand was a piece of type.

– The type-founder strikes the steel punch into it. There, like so, a sunken impression of the letter *a*.

A raven croaked close by and Flood looked up expectantly into the sombre wet trees along the roadside. The coach had gotten stuck in the mud a few miles outside Buda. Djinn had gone with the postilion to fetch help and had not yet returned. The sky, which had been clouded over all day, was now brightening, and Flood felt the familiar anxiousness squeeze his heart and the thought of that limitless sea of blue. He turned back to Pica, who was gnawing a carrot and gazing distantly out at the hills. *Was she even listening?*

– The copper matrix is placed in a mould, he went on, and into the mould is poured the molten alloy. The metal fills the impression, hardens, and there is your piece of type, with the raised letter backwards again on its surface, like the original punch.

– Then why not just use the punch, Pica said, to print with? Wait, I see. You need lots of *a*'s on each page.

– Right. This way the type-cutter can cast as many of each letter as desired, each one exactly the same. Any other questions so far?

– Are you going to eat that potato?

– Take it. Now we place our piece of type, our finished letter *a*, in the composing stick, this way.

– That's upside down.

– The printer's first lesson, Flood said, nodding. Sometimes you have to sneak around your common sense.

He heard a shout from down the road and looked up to see a haywagon pulled by a pair of oxen, and Djinn beside the driver, waving.

She is sitting up in bed with her shift pulled over her shoulders, leaving her back bare. The doctor's fat, greasy fingers probe her ribs, tap her breastbone, squeeze her neck. Sister Beata's horrified whisper slithers out of the shadows behind him.

– Is it . . . the plague?

The doctor pries open her mouth and peers in.

– Thank Providence, no. She has an inflammatory condition of the skin which I do not think to be contagious. These eruptions, I am certain, break out in response to the vaporous, cloistered air in the house. We will begin with bleeding and a cooling astringent, say vitriolated zinc with camphor, or white calx of quicksilver. Or perhaps cold water. If by morning the symptoms have not lessened, take her up to the highest garret in the building, strip her naked, and throw open the shutters to let the winds in.

– Such idleness, doctor, would be worse for her well-being than the disease.

– Then have her practice her scales or whatever it is your musical young ladies do.

– She is no longer in the orchestra. Instead she shall take up other useful arts.

– It matters not what she does, Sister Beata, as long as she stays exposed to the air for at least an hour a day.

She sits on the edge of a cot, a frayed blanket tugged around her, embroidering a handkerchief with tiny roses and raising her eyes now and again to gaze out the window at the snow-cloaked roof of San Giorgio across the canal.

The garret is high in the draughty upper reaches of the Ospedale. Pica shivers, sets her work down beside her, gets up and wanders the room, slapping her hands together to warm them.

Broken and unused instruments hang from the walls. High in one corner is a dusty, battered violin with a single intact string. A jagged crack has split its soundboard. Pica returns to her work, but she cannot keep at it long without stealing another glance at the violin. At last she drags a chair over to the corner, stretches and lifts the instrument from its peg. Sitting back down on the edge of the cot, she turns the violin over and over, traces the purfling with her finger, sniffs the darkness of the sound holes, ponders the odd mark burned into its back:

The Maestro, in a priest's black cassock, stands by the window, his hands clasped behind his back.

– I played that one so hard it cracked. In Milan, I think it was. Yes. Right in the middle of the *Great Mogul*.

Pica holds out the violin and the Maestro takes it, cradles it like an infant or a rare bottle of wine.

– They brought me another instrument, but I could not go on. The audience stared, and then someone laughed. The critics said, *Vivaldi's pact with the devil is expiring at last.* They had no idea what had come over me. I had suddenly understood my own heart.

He tucks the violin under his chin, plucks the string, turns the tuning peg, plucks the string again.

– *Cento donzelle festose e belle,* A hundred maidens cheerful and fair. My joy at being with you each day. Hearing your innocent thoughtless chatter in the morning as you came down for your lessons, beholding your freshly scrubbed and shining faces gazing up at me as I explained harmony and figuration and ritornello. Fool that I was, I did not understand. I played my violin and did not hear my own heart singing out its delight. The world heard, though. The world said I played in a fever, like a man possessed. The world wanted to hear more. *Il prete rosso!* people cried. We want the red priest! They clamoured for me, and so I left the Ospedale, lured away by the promise of gold, fame, love. Everything I thought I wanted.

Far below them in one of the music rooms of the Ospedale a solo voice begins haltingly to climb up and down the scales.

– All your beautiful names. Arcangela dell Cornetto. Lucia Soprano. Anna Maria of the Violin.

Pica steps forward.

– I used to play the violin. I couldn't keep time and the concertmaster dismissed me from the lessons. Now they just call me Pica.

The Maestro returns the violin to her.

– Once I understood where my heart lived I dared not return. I knew that such perfect joy is not permitted a man in this world. Instead, I sent this beauty here, with instructions to the sisters that it not be repaired but put away. I was sure it would betray me, you see. That anyone who heard its music, the music of broken things, would know.

Pica runs her fingers over the crack in the soundboard.

     – Yes. I saw it was broken, and I knew there was a story.

The Maestro's black cloak is the curtain flapping at the edge of the open window. Pica sits up, the violin clutched in her arms. The doctor is bending over her, his sausage fingers on her brow.

     – The child is on fire.

Sister Beata sits beside the bed, her hands entwined in the beads of her rosary.

     – She lapses in and out of this. Speaking to someone who isn't there. I fear the child is . . . possessed.

The doctor makes a throaty noise of annoyance.

     – With all due respect, Sister Beata, we are no longer living in the Dark Ages. The girl is suffering from fever-induced delusions and nothing more. The fresh-air treatment can have that effect, although it has been infrequent in my experience. But to the point: I have consulted with various colleagues and I believe

I have isolated the cause of the symptoms. She has an extremely rare condition known as *batrachia*, which involves waxy glandular secretions and excessive porosity of the skin.

— Will she die of it?

— Not likely, though the irritation may drive her mad. The symptoms are generally most pronounced in children, and then gradually lessen by the time the sufferer reaches adulthood, rather like the pimples one sees so often on the faces of adolescents. I suggest bathing her in warm, watered-down milk three times a week. And mind, she must stay immersed for at least an hour each time if this remedy is to be efficacious.

In the garret she strips naked and climbs wincing into the steaming, silken liquid. Sister Beata stands in the doorway, arms folded, lips pressed bloodless with restraint.

— I haven't the time to watch you loll in a bath all day like the Queen of Sheba. The other girls shall take on this duty.

Night. White sheets hung from the roofbeams to keep out the wind stir gently above her like sails. She is drifting out . . .

— Wake up, magpie.

Francesca enters with her permanent frown, hefting a basin of

hot milk. Pica, sitting submerged to her neck in the wooden
tub, watches her approach through half-closed eyes.

— Do this, Francesca, do that. What do they think I
am, their Nubian slave? I'm the daughter of an arch-
bishop.

Pica's eyes open wide.

— How do you know?

— I know. Sister Beata knows. The Pope himself
probably knows.

— How did you find out?

— The way you find anything out, dummy. First you
find out who knows what you need to know. Then
you find out what they want for it.

— What do they want?

— Money, sometimes. And other things. Sometimes
you have to do the other things to get the money. *(She
curses and cuffs Pica on the back of the head.)* Why am I
telling you this? You get everything done for you,
poor sick baby.

*She dumps what's left in the basin on Pica's head, kicks the side
of the tub, and stalks out. Watery milk sloshes over the rim of*

the tub and drips, *lento*, on the floorboards. Pica sinks down further until she is completely submerged in a warm, white silence. She opens her eyes.

Francesca returns later with another basin of milk. She stops, glances quickly around the room, bends closer to the tub and lets out a shriek. The basin falls with a crash, a comet of milk shooting across the dark floor.

In the dormitory later that night, she listens, pretending to be asleep, while Francesca whispers to the girls gathered at her bedside.

– Prudenza, Zillah, I'm telling you God's truth. She was sleeping like a baby. I could see the bubbles coming up.

Zillah's voice: She was playing a trick on you, idiot.

– I thought of that, hag. I pulled her hair. Shouted. Banged the tub. She didn't budge. I didn't know what to do, I was scared to death, so I hauled her out and all of sudden she started gasping, as if I was drowning her, *in air*. She puked a pailful of milk onto the floor, opened her eyes, and looked at me like she had no idea what had happened. *(She glances over to Pica's blanketed form.)* I'm telling you, that one can breathe underwater.

Prudenza: Maybe she's a changeling.

Zillah: Or a sorceress.

Francesca: I don't care if she's the daughter of the devil himself. All I know is, we can make use of this.

They climbed stiffly from the coach onto the pier, the carpenter eyeing them in suspicious silence. Rightly, Flood thought, if you look at the three of us. A greybeard afraid of his own shadow, a brown man with twelve fingers, a girl in the dress of a boy. Now, as always, he expected a heavy hand on his shoulder, an inexorable summons.

Turini suddenly stepped forward and bowed.

– Countess, I did not know. The Count sent me here to tear up the ship's planks, just before he died. I disobeyed. If you wish us to leave . . .

Pica twisted her hat around in her hands and shook her head.

They could see little of the ship's exterior in the rainy gloom. Turini's wife, Darka, and the children, the twin boy and girl, greeted them on the quarterdeck with respectful bows, which embarrassed Flood but did not seem to bother Pica. Like the carpenter, the woman and children did little more than stare, especially at the girl. *Their new mistress.* Darka took Pica's hand and kissed it. She stepped back, her mouth moving silently, her hands clutched together.

– She wants you to know, Turini said, that she loved your mother very much.

As it was late, the carpenter showed them to the cabin that had been prepared for their arrival and brought them a late supper of bread, cheese, and wine.

Instead of eating Pica explored the cabin, peered under the bunks, opened the drawers in the rough deal table, investigated the wardrobe. She found a narrow horizontal slot in the bottom of the cabin door, slid her hand through it and back out again.

– Do you know what this is for? she asked Turini.

The carpenter shrugged.

– There are many things the Count did. No one knows why. One thing is for certain: you will get lost on this ship. We all did when we first came aboard.

When he had gone, Pica sat down on the edge of her bunk and pulled off her shoes. Flood watched her drift away into her private thoughts. Since they had left the castle she had been their spur and goad, driving them onward. Now that she had reached her destination she suddenly seemed lost.

Djinn sat at the table, gnawing at his bread in gloomy silence. Flood studied him, baffled as always as to what was going on inside the compositor's head. Djinn spoke even less now, if possible, than he had as a boy, and seemed to take everything that happened in his stride, as if this journey into foreign lands was no better or worse than the long years he had spent in the castle. A laugh never escaped him, as far as Flood knew, and rarely even a smile. Djinn had grown into a beautiful young man, and it was clear from her shyness around him that Pica thought so too, but still he seemed to look out at the world with the watchful, innocent eyes of a child.

Flood shivered, took a gulp of wine, and fought back a spasm in his throat. The cabin was cold, damp, ill-lit. Strange lodgings, though the bump of the hull against the pier reminded him all too keenly of the pulse of the castle's machines.

He glanced at Pica tugging off her soiled stockings and suggested that Darka might be able to find her some girl's clothes.

Pica frowned and Flood saw a blush steal into her cheeks.

– I like these clothes. They're loose. My skin is waxy, it needs to breathe. That's what the doctor said.

– Then there is something we have in common.

She looked at him with a sudden eagerness.

– So you can do this?

She jumped up and placed her hand over the candle on the table. Flood gaped, too startled to act, as a filament of greasy smoke threaded upward from her index finger.

– Don't! he shouted, crossing the room.

She glanced back at him with a look of mingled surprise and disappointment, and took her hand away slowly from the candle. A faint blue emanation haloed her fingertips.

She shivers.

In her shift she stands on a stone abutment under a bridge, cradling in her arms a basket weighted with stones. Prudenza ties a thick rope around her waist and knots it tight. She places a hand on Pica's shoulder.

– Pull once on the rope when you want to come up. Pull twice if you get into trouble.

Francesca shoves Prudenza aside.

– Don't get into trouble. And don't come up empty-handed. We'll send you right back down.

Francesca lifts the handle of the basket around Pica's neck. Slowly she crouches and climbs backwards into the freezing water, pausing when she is half-submerged, her fingers frantically clutching the slimy stone of the abutment. The basket is too heavy and she loses her grip, plunging under the surface into a world of echoes and cloudy green light.

She touches bottom, her feet sinking into gelid ooze.

Fear urges her into motion and she begins to walk along the bottom, stirring up plumes of sediment. The sluggish water, warmer now, is still threaded with icy currents that brush against her like ghosts.

She stoops now and again, picks up faceless coins, a rusted rapier hilt, a lady's silk damask shoe embroidered with sequins. Anything that winks at her from the mire.

As the rope goes taut she reaches the piers of another bridge, where the current grates through narrow stone arches with the moan of a bassoon. Beside the bridge lies a skeleton, half-buried in the muck, wrapped in chains. Shreds of lace and the remains of a velvet coat tell her that this was a nobleman. She finds a few coins in a buttoned pocket of the coat. In the cage of the ribs something gleams: a turquoise brooch.

The basket is upended onto the wet stones. Pica sits nearby, soaked and shivering, hands tucked under her arms. With her sleeve Prudenza wipes at a lacquered snuffbox encrusted with yellow grit.

– Look at this. It must be older than Sister Beata.

Francesca laughs. And just as mouldy. We're going to be rich, ladies. As rich as the Doge. As rich as Medici.

Zillah slips a ring on her finger. As rich as Solomon.

– It's as *wise* as Solomon, dolt.

– Who cares, cow. With this stuff we can buy . . . we can buy . . .

Francesca snatches an ivory comb from Zillah's hands.

    – Anything we buy, the nuns will take from us. No, we have to hide our loot for now. Hoard it up until we can think of a really good use for it. We'll get the magpie here to take the basket back down and hide it for now.

Prudenza gestures at Pica and speaks in a whisper.

    – We should give *her* something, shouldn't we?

Pica is handed the dead man's weathered coins.

    – Here's to the magpie!

While Francesca and her friends squabble over their haul, Pica, her back turned, spits the brooch into her wrinkled palm and closes her fingers around it, the pin biting into her cold and trembling flesh.

A sound woke him. A low, tremulous note, like the wind through the hollow of a wave.

He lifted his head and collided with something soft, silk and embroidered. For a moment he breathed in the faint scent of the perfume sachet he had taken from around Irena's neck, heard her breath in his ear as the bed shuddered beneath them.

He opened his eyes. A cushion had been tied with sail thread to the slats of the bunk above his.

He was on the ship. They were heading out to sea. He lay still, his mind struggling upward out of the pool of time in which he had been submerged.

There it came again. That grave, inhuman whistle.

He rose from the bunk and crossed the room unsteadily, his bare feet feeling their way across the uneven planks. The door of the cabin was unlocked. He hobbled along a short passage to a blank end wall which slid aside at his approach. In the centre of a long, low-ceilinged space stood his printing press, braced with timbers and bolted to the deck with iron bars. Setting it up, Turini had suggested, was the only way to keep the press safe from the tossing and pitching of the ship.

Against the hull sides of the room, fastened by huge iron brackets, stood the type cabinets and stout ink casks with huge brass stopcocks in their bellies. Ludwig hung from his hook in the corner, his glassy eyes fixed on the press.

At the work table sat Djinn, cleaning the long-unused type with a brush, a bottle of solvent at his elbow.

– Did you hear that sound? Flood asked.

The compositor glanced up in surprise and then shook his head.

Flood came into the room and looked around with mingled delight and guilt. While he lay curled up in his bunk the first few days, overcome with seasickness, Djinn had obviously been busy. Everything was spotlessly clean. Everything in place and, he realized with a tremor in his heart, ready for work, if he so wished. *Printing at sea*. He shook his head at the thought, and then the memory came to him of his platform at the castle, shuddering to a halt at the striking of the hour.

He noticed then that as Djinn finished cleaning each piece of type he set it into his composing stick.

— What are you working on? he asked.

— Remembering.

Flood followed the elusive sound through the belly of the ship. Climbing the ladders up through the decks, he rose into the glare of sunlight, the flap of canvas, the smells of tarred rope and freshly stone-scrubbed planks. Dread shot through him when he saw that they were out of sight of land.

On the quarterdeck, Turini was down on one knee, knocking together a pair of boards. With his root-like beard and callused hands, the carpenter reminded Flood of a tree, as if in his features one could see the knotty, living wood that became the smoothly planed chairs and shelves he had been making for their use and comfort since they came aboard.

Darka stood beside him at the helm, as unlike her husband as it appeared possible for someone to be. Like water she flowed rather than moved, her supple body seemingly able to take any shape needed, so that it was she who slipped down into the tight spaces her husband could not reach in his endless hunt for loose planks and leaks. When she saw Flood she slid a leg out and nudged her husband with a toe. Turini hastily stood.

— Are you well, Signore Flood?

He nodded. If it were not for Turini and his agile family, they would never have managed to get this far. The morning after they had come aboard he watched the children, a twin boy and girl, scurry up and down the ratlines and along the yards like monkeys, completely at home in their airy world, which to Flood was nothing but a bewildering perplex of ropes and chains. Although they were not deaf-mutes like their mother, Lolo and Miza had learned from her not only their acrobatic skill but also a language of gestures and facial expressions that left them little need to speak. As for their disconcerting resemblance to each other, Flood had soon learned to tell them apart by realizing that he always mistook Miza for her brother.

Flood squinted upward, expecting to find the uncanny children in their element and instead saw Pica hanging in the shrouds like a bird blown there by a storm. Clutched in one hand was the cracked violin she had brought with her from the Ospedale. Teetering from a renewed attack of dizziness, he watched her raise the violin to her lips and blow across the soundhole, a single shearwater note skimming just above silence, until it was lost to the wind.

The book tells its own story.

Examine it closely and you will see the ragged edges of the type, its cracks and bumps and gaps, the letters that lie crookedly or ride higher or lower than the others, the ink's variations in depth, consistency, and hue, the motes of dust and droplets of sweat sealed within the warp and woof of the paper, the tiny insect bodies caught as the platen came down and now immortalized as unnecessary commas and full stops.

In these imperfections lies a human tale of typecutters, squinting compositors, proofreaders and black-faced printer's devils, labouring against time and heartache and disorder, against life, to create that thing not found in nature, yet still subject to its changes.

The pages stain, fox, dry out. Paper flakes like rusty metal. Threads work loose, headbands and tailbands fray. Front and back boards sag from spines, flyleaves and buckram corner-pieces peel away. Dust mites, cockroaches, and termites dine on paper and binding paste. Rats and mice make snug nests in the middle of thick chapters. And unseen, through the chemical action of time, the words themselves are drained of their living sap. In every library, readers sit in placid quiet while all around them a forest decays.

The Well of Stories

Venice, enclosed in a thick, sluggish fog that had already lasted seven days, was growing all too certain about its existence when the strange vessel appeared on the morning of the eighth day and ushered in a joyous revival of doubt. The first people to see the ship, a few early strollers (and late stragglers) on the Riva degli Schiavoni, were convinced they had at last passed through the unrelenting fog of reality into another age. At anchor in the canal was a dream vessel that would have been at home riding the curlicue waves of a serpent-haunted sea in some far corner of an ancient mariner's chart. Her towering sterncastle was that of an antiquated Spanish galleon, her crenellated bulwarks from some ancient floating castle that Marco Polo might have sailed in on his voyage home from Cathay.

The badly painted figurehead was unidentifiable as man, bird, or beast, but the rotund, barnacled hull looked to the watchers on the riva like nothing so much as the jewel-encrusted hide of a dragon, a resemblance aided by the mingled steam and smoke huffing out of her lower portholes. With each exhalation, the ship emitted a wheezing, vaguely musical bellow, like the lowest bass notes from a pipe organ.

She was a small ship, and someone joked that she must be a dragon of a lesser sort, a stinging bee. Those who came aboard the ship to load provisions brought back even more wondrous stories about the crew.

It was soon being whispered that the captain was a sorcerer and his daughter a mermaid with power over tempests. This brought about a debate as to whether mermaids might live above the waves, and what they looked like. It was remembered by the oldest men that a mermaid had once been fished out of the canal, in the time of the Doge Venier. Although the lower extremities of the creature were missing, and it was only ascertained that this was indeed a mermaid when the fish-like half washed up on shore nearby. The incontrovertible proof of its sex was such a scandal to Christendom that the bishop had it hidden away, preserved in a barrel of balsamic vinegar in the vault of his palace.

Others asserted that the girl was not the sorcerer's daughter but in fact a machine that played the violin, and which he stole from the castle of a Hungarian prince in the hope of making a fortune by exhibiting her (or it) in all the great cities.

There was a family of circus performers on board who slept hanging by their feet from the yards like bats. And a clockwork soldier that could walk and talk and breathe fire. And a three-hundred-year-old Chinaman with six fingers on each hand, who had prevented his own decay by lacquering his body, as it was well-known they did in that strange upside-down country.

The ship, it was clear, was some kind of impossible machine. At the helm stood a console with keys and stops that the helmsman played like a church organ to raise and lower the sails. The hold was filled with devilish engines of smoke and fire groaning and hissing away for the purpose of some diabolical alchemy.

Rumour soon fastened onto a few scraps of truth, and it became known that the master of the archaic vessel was a printer who travelled the world selling his damp books, printed in the ink of the squid on pale green seaweed paper and bound in cured sharkskin. As the story spread it was aged like cheese to give it greater piquancy, allowing its tellers to refer to *the long-lost* Bee, as if the tale of Flood the nautical printer was one they had first heard at their grandmother's feet.

The news that uncertainty had returned at last to Venice brought everyone out, and soon the deserted streets were packed with the usual crowds, with buyers and sellers, with the gazers and the gazed at.

In the afternoon, as they made their way along the riva to the Piazza San Marco, Flood and Pica could not help but overhear the stories about them. To Flood it seemed as if his earlier imaginings about pursuing his trade at sea had run on ahead into the future and fulfilled themselves, while he himself lagged behind.

As they passed the grey façade of the Ospedale, Pica tugged her hat lower and hurried by without looking up. In the swarming, noisy piazza they sat at a table under a busy colonnade, where they awaited a reply to the letter, and the spoon, they had sent Kirshner the metallurgist that morning.

Out of nowhere a waiter materialized and took their order. He asked them if they had seen the ship.

— What ship? Pica asked.

— The floating bookshop, the waiter said. The *Bee*.

In the crowded streets, Flood had not only heard rumours about himself but about the metallurgist as well. He was reputed to be of fabulous age, every morning extending his already unnatural lifespan through the drinking of strange fruit juices and the ritual stretching and bending of his limbs. The much-feared Council of Ten had been investigating Kirshner for some time, it appeared. Responsible for the moral health of the city, the Council regularly employed spies, thieves, and arsonists to safeguard and maintain that health. If you learned that you had made it onto their Index of undesirables, one certain truth loomed: someday they would come for you, spirit you away to their prison from which few returned, the Leads.

It could be days or months, Pica had informed him earlier, having heard all about the Council of Ten while growing up at the Ospedale. *Or even years. But they would come for you.*

Flood listened anxiously to these tales of dread, and wished he were back aboard the ship. This briny Venetian murk, like a room that moved with him, blocked out any glimpse of sky, any suggestion of distance, but it did have an alarming tendency not to behave like proper walls, to drift and thin out, allowing apparitions through, like the one who appeared suddenly at their table, a tall figure costumed as the Jew: wide-brimmed black hat, huge hook nose tied on with string, devilish two-pronged beard.

With the threat of the Council hanging over him, why had the metallurgist, or his agent, chosen to disguise himself as his own grotesque double? Flood was about to confirm that this was in fact the person he was supposed to meet here on the stroke of three, as the letter had stipulated, when the costumed man leaned towards him and breathed, in even poorer Italian than his own,

– How much for a night with your girl-boy?

Flood was already turning away when Pica, much to his surprise, spat at the masker a gondolier's insult, *Coglione!* The man stepped back and stared, his eyes darting from Flood to Pica and back again.

– Do you know the metallurgist? Flood said.

The man's tongue began to flick in and out like a snake's, a gesture that was difficult to interpret in a face hidden behind artifice. Just then a hand tapped Flood on the shoulder and a voice whispered a single word. *Kirshner.* He turned to see a boy, a year or two older than Pica, he guessed, in a cloak and tricorn.

The boy held up a tarnished spoon.

– I saw them first, the costumed man protested half-heartedly as the boy led Flood and Pica out of the piazza. Couldn't we share?

– Foreigners, the boy muttered. He tugged down the brim of his hat and increased his pace.

As he hurried to keep up, Flood asked the boy why everyone in the streets seemed to be so restless.

– It's the wind of doubt. Rolls in once every few months. Stirs everyone up.

– I think we brought it with us, Pica said.

– There will be a celebration tonight. The *forse*. The carnival of uncertainty.

They passed a man lighting lanterns despite the fact that it was mid-afternoon, and further on an old woman in rags squatting over a grate and whistling as she loudly emptied her bladder. They were followed for a while by a shabby figure in sackcloth, shouting and crying after them about the eighth level of hell being nearly full. Eventually, after a few more turns and windings, his blood-curling shrieks faded away.

After stumbling in the gloom over two prostrate bodies reeking of drink, they came at last to a narrow bridge barred by a heavy chain. A uniformed man sitting in a sentry box leaned out slowly to look them over, glimpsed the boy, and unhooked the chain to let them through. They crossed an empty, echoing campiello and descended a short flight of uneven stone steps into the narrowest passageway they had seen yet, where the sky was finally shut out by the rain-gutters of the leaning walls.

The boy took them through an arch and under a long sottoportico until he halted at last before an unmarked door set in a wall of featureless lead-coloured stone. Fastened to the doorframe was a small metal tube with a tiny window in its side, in which Flood glimpsed a rolled-up scrap of parchment. The boy unlocked the door and opened it, releasing a grey cat that slid like quicksilver into the shadows.

– You've got a message, Pica said. In your letter-box.

The boy's solemn face broke into a grin.

– Thank you for letting me know.

When they were inside he shut the door and led Flood and Pica along a dim passage. At the end of it they climbed warily down another uneven flight of steps, to a subterranean canal that smelled sharply of mould and damp. The light of a file of torches flung dancing water shadows onto the vault of stone over their heads. Flood stopped and gazed around him, his breath suddenly coming in short gasps. Pica touched his sleeve.

– I'll be fine.

They went along the edge of the canal to a landing where a

small boat was tied. The boy climbed into the rear of the boat and they followed, sitting in front on the narrow wooden slats. The boy poled them along a tunnel lit by ventilation shafts in the arched roof just above their heads. From time to time Pica glanced over her shoulder at him, and whenever his eyes met hers, a suppressed smile would tug at the edges of his mouth.

When they emerged from the tunnel they were in a sunlit garden alive with insect hum and the twitter of sparrows. The world was a green well in which pollen swirled like falling snow. The boy helped them climb from the boat and led them along a curving path bordered by a dark box hedge, at the end of which knelt a white-haired old man, digging with a spade in a bed of tomato plants. Various articles of furniture stood around him on the grass: a type cabinet, a table displaying a dis-ordered array of files and other metalworking tools, a lacquered folding tray on which sat the remains of a meal. The old man raised his head at their approach.

– I've brought them, Grandfather.

– Thank you, Nathan.

The boy turned to go, and as he passed Pica he grinned once more. The old man struggled to his feet and greeted them with a bow. Pica curtsied, a remnant of her Ospedale upbring-ing that Flood had not seen before.

– This is my workroom, Kirshner said, slapping at his dusty breeches, as well as my kitchen garden. Light is important for both. But forgive me.

He patted the empty bench beside him.

They approached and sat, waiting for him to speak again. Kirshner had not yet looked directly at them, and this close Flood could see that the metallurgist's face was pitted with tiny scars, the pupils of his eyes clouded. Something had shattered into atomies in front of him, Flood guessed. A hazard of his profession.

Kirshner felt in the basket at his feet and plucked out two tomatoes.

– Hungry?

Flood declined.

– Too bad. These are the best vegetables in the city. How about you, young lady?

– Please, signore.

– Catch.

He tossed Pica a tomato.

– Thank you.

– You have your mother's voice, my child.

Pica lowered her eyes and blushed.

The old man sighed.

– I wish I could tell you where she is. But I am afraid the last contact I had with the House of Ostrov was when I filled your father's order for type. Twelve years ago now. Though I've thought of you, Mr. Flood, many times since then. And strangely enough, not long ago I had a visit from someone who might be able to help you in your search. The Abbé de Saint-Foix. He told me that you had left the Count's employ, and so he had taken charge of your project. He was eager to learn if you had commissioned anything from me in that regard.

– Did he tell you where he was going?

– He did, in rather loud hints. He wanted me to know that he had been invited to Alexandria by the Ottoman governor. Some prestigious post at court, although he wouldn't say exactly what it was. For my part, I gave away even less by way of help or advice. Not even a spoon.

– The spoon, Flood said. I didn't understand why you sent it.
The old man smiled.
– Neither did I, then.

THE METALLURGIST'S TALE

He was born not far from the Castle Ostrov, on the
other side of the mountains, in a little Polish village. His
father Avram was also a metalsmith. He made candlesticks, cutlery, buckles, and brooches, and often experi-
mented with alloys, on more than one occasion almost
blowing himself up in the process. He travelled often to
Krakow to find out what was in fashion and to hunt for
new commissions. Each time he returned he would sit
Samuel on his knee and tell him about what he had seen
on the way there and on the way back. On every trip he
invariably encountered something odd or amusing to
relate. Avram was a bear of a man, tall and long-bearded,
and Samuel would gaze up at his father as he told his
stories, in a kind of worshipful fear of those glittering
black eyes, that great grinning mouth. Only many years
later did he suspect that most of what he had accepted as
truth was nothing but the purest invention.

Finally, when Samuel was old enough, he was
allowed to accompany his father on the great journey
to Krakow. When they got to the city, he was silent and
sullen, and when his father wanted to know what was
the matter, he asked why they hadn't met that peasant.
What peasant? his father asked. *The one you said you saw
the last time, carrying a saddle on his back.*

The boy had been certain he would see everything his father had seen, as if the sights along the road existed as a fixed and eternal tableau for their eyes. He thought it deceitful of the world not to remain as his father had described it, but he would be fooled no longer. He would believe only in what he had seen for himself.

When Samuel began his apprenticeship, Avram Kirshner would often hold up a soup spoon or a knife that they had just made, and instruct his son to remember how strange and miraculous it was that everything in the universe is really a word, a thought thinking itself in God's mind.

He spent as much time scouring obscure old kabbalistic tomes as he did making brooches and candlesticks. And he was not alone. Half the men in the village came to the house in the evenings to discuss these phantom visions of dead mystics. Avram and his sad-eyed colleagues would sit up all night drinking tea and arguing about the hidden meanings in mystical texts, about the *en-sof*, about the shattering of the vessels of light and the Angel Metatron, whose little finger spans the distance from the earth to Saturn. They talked as if the infinite was as real, as close and solid and undeniably *there* as a table, a chair, a floor you could stomp your foot against.

When he was old enough to leave home, Kirshner moved to Venice, a place where men trafficked in what could be seen, touched, tasted, bought, and sold. As a parting gift from his father he asked for one tarnished spoon.

While the old man was telling his story, the wind rose and a cloud passed across the sun. A drop of rain touched the back of Pica's hand. She stirred, looked up at the changing sky, anxious to be gone now that she knew the old man could not help them. When the sun emerged again its light seemed to be rising out of the earth.

– Perhaps, Mr. Flood, the spoon does taste the broth, Kirshner said. Tell me, the imaginary book your letter mentioned, did you have a name for it?

– The *alam*, Flood said. I called it the *alam*.

– *Alam*. That is good. I like that. There have been many other names for it, of course. *Zohar. The paper-thin garden. Il'bal.*

– Other names. How could there be?

– In imagining your *alam*, Mr. Flood, you became a member of the world's oldest reading society, one that has existed for centuries, under countless names, in every part of the world. A society dedicated to the dreaming of fabulous, impossible, imaginary books. Have you heard of the ninety-eight volume *History of Silence*?

– No.

– There are many others, only a few of which I myself have heard of, and even fewer of which I've read. *The Book of Water. A Universal Chronopticon. The Almanac of Longing. The Formulary of the Ten Thousand Things.* They are all books imagined by the society, and some of them, beginning as insubstantial dreams, have become paper and ink.

– I've done that, too, Pica said. Sometimes, before I open a book, I imagine it's some other book.

Flood stared at her.

– Thank you, Countess, Kirshner said. Over the years I've come to understand that a book itself desires to be. Dream a book, no matter how outlandish or unlikely, and that book will find a way to exist, even if it must wait a thousand years.

A gust of wind stirred the tops of the trees and died away again.

– Twelve years ago I began to think again about infinity, Kirshner said. And books.

He lifted a green cloth from the tabletop to reveal an iron chase about the size of a large folio volume, already filled with a forme of assembled type.

– There's still an empty space, Pica said. There, in the middle.

Kirshner nodded.

– Good. You're observant. I left one letter out.

He pulled open a drawer in the cabinet, plucked out a single sort and dropped it into the tiny square hole in the forme. When he had tightened all the quoins around the edge of the iron frame he held one hand just above the surface of the type, his fingers trembling.

– Like you, Mr. Flood, for years I never suspected the existence of such a society. At least not until I began to work on this, for you. What would once have taken me mere days when I was young and blessed with eyesight has taken a very long time.

He pushed the chase across the table and Flood saw, in place of the expected lines of type, a dull, solid plate of metal.

– I've always found it intriguing, Kirshner said, that an alphabet is both the most durable and the most ephemeral of the world's elements. In the language of my people the alphabet consists of twenty-two letters. Twenty-two rivers, twenty-two bridges.

He smiled at Pica and gestured to the chase.

– Now, if you will, breathe lightly on the forme.

She leaned over the chase and blew softly across its surface. All at once letters began to rise in relief from the metal, until the entire forme had reappeared. Pica laughed.

– Gooseflesh type, she said.

– In my daybook this batch was noted down as *Kirshner galliard roman thirty-seven*, but I like your suggestion much better. Gooseflesh type it shall be.

Flood was unable to tear his eyes from the backwards letters that lay before him, untouched by ink and seeming to blaze in the sunlight so that he could not read them.

The metallurgist's hand brushed lightly over the raised type and the letters rose and sank, bobbing in a pool of mercury. Forme after forme appeared and disappeared, as if within the depths of the metal pages were being turned.

– Is it just random, Flood asked, or is there some order . . . ?

– You could ask the same thing of the universe, Kirshner said. Whatever else infinity may be, it is generous.

Flood watched, spellbound, and thought of the book he had printed for Irena. *Desire.* Her name hidden within it like these letters rising from the metal.

– The pieces are more fragile when they're unassembled, Kirshner said. As they watched, the type solidified again into an ordinary, unmoving block of text.

– Handle them carefully. They are somewhat volatile, as I have discovered.

He held his hands out and Flood saw, burned into his fingertips, slender Hebrew characters.

– The sefirot. Essential ingredients of the alloy, and which I should have taken more care and time to understand. But they did teach me much. We think of the world as *filled*. With things, phenomena, a vast drawing room stuffed with objects, solid and imperishable. When read by the light of the sefirot, however, this world reveals itself to be impermanent, illusory, mostly empty space, until the mind begins to furnish it.

With the quoin key, Kirshner unlocked the chase and slid out the slender wedges of metal furniture.

– If such is the nature of the world, then imaginary books are not absurd dreams but intimations of reality.

He lifted the lid of the typecase and with methodical care began returning the sorts to their compartments. A dragonfly whirred past and vanished into a bed of hollyhocks. When Kirshner had finished he closed the lid of the case and slid it across the table to Flood.

– You want me to have this?

– My work is done. It's up to someone else to find out what can be made of it.

They followed Kirshner through his garden as he finished gathering vegetables for supper. He told them that over the centuries the society had attracted enemies as relentless as they were powerful. If they took the gooseflesh type with them they would have to be on their guard.

– I've been told the Council of Ten is watching you, Flood said.

– They are indeed. And now they will be watching you, too, I'm afraid. I recommend you remain here until the carnival begins. You will more likely go unnoticed in a crowd.

They stayed the evening with the old man, who insisted they dine with him and his grandson. They ate and drank at a table outside until the light declined, then the boy lit torches around the garden. The flames bent and twisted in the night wind. From beyond the walls they heard the rising noise of laughter and merrymaking.

As Flood and Pica were taking their leave of Kirshner they heard a flap of great wings. A pelican glided down over their heads, skimmed the surface of the canal, and rose again, vanishing into the lilac dusk. The first stars began to appear and the boy took them back through the tunnel to the door of the house.

– I will escort you to San Marco, he said, slipping on a cloak.

– I can find it, Pica said, already walking away.

– I think he likes you, Flood whispered when he had caught up to her.

– I really can find the way, she said. I have it in my head now. You'll see.

Flood steered for the streets where the crowds were thickest, Pica close at his side and the case of gooseflesh type clutched tightly under his arm. He was not sure just what he had been given, but the familiar heft of the case, the muffled rattle of the sorts, reassured him.

Grotesque and comical faces swam up at them and vanished. The familiar harlequins, beaked plague doctors and zanies were in abundance, but every so often masks swept past that left them only with a vague sense of recognition and unease, as if they had encountered these faces before in dreams.

They were hurrying along an unlit arcade, hoping to elude any pursuers, when two cowled figures and a man dressed as Don Quixote stumbled drunkenly out of the shadows into their path. All three carried thick wooden staves. The lanky knight stepped forward and in a slurred voice demanded that they all go for a drink, even the lad. Flood refused and asked to be left in peace, as he was on urgent business. He was not sure what sign indicated it to him, but in the next instant he knew that the three men were as sober as he was.

– We can guess your urgent business, Don Quixote said. You were in the Jewish quarter. You brought something out with you. Alchemist's gold, perhaps, to ferret out of the city.

– We have nothing you would want.

Don Quixote scratched his chin.

– Are you absolutely sure of that, friend? After all, this is the night of *forse*. I think my friends and I will have to see for ourselves.

Flood leaned down to whisper in Pica's ear.

– Run. Warn Djinn.

– But –

– Do it.

As she darted away, Flood turned back the way they had come and was instantly seized from behind. Over his shoulder he caught a glimpse of Pica bolting down the arcade, then their staves cracked against his skull, his shoulders, drove into his stomach. Pain dazzling as lightning illuminated the borders of a realm he had not imagined, the dark ranges of agony. When it had subsided he was lying with his face pressed against the cold stones, tasting his own blood.

– What are they?

– Lead slugs. Trash.

He heard the case crack as it hit the ground, the scuff of footsteps receding.

Slowly, with laboured breathing, he climbed to his knees. The case lay open and overturned nearby, its lid split down the middle. His attackers had kicked the slugs in every direction before fleeing. *Pie*, he thought absurdly, his father's word for a mess of spilled type.

On hands and knees he began to gather the sorts that were scattered over the stones, dropping them with trembling fingers back into the case without concern for the proper order. A few stray pieces lay at the canal's edge. Just beyond his reach the moon slithered on black water. He watched its silent dance for a moment, spellbound.

It was likely that some of the type was lost forever, lying now in the murk and mire at the bottom of the canal. Perhaps he could bring Pica here in daylight to search for the missing pieces.

Pica.

He heard the sound of footsteps and climbed unsteadily to his feet. He lurched into a staggering run and as his legs gave way a sturdy pair of arms caught him.

— I'm ready now, he said. Lock me up and don't let me out this time.

φ

They brought him back to the ship, where he lay, delirious, in his bunk, while Turini set sail and took them out to sea.

Three days later he awoke with a throbbing head and a terrible thirst, to find that they were bound for Alexandria.

When he was well enough, he had Pica bring him the gooseflesh type. Under his direction, he had her set a forme. As she had done at the metallurgist's garden, she tried breathing on it, then shaking it, and brushing the letters with ink. She and Djinn heated the chase, immersed it in brine, and set it out in the sun. Nothing produced the slightest tremor in the metal. The slugs, some with letters and others blank, remained as they were, dull and inert.

– We'll keep rearranging the letters, Flood said, like the pieces of a puzzle, until something happens.

φ

She remembered how she had first glimpsed him through the spyhole in his cell at the Castle Ostrov, oblivious to everything else around him as he printed an invisible book.

She had been searching the *Bee* up and down ever since they first came on board, with no idea what she was hoping to find. Now she spent all her spare time prowling the decks, learning every passageway, every sliding panel and trapdoor, every secret recess where someone or something might have been hidden away.

A letter. A map. Some sort of clue. The more she learned of the ship's devious intricacies, the greater was her sense that there was something hidden just beyond her knowledge. Sometimes when she was climbing through one of the sliding panels she had the feeling that her mother had just disappeared behind another panel or through a hidden door, that she was actually somewhere on the ship and that they were both looking for each other but never quite meeting.

She spent most of her time with the Turinis, aware of the way the four of them existed as a kind of single being. They had soon overcome their fear of her, although the carpenter still insisted on addressing her as Countess. From him and Darka she learned to steer, keep the sails trim, and judge the wind. With the encouragement of the children she began to feel at home high up in the rigging. She sensed, running through the daily shipboard routines, the invisible web that bound the parents together, the parents to the twins, and the twins to each other. Lolo and Miza often woke her early in the morning, crawling into her bed and asking for the stories she had learned as a child. She would rise with the family, eat with them, share their talk and laughter, their squabbles and reconciliations. Often she would spend an entire day among them without once seeing her father. In the evening, she would bring him a meal and he would grope for his cup of tea with his eyes on the forme of type before him.

Then night would come, broken up into its long, tedious watches. The children would finally fall asleep, and she would take her turn alone at the helm, keeping the lanterns lit and the sails braced. And then she would hear, amid the other moans, murmurs and stirrings of the dreaming ship, the dull clink of the sorts.

φ

Djinn suggested trying a different ink. He was thinking of a formula he had glimpsed in an occult treatise on geometry in the Count's library. The author, Johannes Trithemius, suggested that this forbidden ink, which was reputed to be of the same chemical composition as a fallen angel's blood, might be efficacious in the summoning of mournful, tormented spirits.

> *Ad faciendum atramentum divinum, recipe gallas et contere minute in pulverum; funde desuper aquam mutabilem, cerevisiam teneum, et oleum igneum, et impone de vitalo quantum sufficit juxta existationem. . . .*

Flood, his Latin grown rusty, attempted to translate for Pica's benefit. *To make supernatural ink, gather oak-galls, and grind minutely . . .*

– *Aquam mutabilem*?

– We could try vinegar, Djinn said.

– Good. Now, *put in as much – vitalo*? What is that? Vitality? Life? – *as is sufficient to your judgement and permit it to stand for some days* . . .

φ

Alexandria was white, a city of salt on the edge of the sea.

On the first day, Flood, Djinn, and Pica left the *Bee* only for short forays into the narrow alleyways around the harbour, dazed into near-imbecility by the heat. Flood's right leg had remained stiff and sore since the attack, and now the pain flared up again, so that he limped along. Before they left the ship, Pica had looked through the seventh volume of the encyclopedia, in search of something that would help them orient themselves in this unfamiliar world. All she could come up with was the entry on language, which speculated that the tower of Babel might have been in Egypt.

Alexandria had been cobbled together from the ruins of its ancient lives, so that one might see the stumps of Roman columns framing a doorway, or bits of ancient mosaic tile stuck into the plaster of a wall. To ascend these crumbling colonnades, where cloaked and veiled figures drifted past or lurked in curtained recesses, was to imagine that they had come to a cemetery where the dead had not quite settled down to rest. The impression of their own swiftness in relation to these spectres continued until they reached the souk, where the sun finally pummelled them into submission and they took refuge under an awning's thin moon of shade.

As they rested, panting like dogs, Djinn found his vision

splitting in two like the halves of a lemon, so that it seemed everything was happening to him in two places at once. Like a man carrying a mirror on his shoulder, he moved through two worlds unfolding from one. In the lifeless dust he caught the delicious scent of rain. A curving pathway of sand shimmered for a moment with the tree-shaded green of a canal. Above him a pagoda rose, a horned and scaly dragon perched among the slender minarets. Out of the buzz and murmur of tongues he had carried in his head since childhood, two words came together, spoken in a voice so clear that he started as if it had been whispered in his ear.

Xian Shu.

– My name, he said.

– What's that? Flood said, looking up.

– I know my name.

The sun slid from its zenith and the marketplace began to fill with people. The three of them rose from their shelter and set out again, keeping the twin spires of the palace before them above the flat rooftops. By now Djinn was caught in a maze of reflections so persistent that every doorway of beaded curtains, every yawning camel, every pair of eyes flashing from the covert of a yashmak, had its counterpart in his memory. This was both a leafy city in China and salt-crusted Alexandria, and thus somewhere other than both, and Djinn sensed in this joining and splintering of worlds that his history was more than a single sad tale, or even a chain of such stories told one after another.

Flood spoke, and the vision folded in upon itself again, the jade towers of China melting away like ice spires in the heat.

– Here it is.

They were at the gates of the palace.

– Do you have an appointment? the doorwarden asked. You have to have an appointment.

– How do we get one?

– You have to see the *vekil* of appointments.

– Then we'd like to see him.

– Do you have an appointment?

Unable to puncture this hermetically sealed logic, they retreated.

– Don't worry, Djinn said as they turned away. He will let us in tomorrow.

– How do you know that? Flood asked.

– I remember.

On the morning of the second day, in the crowded souk, Flood lost her. He and Djinn turned this way and that, jumped to look over heads, called her name into the chorus of a hundred voices crying their wares.

On the edge of the marketplace they were caught up in a hurrying mob. From the gossip around them Djinn was able to glean that there was to be an unexpected public execution. The condemned man, a supplier of coffee to the Mamluk garrison, had been caught dealing with the despised Turkish janissaries. This was not an execution, in other words, so much as a message from the powerful Egyptian troops to the Ottoman pasha, and it was clear the people in the streets were eager to see it delivered. Flood and Djinn shouldered through to the front of the crowd just as the curved blade flashed down. After a long still moment the spectators stirred, the talking and jostling beginning anew as the crowd transformed from a single body into people heading every which way back to their lives.

He caught sight of her then, not far from him, staring at the headless body slumped on the stone, the blood darkening in the sand.

He took hold of her wrist and led her out of the square.

The next day the three of them set out again for the palace.

— Do we have an appointment? Djinn asked the doorwarden.

— With who?

— The *vekil* of appointments.

— How the devil should I know? the doorwarden growled. Ask him.

In the outer reception hall they met the indifference of court protocol, a cold so palpable that Flood almost wished the clerk he had snagged by the sleeve would wave them off and thus waft some of his studied iciness their way. The clerk, a thick sheaf of documents stuffed under his arm, listened without expression as Flood described the Abbé, then informed them he had never seen nor heard of such a person, and continued on his way.

Back outside in the public court, they sat by a fountain under a sycamore and debated whether to return to the ship or find lodgings in the city. They were no longer in a hurry, content for the moment to be out of the furnace of the streets. As they lingered near the fountain, reluctant to leave its cool spray, the clerk Flood had spoken to earlier came hurrying by, now without his bundle of documents. He gave Djinn the briefest of sideways glances as he passed and kept on, but at the gate of the court he stopped, turned, and came back.

— No one will help you, he said in French, if you keep doing foolish things.

— Such as? Flood asked.

– Asking for Safwa Effendi.

The clerk's name was Selim. He told them he spoke French because it was required at the present pasha's court to know the language of that refined nation, Alexandria's favoured trading partner. He asked their names and inquired after their business, but was careful, Flood noted, not to ask too much. He told them that the Abbé's knowledge of obscure arts and sciences made him a closely guarded resource.

– Like the porcelain-makers of Germany, he said, imprisoned by greedy kings to keep the process secret.

If they wished to see Safwa Effendi, they had to gain entrance to the inner palace, and in order to accomplish that, they would have to be invited by the pasha.

– The cool of the evening is almost here, the clerk said. We may walk together in the streets now without attracting notice.

Djinn fetched the Turinis from the ship, and they all ate dinner at the clerk's house, a loft above the *khan* of an Armenian wool merchant, where doves crowded the ledges of the latticed windows. Lolo and Miza, having spent so much of their life on board the ship, were terrified of the city's unyielding solidity and clung to Pica the entire evening.

Selim lived with his three unmarried older sisters, who welcomed the visitors with nods and bows, but soon retired to a far corner of the room and sat together, stealing curious glances at Pica. They sat apart during the meal as well, and from the bits of family history Selim dropped here and there, Flood learned that all three sisters were widows of the pasha's numerous military excursions, and that their brother's greatest concern was to find each of them a husband.

– I could die in peace tomorrow, he said, eyeing Djinn and then Flood, if I found a soul brave enough to take all three.

The pasha, Selim informed them, had one all-consuming passion: his own death, for which he was determined to be better prepared than any man had been before. As a result, he was an insatiable collector of things that would assist his meditations on the inevitable. Lugubrious poetry, dismal music, the bones of suicides, and courtesans dead of the plague. By now the pasha was said to have an unrivalled collection of such morbid treasures, and so something that would tempt him would have to be very unusual indeed.

The next morning Pica found her father in the press room, unshaven and dressed in the clothes he had on the day before, having stayed up all night wrestling with the challenge of creating something very unusual. He had expected Djinn's help, but for the first time since Flood had known him, the compositor seemed uninterested in printing, and took to strolling alone through the streets. He would be gone most of the day and then return to the ship in the evening, bringing sugary treats, toys, or unusual shells for the twins. Lolo and Miza now rushed to greet him, tugging at his sleeves and chanting his name. Selim had been telling them stories from *The Thousand and One Nights*, and they were convinced that the compositor might, if pestered enough, live up to his name and perform the kind of djinnistical feats performed in these tales, like growing to the height of Diocletian's pillar, or drinking up the Mareotic Lake in one mighty gulp.

One evening when Pica and the twins were visiting the clerk, Djinn showed up with a sheaf of long yellow leaves tucked in his belt and a dazed, far-off look in his eyes. Selim pushed and patted the compositor down into a chair and brewed him some of his frightful black coffee. Once he had been rescued from the children, Djinn shrugged off his stupor and related how, while nosing around in the souk, he had caught the scent of something that would not let him go and had traced it, delving further and further into the windings of the streets, along narrower and narrower passageways, having picked out of the cloud of aromas a scent that seemed to him to come not from the here and now but from the hazy borderlands of his own past.

– I thought I was fooling myself, he said, but it was maddening. Like a face you can't quite remember.

He ended up in the arcade of a public bath, at a tiny stall that sold baskets woven of a slender yellow sedge. The aged merchant spoke a tongue of which Djinn could only understand a few words, but he patiently showed the compositor how they used the roots of the plant for firewood and building material, and the long blades of the leaves for baskets, rope, and paper.

The sedge was papyrus.

When Djinn's reservoir of words ran dry, the old man brought out some leaves of papyrus, a reed pen, and a clay ink bottle. Djinn sniffed the ink and knew at once it was the recipe for which he and Flood had been seeking. This was the fallen-angel ink, its faint scent that of a time of absolute joy now dead and gone, darkened by the sulphurous odour of mingled blood and pitch. With halting words and hand signs, he asked what the ink was made from, and the old man drew

By nightfall they had passed through the gate of the moon, seated in a houseboat of plaited reeds, the guests of three people with whom they had hardly spoken a word: the ancient basket merchant, a woman who appeared to be even older, and a young woman, veiled and silent. Flood and Pica sat together in the stern, watching Djinn converse haltingly with the old man in a tongue that he seemed to be remembering as they spoke. The boat floated through a forest of towering rushes, water lilies drifting past in the darkness like luminous planets.

They arrived at dawn in a tiny village among the reeds where one of the last of the papyrus craftsmen lived. Greeted as one long lost by the villagers, Djinn was taken to his reed hut and permitted to watch while he worked.

The craftsman split the green leaves with a bone needle into long, narrow strips and held them up for Djinn's inspection. The quality of the papyrus, Djinn learned, was best when made from the inner pith. This was used to make the *hieratic* paper, reserved exclusively from ancient times for sacred texts. From there, the various grades deteriorated until one reached the outer husks, which were used for *emporitica*, paper for wrapping fish and other perishable merchandise.

The thin strips of papyrus were spread out on a wet stone table. As the craftsman wove them together, his assistant, a little boy, spread watery mud on each layer. The woven plaits were then pressed beneath heavy wooden boards, left to dry in the sun, and finally stitched together into a long roll.

Djinn held a freshly dried sheet of papyrus to his nose and inhaled, and something older than his own past was breathed to him. The slightly briny reek of the fibres hinted of a time so distant he grew dizzy at the thought. *This paper comes from a place where we all began*, he thought. *Not quite land, not quite sea.*

The three people they had travelled with erected a sheep-skin tent on the edge of the village and made a fire with thin sticks of wood and cakes of dried dung. When they had eaten their evening meal, the young woman rose, slipped silently into the tent, and returned a few moments later. Her face was still veiled but the rest of her body was draped only in a sheet of the thinnest muslin. She approached the fire, and when she let fall her sheer covering, they could see that her umber skin was tattooed from neck to ankles with tiny blue-black interweaving symbols. The basket merchant beckoned to Djinn and made a sign to him that he should also disrobe. Djinn glanced at Flood and Pica, then slipped out of his shirt and breeches and stood clutching the bundle of his clothes. The merchant untied a small leather pouch and set out on the sand before him an array of knives and bone needles.

At his bidding, Djinn lay down on his side near the fire. With a finger, the old woman began to trace the flowing script on the tattooed woman's flesh, and as she did so she spoke to the old man, who sat cross-legged beside Djinn with his tattooing instruments and pouch of ink.

As each word was passed to him, he made an incision into Djinn's flesh.

φ

The true weeping ink, the basket merchant called it.

Djinn was not able to read the ancient script, but as if the ink had seeped through his skin and added its own dark tincture to his blood, he would spend hours in a lethargic trance, only to wake suddenly, leave the ship, and prowl through the marketplace, on the trail of a certain herb, gum, or oil that would be added to the mixture brewing in the iron pot he had placed on the type-founding furnace.

Both Flood and Pica noticed that the compositor had grown even more quiet and withdrawn since his tattooing, and assumed that the ink was indeed to blame. Hoping to draw him out, Pica began preparing the ingredients he gathered and mixing them in the quantities he prescribed.

The resulting fluid was so volatile they had difficulty pouring it into the storage vat. The ink leapt as if alive, splattering and slithering away along the seams of the planks, where it quickly vanished, as if absorbed into the frame of the ship itself.

Finally, Flood managed to confine a few ounces in a stoppered glass bottle, and by careful siphoning was able to coat a forme of gooseflesh type. A sheet from the roll of papyrus the paper-maker had given them was prepared and set in place, and while Pica and Djinn watched from a safe distance, Flood slid the carriage under the press, heaved on the bar, and released it.

He unclipped the damp sheet from the tympan and peeled it away. The paper was as blank as it had been when it went in. The ink had not held, they thought at first, until Pica noticed a tiny speck near the bottom of the page. At first they thought it was an eyelash or something that had fallen on the sheet just before printing.

– It's a comma, Flood said, closing one eye and peering closely at the speck. A Griffo, or a Jenson, I think.

He brought out a small cylindrical microscope of tooled copper, peered through the aperture at the paper, and let out a soft *hmph* of surprise. Djinn had a look, and then it was Pica's turn. She squinted into the eyepiece and was startled to see that the comma, which to her unaided eyes had looked smooth and sharp-edged, had become a spiny sea creature, scaly and ten-drilled. The paper itself had been transformed into a bumpy plain of rises and hollows. This was what happened, she understood at last, when inked metal letters were pressed into paper. They crushed it and bled hair-thin capillaries of ink into its fibres.

Then she saw something else. The comma was breathing, its sea-horse shape expanding and contracting with a slow pulse.

– Did you see? she asked her father breathlessly.

– Yes. And look at the type.

Flood drew their attention back to the forme. They gathered around the press to see that the blank plate of metal within the chase was now shimmering, restless, liquid, as it had been in Kirshner's garden.

φ

She opened her father's pocketwatch, examined the face by the light from the overhead hatch, and shut the lid. Dangling the watch by its chain, she quickly lowered it into the glimmering pool of metal.

She waited, holding her breath. After something more than a minute she lifted the watch out, checked the time, and smiled to herself. Again she leaned over the chase of gooseflesh type, studied it for a few moments, then pursed her lips and let drop a gob of spittle.

There was a cough from the doorway and she turned to see her father watching her.

– I wanted to see what would happen, she said.

– And what did?

– Time slows down in there.

– And the spit?

– I don't know. I felt like doing that.

He smiled.

– Keep the watch. You can use it.

Once the ink was ready, Djinn began to set a text. He mingled gooseflesh and ordinary type in formes that he printed onto the papyrus and then stitched into a growing scroll. When Flood asked him where he was getting the story, the compositor explained that it was drawn from his own life.

With the help of the ink and Kirshner's type, Djinn had managed to go back further than ever, through his youth and into his vanished childhood, to the first sounds he had ever uttered, while he was still in his mother's womb. He had recaptured it all, he told Flood.

– The taste of milk from my mother's breast. The first sight of my father, dancing a tiny jade horse before me. The cool silk cocoon my mother carried me in.

He knew now that his father was Chinese and his mother Ethiopian. They had met in Alexandria, had a child, and had travelled during Djinn's early childhood. His father was a silk merchant, he believed. One terrible day he had been separated from them, and then, much later, from his memory of them.

– How did you lose them? Flood asked.

Djinn would say nothing more.

– I don't like to tell the story forwards.

– But you're printing it.

He was not. Instead, he was printing the melancholy story of his life yet to come.

– When you look far enough into the past, Djinn said, the future overtakes you. Since I'm of a melancholy humour at present, it had to be the result of both sorrow past and sorrow to come.

– I'm no philosopher, Flood said, but it seems to me that a cause can't come after an effect.

Djinn shrugged.

– It's comforting to know you won't be taken by surprise.

– So what is the story you're working on, then?

– There's a woman. It's difficult to explain –

Pica, polishing the timbers of the press, stopped to listen.

– This is news, Flood said. Who is she?

– I haven't met her yet.

Turini, passing through the press room on his never-ending campaign against leaks, offered his own advice.

– The best cure for melancholy is a good bleeding. Get the black bile out. That's what Darka does for me.

In this way the problem of *vitalo* was solved. Darka cut open a vein in the compositor's forearm. Blood of an alarmingly black colour spurted out of him and joined the rest of the ingredients simmering in the pot.

To test the ink's affinity for paper, they printed, with a combination of gooseflesh type and ordinary ten-point Bembo, a copy of Djinn's *Book of Tears*, which they bound in scroll form. When Flood added his device to the last leaf he realized that this was the first time he had done so in twelve years. After the countless hours he had spent in the cell printing off sheaves of intangible paper, this slender roll of papyrus, someone else's book, was all he had to show the world.

Djinn gave Pica the scroll to read first. She scanned the first few pages, a hazy description of a green, meandering river, and then suddenly drew her head back, her eyes filling with tears.

– It's like peeling an onion. Is that really what you want?

– It will have to do, Djinn said.

Selim took the *Book of Tears* with him to the palace. They prepared themselves for another long wait, but the clerk returned to the ship the very next day with the news that the Reader of Souls, the court censor, had approved the book and that they had been granted an audience with the pasha. Or rather, Flood and Pica had been granted that tremendous honour. As the slave of a European, Djinn could not be brought in the pasha's presence.

Flood protested that Djinn was the book's creator, but the compositor did not seem to care.

– Just go. It doesn't matter.

Now, as if by magic, the forbidden inner regions of the palace were opened to them. Led by a solemn doorwarden shoulder- ing a gold mace, Flood and Pica passed through the flock of whispering clerks in the outer reception hall and across a parade ground open to the sky, where a group of janissaries stood around in idle conversation, grooming their horses. At the gate of the inner seraglio the guards ordered them to remove their buckled shoes and put on green felt slippers. Here, where absolute silence reigned, they were led through a succes- sion of anterooms and connecting corridors to the Hall of the Divan, an oblong vault of dull stone hung with black brocades, weakly illuminated through a deep skylight in the roof. At the door, Selim appeared and leaned towards Flood, speaking in a whisper.

– Remember to bow. Often.

As they proceeded down the length of the hall, led by the doorwarden, courtiers in robes of dark red and brown drifted like dispersing mourners out of their path.

The plump ruler of Alexandria lay on his side on a cushioned cedar sofa, already half-mummified in wet cloths soaked with some bitter-smelling embrocation. At the doorwarden's whispered announcement, he raised a many-ringed finger to signal that the printer should approach.

Flood stepped forward, and Pica shrank back behind him.

– And the boy, the doorwarden said.

Pica came out from behind Flood. The pasha studied her for a long time, then whispered to Selim, who bowed so low to reach his master's ear that Flood wondered if he would manage to right himself again.

– We have seen your book, the pasha breathed in French. We thank you for it.

Flood caught sight of Selim's frantic grimace, remembered that he was supposed to bow, and did so, emptied of fear and desire. In the old man's half-throttled wisp of a voice he had heard the weary effort to remain interested in the world, in anything, no matter how trivial, as if life might be clung to by the thread of mere curiosity. But beyond all of this ceremony, the end was still coming. The end that could best be delayed by making each day so very like one's last that to survive it seemed a miraculous reprieve.

Hold back death by dying every day.

Flood felt himself drained of everything but the cold certainty that the Count's final riddle would remain unsolved. He glanced at Pica, saw the frightened determination in her eyes, and looked away. Why had he brought her here? The world as it truly was, a broken labyrinth of unfinished stories, would continue to baffle them, lead them astray, and at last turn their hopes to dust, as it had done to everything he had ever worked towards. The pasha alone had seen this truth clearly, that it was better to welcome oblivion than to go on deceiving oneself.

Flood forced himself to take the next few steps forward. It barely concerned him any longer to wonder how their offering would be received, and he stood as if bereft of will as Selim bent to receive another whispered command.

– You will remain here, the clerk said. As the pasha's guest.

For a moment the old man's eyes glimmered with something like anticipation, then fluttered back to rest in a dim unseeing.

– Now I beg you to leave us, the pasha said, waving a hand vaguely in their direction.

– Open all the windows, he went on, his wattles shaking and his voice tremulously grasping for strength, as if an unexpected fit of purpose had seized hold of him. Around the room, gilded ropes were tugged, heavy tapestries crumpled upward and light crashed into the room.

– Open them to the winds, he added in a fainter voice, for I feel as if heaven lies close upon the earth and I between the two, breathing through the eye of a needle.

He smiled to himself, and all at once Flood understood the bizarre hope that the pasha's unrehearsed flight of eloquence had given him. Such fine last words were too beautiful, too perfect to possibly be one's actual last words. The moment would pass and the dreary farce would go on, to some doubtless more ignoble conclusion. As he stood with his head bowed, it seemed to him that time had filled to the brim and was trembling, about to spill over into the next moment. The pasha was wrong. There was always something more. Flood's fit of despondency suddenly left him and he held his breath, seized with the desire to know what was about to happen.

On his sofa the pasha continued to smile. Selim bent almost double again to await the next command, then lifted his eyes to the pasha's glassy stare, started, shot a look of terror at the doorwarden, who followed suit with his closest neighbour in the entourage around the throne. In the flurry of somewhat restrained distress that followed, the foreigners were forgotten by everyone except Selim, who glided coolly through the sudden swarm of murmuring courtiers.

– Wait a moment, then follow me.

The clerk slipped out of the hall through a curtained recess, and after a few seconds they joined him. Without a word he led them through a sequence of stone passageways that widened and grew brighter as the echoing clamour in the audience chamber faded. To Flood, the sensation was one of an ascent towards freedom, but when Selim finally halted before a narrow door of oak banded with iron, he had the sudden terrible thought that he was about to meet the same fate that had closed around him at the castle. Selim unlocked the door and stood aside.

– I cannot remain with you a moment longer. Go.

To Flood's surprise Pica took the lead, plunging ahead of him into blackness. Flood followed more cautiously, groping for the side walls of the narrow passage and whispering to her. *Pica. Where are –?* His hands encountered empty air and he stopped, hearing her voice from somewhere below him. *There are stairs here.* He descended in darkness, the sweat cooling on his neck, his slippered feet gingerly testing for the next stair, until there were no more steps and he felt Pica's cool hand on his.

– There's another door here.

This time she let him proceed and his fingers found a latch. He opened the unwilling door with a shove and stumbled forward. They were in absolute darkness, on the edge of an unseen open space where a cold, dank wind keened.

– There's nothing here, Flood said. We have to go back.

Pica clutched his arm.

– Wait. Listen.

They heard the squeal of a pulley and the clatter of moving chains, and a dim yellow glow appeared below them, growing out of the darkness. As the light neared they could see that they were standing on a narrow wooden platform, on the rim of a cylindrical shaft. The dark clay walls were dotted with innumerable tiny holes, like the nests of wrens. The chains they had heard were moving up and down in the shaft, drawing the light upward from below.

The light came from a lantern, hanging in a metal cage.

In the cage stood the Abbé de Saint-Foix, in a turban and caftan powdered with grey dust. When the cage came up level with their platform it jolted to a halt.

– I call it the well of stories, the Abbé said, brushing dust from his sleeves. I don't know how far down it goes. When I reach a certain depth candles go out from lack of air. The present ruler's grandfather unearthed it, but he used the well only to get rid of . . . inconvenient people.

He bowed towards Pica.

– Countess. You have grown.

Flood inhaled the smell of oiled chains and ancient damp and fought off a rush of vertigo. It was as if the floor of his cell in the castle had dropped away.

– The Count would approve, he said.

– Except that here, the Abbé said, time has been banished. The pasha shares my dislike of clocks, and has graciously allowed me to explore the well at my leisure.

Flood saw then that at the Abbé's feet lay tools – brushes, a sweeping pan, a hammer and chisel – amid bits of rock and dried clay.

– You're a prisoner, Abbé.

– Only when I work in the well. And only for my own safety. Otherwise I have the freedom of the palace.

– I find it hard to believe you would submit to this.

– I have accepted certain constraints on my liberty. As will you, Flood, when you join me here.

– Why would I do that?

– Like me, you won't be able to resist. These pigeonholes around us contain parchment scrolls and codices that have been embedded in wet clay for an untold number of centuries. Someone, we know not who, or when, intended them to be drowned and lost forever. Ironic, don't you think, seeing how the world believes the ancient library was consumed in fire? Just think of the fame that would come to the man who printed the lost library of Alexandria.

– I have been locked away long enough. No book is worth that again.

– A price must always be paid for knowledge. Of whatever kind. You know that.

– You knew that the Count had imprisoned me, and you did nothing.

– You were in that cell for twelve years, but only for some of that time were you the Count's prisoner. By the time I found out what had happened to you, you had become your own jailer. It seemed wiser, certainly kinder, to leave you be. And then the pasha offered me this opportunity.

– To do what?

– The pasha, true as ever to his ruling passion, is looking for what is known here as *sihr*. Books of magic. So far I've managed to extricate fragments of histories, legends, records of famines or droughts. The pasha and I have reason to believe there is more to be found here. From the earliest days of the Ottoman conquest, as you may know, the rulers of Alexandria have been known for an all-consuming preoccupation with their own mortality.

THE LEGEND OF SESHAT

From their Egyptian subjects, it was said, the Ottomans had caught the disease of haunting their own tombs in advance. An Ottoman warrior was supposed to sneer at death, which came when it came, as Allah willed it. The important thing was to be doing something worthy of paradise when death arrived.

The Turkish overlords, looking about them in this conquered land where the dead seemed to outnumber the living, had forgotten this truth. Long after the ancient library had been gutted, its contents burned and the ashes scattered, they continued to search for a fabled scroll that was said to hold the secret of immortality.

They knew there had been books housed in the ancient library that had been filed away in the laby-rinthine catacombs in a time already remote from the knowledge of the librarians of antiquity. According to Zenodotus, one of the first chroniclers of the fate of the library, fires often started when weary scribes knocked over oil lamps, and over time many of the precious books were damaged or lost. The depredations of conquerors also took their toll. Then came the rumour that the Christian monks, whose power and influence in the city had been growing, intended to destroy the library, the fount of pagan knowledge, once and for all. One of the old librarians, whose name has not come down to us, wished that somehow he could keep the books in his care safely tucked away in their nests and holes, while at the same time freeing them from their vulnerable immobility, so that they would escape any catastrophe which might befall the library itself. One day he noticed the ink stains on the hands of the many scribes who toiled at copying the books, and a wild idea came into his head.

The librarian called together all his assistants, all the scribes, copyists, and book-menders. Employing tattoo artists equipped with the quills of porcupine fish and ink made of acacia oil, the librarian ordered the text of one book to be inscribed on the flesh of each man. Only those parts of the body that would not be hidden by clothing were left unmarked. The dictating and inscribing took many days. Only a small amount could be copied at a time, as the pain was terrible and caused the men to twitch and writhe, marring the tattoo artist's delicate work.

The history that follows I am sure you know. The library was burned not once but several times as one empire after another plucked the jewel of Alexandria for itself. The remaining papyrus scrolls and parchment codices were utterly consumed by fire, decay, and time.

The scholars and librarians were stoned to death or driven into exile. The secret of the tattooed men might have been safe but for the unlucky moment when one of them, driven by the thirst of curiosity, stood naked in front of a brass mirror and began to read, laboriously translating aloud the sinuous, backwards script that coiled around his body.

He found it to be a verse epic celebrating the numerous episodes of intimate congress between gods and mortals. Yet there were, to his dismay, sections of the book, on the small of his back, his shoulder blades, and elsewhere, which no amount of agonizing contortion allowed him to glimpse. Desperate to fill in the missing verses, he visited a brothel and requested a woman who could read. He did not know that the enemy, from long experience of the places where valuable secrets are revealed, had stocked every house of pleasure in the city with spies.

Under torture the tattooed man surrendered the details of the librarian's plan. A list of all the book-men was swiftly drawn up. One by one they were hunted down and killed, the skin then stripped from their bodies and burned to ashes.

Legend has it, however, that a woman, an Abyssinian slave, who was chosen only out of necessity because the librarian ran out of time and men's bodies, was the last to be inscribed. This woman alone of the tattooed fraternity managed to escape with her life and her secret. She took the name Seshat, goddess of archives, sister of Thoth, or as the Greeks called him, Hermes Trismegistus.

Seshat wandered for years through the empire of the conquering faith, carrying the last of the librarian's books concealed from her enemies, and over time she gathered around her a small group of readers to whom she revealed the secret.

The book she bore upon her flesh was rumoured to be a treatise by Hermes himself on the lost art of never dying. No one knows if that is true, but the legend tells us that when Seshat grew older, she had the markings copied onto one of her younger followers, with instructions to do likewise. And when Seshat died, her body, as she requested, was wrapped in the traditional manner, in ribbons of muslin sprinkled with hyssop.

Since it is the binding which usually announces, before anything else, the presence of a book, Seshat and her followers must be the exception to this rule. For only if their bindings are removed may one discover that beneath them a book lies concealed.

From his cassock the Abbé drew out Djinn's *Book of Tears*.

– Alexandria is not the first place I have served as an interpreter of ancient texts. Since we parted at the castle I have travelled the globe. Jerusalem, the Orient, Brazil, New Spain.

The Abbé unrolled the scroll to the innermost leaf.

– Do you know that the ancient Mexicans worshipped a god whose image very much resembles the symbol you put on your books? Xolotol, the god of transformations. In their mythology he was a hideous, giant amphibian that could leave the water, change shape and become a dog, a woman of fire, the future. I've taken him as an emblem, you see, of my search.

He's slipped away from me and I've caught sight of him again, many times. I had begun to think I was wasting my time here, since I had found little trace of him thus far. Then you arrived with your marvellous scroll.

– What do you want from me, Abbé?

The Abbé shook his head.

– You should ask instead what I can give you, and your daughter. I have the means to find out what goes on outside the palace. I know, for instance, that you brought something from Venice, something that helped you make *this*. And I know about the disease that plagues your daughter's skin. Why go roaming about the world, endangering your work and her health, when everything you need is right here?

– So you would take the place of the Count. I didn't want to think you capable of that, Abbé.

– It would be for your own good, Flood. The superstitious populace already looks upon the inventions of Europe as tools of Satan. Imagine their response should they find out what you could bring into the world. Books that say to all boundaries, all truths, *There is something more.*

– Is that what you think I'm doing?

The Abbé slowly rolled up the scroll, his gaze fixed on Flood.

– You don't see it, do you? he said. The possibility that this . . . this trial effort hints at.

– I'm sure you're planning to enlighten me.

The Abbé smiled.

– That remains to be seen.

He toed a chunk of dried clay to the edge of his cage, nudged it over into the well, where it dropped into silence.

– My time here is growing short, he said. There are underground sluices running from the river that could drown this well again in a matter of minutes. I expect that is what will happen if the anti-European faction wins out at court.

– It probably has, Flood said. The pasha is dead.

The Abbé blinked.

– Dead?

– Just now, in the Hall of the Divan.

The Abbé gazed upward into the darkness, and a cold laugh burst from him.

– Just now. And so time wins again.

Pica stepped in front of Flood.

– You were on the ship, she said. When I was born.

The Abbé stared at Pica open-mouthed and then, recovering himself, bowed slightly towards her.

– You have an astounding memory, mademoiselle.

– You were there. The man in black.

– Ah. Yes. The midwife. I knew she was not to be trusted, but yours was a difficult birth, and something had to be done to preserve, if possible, both mother and daughter. In other words, you should be thankful I was there, Countess, since it was my task to make sure you were both safely . . . delivered.

– Then it's true, Pica said.

– What story did they tell you at the Ospedale, about your mother? That she was dead, no doubt. Forgive my bluntness, but did it ever occur to you that they might be telling the truth? Or that they were, but in another sense. Perhaps, child, they were hoping to spare you further pain and loss.

Pica stared at him, her eyes searching his. The Abbé turned to Flood.

– Surely you've prepared the girl for the possibility that her mother does not want to be found. Especially by the daughter she cannot acknowledge as hers.

– I don't believe you, Pica said.

– As you please. But believe me when I say I do not know where the Countess is. I cannot even tell you whether she is living or dead.

He gestured to the darkness around them.

– This is the world, mademoiselle. Few questions find answers. Few stories end the way we might wish. Ask your father.

The chains jerked and squealed and the Abbé's cage began to ascend ponderously into the upper darkness.

– I am called to my accounting, he said, tucking the scroll into his sleeve. But I would advise you to stay where you are. There is, after all, nowhere else to go.

φ

Selim found them wandering the corridors and led them safely through the palace.

– As you see, I don't exist, he whispered to them as they slipped across the parade ground where the janissaries preened with their horses. At least not here.

They took a devious route to his house to collect Djinn.

The clerk insisted they stay with him until the excitement over the pasha's death quieted down. There was no need, he went on, for them to leave at all, really. There was certainly plenty of work for a printer in Alexandria.

– We can't stay, Flood said. Someone will come for us sooner or later.

– At least you, Selim said, embracing Djinn with tears in his eyes. You belong here. That much I know.

Djinn smiled.

— I wish I did.

When they returned to the *Bee*, a huge warship, crowded with sails, was just gliding into the Port of the Infidels. She had clearly been on a long and eventful journey: the hull, pockmarked by cannonfire, was bleached to a driftwood paleness by salt and long exposure to the elements.

The *Bee* was standing away from the mole as the white ship passed them, so near that the hull towered overhead like a great chalk cliff. The figurehead, a mad-eyed harpy, grinned down for a moment and then turned its shoulder to them. The *Bee* lurched through the warship's wake, caught a favourable breeze, and began to make way.

By late afternoon, as Alexandria dwindled to a white mirage on the horizon, Flood looked for Pica and found her at last in the last place he expected, the galley, slicing up a cuttlefish Djinn had bought in the souk before they left.

— We're heading for London, he said. There's nowhere else to go, now.

Pica turned the cuttlefish over, plunged her knife into the pale underside.

— I can set up shop there again, he went on when she had not spoken. If you want, you can help me. Work in the shop. We can't sail around the world, after all.

She drew out the translucent, quivering ink sac.

— Why not?

She could not sleep.

She knew the *Bee* so well by this time that she could move easily, even in the near-darkness, through its formerly baffling interior. Every night she made her rounds, often closing her eyes, which had too often missed the ship's well-disguised secrets, searching only with her fingers and toes for hidden recesses, sliding panels, undiscovered passages between decks. So far she had told no one about her nightly wanderings, nor about the phantom prowling just ahead of her through the sleeping vessel, not knowing for certain whether her fancy or the ship itself was playing tricks on her.

She thought for a while that it might be Darka, who could often be found in out-of-the-way corners of the ship, picking up after the children. But it made no sense for her to be doing this in the middle of the night, even considering her fanatical tidiness. And besides, Darka usually took watch on deck while Pica was creeping around below.

She took her turn at the helm, only half-listening as Turini lingered to puzzle over the fact that ever since Alexandria the *Bee* seemed to have developed a will of its own. Every day he fought against the winds and currents bent on driving them east, only to shorten sail for the night and the next morning find the ship had accomplished what he could not, having righted itself to their northwesterly course.

The next night she stood impatiently at the helm through her watch, and when at last the carpenter relieved her she went below and continued her search, creeping along passageways, listening, and then breathlessly hurrying after the fading creak of footfalls on the planks. Dawn neared, and heading at last for bed, on a sudden impulse she crouched in one of the hidden crawlspaces and waited without moving. After a while she heard the laboured breathing of someone moving through the cramped passage towards her. As the someone shuffled close she reached out a hand and clutched a bony wrist.

The phantom struggled, struck Pica on the breastbone with a flailing hand, pulled her hair. She would not let go.

– Very well, a woman's voice muttered. You caught me.

She followed her unseen captive out of the crawlspace and into the light of the companionway lantern. The woman was dark-skinned, and wore a white blouse that hung untucked to her knees. Her face was streaked with dirt and shadowed by a tangle of woolly hair, through which her dark eyes glittered. There was no doubt any longer that the phantom was flesh and blood.

φ

She would not tell them her name.

When everyone had been roused from sleep, they all gathered in the great cabin, watching the young black woman wolf down the bread and cheese that had been her first request. When she had finished her meal she sat back, belched, and commenced chewing at a fingernail, staring at each of them in turn from behind the matted ropes of her hair. Turini was the first to break the silence.

– You've been righting the ship's course, he said. Why?

The young woman spat out a sliver of fingernail.

– You're going to London, she said. So am I.

She would answer no more questions, and snatching up the spyglass on the chart table, she dashed from the great cabin and climbed out onto the quarterdeck. Like lost sheep they all followed.

She had the spyglass trained to the stern, where sea and sky were merged in a grey dawn haze.

– This ship is a madhouse, she muttered, lowering the spyglass. It took me days to figure out how everything worked. We've lost so much time.

– Time for what? Flood asked.

She looked at Pica and the twins and then turned again to Turini.

– Those guns in the hold. We need them up here.

– Antiques, the carpenter said. Ballast. They'll probably explode the first time they're fired.

– We will see.

Just then Miza pointed to the stern.

– Look.

They all turned and to Flood at first it seemed that a fragment of Alexandria had somehow broken away and followed after them. Out of the haze a shining white pyramid had materialized. He snatched the spyglass from the young woman. Into the scope jumped a huge ship under full sail, flying British colours.

– She's called the *Acheron*, the young woman said. She's after me.

THE TRUE HISTORY OF THE NOTORIOUS
FEMALE BUCCANEER, AMPHITRITE SNOW,
AND HER BLOODTHIRSTY CREW OF
ADVENTURESSES, HARLOTS, AND JEZEBELS

The cargo ship *Gold Coast*, out of Southampton, was bound for New Providence in the Bahamas with a cargo of beef, beer, and women. It is not recorded that the beef or beer gave any trouble, but the young women were another matter. Most of them were serving girls, promised well-paying positions in good homes, although the real plan was to help redress the lamentable shortage of white female flesh in the troubled colony. In a letter to the king, the governor had warned that if something wasn't done soon to provide the male population with marriageable (or at least beddable) white women, the entire island would soon be overrun with mulatto bastards.

Despite this commission, the *Gold Coast* also carried a few black females, to help defray the cost of the voyage. They were kept under watch in the hold, as somewhat less valuable cargo. The girl who would become Amphitrite Snow was one of them. She had been stripped of her real name and dubbed *Amphitrite* in the house of the nobleman who had first purchased her, an admiral in the navy. *A goddess of the sea*, he had called her one day when he and his wife were inspecting the kitchens. The admiral's wife had watched her closely after that day and she was let go soon after, and brought aboard the *Gold Coast*.

The crew was loud and often drunk, and from the hold Snow could hear much of what went on elsewhere in the ship. Screams and sounds of struggle soon made it clear to everyone on board that the captain had permitted his men to enjoy some of the cargo, as compensation for the rigours of the voyage.

Those lads in New Poxidence, he could be heard encouraging them, *aren't likely to be too picky about used goods.*

The crew eyed her often but never spoke to her as they did the others. When she was let up on deck for air one of the men gripped her arm and winked at her.

—You must be white as snow on the inside, my dear. The captain's been saving himself for you.

So she acquired her names. Before being taken below decks, Amphitrite Snow got hold of a nail the ship's carpenter had mislaid. The captain sent for her that night, had her brought to his cabin. When he climbed on top of her she drove the nail through the back of his hand and in between her ribs.

Goodness, you've crucified us, he said, plucking out the nail with a ghastly smile. She closed her eyes and tried to fall out of her body, certain of a beating, but only silence descended. She opened her eyes. The captain was inspecting the wound she had given herself.

Not as bad as it could have been.

He had a basin of hot water and a cloth brought to the cabin, and washed the blood from her body himself. She sat motionless, the water cooling on her skin.

We can't mar the goods, he finally said, standing back to look at her. *At least not until I've been paid. So first we'll get you sold. Then, rest assured, I'll be coming to pay you a visit, to catch up on old times.*

Not long afterward the crew indulged in its most riotous night of drinking. Since there were no male slaves aboard, even the watch had been allowed a tot of rum or several, and were soon sprawled about the decks, incapacitated.

Snow led a party of seven other women who broke into the weapons locker and armed themselves. In a few minutes they had taken over the vessel and rounded up the half-uncomprehending crew. The first man who rushed them she shot at, hitting him in the belly. He sat down on the deck, holding his gut and crying until the captain growled at him to shut up. Once she had fired the gun her fear was gone, leaving the same emptiness she had felt when she was taken from her own country.

They drifted for the first few days, debating what to do next and where they might go, with the captain and his men howling at them from their prison in the hold. *You'll hang. You'll be torn apart by horses. You'll be burned at the stake as witches.* Some of the women were for surrendering, for making some kind of arrangement with the captain so that the whole thing would be forgotten. She lowered a boat for them, told them to gather what they would need. No one took her up on it.

Eventually the men were brought out of the hold, herded at gunpoint into a longboat, and set adrift in the icy North Atlantic. All but the sailmaker, who was half-blind, and the doctor. Snow reasoned their skills would be needed, at least until the new crew of the *Gold Coast* could fend for itself.

They wandered the seas for months, afraid to anchor in any but the most remote places. When other ships approached, they ran up a plague flag. In time, however, they had enough contact with the rest of the world to hear about the reward of one hundred guineas *for the capture, dead or alive, of Amphitrite Snow & her crew, for the Disruption of Trade & Commerce on the High Seas; & for their diverse Abductions of Young Women, with the manifest*

Intent of corrupting Morals & Persuading Others to a Life of Crime, Villainy & Murder.

They also heard two stories that interested them greatly.

The first was a rumour about the great arch-pirate, Henry Avery, who had never been caught. It was said he had sailed away to the South Seas in his ship, the *Fancy*, and founded a pirate republic on a remote tropical island.

– The island of Shekinar, Snow told the *Bee*'s crew. The world's only truly free state. No kings, no magistrates, no jails. No buying and selling of men or women.

Their wandering now had a goal, however remote and unlikely. Perhaps somewhere in the world, they hoped, there was a place where they would be safe from retribution. But on remote beaches and in dark taverns at the edges of the world they also heard legends of the man known only as the Commander.

He could sniff out pirates a hundred miles distant through a raging gale. Predict the outcome of battles that had not yet begun.

. . . It was thirty-three days and nights in a longboat, drifting through ice and darkness. That's what gave him his uncanny powers. Four of his men froze to death. One thought he was Christ and stepped off the boat into the sea. Another cut off the fingers on his left hand, to save for when they ran out of rations. He bled to death while they watched.

Parts of the Commander himself were frostbitten so badly that when the survivors were finally rescued, by a brig hauling salt to the Newfoundland fishery, bits of the man had to be pared away, like the stale corners of a block of cheese, to save the remainder.

Bits of me, he would repeat when he told the tale, as if the worst of it lay there. *Not a hand, an entire eye, a complete limb. Just slices and scraps, here and there. Thirteen chunks of dumb flesh in all and no words to mourn their loss. Do you see? Hacked in two would have been preferable. But I was merely diminished, chipped away at, my name associated with no missing appurtenance of any definitive shape. The black witch knew what she was doing. If you're going to lop away at a seafaring man, take something to which legend can give a name. Harry Two-Hooks. Noseless Ned. One-Stone Jack.*

The Admiralty gave him command of the *Acheron,* their newest and most well-armed weapon against pirates, or at least those who did not have government sanction. In time, as one infamous sea-devil after another met the rope, the definite article became attached to the title and the real name of the former captain of the *Gold Coast* was all but forgotten. It was merely necessary to say *The Commander* and wary men in every port would nod, glance over their shoulders, and whisper their own stories about him.

The Commander's dread fame, though, had come at a high price. The agonies of his abandonment at sea, it was said, combined with the humiliation of the aftermath, had seared something in him to such a white heat that his inner vision had acquired the ability to see, simply by sighting a coastline with his spyglass, whether or not that particular island or peninsula or country or continent would ever be part of the British dominions. Or, if the territory in question was already under the Union Jack, the Commander somehow knew whether or not it would cease to be British at some time in the future, date unspecified. From Cork to Madras he'd made his predictions of imperial acquisition and relinquishment with a recklessness so undisciplined that the Admiralty had at last been constrained to order the *Acheron* home to Spithead. What he was doing, did he not understand, was very bad for public morale. Not to mention the other nations with an interest in his predictions, such as the French, who were less than delighted to be advised that New France was fated to become Even Newer Britannia.

The Commander was disinclined to obey the homeward order from his superiors. He hadn't found her yet, and until he had, the log of the *Acheron* would record only that the vessel was unable to return to port due to strong headwinds and the need for extensive repairs. Thus he became a renegade, a threat. The Admiralty issued orders to all its ships that the *Acheron* be attacked on sight.

There's going to be war, soon, with France, he often said. *Britannia's going to win all of North America, and then she's going to lose it. That was the one that tore their mainsheets, and I didn't even have to use the gift to see it. The fact is baldly obvious. Remove the French threat and the colonials to the south will start looking around for someone else to go to war with. That's why they will beg me to come back. Just you wait. They need someone with vision, a clear head.*

His midday navigational ritual, so the stories told, took place on the quarterdeck around a table draped in white cloth like an altar, with an equally formidable array of arcane instruments lined up and ready for a mariner's Mass. The ceremonies included compass readings, sextant readings, log and lead measurements, and lastly, the cocking of his truncated but supersensitive nose slantwise to the plane of the ecliptic, testing the telltale winds, as he liked to say, for traces of Snow.

He caught up to her at last off Cyprus, and the rest is swiftly told.

– They blasted us to bits, Snow said, as they watched the *Acheron* grow off their port quarter.

The *Gold Coast* was sunk. Those of the crew who did not perish in the waves, she assumed, were saved for the gibbet. Cat Nutley and Crook-Fingered Jane. Brigid O'Byrne. Lucy Teach.

– But not me, she said. He wasn't finished with me yet.

First a brief stop at Alexandria to take on provisions, and then the *Acheron* was on its way home.

φ

The first volley came when the warship was still a considerable distance off, taking even Snow by surprise. The whizzing shot fell short, sending up spray that drifted down like a mist over the decks.

– He's impatient, Amphitrite said. He wants us to shorten sail and get this over with as quickly as possible.

– He wants you alive, Flood said, doesn't he?

– I hope not.

As the *Acheron* closed, Amphitrite's meagre armament of antiquated guns responded with a smattering of fire that appeared to have no effect on her massive adversary. Through the smoke of their ineffectual volley they watched the warship come on with carriage regally unhurried, her bows turning in a long slow arc to flank them, her starboard gunports snapping open briskly, ready for business.

Pica slipped unnoticed from the quarterdeck and descended the main hatchway. As she reached the press room there was a roar, the ship heeled violently, and she pitched forward onto the planks.

A ball from the *Acheron* had struck them somewhere, she knew. She picked herself up and saw that the impact had knocked over her father's work table and dislodged two of the ink casks, which had smashed on the planks and were now furiously gushing ink. In the swirling black pool that was forming lay Ludwig the automaton, his head turned back to front, one of his arms pumping uselessly in the air.

She hurried over to the press, her heart pounding wildly. The forme of gooseflesh type Djinn had just set was still in the carriage, the metal within the frame of the chase a dull and solid-looking plate. A poke of her finger in the centre sent a lethargic wave radiating outward.

She placed her hands on her hips, and then on the two long sides of the chase. The iron frame was slightly wider. Like one of the ship's trapdoors. She would just fit.

Pica kicked her shoes into a corner, peeled off her stockings, and climbed up onto the bed of the press. Gripping the bar to keep her balance, she leaned forward and breathed on the forme. The metal continued to deliquesce until wavelets agitated its surface with every shudder of the hull.

Cautiously she dipped in a toe.

– Cold.

Gripping the sides of the chase, she leaned forward and gazed at her wavering reflection in the surface of the metal. On a sudden thought she hung her pocketwatch by its chain from the bar.

– Time slows down there, she whispered.

Taking a great gulp of air she plunged in headfirst.

As the metal closed over her she remembered someone, a girl who searched for trinkets at the bottom of a filthy canal, in a story told long ago.

She surfaced in the press room. At first she thought that in the depths of the metal she had somehow gotten turned around and come back out the way she had gone in. But hauling herself onto the bed of the press she saw the pocketwatch, halted at one end of its chain's swing. The hands had stopped, seven seconds later than when she had gone in. She was on the other side. In the well of stories.

Where had she been for those seven seconds? There had been a darkness, and then a coming back to herself as if from a long sleep.

Shakily she climbed down from the press. Nothing moved, and there was no sound. Something had happened to the light in the cabin: it had darkened to thick gold and taken on texture, a fine, grainy substantiality like translucent jelly.

She moved forward and something brushed cobweb-like against her skin. As she lifted a hand to sweep it aside, everything in front of her, the press, the ink barrels, the long room and the layered and gelatinous light itself, bent and elongated slightly, like an image painted on taut, transparent fabric. That faint spidery sensation, she understood, was the impress of the light itself on her skin.

She squeezed her hand into a fist, and when she opened it a knot of light sat pulsing in her palm.

Ludwig lay motionless in the pool of ink that was fused to him now, and solid as black glass. She knelt and tugged the automaton's head around. His eternal smile of youth had been split by a hairline crack running from forehead to chin.

She left him and climbed the hatchway. A dark figure hung, silhouetted against sunlight, at the top. Her father, still and silent, one foot raised over vacancy, about to descend the stairs to the press room to find out where she had gone.

When she reached him she examined his shadowed face, the line of muscle in his jaw revealing teeth clenched hard. His eyes looking into hers, not seeing, the dilation of the pupils arrested as he was turning away from the light. The fear there, for her. Or of her. Fear of what he would find when he reached the press room.

For the first time she touched his hand, felt the ridges of the veins, the callused knuckles. Cold and lifeless as stone. She saw the fraying threads of his shirt cuff, the tiny dots of ink on the sleeve.

Finally she stepped past him and climbed onto the quarter-deck. The ship lay at the beginning of a larboard heel, Snow and Turini frozen at the helm, Darka and the twins stopped where they had been racing along the gangway, frozen into positions impossible even for them. Puffballs of black smoke hung in the air. She pushed at one just above her head and her hand sank into it, leaving a hand-shaped hollow.

She could look at the sun without flinching, its face a dark burnished gold, its light hanging visible in the air like strands of honey.

The silence.

She was alone. Everyone else suspended while she remained here. Waiting for her to bring them back to life.

She looked at the frozen sky and all at once she remembered something that happened to her at the Ospedale in Venice. She had been sitting in the garret, reading one of Francesca's forbidden novels. Bored with its tale of fearless knights and virtuous ladies, she had taken the Maestro's violin down from the wall and was lying on her back, her head hanging over the foot of the bed so that she was looking upside down out one of the open window casements. She plucked the one remaining string of the violin, wondering if the sound would summon the Maestro's shade again. Out the window, she remembered, was a lake of blue sky. The ceaseless burble of the city had dwindled to an immense distance. She felt the thrum of the plucked string pass from the instrument's belly to her cheek, listened as the note faded in the still air. The sound like time itself, each moment a wire, taut with possibility and then plucked and already fading into the past. As the notes died away she suddenly felt lighter than air, about to rise off the bed and float away through the window. *She was free.*

In the well the world was like that empty blue vault, like a string pulled taut, not yet plucked.

She had to be careful. Without time, she sensed, the world was defenceless against suggestion. The skin of the moment was fragile. She alone could choose. *Like reading a book*, she told herself. *I make the next thing happen.*

She leaned out between two bulwarks. The surface of the ocean gleamed like a shell of translucent green glass. Just beneath the surface she saw the black egg of an incubus, its shell already cracking open along red volcanic seams, inches from the *Bee*'s hull.

She squinted through the intervening forest of smoke to the white hull of the warship, lit with the motionless stars of its own gunfire. Terrified, she saw herself walking across the water's surface, climbing aboard the *Acheron*, disabling their guns. Taking the Commander hostage. Making him re-enter time with a sword through his guts. She rejected her next idea as soon as it formed in her mind, tempting her with its awful simplicity: striking a match in their powder magazine and leaving it hang there, about to fall, an icicle of fire.

Her gaze moved past the *Acheron* to the sea. A storm to the northeast stood like a vast grey ship, anchored to the sea by a white cable of lightning. She thought of the great round globe, the cities, towns, and villages and all the people in them, the farms and vineyards and forests and deserts, the creatures down in the abysses of the sea and on the plains and high in the air. Everyone and everything still as a painting now. Drops of rain suspended inches above the earth. Trees bowed by invisible shoulders of wind. Deer caught in mid-leap. Newborns halted in their first tiny wails. Condemned men reprieved for now from a drop through the final door of the gallows.

The earth itself not turning, she thought in wonder, turning away from the rail. She felt the blood within her slowing, the seeping away of time from her flesh and bones. She sensed deep within that if she were to stay here, she would never sicken, never grow old. She would stay a girl forever.

Someone was missing. Djinn.

She slid down the companion ladder and ducked through the hatch to the great cabin.

In the gloom she groped for Amphitrite's chart table, and as her sight returned she found it, her fingers touching the painted plaster globe of the world that sat there.

She found Djinn crouched under the chart table, his hands over his ears, his mouth open in a silent scream. Like a terrified little boy. She knelt and kissed him softly on the forehead.

The silence had been working on her, she realized, filling her with the deepest loneliness she has ever known. She was glad her father would not be far away when she climbed back out.

Before leaving she looked at the books lined up on the shelf behind the chart table. Turini's books of navigation and weather lore. Her own books were down in the press room, in a glass-fronted cabinet that Turini had made for her, to protect them from damp and rot. *Gulliver's Travels. Robinson Crusoe. The Thousand and One Nights.* The seventh volume of the *Libraria Technicum.*

To keep them all safe, she could just stay here and read. Forever.

She was free here to take hold of the hem of things, pull the world around her like a cloak, search through its dark folds and creases for what she has lost. The earth her clockwork toy, spinning as she wished, all mysteries and sorrows burned away in the cold flames of her desire.

She touched the globe, sent it revolving slowly, wobbling slightly from the tap of her finger. Rivers, mountain ranges, names of places she had never been drifted past. *Cathay. London. New France.*

The empty expanse of the Pacific rolled past. Where, she wondered, was Amphitrite's fabled island of Shekinar? If she stayed here long enough, she could find it, or make it exist.

Her heart began to pound and a wave of cold panic crawled over her skin. She had to leave now, while she still could.

With a slap she sent the globe spinning.

Back in the press room she took another deep breath and plunged headfirst into the metal. When she climbed out she saw the hands of the pocketwatch moving, and heard the metallic stutter of Ludwig the automaton. The clock of the world was ticking again.

Sometimes you wish to escape to another part of the book.

You stop reading and riffle the pages, catching sight of the story as it races ahead, not above the world but through it, through forests and complications, the chaos of intentions and cities.

As you near the last few pages you are hurtling through the book at increasing speed, until all is a blur of restlessness, and then suddenly your thumb loses its grip and you sail out of the story and back into yourself. The book is once again a fragile vessel of cloth and paper. You have gone everywhere and nowhere.

THE PAPER-THIN GARDEN

There had been a battle at sea. They were all agreed about that. But no one could quite remember how long ago it had happened, or how it had ended, other than with their escape.

Pica had joined the others on deck, where they stood about like recently awakened sleepers. The battered *Bee* was listing slightly to starboard. The air hung heavy and still, but despite the heat the masts were furred with rime.

That evening and for days afterward, while they made repairs to the damaged timbers and shifted the ballast in the hold, they kept stumbling across objects no one remembered seeing before: an arrow stuck high in the mizzen-mast, drifts of snow in shaded corners of the upper decks, a snakeskin glove without its fellow. This collective memory loss, Snow decided, was an early sign of scurvy, and they had better hope to find fresh rations soon.

One morning they found themselves in a region of great ice islands, through which they crept like wayfarers in a frozen city of giants. During a blizzard they anchored in the lee of a rocky islet, the home of a colony of seals that could not be seen through the flying snow, but whose bellows and honks went on incessantly throughout the storm. In the morning the air was clear and the wind knife-sharp. Amphitrite Snow went alone to the far side of the islet in a longboat, taking with her the ship's one working gun, Turini's ancient musket. They heard five shots, a long silence between each. Soon afterward Snow returned, with three of the beasts in the bottom of the boat. When Turini hauled her up she heaved one of the seals over the gunwale onto the deck. It lay there, a huge, bloody bag of fur.

Snow crouched, rolled the animal over, and with her knife sliced along the pale underside from gullet to rump. Pica watched the knife tug and twist, the guts spilling forth, collapsing into a coiled grey mound, striped with ropy gouts of blood. The liver followed, lying like a smoking island in a lake of blood, then the lungs and the heart.

— Best to eat it raw, Snow said, holding up the liver. Helps against scurvy.

She bit into the dark slab of flesh, and through a gory mouthful, insisted that everyone else take a bite.

One by one the others tried a bit of the raw liver, and then, disgusted, Turini lit a fire in the galley and roasted what remained. Everyone ate, cramming the steaming strips of flesh into their huffing mouths.

After the meal Snow lifted up the skin, showed it to Darka and mimed the action of putting on a coat.

— If she needs more skins, Snow said to Turini, I can get more.

The coats the contortionists made for everyone kept them warm and comfortable while they ploughed onward through the bitter cold. The largest of the ice islands stood off their port quarter for three days, until they began to wonder if there were any end to it. On the fourth day, Snow roused everyone with the discovery that the *Bee* and the ice island had drifted much closer to one another in the night. What from a distance had appeared to be solid and unmoving was as subject to the heaving and tossing of the sea as they were. The wall of the island rose ponderously before them on the swell of the waves and sank again with a roar that shook the *Bee*'s timbers. In its shadow the shriek of the wind dropped to a muted moan, punctuated by the rumbling and creaking of the ice.

At the helm Snow frantically attempted to claw them away from disaster. Underneath the waves the hull groaned, scraping against something for a long terrible time. As they finally began to shear away from the overhanging wall, a shower of crystal needles glittered down around them. The twins shrieked, leaping to catch the ice diamonds in their hands and on their tongues. Snow hissed at them to be quiet, then looked up and shouted a warning. There was a crack like thunder as far above them a vast plate of ice broke free from the white cliff.

Turini and Darka grabbed the twins and shielded them with their bodies. Djinn and Snow dived to the deck. Pica crouched with Flood in the lee of the forward companionway.

An obelisk of ice hit the stern rail of the *Bee* and shattered it into flying splinters. A white mass the size of a house plunged just to the stern. A cataract of freezing brine roared over the deck.

In another moment they had emerged from a cloud of churning mist and into the waning light of day. Pica, clutching

Flood's hand, raised her head to see jagged stalactites sticking upright in the planks of the quarterdeck. Snow and Djinn were picking themselves up and brushing ice chips from their hair.

After they left the sea of ice they were dogged by a lingering drowsiness. Days passed during which the watch was neglected, the sails and rigging untended, the ship's course left to the random nudgings of wind and waves. They slept undisturbed through a gale that spun them around and tore the sails to shreds. When they gathered for meals in the galley they would try to reconstruct an objective history of the last few hours, with everyone contributing minutes of lucid certainty here and there. Often this collective remembering was frustrated by the way they had begun mixing up their sleeping and waking lives. Each morning the twins reported their odd dreams, about how the ship had gone very fast through forests and cities, and eventually someone else would admit that they had had similar dreams of terrifying speed. The only one who never had any nocturnal visions to report was Pica. At breakfast she sensed that they were waiting for her to contribute her dreams, and when she did not there would be an awkward silence.

Despite the disappearance of the *Acheron*, Amphitrite Snow remained vigilant when on her watch, but during her off-hours took to sleepwalking in earnest, sometimes in the middle of the day. One morning Flood found Ludwig missing from the press room and followed inky prints of bare feet to Snow's cabin, where he found her snoring peacefully with the automaton in her arms.

The only one who seemed not at all baffled by their circumstances was Djinn.

– I knew something like this would happen, he said. It was to be expected. We're utterly lost.

φ

The stars had changed.

They drifted on the swell of the sea for days without breath of wind or sight of land. The water in the butts dropped to an alarming level and the provisions they had taken on in Alexandria were nearly gone.

One morning Pica awoke to the sound of rain and went out on deck to find the *Bee* resting in the middle of a plain of lush green grass. Snow was already at the rail, lowering a lead line.

– It must be the calenture, she said. Sea fever. I've seen it happen. You think the sea is a lovely meadow, so you climb overboard to go for a pleasant stroll and you drown.

– It looks real to me, Pica said.

There was only one way to find out. Snow had Turini lower her in a longboat, which sat solidly in the grass and did not bob as she had expected. She trailed a hand over the side and came up with a fistful of stalks. Finally she climbed out of the boat and walked all the way around it.

It was a bed of seaweed, she finally admitted. The surface had a spongy give and she could hear a watery squelch at every step. It was grown so thick that other vegetable life had been able to thrive upon it.

By this time the rain had drawn off, the Turinis were up and soon joined Amphitrite for a stroll. Turini brought out poles and sailcloth and erected a pavilion to keep the sun off. By the time Flood awoke he found everyone out on the grass, having a picnic. He climbed down to find Djinn brewing tea on the stove he used to recast type. The children had gathered leaves, tubers, and iridescent snails to make a salad. Turini and Darka were giggling and cooing over each other like young lovers.

Pica sat apart, propped against an empty ink cask, immersed in one of her beloved novels. Flood left her alone, reminded of how Irena had looked the day he watched her reading among the silent shelves.

They spent all day and most of the evening away from the ship, lolling about in the cool grass. Djinn and Turini went on a trek and returned at sunset with the news that they had found the rotting remains of other vessels. The seaweed island was a graveyard of ship carcasses, the oldest a galley that appeared to be of Roman vintage.

Days went by while they waited to see if the weeds would let them go. Not even Djinn could offer any guess as to their fate. Turini took advantage of the enforced idleness to patch up the ship, although it soon became clear that the carpenter had grander plans in mind. His intent had been to refit their ship with salvageable material from the scattered wrecks, but to accomplish this such extensive dismantling was necessary that the *Bee* was stripped down to little more than a skeleton. When Flood wondered out loud, over supper, whether such drastic measures were really needed, Snow came to the carpenter's defence by citing the one great law of the ocean, the one that even the whales understood: *Sooner or later you're going to run into someone you know.* It would be a good idea, she mused, to change appearances and confuse the perceptions of the Commander as much as possible. If he was still out there hoping to swat a bee, they would transmogrify into some other creature.

While Turini worked, the winds rose and brought storms over the island of weeds. At night, while the elements raged, they huddled under the scant shelter that was left in the half-dismantled ship and felt the ground beneath them shudder with the rolling of a deep current. In the morning the weed bed would show gaps here and there, ponds and creeks that had not existed the night before. The daily strolls that had relieved the tedium were forbidden now.

Turini worked on the ship at a feverish pace. The unknown creature that had graced their bows was knocked away and replaced with the figurehead from a Dutch flute, a rubicund mermaid with flowing scarlet tresses. The mermaid was too long to sit well in her housing under the bowsprit and so she suffered a curtailment under Turini's adze. Pica and the twins pitched in to give her a new coat of paint, which they had to finish from a longboat, as the island was by now shredding away under the force of the waves.

The only potent liquor they had left in stores was the weeping ink. With a bottle of it they christened the new *Bee*.

That night, under a swollen moon, the ship drifted clear of the weeds and in the morning they found themselves once again on a barren ocean.

φ

The island where they anchored next for food and water turned out to be the habitation of innumerable tiny bats, the size of sparrows, with wings as thin as gossamer. As soon as the sun had set they would begin to take flight from the caves in immense silent black swarms. The crew of the *Bee* watched them rising until they merged with the deepening night. At sunrise they would be seen returning in a great cloud.

Flood continued to work with the gooseflesh type and the weeping ink. Long after Djinn had gone off to bed he would be sorting and resorting the type and printing trial sheets, finally collapsing at dawn and sleeping through the day before awakening in the afternoon to start all over again. By lantern-light he sat scribbling notes and figures at his work table, oblivious to the dozens of bats nestled in the crannies of the room and sometimes in his hair.

Pica brought him his meals, aware that he had grown forgetful and even more solitary than usual since she had gone into the well. She would look with suspicion at the pieces of gooseflesh type laid out on his work table. When he wasn't looking she would read the lines of words he had arranged in formes, and realized that he was taking as his texts passages from the books on his shelf. Geometry. Typography. Calculus. Without knowing quite why, she left one of her own books, *Gulliver's Travels*, in the press room where he would see it.

At last they caught a favourable wind that sent the *Bee* ploughing northwest into warmer waters. One evening Amphitrite, up on the masthead, sighted the spouts of whales. When they drew nearer to the great beasts they caught the foul reek of their spray.

Later that same day gulls appeared and wheeled around the ship, uttering raucous cries of welcome. Amphitrite sounded every hour and at last touched ground at twelve fathoms, the lead bringing up sand and iridescent bits of shell.

They anchored off a shore of white sand that stretched away on either hand in an unbroken line to the horizon. One hundred paces inland, searching for fresh water, they struggled up a ridge of soft sand and found themselves on a shore again.

On this island that was nothing more than a narrow strip of beach they met with a marooned Scotsman.

He called himself Mister Zero because he had forgotten his real name. Following him down the beach they came to the stilt hut he had built from the timbers of the ship that had broken here, spilling him out into the waves, where luckily he had been snagged like a fly on this spider's thread of land. His diet consisted of whatever polyped and crustaceous life the sea left stranded on the coasts of his lean continent.

Mister Zero invited them to share his lunch of boiled crab and seawrack, and related the story, as well as he could draw it out of his waterlogged memory, of how he had ended up the sole citizen of Exilium, as he had named the island. At times, depending on the winds and currents, his island would be submerged, slowly sinking under the waves from both ends. On those occasions he was forced to run back and forth until he was certain where the high ground would be this time.

— It's rather bracing, he said. Being monarch of a mound, while the waves lap at your ankles. But we are safe for now, I assure you. High tide isn't for another three days.

The vessel he was aboard as supercargo had set out from the East India Company station at Canton with a fleet of four others, their goal the newly discovered continent in the South Seas that Dutch explorers, with outrageous presumption, had named New Holland. Lured by tales of ruby mountains and deserts of gold dust, they ventured beyond the southern edge of their maps.

— We discovered it, Mister Zero said. And there were deserts all right.

As a consolation they found the sport very much to their liking. On the day they first landed Zero shot three eagles.

— Is it true, Pica asked, about the giant rabbit that lives there, the one that keeps its young in a pocket?

— Quite true, Zero said. *Gan-gurroo* the natives call these remarkable creatures. I shot a tidy number of them myself and often heard the babies mewing in their dead mother's pouch.

– And the animal that's part duck, Djinn asked, and part beaver?

– Never saw a hair of one of those. They might already all be shot.

On the return voyage to Canton, his ship was separated from the rest of the fleet by a violent hurricane off the Admiralty Islands. Dismasted, leaking in a dozen places, the ship drifted for days without fresh water or provisions, until the desperate cook caught and cooked up some sort of foul-smelling jellyfish which gave everyone fever and hallucinations. Half the crew leaped overboard. The captain hanged himself while up in the crosstrees trying to summon rainclouds.

For his part, Zero became convinced the crew was trying to kill him. Locking himself in his cabin, he stood in front of his travelling mirror and in agony pulled from his ear a tiny dagger of yellow wax. He was going mad, he knew, and considered that his misfortunes – the fatal idea of expanding his Turkey and Levant Company around the Cape of Good Hope to these antipodal waters, with the subsequent loss of everything – had at last turned his wits. *This is what comes*, he told himself, *of trusting these newfangled nautical chronometers, as I warned Captain Tristram – damn that unlucky name – on many occasions.* That night, unpiloted and driven before the winds, the ship struck a shoal in the sea and foundered.

– Everyone was swept overboard and lost, Mister Zero told them, myself included.

– Only you survived? Flood asked.

– I said everyone was lost, myself included. By which I meant to imply that rather than clinging to a cask and washing up on this shore, I believe that I became a citizen of the land of the dead.

– And what about us?

– I doubt my powers of fancy bold enough to dream up such an apparition as your ship and crew. No, I am sure you are living sojourners through this terraqueous netherworld, and that however it has come about, you have happened here fortuitously for my sake. The postal ships don't stop in this vicinity, and it so happens I have a letter that I would like to have delivered to someone residing in the country of the living.

– Which we've been hoping to find, Snow hinted.

– Head due north from here – once you find your way around the island – and you should eventually bang up against China. The British traders at Canton will help you if you use my name as an introduction. The letter is for my son. He was nearing his fourth birthday when I left home for what I could not contemplate would be the last time.

Zero tugged a folded scrap of paper out of his boot. Gently he pried apart its folds.

– His name is Robert. The letter is addressed to the office of the Expanded Turkey and Levant Trading Company in Canton, since I no longer remember where it was that I lived. When I lived.

Djinn asked to see the letter and turned it over in his hand. The late-afternoon light slanted across the paper, transforming its surface into hillocks and hollows, a desert, the thin letters crossing it like a caravan and its long shadows. As in Alexandria, he heard his first name called from a great distance. *Xian Shu* . . .

– This is extremely fine paper, he said. Where did you get it?

Zero's eyes brightened.

– A connoisseur, I see. Yes, this is of rare manufacture, isn't it? Finest Tortoise, the Chinese call it. They alone know the secret of its making. The likes of us, foreign dogs all, are not even supposed to set eyes on the stuff, but on a trip to Canton I was able, with a great deal of trouble, to get my as yet living hands on a few sheets. That was seventeen years ago. The sheaf looked like it might be good for twice a dozen pages at most, but the paper is so incredibly fine that with careful economy I've made it last until today. This is my last scrap of Finest Tortoise, hoarded for this very opportunity.

Before allowing them to leave, Zero took a stick of burnt wood and drew up a map on the wind-whitened door of his hut. If his memory served, this was an accurate chart of what they might encounter on their course for China.

He warned them to keep well away from the terrible island of Durge, where the people live perpetually buried up to their necks in black volcanic soil, with hot ashes raining down on their heads night and day. At dusk, he told them, yellow-eyed jackals come down from the mountain in hungry packs, and then the inhabitants of Durge, contorting their faces with desperate animation, begin a ceaseless prattle to which the jackals will patiently listen as though spellbound by every word. Some have memorized their chatter and numbly repeat the same litany night after endless night, while others, the more adventurous or forgetful, come up with a new stream of babble on each occasion.

– But woe to those whose tongues tire out, Zero said, or who find themselves at a loss for words, for the jackals are quick to gather about the silent and eat their heads.

And they should watch out for the treacherous rocks that lay hidden near Oronymy, a chain of steep mountains rising like a wall out of the sea. This was the home of the Glose, a race of sleepers who dwelt high up on the sheer precipices in hollows worn out of the rock by their own bodies as they squirmed and writhed in their dreams. The Glose rarely awakened, but when they did, and became aware of their precarious situation, they lost their nerve, and their balance, and toppled headlong into the sea.

– On my way here, he told them, I penetrated to the interior of Oronymy, and came to a silent city. I spent some time there, wandering from street to street, house to house, but finding nary a soul who was not utterly plunged in fathomless slumber. Each night I would sit in a different drawing room, a snoring dog curled at my feet, smoking my pipe and listening to a symphony of breathing. From time to time I would tuck the blankets back around a child that had cried out in its dreams. At last, however, the sadness of this city overcame me and I left.

If forced to it by bad weather or some other mishap, he went on, they could safely lay to at a nearby island of fussy cannibals who dined only on each other, finding the meat of strangers vastly inferior to the local variety.

– Although the island may be deserted by now, he mused.

In an emergency, they could do worse than to anchor off Alluvion, a great, ring-shaped reef composed entirely of refuse, filth, and human dung. The inhabitants of an industrious, over-populated nation not many leagues to the east began hauling their voluminous mountains of waste by ship to Alluvion many decades before, as the only way to avoid being buried in it. Zero was not certain who the original constructors of the reef were, but Alluvion was home at the present time to highly intelligent monkeys and seagulls who lived together as one nation.

Amphitrite Snow asked him if he had visited Shekinar.

– I believe I've heard of it, Zero told her. The pirate utopia, where all men live in peace and harmony?

– Yes.

He gave her a gentle smile and went on to the next point of interest on his chart.

Back aboard the *Bee*, Pica watched Djinn and her father hurry back down into the press room. She followed them and found them examining the fibres of the letter paper through the pocket microscope. As she entered the room they looked up.

– We're going to China, aren't we, she said.

φ

The world's most expensive paper, Finest Tortoise, was said to be fashioned of a blending of crushed hummingbird-egg shells, dragonfly wings, and the inner lining of wasp nests. Its exact composition and delicate method of preparation remained a secret passed down through the generations from the earliest, legendary masters of the craft. The price for a ream was breathtaking, but Flood had made up his mind he must acquire at least a few sheets of it. Unfortunately, Finest Tortoise was not for sale, he was told by the English stationer in Canton.

– How about the next best thing?

– That would be what they call Breath-That-Folds, but I haven't any of that either.

The *Bee* had arrived in the Portuguese colony of Macao a week before. It had taken that long for them to clear customs and be allowed to sail up the mouth of the Pearl River to Canton. Now the ship lay at anchor in a floating city of frigates, ferries, junks, government vessels, barbers' boats, and the sampans of actors and fortune tellers from Hanan Island. As soon as they had permission to set foot on Chinese soil, Flood and Djinn sought out the stationer's shop in Thirteen Factory Street.

At the moment there was no paper of any kind for sale in the foreign enclave.

– Why the ban?

– The Chinese governor's decree, the stationer told them. He loves to play this chess game with the white traders. If Westerners want China's miraculous porcelain, they have to earn it by behaving as befits their status.

– Which is?

– According to the latest imperial edict, slightly above dogs with the mange. The traders don't like crawling on their bellies, and every so often they kick against the rules and the governor goes off like a firecracker and tells us we can no longer buy or sell things invented by his people. Last month it was gunpowder. The month before, compasses. If you wait long enough, the ban on paper will be lifted and get put on something else. Ice cream. Parasols. Ploughs. Nobody knows what's next. Nobody has a clue. We live in a murky ambiguity lit by occasional flashes of utter incomprehension.

The stationer told Flood and Djinn that the only Finest Tortoise within a hundred miles of Canton was to be found at the palace of a great mandarin in a neighbouring province. In his employ were the only artisans who knew the secret of making the precious writing material.

The mandarin's library contained great treasures, it was rumoured. An encyclopedia in eleven thousand volumes. A book made of jade that could predict the future. The world's lengthiest erotic novel, banned by imperial decree for its power to turn readers, men and women both, into shamelessly rutting beasts. It was said to have been written by the god of tumescence during the brief rests he took from his unending sexual exercise, and printed during the Xia dynasty on Finest Tortoise.

The title of this monumental sutra of the flesh was *Dragon Vein Stretching a Thousand Miles*.

– So what do you write on in the meantime? Djinn asked the stationer.

– Wood. Unless it's lacquered. That's banned too at the moment.

Flood glanced around the shop, noticing for the first time the number of solitary, unescorted Chinese women rifling distractedly through the boxes of pens and sealing wax. He leaned towards the stationer and said in a low voice,

– You're absolutely sure there's no paper? Not even in, let us say, unofficial transactions?

– Absolutely certain of it, sir. And even if there were, the price would be triple what I just quoted you.

– Good Lord.

– Indeed. Commerce out here is like the climate. It has done in many an iron constitution.

– This is a stationer's shop and you can't sell me paper?

– I can sell you fireworks. And kites. For now.

Flood turned to go and discovered that Djinn was no longer beside him. The compositor had wandered away into the shop and was now looking up at the kites that hung on strings from the ceiling. Amid the brightly coloured swallows and dragons and goldfish was a huge box kite of black silk and bamboo, unadorned and slowly turning at the end of its string.

A tiny inscription in red ran along one edge. The stationer translated it for Djinn:

The tiger opens the casket of dreams.

– I will take that one, Djinn said.

That evening Djinn brought back to the ship a cartouche of bamboo rockets and the silk box kite, but as it was raining, the show he had hoped to put on for the twins had to be postponed.

For days they waited with the fleet of homeward-bound English merchantmen, delayed by port officials and their elaborate ceremonies, and by the lateness of the monsoon winds that were to drive them across the Indian Ocean and around Africa. Pica, Snow, and Darka, confined below decks most of the time by the stricture against foreign women in Canton, shared a cabin to keep one another company. When she rose in the yellow light of dawn, Pica expected Snow to have slipped away in the night, vanished into the teeming city of ships in search of another berth, a vessel ready to sail for London. But every morning the young woman was still there, sitting up in bed, smoking a pipe and lost in thought. Pica cautiously hinted at this one day, and Snow laughed.

– Haven't you learned any patience, little girl?

In the meantime, Flood found the post office of the East India Company and delivered Mister Zero's letter. The clerk looked it over, stroking his quill pen against his cheek.

– Zero, Zero, he mused softly. Where did you say this encounter took place?

Flood glanced in dismay at the map of the southern hemisphere tacked to the wall, covered in pencilled circles and arrows and forested with pins. He described, as well as he could with having spent most of it below decks, the journey they had made from Exilium to Canton. The clerk turned to a tall oak filing cabinet behind his desk, pulled open a drawer, then another. His fingers snapped the sheets briskly forward, then back.

– We keep records of all our castaways, he said, slamming the second drawer shut and trying a third. There are currently over a hundred solitaries in the general area of which you speak.

A few double numbers here and there, and one sextet. Not a happy island, from all reports. Let me see now. Let me see.

Since they were not going anywhere soon, Flood decided there was time to journey into the interior in search of Finest Tortoise. The only problem was that the Emperor had once again rescinded the Edict of Toleration and hustled the Jesuits out by their clerical collars. General hostility toward *fan kwae lo*, the foreign devils, was being encouraged, and in light of these political developments, the celestial empire was off limits to any but the foolhardy.

On their first trip to the stationer's shop, Flood and Djinn had brought along Ludwig the automaton to help them carry the reams of paper they had expected to purchase. Flood quickly noticed that a man made of porcelain caused not the least astonishment in the streets. The next time he went to the stationer's to inquire about the feasibility of travelling inland he learned the reason for this surprising lack of interest in what would be a marvel in any European city.

This was *China*, the stationer reminded Flood. They invented the stuff. And they were fascinated by the clockwork gadgets of the west. They called them *sing-song*, and a European who wanted decent treatment from a local dignitary had better have some to hand out as gifts. The Chinese had applied Europe's ingenuity to their own way of life, and as a result porcelain automatons were as common as spades in some districts. Government officials used them as long-distance messengers. They never got distracted, for one thing, and they could never be bribed or recruited as spies.

– What happens when they wind down, or stray off the road?

Everyone knew the messengers were on important imperial business, so passersby always paused to crank them up again or set them back on course. Heaven and earth had to run efficiently.

Back on board the ship Flood took his straight-edge rule and measured Djinn's height.

– You speak Chinese, don't you?

– Which Chinese?

– How many languages do they have here?

– Several, I believe.

– As long as you know one of them.

When the compositor understood what Flood wanted of him, he made no complaint.

– I will meet my fate here, he said.

It turned out that Djinn was slightly shorter and slenderer than Ludwig. Turini carefully dismantled the automaton, removed his cogs and gears, and fitted his porcelain shell around Djinn like a suit of armour. Ludwig's painted metal eyeballs were replaced with transparent disks of glass to allow the compositor to see where he was going. A latch and hinge were fitted to the mouthpiece to allow him to eat and drink, and another similar trapdoor cut in the posterior for the subsequent necessities. As a final touch, Darka concealed Ludwig's military paint behind Chinese garments, and placed a straw hat like that worn by the locals on his head to hide the automaton's European features.

They escorted him through the streets to the high white-washed wall that enclosed the district of the traders, and saw him off at a gatehouse with a humpbacked roof of red tiles. All that Pica could glimpse before the doors shut was a low hedge glistening darkly in the rain.

THE ADVENTURE OF DJINN

After several days of solitary travel he came at dusk to the bank of a wide river, where a ferryman sat waiting in his boat. The fading light, the lonely slap of water against the side of the ferry, the dim red lantern of the ferry boat all produced in Djinn a feeling that his melancholy destiny was near, and he brightened at the thought. As he hurried down the steep, stony bank, the ferryman appeared, a naked sword in his hand.

– An upside-down night, the bearded, red-eyed ferryman growled, his teeth bared in a terrible grimace. A moonlit day.

Djinn hesitated at the sight of this apparition. Fearing to betray himself he remained silent. The ferryman repeated his salutation and then leaned closer, sniffing.

– Ah. Only a wind-up messenger. I can't see anything in this gloom.

As the boat slipped out into the stream, the ferryman took a longer look at his passenger by the light of the stern lantern.

– You're not really an automaton, are you? he asked, his frightful red eyes narrowing.

Djinn did not speak.

– A foreigner?

– Of course not, Djinn blurted in his best attempt at Cantonese. – You see, I'm actually from –

– Another foreigner, the ferryman muttered, shaking his head. Tell me, why do you people persist in coming here?

You will find only what you would find anywhere else. Pain and sorrow.

The ferryman seemed to want to continue, and so Djinn said nothing, knowing silence to be the surest prompter of speech.

– Three years ago, he said, my beautiful young wife drowned in this river. Here at this very crossing.

Djinn slowly sat, abandoning all pretense of machinehood.

– Years ago, the ferryman went on, I was a wealthy and respected salt merchant. I had been married since my youth to a kind and hard-working woman. When death took her suddenly from me, I mourned for a long time, certain that I would spend my remaining years in solitude, comforted only by memories of my dear helpmeet. If only heaven had seen fit to allow my old age this lonely but dignified retirement from the world.

He ceased for a moment, and all around them in the humid night Djinn heard the croaking of multitudes of frogs.

– As heaven willed it, the ferryman went on, one day I saw a face. A face that stopped me dead in the street. I stumbled home, forgetting my business. I made inquiries. The young woman was from a distant province, and her noble but impoverished family had come to my prosperous town in search of better fortune.

Her name was Pool of Jade. At night her perfect white face hovered before him, driving away sleep. By day he tended his business in a state he had all but forgotten: the giddy drunkenness of infatuation. In a kind of fever he went again and again to her house, wooed her, lavished gifts on her family, and was at last accepted.

On fire, he married hastily, against the advice of his older brother, a monk, who tactfully reminded him of the wide river of years between his betrothed and himself, and cautioned him to maintain a stern lordship over her at all times. The salt merchant demanded of his cloistered brother what he could possibly know about love, and devoted himself entirely to his wife's happiness.

— I see now that I fussed over her far too much, made myself an obsequious and tiresome fool in her eyes. No doubt she soon wearied of such timid attentions from a man whose hair was already grey.

After her death he found letters full of indecent hints and suggestions she could only have exchanged with some shameless libertine of the town. It was clear to him then that she had found what she really longed for, a youthful lover.

— Who he was, I have not yet discovered. Not yet.

He knew only that at night she would slip out with her devoted maid to meet this scoundrel at the river, where he waited with a boat to take them to their trysting place. There was no ferry at this crossing then. People in these parts had always called this the Ford of Amorous Longing and he had never known why.

— I know now, to my sorrow, the ferryman said. Why was I not aware of her absences, you may well ask. It seems she had bought from some apothecary a vial of sleeping potion, a few drops of which in my evening tea would topple me like a stone into unhearing, dreamless slumber until the dawn.

Toiling each day at his shop, mollifying customers and government inspectors, browbeating his labourers, he was too busy to be suspicious of this unusual drowsiness and only assumed that age was at last laying its heavy hand upon his shoulder.

— One spring night, as my wife and her maid slipped out to their clandestine rendezvous, a thunderstorm rose up and hid the moon. My wife, not seeing her lover's lantern in the rain and darkness, fell into the river and was swept away. I assume her brave paramour heard her screams for help and fled, rather than risk his own precious life to save her.

The maid returned to the house and woke him, told him in gasps what had befallen her mistress. So dull-witted was he that he did not even think to ask why his wife would be out of doors at night. He dressed in haste and rushed out into the rain, the maid running after him, babbling nonsense about river spirits. At dawn, after searching through the night, he found her at last, lying amid the reeds.

The ferryman fell silent, and gazed out into the black waves of the river.

— Her robe had come loose from her shoulder, he said at last, and when I lifted her in my arms I saw the mark of teeth, a bite no doubt inflicted during the heedless frenzy of passion.

The maid had fled, doubtless terrified of the punishment that would fall upon her for her part in all that had transpired. He never saw the woman again. And so he was left with only the memory of that livid bite mark as a clue, a mark so powerfully impressed into his mind that it was as if he himself had been bitten. A single character to lead him to the man he vowed to kill.

— But surely such a clue is not enough, Djinn could not help saying, given that one man's teeth must be very like another's.

— Except in this case, the ferryman said with a bitter smile. My quarry left a very distinctive bite mark, you see.

One of his eye teeth had been filed to an unusual double point, most likely to serve as a kind of seal, a sign of conquest on each woman he seduced. And it was only possible to see this double point by two methods: close examination of the offending fang, or by the impression left by a bite.

— What could I do to catch the cowardly dog who destroyed my happiness? If I asked to see the teeth of every man who entered my shop, they would quite rightly consider me mad, and complain to the government, who would revoke my salt licence and probably behead me into the bargain.

He thought for a while of opening a tea house or a bakery, in which sort of establishment he might have the opportunity to examine bites left in cakes or crusts of stale bread. But could he always be certain whose teeth had left which bite in a discarded crust? That strategy was far too susceptible to error for his liking.

Guessing that the culprit must live near the river, he hit upon a different plan, one which seemed much more probable of success. First of all, he sold his prospering salt business and told all his friends and acquaintances that he was leaving to return to the far province of his ancestors. Then he vanished from the town and took up residence in his brother's monastery in the mountains, where the monks were only too happy to conceal him in exchange for his generous donations. A year later, with a new name and his face disguised with a shock of wild hair, he established a ferry at the Ford of Amorous Longing.

— At first my hope was that *he* and his latest conquest would avail themselves of this boat some night, and I would have him for certain. But I have found that the nights are quiet on this stretch of the river. Suspiciously quiet.

He paused for a moment, as if listening to the frogs, the burble of the stream, the wind sighing in the trees.

— But day and night I greet every man who passes this way with an unholy grin and a pointless jest, he went on, in the hope of provoking a like smile, so that I may examine his teeth.

If that ploy fails, I tell indecent stories while I pole us across the river. My quarry is doubtless a man to laugh heartily at the weakness of the flesh and the humiliation of women. And those who take offence, well, what can they say? After all, if you don't like the ferryman's manners, you can't very well tell him so halfway across the river, can you? The local magistrate has listened to numerous complaints about me, to be sure, but since he is nestled snugly in my still-capacious purse, I need not fear being removed from my post any day soon.

– And so I await my opportunity. Sooner or later this shadow, this wily demon in a man's skin, will find it necessary to cross the river, perhaps on his way to another illicit conquest of the heart. Would he suspect that the rich and haughty merchant he so blithely cuckolded all those years ago would stoop to such an ignoble station in life? No, he will think what everyone who passes this way thinks, what you yourself no doubt thought when I first addressed you. This hairy wretch is insane, he will say to himself, and in order that I may hurry to a warm fire or to a good supper or to bed and the waiting arms of my lover, I will humour him. I will laugh at him while pretending to laugh with him, and then be on my way.

The boat bumped up against the wooden platform on the far bank.

– And that baring of white teeth, the ferryman said, driving his pole like a spear into the wet bank, will be his last false smile on this earth.

Djinn climbed unsteadily out of the boat and turned to the ferryman.

– What about all those men who never laugh?

– I am patient, the ferryman said. It may be that *he* has already passed here numerous times, and will again and again before I wrench a grin out of him. After all, the wicked must travel more than the virtuous.

– Do women pass this way?

– Often, the ferryman said with a shrug at the obvious. Out of respect for both my wives I refrain from offending feminine delicacy . . .

The ferryman's last words trailed off. His eyes opened wide, the pole slipped from his hand and clattered to the floor of the boat. And with the ferryman in that state, transfixed and speechless in the waning darkness, Djinn left him and went on his way.

He reached a mountainous region and came to Ching-te chen, the City of Porcelain, where the mandarin had his palace.

The narrow valley in which the city lay was clouded with the smoke of hundreds of kilns. As Djinn slowly made his way up along the main road, he witnessed the steps in the creation of an automaton. The manufacturing of each porcelain shell had been divided into a sequence of discrete operations, each of which took place in its own district, inhabited by labourers whose most common occupational hazard gave their city-within-a-city its name.

In the City of the Maimed they hacked clay and rock out of the mountainsides and pounded it into paste.

In the City of the Arthritic, artisans shaped the raw porcelain in moulds for the various sections of the automaton's body.

The pieces were fired in red-hot kilns in the ash-choked City of the Blind.

In the City of the Hunchbacks they applied the delicate strokes and curlicues of paint and the final glaze.

Beyond the City of the Disgruntled, where the porcelain was packaged, labelled, and loaded aboard barges, Djinn eventually reached the palace, but in his guise as a mechanical messenger, he found it impossible to contrive a way into the library or the printing house. The various functionaries and guards who barred his way, discovering he carried no official documents, considered him defective and steered him back outside onto the palace grounds. Here he stayed for several days, in rain and sun, furtively snatching nuts and fallen fruit when no one was about.

Eventually his curiosity led him to a walled-off area of the grounds, which he found to his surprise to be an artificial garden. The earth in this enclosure was covered in tiles of polished malachite to create a bright green lawn that would never wither or go to seed. Trees of copper and brass had been erected, painted in life-like colours and hung with censers, so that if any members of the mandarin's staff chanced to walk that way they would inhale sweet odours of jasmine, peach blossom, and honey. The flowers that lined the marble pathways were fashioned of delicate shards of jade, crystal, and amethyst. Ceramic birds perched on metallic tree boughs, and in the ponds of glass bronze goldfish flitted.

Djinn imagined that here he would be free of vigilant eyes, since no one would be needed to tend a landscape of artifice, but it was not long before he realized his mistake. Gardeners were everywhere, with brooms, brushes, nets, and tongs, roaming through the enclosure at all hours, making sure everything was kept polished, free from stain or blemish. He watched them at their work, as any dry leaves, twigs, insects, or nests of mice that happened to stray over or under the walls were swiftly hunted down and rooted out.

One of these gardeners appeared so suddenly that Djinn was nearly caught in the unautomaton-like act of relieving himself through the lower hatch of the porcelain suit.

– I don't know how you ended up in this place, the gardener said to him, but you are certainly at home here. I'll wind you up presently, but you might as well stay for now, while I rest.

The gardener glanced around furtively, then sat down heavily on a nearby bench and leaned his broom beside him.

– Since I dare not tell my secret to anyone whose ears could really hear me, the gardener sighed, I will have to confide in you, my mechanical friend.

Djinn held his breath and tried his best not to move.

– You see, I cannot let the world know what I have found here in the Garden of Heavenly Perfection.

. . . I was picking straw blown over the wall by the autumn winds, when I saw the crimson tongue of its place-marking ribbon poking up between two slabs of stone. The sight was partially hidden by a mimosa of artfully wrought opal. Under pretence of inspecting the base of the plant for stray wisps of straw, I knelt and levered up a tile with my trowel, exposing one angular corner of the intruder. With much effort I was able to dig the book free of the thick, fibrous roots anchoring it to the dark earth. I only had time for a quick glance at my find before concealing it in my tunic. The book's cover was made of wood, its damp, heavy pages giving off a pungent odour of earth, rain, leaf rot. As I hurried back to my cell, I debated what I should do with my find. Cart it, with all the other chaff, to the bonfire outside the garden wall? Or give it to the superintendent to pass on upward through the clerks and ministers to the mandarin, to add to his unread library? After a morning of indecision, I did neither and instead kept my discovery hidden.

In private moments I take up the volume and the rough, thorny binding hums in my hand like a beehive. As I turn the pages coniferous sap sticks to my fingers. In the rustle of its paper I hear the nocturnal stirring of owls. Letters become iridescent beetles that uncase their wings with a click and whirr into the air. This book is a wild tangle of words, a shadowy ravine through which unseen beasts prowl, rustling the pages as they pass.

In the middle of the book I found the story of an ancient hermit of the forest, and he too is reading by candlelight in the evening, and in the book he is reading there is described a still pool of water in the midst of aromatic night blossoms, where he imagines himself sitting at twilight, bending to cup his hands and drink, and when he looks at his reflection he sees staring back at him a youth of great beauty.

As I read, each page slowly turns yellow and sere and falls softly from the book to the tiled lawn. I hurriedly gather these fallen leaves and bury them secretly in the place where I first saw the book. I have been reading all through the summer, and now approaches the time of year when not even imperial decree may halt the inevitable. This is the season when the mandarin takes flight to his summer house far to the south, to escape the sight of grey skies and trees, even artificial trees, laden with snow. This is the season when we gardeners must battle vigilantly against ice and sleet, against rust and rot.

I have no doubt that in the spring the book will be the first sign of green to emerge from winter's white sleep, the pale, dog-eared corners of its pages shivering in the cool wind. During the rains I will come out with my umbrella to inspect the tender shoots, watch the snails crawl across their delicately veined surfaces, knowing that soon I will be reading it again, a book both familiar and entirely new.

I used to wonder how this book reached me and who authored it, but I soon grew weary of pondering these unimportant matters. I know only that the book's leaves have come from another garden, a far-off, legendary garden as thin as paper, a garden weaving across thousands of miles like a serpentine wall that keeps no one out and nothing in. A garden I dream of every night in my narrow cell, and which I know to be real, if unapproachable. It is not inscribed on any chart, you cannot see it, but when you pass unsuspecting through its shimmering verdant curtain you will know, and remember. There will be an instant, the most fleeting of moments, when all your senses will tremble with infinite delight.

In the evenings, when I tuck the book away under my straw mattress and blow out the candle, I can see, through my cell window, the tiled roof of the mandarin's palace above the artificial forest. And on certain wet and gusty nights I see a light appear in a high window, a light that burns until morning. And then I know that in his great canopied bed, under sheets of the purest peach-blossom silk, the mandarin too has dreamt of this garden, and has woken in terror.

Having come to the end of his confession, the gardener rose from the bench and gently wound the key of the automaton. Djinn made a feint of shuddering to life. The gardener smiled wistfully and stepped up close to his earpiece.

– Take my secret with you, foreigner.

One evening on his return journey Djinn was climbing a steep, rocky path along the edge of a pine forest. Two men carrying heavy sacks appeared over the brow of the hill, headed in the opposite direction. As they passed him one of them reached out, halted him, and spoke in a furtive growl.

– Hey, you ridiculous smiling teapot, how long ago did you leave the last traveller's rest house?

– Should we take him with us? the other man asked. He could carry these blasted sacks.

– Probably not a wise idea. If we were caught interfering with an imperial messenger we'd be in worse trouble than we would be for having stolen all this stuff.

– Well, he's lucky, the first man said. A machine doesn't have to worry about the terror that stalks this forest.

Djinn carried on with great trepidation. Night fell, the moon climbed into a clear, starry sky, and the wind rose. The tops of the pine trees along the path tossed and scraped against one another. The cold fogged the lenses of his eyeholes so that he could barely see the path in front of him. Suddenly a silvery black shadow slipped across the narrow frame of his vision.

He halted, holding his breath, turning his head this way and that. He heard a scrape of gravel behind him and whirled around, but could see nothing. He turned again to hurry away and there before him in the path was a crouched tiger, its striped hide silvered by moonlight. Djinn stared, rooted to the spot more by wonder than fear. With a loping spring that seemed to happen very slowly, the huge beast leapt up on its hind legs, swung a paw, and batted Djinn to the earth.

He lay staring up at the stars, his breath slapped out of his body, and then the tiger was over him, a blur of shadows, its great mouth breathing fetid gusts that steamed over the lenses of the eyeholes. Djinn shut his eyes and waited, expecting at any moment to feel talons peeling him out of his shell like a soft-boiled egg. Instead he heard the beast's bristled snout scraping against the face plate, and a loud wet snuff. One of the tiger's whiskers slipped through a breathing hole, tickling Djinn's nose. Unable to stop himself, he sneezed, the sound amplified in the spirals of the automaton's vocal passage to a staccato gunshot. The tiger recoiled with a grunt, its claws scrabbling on the loose stones of the path, and then it turned tail and bounded back into the darkness.

It won't be long before he gets over his surprise, Djinn thought, and he scrambled to his feet. Awkwardly he hoisted himself into the upper branches of a nearby tree and clung there, shivering in the night air and wondering how his sense of the path his own life was to take could have failed to predict this gruesome and spectacular end. Here he was, alone, in a forest in the middle of a vast country that knew nothing of him, friendless, unloved, almost certain to be eaten by a ravenous beast of prey and perish unmourned. It was not in character, to be sure, but yet it was perfect in its own way, he admitted to himself, his only regret being that no one was here to find out how right he had been about his future.

Not long afterward the tiger returned, padding along the forest floor at a much more sedate pace and followed by a slender figure, cloaked and hooded in green, carrying a bow and a quiver of arrows. The tiger slunk to the base of the tree where Djinn had imagined himself concealed by leaves and shadows.

The green figure reached the tiger's side, peered up into the tree, tapped its bow against the trunk.

— It's no use, a muffled voice said. If you don't climb down, I'll shoot you down.

A woman, Djinn realized.

— The tiger will not hurt you, she said.

— Then why did he pounce on me just now?

— He's seen plenty of people disguised as automatons before, so there must've been something different about you. The two of us like to keep this forest free of murderers, thieves, and generally suspicious characters. Which are you?

— Neither, blurted Djinn. None, I mean.

— Then you have nothing to fear. Now climb down or I'll begin to think you've got something to hide and I'll send my friend here up after you.

When Djinn had inched his way painstakingly to the ground, he saw that the woman, like him, was encased from head to foot in porcelain. The face was that of an archer with a pencil-thin beard and, like Ludwig, a smile.

— I'll wager you're another foreigner in disguise.

Djinn nodded wearily. Exhausted by his ordeal, he allowed himself to be led without protest to a cave deep in the woods.

A well-furnished cave, he saw with surprise when they had ducked through the mossy entrance, tapestried and cushioned and warmed by cheerful yellow lanterns. The woman bade him sit where he liked, lit a small fire in a woodstove and brewed tea. In one corner lay a heap of gears, springs, and glazed potsherds that had obviously once been part of one or more porcelain messengers.

– I find them abandoned quite often, the woman said, noticing the direction of his gaze, and I bring them here. I use the parts for everything from knives to dishes. My friend must have thought you were defective in some way, and that's why he pounced.

– Defective?

The woman unclipped her armour piece by piece, ending with her face plate, then shook out her matted hair. Beneath the porcelain shell she was tightly wrapped in a gauze-like fabric, the ends of which she proceeded to unwind and then to fan herself with. When she saw Djinn's stare she excused herself, went behind a folding paper screen, and re-emerged in a tunic and breeches.

– One carries one's upbringing, she said. Even into the forest.

Djinn and the woman sat on straw mats and sipped tea from tiny clay bowls. The tiger stretched out at their feet and commenced licking its great shaggy paws.

– I was wondering how you managed to feed yourself in that thing, the woman said. It looks a lot less removable than mine.

– I was worried about that myself, Djinn said. But along the way children would run up and slip nuts and seeds through my faceplate. They knew an automaton must get hungry like everyone else.

While they drank he told the woman where he had journeyed from, and spoke of Flood and his search for Finest Tortoise.

– You're not the only one who guessed my secret, Djinn said. There was a ferryman who figured it out pretty quickly, but then he himself was in disguise.

– In disguise, echoed the woman. Don't tell me. He had once been a salt merchant.

– That's right. How did you know?

The woman remained silent.

– You were the maid, Djinn said.

– His wife loved him, she muttered with an angry shake of the head. Truly, devotedly. And he rewarded that love with jealousy.

Possessiveness ruled his heart as it always had, and made him unable to love. He wanted only the desirable wife, not the desiring woman. Each night he would wish her a restful sleep and retire to his own chamber to go over his accounts, as if careful management of his business was all that was needed to guarantee a harmonious home life.

– The poor girl was desperate to give him a child, and begged me for help. My first thought was that she was not yet comfortable with the act of love, and so I penned letters, purportedly from the salt merchant, letters of such passion that they might accomplish what that dried old carp could not. She saw through my scheme and begged me to think of some other means to her desire. I told her what I knew of the arts of love, but she refused to hear a maid speak so plainly of such intimacies.

As a last desperate resort they drugged her husband at night so that they could slip away undetected and carry out the maid's next plan. She knew that since time immemorial, women who wished for love would go down to the Ford of Amorous Longing. Its waters were said to anoint the soul of a woman with an irresistible allure. Every night they came secretly to the river's edge and Pool of Jade would bathe in the frigid water until her perfect alabaster skin turned blue.

– That last night, with the wind and high water, the current proved too strong. On her way back to the bank she lost her balance and was swept out of my sight.

The woman reached out and scratched behind the tiger's ears. The great beast purred contentedly.

– But the tooth mark, Djinn said. Whose teeth left that bite?

The woman smiled bitterly.

– Before I came to work for her, I was a seamstress. The faster I worked, the more money I made for my family. I bit through so many threads, chewed so many pins, I wore a groove in this tooth, here.

She opened her mouth and tapped one of her eye teeth.

– You bit her.

The woman nodded, staring into her teacup.

– I loved her as a maid should love her mistress and protector, and for a long time I did not suspect the true nature of my feelings.

When she penned those passionate letters she did not understand she was giving voice to her own unacknowledged desires. One night she attempted to teach her mistress various methods of seduction. To show Pool of Jade where and how to touch a man, she touched her. They embraced. They kissed. All at once both of them knew this was no longer a lesson. For one moment they belonged only to one another. And already in that moment they knew this could not be.

– If we were to live, it had to begin and end right then and there. And so I fled and hid in my chamber. Much later she came to my room and, saying not a word, bared her shoulder. Softly I kissed her burning skin. Like a butterfly her fingers alighted on my neck. Then I felt her nails sink into my flesh and I bared my teeth and inflicted the bite that her husband found upon her. She cried out and tore herself away. We never spoke again of that night.

The woman shook her head sadly, and poured out the dregs of her tea.

– After her death I wandered and finally came to live here, in this forest, where I befriended a tiger cub whose mother had been killed by hunters. I began to find the empty shells of automatons and I vowed then to become the protector of the lost in these woods.

– Of all people, Djinn said, that I should encounter you.

– It is not surprising. The road you were on is known in these parts as the Dragon Vein Stretching a Thousand Miles. Every mile of it is crowded with people like me, like the ferryman, like yourself, people with stories. And all of these stories are in some hidden way linked to one another, like the blood of the dragon flowing beneath its impenetrable hide.

Inside Ludwig, Djinn smiled.

– And now my story is here as well, he said.

– Although we don't know the ending yet.

The tiger opened its jaws in a vast yawn.

– Right, my friend, the woman said, patting the tiger's flank. Time for bed.

Without further ceremony she fluffed up a heap of pillows and settled into them, tucking her hands under her head.

Djinn lay back on the stone floor. His porcelain armour had been chafing him ever since he set out on this journey, and made for very uncomfortable sleeping. He lay on one side and then the other, grunting angrily each time he was forced to try another position.

The woman sat up.

— Can't you take any of that off?

— Not without help, Djinn said.

She stirred the coals in the stove and slid over to him.

— There's a little metal pin in back, where the queue is painted on, Djinn said, reaching around to the rear headpiece. The woman's hair brushed against his ear. Her skin smelled of pine and mossy earth and something like dappled spring sunlight.

— It's really wedged in, and I can't quite . . .

— I see, the woman said. Here, I've got it.

She pried open and lifted away the halves of Ludwig's skull. Djinn felt his face and hair steam in the night air.

— Thank you, he said. I'm Djinn.

— My name is Peony. She hefted the automaton's face plate. This is an unwieldy design. Here we make them easier to get in and out of.

— A lot of people go around disguised as clockwork messengers?

She laughed.

— There haven't been any clockwork messengers for a long time. Most people know that, but it's convenient to pretend otherwise. One never knows when one might need a little concealment. And it occurs to me that with a little stealth, and luck, it wouldn't be so difficult to get our hands on some of that paper you're after.

— You think so?

— Your idea was good, but this . . . this was all wrong.

She handed him the automaton's faceplate and he looked at it for the first time since Flood had taken his height and then entombed him in this glazed sarcophagus. Here was the smile he had worn every league of his journey. No wonder the children had come running to him. He felt a pang of belated affection for Ludwig, and at the same time a desire to liberate his flesh once and for all. To remember, through the simple caress of air on naked skin, just who had been inhabiting this shell.

— If it's not too much trouble, Djinn said, those hinge things in the back, between the shoulder blades . . . ?

— Just a moment.

Soon Djinn was naked to the waist and Ludwig's breastplate and arms lay on the floor of the cave. Peony looked him up and down.

— Those are beautiful tattoos.

He started to speak and then hesitated. His shoulders slumped.

— I understand, she said. A very long story, like the dragon vein. We can continue our talk in the morning. I have many questions about the world beyond China.

She leaned towards the lantern, her hair sliding across her face, her shoulder catching the light.

— I could answer a question or two now, Djinn said. It's really no trouble.

— Well, for one thing, Peony said, sitting up again, I've often wondered if all men are as obtuse about matters of the heart as they are in my country. I've always cursed that stupid salt merchant. He had love right in front of him and he couldn't see it.

— Foolish, Djinn agreed, blissfully scratching his nose for the first time in weeks.

– I mean to say, Peony continued, that opportunities for the incomparable delights of love arise so fleetingly, and often so miraculously, that we truly insult heaven if we let them slip through our fingers.

The tiger raised its head and sniffed. It rose up, stretched, and padded slowly out of the cave.

– It's almost as if he understood you, Djinn said, twisting his aching neck from side to side, and decided to go in search of a mate.

– I wish him good fortune, Peony said, drawing closer to Djinn and laying a hand on his cold porcelain thigh. And bliss. Now let's see about the rest of these hinges.

φ

The automaton returned on a rainy morning. Under her umbrella, her hat pulled low to hide her face, Pica was waiting as she had been every day since Djinn set out, near the gatehouse in the wall.

In a downpour too loud for conversation, she took Ludwig by the arm, alarmed at Djinn's lightness – *they'd almost starved him with this crazy scheme* – and returned to the ship.

The compositor was not inside. The clockwork mechanisms that had taken his place were unfamiliar. Flood spun the tiny wheels of brass and prodded delicate copper cylinders, while Pica peered into the hollow limbs. In one leg they found a note in the compositor's hand explaining, with a rare joke that revealed to them the seriousness of his decision, that he would be staying behind in China rather than returning in porcelain.

At the bottom of the page Djinn had scribbled an afterthought.

I was wrong about the future. Or it was wrong about me.

Inside the other leg of the automaton they found a sealed bamboo tube, and inside it a roll of paper that gave off a faint scent of something vaguely familiar for which Flood could not find a name. Amphitrite Snow sniffed the paper.

– *Kong hu.* Black tea. It's the only thing we had to drink aboard the *Gold Coast*, once the rum was gone.

The paper was extremely light and thin, yet durable, without being any more translucent than a standard rag stock.

Pica remembered her first sight of the compositor and the automaton together, at the castle. Djinn had been printing a trial page on the press before he took it apart, to make certain it would work when they put it back together in her father's cell. She had watched the two of them in a kind of trance, these beings of unearthly beauty, working together in silence.

It was only now, when they understood that Djinn would not be returning, and she and her father reassembled Ludwig and polished him up, that Pica realized how much she already missed whoever it was that the two of them, man and machine, had made.

That evening, when she brought her father his customary late supper, Pica was surprised to see that all the lamps were out. Ludwig was not at the ready alongside the press where she expected to find him, but hanging from his hook, swaying slightly with the rocking of the ship. The air smelled of steam and hot metal, reminding her of the laundry at the Ospedale.

She found her father at the far end of the press room, holding a sheet of paper under the moonlight sieved by the grille of the overhead hatch. He did not move as she came near, and in the cold silver light his skin had taken on the automaton's rigid pallor.

– The paper was the key, he said, as if to himself. It's beginning.

– What is?

– The *alam*.

· He stirred at the sound of her approach and turned stiffly, blinking at her as if unable to quite remember who she was.

φ

He lived in the press room now, catching brief snatches of sleep in a hammock. He worked with Ludwig alone and seemed to prefer it that way, no longer bothering to ask if Pica wished to help. Once in a long while he would appear on deck, unshaven and dazed, and stare out at the city, hazy and steaming in the endless drizzle, or at the crowded waterway with its changing warp and weft of sails. He would dunk his head in the water-butt, come up dripping, and then suddenly disappear down the hatchway without a word, like a ghost departing at cockcrow.

On the rare occasions he joined the rest of them at supper he fidgeted like a little boy and laughed giddily at his own feeble jokes. Whenever he showed up at the table, Pica would find an excuse to leave early and go up on deck to sit alone until she heard his press start up again.

When the English fleet was at last ready to get under way, Pica learned from Turini that the birthday of the twins had just passed. She threw off her dampened spirits, determined to give Lolo and Miza something she had never had.

– It will be a farewell party, too, she said. For Djinn. With Ludwig as the guest of honour.

The *Bee* was decked from bow to stern with paper garlands

and the shrouds and stays hung with multicoloured lanterns. Flood brought out the fireworks he and Djinn had purchased weeks before and Darka hung them all over the ship. While Darka and Snow prepared a feast in the galley, the twins and Pica, in her boy's clothes, tried out Djinn's kite on the quay. The wind rose with such sudden ferocity that Lolo was nearly carried off into the sky. They were reeling him and the kite in for another try when Turini called them back to the ship. In the channel hundreds of vessels of every shape and size could be seen heading shoreward like a great invasion fleet. Soon the *Bee* was surrounded by a crowd of boats bumping into one another, snagging each other's yards and rigging in their haste to find anchorage.

The sea began to heave. The masts swayed and the lanterns in the rigging swung wildly, some snapping free. They felt the tug of the ship straining against its anchor chains.

In an ominous twilight they sat down to the birthday feast, then hurried back out on deck. A wall of black cloud had risen out of the southeast and soon brought a slashing rainstorm down upon the harbour. The gale that followed drove the waters before it, sending wave after wave breaking over the decks.

While Turini and Darka rushed to lash down the sails and make fast the rigging, a white ship appeared out of the veils of rain at the entrance to the harbour, rising and dropping out of sight again. The guns of the Cloud Island fort fired the one-volley alarm for a ship in distress, then as an afterthought the two-volley alarm for pirates. A mountainous swell rose in the river, and when it subsided, after disgorging great numbers of fish onto the dockside streets, the white ship had vanished.

By dawn the next morning the wind had dropped to a fresh breeze and the sky was clear. Aboard the *Bee* they were confronted with a mess of shredded sails, snapped and snarled rigging, and wet, limp, washed-out paper garlands. The rockets that Flood had been assured by the stationer would burst in the shapes of fantastic birds were soaked and useless. All but one, as they discovered, which Lolo had taken the night before and hidden under his pillow. Despite the fact that it was daylight, they gave in to his inarticulate entreaties and fired it for him. It flew upward in a wobbly spiral, sputtering smoke but failing to burst, then plummeted and vanished into the water with a hiss.

Turini and Darka spent the morning making repairs in preparation for a hasty departure. A few minutes into the forenoon watch, as they were about to weigh anchor, a closed carriage rattled up on the stone quay, bumping over the ropes of dried seaweed that still lay strewn everywhere. An indistinct voice hailed the ship, and Snow leaned over the quarterdeck rail to see an elegantly dressed young man tumble from the carriage, followed by an empty brandy bottle that wobbled chummily over to a bollard, against which it stopped with a hollow thunk. The young man crawled over to the bottle with an exaggerated mockery of feline stealth, lunged, and caught it in his hands. He scrambled to his feet and held aloft his prize, which immediately slipped out of his grasp and shattered on the stones.

The mishap was applauded by the other occupants of the carriage, three rouged and powdered women peeking over the fringes of scallopshell fans. The young man bowed extravagantly to them, spun teetering on his heel, and waved up at the crew of the *Bee*.

— Pardon me, mariners, he shouted, but I was told there was an absolute smasher of a party going on here. Are we too late for it?

– You're English, I think, Flood said.

– So do I, sir, although I confess I am no longer certain. They say this climate kills men of my nation and I'm still here. Dear Papa thought it would be so improving to send me out to the antipodes for a few years to learn commerce from the Chinamen. Do me a world of good, he insisted. Do him good, the old bugger, after I strolled into the orangery one afternoon and found him at it like donkeys with the gardener.

At that moment Pica came up beside Snow. The young man's eyes went wide and he staggered back theatrically, placing a hand on his breast.

– God's wattles, he said, if you aren't the spitting image of Madame Beaufort. I last saw her on the day I left London, to ask her would I have a safe voyage. And I swear, if you couldn't pass for her daughter, my little lass, then I am an orangutan.

*T*he book invents another book.

Now and then you glimpse it, this other book that desires you as reader. It is there before the book is opened, there after it is closed. Letters of ink on white paper may fleetingly seem the shadows cast by its radiance, passing through the net of the world.

Sages have spoken of the Four Noble Books: the Material Book, the Fluid Book, the Fiery Book, the Invisible Book. And in their merging is said to be found the Unread Book within all others. Heard in the creak of the binding, felt in the fibres of the paper, beheld entire for an instant on the edge of a turning page.

There are those who say that the printing press, like a mirror that produces only false copies, is the enemy of the Unread Book. It is wise to remember, however, that even the most commonplace volume partakes of the substance of the Material Book. Out of that subtle affinity much has been dreamed. I have heard of holy fools who read with their legs stretched naked in the dust. They read from the sole of the foot upward, from the crown of the scalp downward. A book, they say, consists of nails, teeth, skin, tendon, marrow; of heart and lungs, liver, spleen, and kidneys, stomach and intestines; of the fire of the breath and the wind of the bowels; of sweat, spittle, tears, mucus, urine, bile, lymph, oil of the joints, and fluids of generation.

They burrow into the book held warm and living in their hands, peel its leaves back like layers of flesh, come at last to blankness, a page of bone.

THE CABINET OF WONDERS

It was inevitable that he would lose count, and so he did, somewhere past the twelve thousandth sheet. Still his pace did not slacken. Kirshner's type continued to bring forth forme after forme, rising unbidden from the metal, and he continued to print, to cut into small folio pages, pausing only long enough to notice that the stack of paper which he had expected would soon overflow his work table did not seem to grow measurably once it had reached the thickness of a Bible, or one of Samuel Richardson's novels. It occurred to him that this could only be possible if each sheet he cut from the roll of Finest Tortoise was thinner than the one before it. He wondered what he would find when he reached the innermost curl of the roll, if he ever did.

When he rested briefly from his labours he would ask his daughter if she wished to look through the sheets just printed.

Pica always declined, although she would watch him at his work, and once she asked how he would know when he was finished. He held up the apple she had just brought him for lunch.

– If the book was shaped like this, he said, would you ask that question?

She went away puzzling over that, and then realized that the solution, if there was one, did not matter as much as the fact that her father was answering her now in riddles.

He had begun to inhabit another world, a waning moon. His gaze went through things. On the rare occasions he spoke, his words came from a lunar distance. He was indifferent to food, and as usual barely slept, but now without apparently needing to sleep.

On the day he had set her the riddle of the book's shape she returned later with coffee, and saw that the apple, shiny and unblemished a few hours before, now resembled one of the shrunken heads she had seen in the window of a curio shop in Canton.

After that revelation she found excuses to linger in the press room and silently observe. Candles burned down to stubs here twice as fast as they did anywhere else on the ship. The timbers of the press had begun to crack and warp. Cobwebs hung everywhere and an odour of ancient decay like that of the Abbé's subterranean library clung to the room, even after she opened all the gunports and scrubbed the planks. When she watched Ludwig at the press she saw that the automaton's movements had increased in speed to the point where, after a long run of printing, his fingertips were hot to the touch. A mosaic of hair-thin cracks had begun to appear all over his faded enamel.

For the first few days out of Canton, the *Bee* had kept along with the East India Company fleet, but soon she outpaced the huge, lumbering trading vessels with their laden holds. The white spray flew from the ship's bows as day after day the *Bee* sliced through the waves, her taut sails straining.

Once through the Strait of Sunda they rode the monsoons northwest to Ceylon, laying over to caulk the leaking seams of the hull at the port of Trincomalee. Pica, Darka, and the twins sat under a sailcloth awning on deck, twining strands of tarred rope to make oakum, which Snow and Turini hammered into the loosened joints and cracks between the planks. Eventually even Flood was driven out of the sweltering tomb below decks, and took a hand in the repairs. At the end of the day they all lay prostrate on the deck, drinking the milk of coconuts.

– It's too bad, Pica said, we can't sew the ship up like a book.

The next day, to her surprise, her father led them on an excursion through the town. Soon leaving behind the tidy lanes of houses around the harbour, they entered the borderland of the half-castes, a narrow zone of unroofed light between the angled black shadows of the European streets and the hushed, towering forest. On a road curving up a bare hill, a thin snake of blood slid through the dust at their feet. At the crest of the hill they found the source, a ramshackle tannery. The reek of blood and the moans of animals about to meet the knife pro-pelled them forward, but Flood lingered, his eye caught by a display of undyed skins on racks by the entrance.

Pica's comment the evening before reminded him he had yet to consider how he was going to bind his stack of pages.

While the others waited, he fingered the pale yellow skins, tugged at them, gathered an impression of resilience and supple pliability. The Sinhalese tanner, his own skin dyed a deep blue, knew a few words in English, French, and Dutch, and by trading these scraps of language back and forth Flood learned that these were the skins of rare monkeys from the interior hills. If he wanted to know more, the tanner told him, he would have to consult the *alam*.

— The what?

— *Alam*, the tanner repeated. He sighed, beckoned Flood though a beaded archway and up a curving staircase. On the roof, under a parasol, an old naked man sat cross-legged on a carpet of palm leaves.

— Father-in-law, the tanner said.

Flood crouched in front of the old man, who was mumbling softly to himself, his head sunk forward, his long, root-like beard covering his naked body.

— Are you . . . the *alam*?

The old man's muttering ceased and he slowly raised his head. A pair of depthless brown eyes blinked and focused on Flood.

— *Alam*. . . . Yes. She whispered it, my name, like a secret, in the garden of the English consul. Her lips on my ear. The jacaranda petals were about to fall.

The old man's head drooped again.

THE TALE OF THE TANNER'S FATHER-IN-LAW

He was the chief huntsman of the white overlords. She was the governor's neice. He circled her noiselessly, as if she were a wild animal. One evening after the hunt he was invited among the pavilions, to tell the quaint old stories. She was there, reclined on dark silk laid on the cool, wet grass, a little brown monkey playing about her white arms. Her eyes were upon him as he told of Prince Rama and loyal Hanuman. How they built a bridge of stones across the sea to Lanka, to rescue lovely Sita from the ten-headed Ravana and his demons.

He told of Hanuman's monkey army, dying in their thousands on the bloody field of battle, and how their grieving commander, to save them, fetched an entire mountain from the far Himalayas. A mountain on which grew a herb that cured all sickness and restored life to the dead.

Does that mean, she asked him, that my little friend here, being one of their descendants, is immortal?

They all laughed at that. He answered before he could relax the bowstring of his anger.

You should ask the people of the forest, he said. They were here before any of us.

They watched him more carefully after that day, but in her eyes he saw that only she had guessed the truth. The secret he had kept from his new masters, the name a seed wrapped in betel leaves.

She came to him, and he told her his hidden name. They fled together to the forest of his people. He found their way by the trees that held the ancient tattoos. Eyes and arrows. In the forest she gave birth to their child, but there was not enough life in her for both of them.

After she died he killed the monkey, the beloved pet she had not been able to leave behind. He roasted it, chewed its flesh and fed it to the child. A delicacy among his people. Then he took his bow and hunted its brothers. Old rhymes, nonsense for children, drew them down from the branches.

– I shot them and skinned them, the old man said, and with our child in my arms I came down out of the forest. The Portuguese and the Dutch and the English marvelled at the beautiful skins and bought them, and sent me back into the forest to find more.

The old man fell silent, seemed not to hear Flood's further questions. Behind them the tanner coughed pointedly.

That evening Flood brought several of the undyed skins back to the *Bee*. He stretched one of them on a board, in preparation for making parchment endpapers. Then he found Darka and had her bring him the sealskin left over from the making of the coats.

φ

From Trincomalee they stood southwest for Madagascar, hoping to pass quickly through the equatorial zone, where the weather refused to obey the almanacs. Day after day they were driven before the wind and drenched with rain. When the storms at last ceased the *Bee* was becalmed under a yellow haze. The sea turned bile green, hardly seeming to stir. In the sultry heat their wet clothing refused to dry. When they took it down from the shrouds in the morning it would still be damp, giving them rashes, and chills when night came.

At noon, not even the merest horsetail swish of breeze stirred the air. They went about their daily chores in a surly silence, avoiding one another's eyes, their conversation at supper pared down to the mere necessities of table etiquette. Finally Darka stitched some odd scraps of canvas together, and Turini hung the resulting patchwork bag from two spars over the side. Now they had a makeshift bathtub that was theoretically proof from sharks, and in which everyone except Flood spent the hottest hours of the day.

They sighted the coast of Madagascar, anchored to take on fresh water, and continued south. The nights grew colder, and with the relentless damp everyone, with the exception of Flood, succumbed to fever. The twins were struck the worst blow. They lay in their hammocks shivering and crying out now and again from the depths of nightmares that they appeared to be sharing. At a suggestion from Snow, Turini heated chain shot in the furnace and hung the linked cannonballs in their sleeping compartment, where for hours they radiated a dull flatiron warmth.

A southeast gale blew them into Cape Town, where they lay to for a fortnight while the twins recovered. The weather seemed to come in waves here at the land's end: a day of heat and unearthly stillness giving way to wind and icy rain.

It was in Cape Town that Flood, who had so far escaped the fever, finally succumbed to the rigours of the voyage. Despite his bad leg, he insisted on climbing with Pica up the side of Table Mountain for a view of the land beyond the colony. To the north all of Africa seemed to stretch away before them, sand flats and tawny hills giving way to faint smoke-blue ranges.

As they were descending, the sky swiftly darkened and they looked up to see a milky cloud pouring over the long flat rim of the mountain. Wet flakes of snow drifted around them as they scrambled down the path. Flood stumbled several times and Pica had to help him down the rocky slope.

As they reached the road back to town the sun splintered the clouds and birds rose everywhere from the steaming grass. Rounding a curve, they glimpsed a group of what looked like children in ragged sheepskins flitting across the road and disappearing into the bramble hedge on the other side. The last of the children paused at the edge of the impenetrable green wall, glancing over her shoulder as they passed. Pica saw that she was a young woman. Under the brim of her goatskin hat her buttery skin gleamed.

She turned to her father to tell him what she had seen and found him lying face down in the road.

They were rescued by a Dutchwoman who happened to be riding past in her carriage. She took them to her house on the outskirts of the colony and had Flood out to bed and tended by her Hottentot servants. Pica rode back to the ship in the Dutchwoman's carriage to let the others know what had happened. She returned in the evening to find her father awake and seemingly recovered. They were sitting together, chatting, on the enormous whitewashed verandah. As Pica approached she noted that the Dutchwoman had a frontage every bit as impressive as her house.

– Your daughter, the woman said, is a rare blossom. She would be married by now if she lived here.

– I would not, Pica said.

The woman laughed and touched Flood on the shoulder.

– They all say that at her age. I certainly did. But I grew to love my husband in time, more than I thought possible.

THE CURIOUS CONFESSION
OF THE WIDOW JANSSENS

When he retired from the ivory trade, her husband had set off one last time to fulfil his dream of finding the source of the Nile. Like so many of his fellow hunters, he was convinced the headwaters of the great river had to lie not much farther north than they had already ventured from the Cape. How vast, after all, could Africa be?

She was born in this country. She knew that it bred men who made such journeys. Her father had been one of them. It did not matter where they thought they were headed or what direction they took. The destination was always the same.

One of her Hottentot women came to speak with her a few days before his expedition set off. She gave the widow a little grey egg-shaped stone with a hole in either end, and told her about the little animal that lived inside it.

Her people kept these stones with them whenever a loved one went on a journey. The insect inside them, the *kamma*, spun its own thread from the thread of the loved one's path through the world. A thread as difficult to see as the Hottentots themselves could be when it suited them. One of them could be standing at your elbow for hours and you would not be aware of it.

– The people with shiny skin, Pica ventured.
The widow sipped at her coffee and nodded.
– They grease themselves in sheepfat. Stinks to heaven but keeps the fleas off, and believe me, you want to do that here. They're the most practical people in the world.

While the loved one was away, those left behind wove the thread of the *kamma* into their clothing, their hair, sometimes their skin. In this way they bound the wanderer to their lives, their bodies.

Without saying anything to her husband, who despised heathen customs, she tore out the stitching of her wedding gown and after he was gone replaced it slowly, a few stitches each day, with the thread of the *kamma*.

For a while he was able to send back letters with those among his party who gave up the search and returned. She learned that they had travelled for weeks and weeks, and there was always more veld, more deserts and more mountains, with rivers flowing from them to the east and the west. Never to the north.

Then the letters stopped, and she had only the thread of the *kamma* to tell her that he was alive.

As the weeks and months wore on the thread grew thinner and she knew that, one by one, his companions were leaving him. In the trembling of the gossamer filament she heard the thunder of sudden torrents down dry streambeds, sweeping men and horses away. When the thread made her fingertips itch, she saw bodies blackening in the sun, half-eaten by carnivorous ants. A prick of the needle showed her a vision of men lying naked, quilled like porcupines with Xhosa arrows.

Then the thread of his journey thickened again, as through it twined another thread, hair-thin and black. She guessed that someone had joined him, and that this someone was a woman. When the end of the thread slid out of the stone and there was no more, she knew that he would never return.

– I hated him then for betraying me, the widow said. But over the years I understood what I had done. How I had betrayed him, too. I had bound him to me with the finely spun guts of a continent. He was not leaving me so much as joining an endless web.

As it was dark by the time the widow finished her tale, she convinced Flood and Pica to stay the night. In the morning she treated them to a vast breakfast, again on the verandah, and insisted they remain with her for a few more days before setting off again on so long a journey.

The widow Janssens leaned across the breakfast table and held Flood's wrist in her hand.

– Your father's pulse, she said to Pica. Still fluttering like a bird's. You cannot let him leave.

Pica was relieved when Flood turned down the widow's invitation, although he did accept a skein of *kamma* thread as a token of remembrance.

When at last the *Bee* stood off from the Cape, a line of ships with tattered sails ranged up on her stern. It was the merchant fleet. The captain of the flagship came across in a cutter to find out how they had accomplished their record passage into homeward waters.

They headed northwest into the Atlantic and once more, after a few days of scurrying along in the midst of lumbering giants, they left the fleet behind.

On the island of St. Helena, where they watered, Snow prowled the harbour lanes with Pica in tow, and learned that the *Acheron* had been sighted three days earlier, headed south.

As they neared the English coast, Flood began to tell stories of London, delivering them unbidden and without warning, like prophecies.

He spoke of the navy press gangs with their cudgels, filling the rosters of warships with the bruised. The pimps and bawds prowling like sharks for hungry, credulous girls. And boys. The Mohocks, aristocrats who daubed their faces with paint and stalked the streets at night, slitting off the noses of their victims, gouging out eyes.

φ

London was smoke.

At dawn they passed Execution Dock, where the tarred bodies of pirates hung in gibbets, and passed into a world of ghosts. Pale ash whitened the rails and rigging. Fog drifted upon the waves like wraiths. Near the custom house the *Bee* slid unnoticed between two towering coal hulks riding at anchor, their masts vanishing into a yellow haze. On the dock great vats of caulking tar bubbled and steamed, stirred by boys with blackened faces.

They could not see the city, but all their other senses told them it was there. They could smell its filthy gutters and burning rubbish heaps, hear its human clamour, feel the tremor of innumerable feet and hooves and carriage wheels. And then there were Flood's stories, to fill the streets they could not see with menace.

Pica disappeared into the great cabin with Darka, and when they emerged an hour later everyone was startled by the unexpected appearance of a girl decked out in a hooped gown of yellow tabby silk, lavender petticoats, and shoes of silk damask.

Pica's unkempt hair, which had grown long during the voyage, had been upswept into a powdered coiffure and topped with a pinner of lace. Darka, it turned out, had kept a secret in the days before they reached London, altering one of her old costumes to Pica's size. To find Madame Beaufort, she reasoned, Pica might need to get in through any number of doors, most of which would be closed to an unbrushed tomboy in patched breeches.

The contortionist had watched the others listen in dread to his stories, Flood realized, and had grasped his underlying lesson. This was a city extending not so much in the familiar directions of the compass as in sundered zones of fortune and desolation, with hidden passageways that could transport you from one to the other in an eyeblink.

Snow turned Pica around, inspected her, and gave an unexpected nod of approval.

– You could hide a brace of pistols under all that stuff.

Flood ventured out and hired a wherry to take them upriver. As they climbed into the boat, Snow took her leave of them and went off alone. She had reached an agreement with Flood: once the printer had found a place to set up shop, the *Bee* was hers to take where she wished, provided she could gather a crew.

The wherry slid through the oily smoke standing on the river, skirting the sudden phantom shapes of barges, skiffs, and other passenger boats plying the sullen waves. In reply to Flood's question about the smoke, the boatman told them that it had been an unusually hot and dry spring, which was always good for a rash of fires around town. Most of the murk, though, came from the bonfires and the rockets sent up last night, a burst of patriotic fervour following the latest news from the American colonies.

As if unable to contain himself, he launched into a tune.

Soon we'll teach these bragging foes
That Beef and Beer give Heavier Blows
Than Soup and Roasted Frogs

While the boatman piled verse upon verse, the wherry ran the foaming cataract between the derelict piers of London Bridge, and slid at last into the crush of boats at Blackfriars Stairs.

In an ashen twilight they climbed to Ludgate Hill, following Flood's memory of the streets. Every now and then they skirted dark alleys lit by fires around which ragged figures huddled, staring sullenly out at the traffic in the street. They passed a man dressed as a dervish, ringed by a pack of gaping children, about to swallow a sputtering rag torch. On their left hand, below the crumbling embankment, the filth-choked, reeking Fleet Ditch steamed in the morning chill like a river of the underworld.

At the top of the hill they stood at the edge of a great thoroughfare, uncertain what direction to take. Pica was shoved from behind and stumbled forward into the street, so that only Snow's quick clutching of her cloak saved her from a collision with a passing coach horse. They looked around to see who had caused the mishap, but the crowd was too thick for any one culprit to be singled out.

They stopped the next hackney coach that came along, driven by a man with a hand of dirty, frayed playing-cards pinned to his hat. When he asked them where they would like to go, no one spoke. Overwhelmed by the city itself, they had not thought that far ahead.

– We're looking for someone, Pica finally said. We don't know where to begin.

The coachman replied that if it was someone who might prove difficult to find, they should visit the booksellers around St. Paul's.

– A book is a confession, after all. Those fellows know all the secrets.

– They used to say you could get anything here, Flood observed.

– Still true, sir, the coachman said, nodding solemnly. Even the Spanish pox.

Flood asked about the news from the colonies.

– A young major, name of Washington, the coachman said, surprised a troop of Frenchies in hiding and peppered them good. Supposedly shot their commander just as he was waving some sort of official paper he'd been sent to deliver. If that's the case, I ask, why was he hiding in the woods? But now Paris is howling bloody murder. There'll be out-and-out war at this rate, mark my words. They're rioting for it on both sides of the channel.

At the bottom of the hill they passed an inn gutted by fire. A man in a soot-blackened apron sat on the pavement with his head in his hands.

– Tragedy at the Belle Savage, the coachman shouted down to them like a tour guide. Handsome officer and young gentlewoman, pretty little biscuit. Take a room as man and wife, up from the country for the celebration. Round midnight the husband arrives, forces his way upstairs, and catches the lovers in a state of dishabby, which is French for your clothes mostly off. Furious oaths. Blood-curdling shrieks. Flash of rapiers in the candlelight. *Ting, tang, skling, sklang.* And finally *sshhtuck.* Husband mortally wounded, expiring on the floor. Night watch rushes in, apprehends the captain fleeing out the window in his nightshirt. In the confusion, candle knocked over, curtains catch fire. Conflagration.

The coachman tapped the cards on his hat as he dealt out the remainder.

– Pretty gentlewoman brought home insensible. Yesterday learns of her gallant officer: Newgate's newest tenant. Public rendezvous with a rope expected shortly. Despair of the gentlewoman knows no bounds. Takes poison with her afternoon tea. Dying whisper to nursie: *Bring me my little girl.* Last kiss. Poor lame poppet left an orphan.

The coach drew up suddenly as a fancy carriage crossed their path, its gilt facings in the shapes of unicorns and gryphons flashing at them through the murk. Like spectators in the dark of a theatre pit they gaped as a mythological tableau traversed the stage.

– Where will she go? Pica asked. The little girl.

– If she's lucky there're rich relations to take her in. Though with a start like she's had I wouldn't wager her a happy life.

Their progress was halted next by a crowd of people milling in the street. The cries of hawkers selling oranges, chestnuts, and ballad sheets competed with the shouting and banter of the crowd, the wails of children lost in the crush, the barking of dogs. The Turinis shrank together in their seat, staring out the window in frightened wonder at the roaring tide of humanity as it seethed around the coach.

– Newgate just up the street, the coachman shouted over the din. A load of condemned men being carted off to Tyburn this morning. And there's the summoning bell. Won't be long now.

They spent the rest of the morning in the narrow, winding

lanes around St. Paul's, going from bookshop to bookshop, asking everyone they met if they knew of a Madame Beaufort. Once in a while the proprietor recognized Flood and grumbled that it was a long time since he had seen fit to grace them with his merchandise. At Pica's insistence they stopped in at all the other shops as well, print sellers and sheet-music sellers, jewellers and clockmakers, engravers and silversmiths, gathering a few unpromising scraps of rumour and hearsay. A certain duke owned a prize racehorse named Beaufort, and Beaufort was also the name of a lady's wigmaker in St. Martin's Lane, famous for the scandalous shapes of his creations. By noon the smoke had thinned enough that the dome of the cathedral appeared, its golden cross flickering in the haphazard sunlight like a cold, distant flame.

With the clearing of the sky, a damp, sweltering heat descended. The jostling crowd around them reeked and steamed like cattle, and with the exception of Pica, who seemed to thrive on the noise and confusion, they all began to droop. Turini and his wife, their faces pale with shock and exhaustion, clung to the young twins, who by now had overcome their earlier fear and strained to be let loose.

Flood found himself in a borderland between this city and the one he remembered, only now and then recognizing streets, shop signs, monuments, like beckoning islands in an unfamiliar sea.

They were rolling past the dust and flying straw of Smithfield Market when Flood suddenly spoke.

– It was near here, he said. My old shop.

Pica wanted to stop, but Flood pictured her disappointment when she saw the sort of place he was asking to live. He insisted they go on.

– There's nothing there.

It was clear to him that she had not yet grasped the futility of this random pursuit of a vague clue, a name, in the biggest city on earth. There were other ways, more likely places to search, but he held off mentioning them for now, unwilling to snatch hope away from her too soon.

The shops around the cathedral had turned up very little, and so the coachman again became their guide.

– Covent Garden, he suggested. Rumour mill of the city.

From Fleet Street to the Strand the coach was swept along in a rushing river of foot, horse, and vehicle traffic, besieged by a thousand contending sights, clashing sounds, and odours borne to them on the broiling air. London was every place they had been: the crowds and the murkiness of Venice. The heat of Alexandria. The many-tongued babble of Canton.

When they struck a shoal of oyster stalls on the edge of the Haymarket, they abandoned the coach and set out on foot, but not before engaging the coachman's services for an indefinite period. It was agreed that he would meet them at Blackfriars Stairs every morning at eight.

They passed through a maze of winding alleys lined with shops selling oddities and marvels. At each grimy window the twins would stop and press their faces against the glass, gaping at comical masks and animal disguises, ingenious toys, marvellously iced pastries and chocolate-dipped sweetmeats, until their mother or father tugged them away by the hand.

Their way led them through a sort of roofed tunnel with shops on either hand. A sallow-faced young woman stood leaning in a doorway, watching them pass with cold, unswerving eyes. A long, livid scar ran down one side of her face. At the tunnel's end Pica glanced back and saw that she had vanished.

In Covent Garden the carpenter and his wife at last discovered a London they could understand: the realm of amazement. Under the colonnades of the Piazza inventors, clowns, conjurers, and snake charmers jostled for elbow room. Everywhere they turned another spectacle greeted them. On a raised stage near the centre of the square two Amazons in tinsel armour trading meaty smacks. Gaudy puppet theatres staging Noah's Flood and the Siege of Troy. Waxwork booths promising gory tableaux of famous executions. Barkers thundering from curtained platforms where giantesses, two-headed men, and other human monstrosities would display themselves to the public for six-pence, with Turkey-chairs at the ready for fainting women.

As a trial, the Turinis appropriated a tiny patch of open ground, strategically close to a seller of sugared ices, where Darka and the twins prepared a hastily improvised tumbling act. Lolo sulked at first, lamenting a brightly coloured paper whirligig he had seen spinning in a toy-shop window. When Turini suggested the toy could be his if he earned it, he threw off his moodiness and joined his mother and sister. Thanks in part to the ice seller, they swiftly attracted a crowd, and Turini's overturned hat soon began clinking out the music of tossed pennies.

Pica had her first success as well. She spoke to a girl in a bird costume, posting handbills for a *Pageant of the Fall of Rome*, who told her that a grand lady like the Duchess of Beaufort would never set foot in a sinkhole like this. The place to go was Ranelagh Gardens, where the quality went to look at each other. And to eat. She knew. She had acted there for them, while they sat guzzling wine and stuffing themselves silly with goose.

– I don't know the place, Flood told Pica. It wasn't here in my time.

It was getting late in the day, he told her, and the best course was to return to the ship and look for Ranelagh in the morning. To his surprise, she gave in without protest and he looked at her more closely, realizing from the sag of her shoulders that the city had finally worn her down. They were returning to where they had left the Turinis when Flood halted suddenly in front of a narrow shopfront under a dirty blue-and-grey awning. The brass plate on the door read *A. Martin. Colle, Carton, Cartes á jouer.*

– What is it? Pica asked, but Flood was already pushing open the door.

Monsieur Martin was confined to a wheeled chair, but still supervised his four sons at the making of the finest playing cards in London. When he recognized Flood, the old man began to weep.

– *Nicolas*, he growled, wiping his eyes. My boy, I thought you were dead.

– Not yet, Papa Martin. I've been away a long time.

The old man leaned forward in his chair and squinted at Pica, his brows knitting.

– Can this be . . . Marguerite?

– This is my daughter, Papa Martin.

The old man patted the air with a shaky hand.

– Of course, of course. Forgive a witless old dotard. Are you still printing books, *Nicolas*?

– I am. And I'm in need of your finest paste.

– For something very special, eh? Your father would be proud.

Old Martin clapped his hands and one of his sons appeared through a doorway curtained in strips of leather.

– Jean, a bottle of the family stock. *Vingt-neuf.*

When his son had bowed and gone out again, the old man turned to Pica.

– Did your father tell you, *ma petite miette*, why so many of our people went into trades that involve paste?

– No, monsieur.

– In France, in the terrible days, they wouldn't let us bury our dead. We had to take them with us. Until it was safe to lay them properly to rest. Can you guess how we kept them hidden?

– Bones, Pica said, after a moment's thought. Paste is made from bones.

– A clever little *coquille*, *Nicolas*, the old man chuckled. I can see she is yours. Yes, child. What better way to hide the bones we weren't supposed to have than in a heap of other bones? To be sure, from time to time a bit of one's ancestors ended up by accident in the glue vat. . . .

A catarrhal laugh shook him as he struggled to finish.

– We Huguenots, he choked out, can truly say that we bury ourselves in our work.

Old Martin's son returned with a squat, neatly labelled brown bottle. As Flood dug for his coin-purse, the old man waved his hand, his eyes brimming again with tears.

– Take it, *Nicolas*. It was good of you to visit. Corpses like me only live when people remember.

– I'll come again soon, Papa Martin.

The old man was already wheeling himself backwards into the gloom of the shop, no longer looking at them.

– Yes. Yes. Soon.

– Who is Marguerite? Pica asked when they were back outside among the crowds.

– My sister, Meg. She died when we were children.

φ

As a lid of smoke closed again over the streets, they rejoined the Turinis and made their way to Blackfriars Stairs, dazed and footsore. When they arrived at the ship they found Snow had already returned, with even less to show for her day. Those sailors, she found, who weren't already indentured to other vessels were in hiding from the press gangs. The few she was able to buttonhole in taverns and gambling dens eyed her with distrust and refused to go have a look at the *Bee*, plainly suspecting that a woman, *a black woman at that*, could only be the navy's latest lure.

That night Pica sat up in her bunk, aware as always of the sounds of her father's nightly vigil. The rhythmic creaking of the press timbers had lulled her to sleep often on their journey. Tonight she was restless, her pulse seeming to beat out of time with that of the press.

All day her eyes had been open so wide that even in the dark she could not will them closed. The city was within her now. Its smoke, its clatter and hum and flash. The quicksilver of its being had seeped through her skin and into her blood. Her father's history, its sombre current, now ran there as well.

Goaded by her whirling thoughts she left her bed and climbed on deck. Beyond the slap of the waves, the hull's familiar hollow bump against the pier, she could hear the alien sounds of London. A foreign language. Scraps of voices raised in brawling, laughter, and song drifted brokenly to her. The smash of glass. The clatter of carriages transporting merry-makers to yet another party.

The wall of night was lit here and there with the glow of ceaselessly burning outdoor fires. Dizzily she felt herself floating in the blackness between the stars. She thought of the children out there, living in the streets. Foraging. She had seen them during the day, distinguishable only in size from the grown-ups around them. The same cold watchfulness in their eyes.

Madame Beaufort was out there, too. Somewhere.

She remembered a woman she had seen in the morning near the cathedral, leaving a milliner's shop with a hatbox wrapped in pale blue paper. Tall, graceful, about the right age, she thought. While her father ducked into another bookshop she had followed the woman down the street, rehearsing in her head the moment when she caught her up, spoke to her. *Pardon me, ma'am, but I was wondering . . .*

She was about to make her approach when a man stepped up to the woman, leaned his face close to hers and spoke harshly. The woman frowned, took his arm, and they went off together around the corner. Pica turned and went back to the bookshop where she had left her father. He stood waiting for her at the door. When she came up he put a hand on her shoulder. *That wasn't her*, he had said quietly.

The creak of a plank behind her. She turned. Amphitrite Snow stood there in her father's hat and redingote.

– Caught me again, little girl.

– Where are you going?

Snow plucked Turini's hat and storm-cloak from their hook under the binnacle.

– You want to find out, put these on.

Pica obeyed, following the young woman over the side and into the darkness of the dockside streets.

– I was thinking about that drunken fool we met in Canton, Snow whispered. There are plenty more where he came from, I would imagine.

She kept on swiftly through the blackness as if possessed of cat's eyes, halting now and then at corners and reaching a hand back to stop Pica, while a carriage or a man being lighted home by a link-boy passed in front of them. Once they had to crouch in a doorway, holding their breath as another clutch of night prowlers glided past, the reek of gunpowder the only certain evidence of their presence. Pica could not help thinking of her father's stories of London's terrors. She had listened to them as if they were tales from a vanished age. Now that city of words was all around her in the dark, as close as a breath. She was on the point of insisting they turn back, but she held her tongue and crept along in silence.

Finally, in a covered archway between two courts, Snow found what she was looking for. A hatless man came staggering up the tunnel, splashing in and out of the gutter on a weaving course towards them.

– Silver buckles, I believe, Snow said. And gold trim. He's our fop.

Pica felt something poke her in the ribs. From her coat Snow had produced the two ancient flintlock pistols that usually hung above the door of the great cabin.

– I thought those didn't work.

– They'll work well enough.

A few steps from where they crouched the man suddenly stopped and turned towards the wall. They heard soft curses as he fumbled with his clothes, then a moan of pleasure as his stream began to splatter against the wall.

Snow nudged Pica.

– Here we go.

– No.

She grabbed Pica's cloak sleeve and tugged her into the alley. They froze as the man's voice hacked through the silence.

– Not worth a piss.

He was leaning forward, his head touching the wall.

– You hear me? Not worth a poxy piss. In a 'pothecary's pot. Say, that's rather good, isn't it? Have to tell it to the mistress.

Snow darted forward and shoved both pistols into the man's back.

– Your money, she said, her voice lowered to a growl. The man started and then laughed sourly.

– May I finish first?

His stream died to a trickle and then ceased. He shook himself once expertly and calmly began buttoning up his breeches.

– Thank you. You're a lad of good breeding.

– Thanks to my mother, Snow said. Now hand it over.

– What? The goodfellow?

– Your money. And don't turn around.

The man dug in the breast pocket of his jacket and hoisted a leather pouch over his shoulder.

– Always the cash. The world never wants anything else. My philosophy of life. The noble sentiments of my heart. The lessons that bitter experience has stamped upon my soul.

– Pocketwatch, too. And rings.

The watch was delivered. There were no rings. The man, still leaning with his head up against the wall, mumbled something Pica did not catch. Forgetting herself, she whispered to Snow.

— What did he say?

— I said, go ahead and do it. Finish the job, my dears.

Back in the great cabin, Snow spilled the contents of the pouch on the table and began sorting the coins.

— Pretty good. Not great, but a decent start.

Pica stood in the doorway, hugging herself against the chill. Snow glanced up and rolled her eyes.

— We didn't hurt anyone, she said. He would've spent this on gambling or drink anyways.

Pica looked away.

— Without money, Snow said, I can't hire a crew.

Pica felt sure the young woman was keeping something from them. She had been so eager to reach London, the one place on the globe the renegade Commander dared not pursue her. And now that she was here, she was just as eager to set sail again.

— When you leave, Pica said, where will you go?

— Are you thinking of coming with me?

— I . . .

— Not sure, eh?

Snow picked up a coin.

— Here's one way to decide.

With a flick of her thumb she sent the coin spinning and caught it in a fist.

φ

The next morning the Turinis rose earlier than anyone to claim their valuable piece of ground in Covent Garden. At the end of that first promising day, Darka had unpacked and mended their costumes and Turini accompanied them with a collapsible platform on wheels that he had hammered together out of planks left over from the refit of the *Bee*.

Flood and Pica found the coachman waiting for them at the Stairs, huddled in his cloak against the morning chill. He roused himself and his horse and drove them south, through Charing Cross and into the genteel streets and squares of Westminster. At the gates of Ranelagh Gardens they asked the coachman to wait for them, bought tickets, and strolled with surprise into another realm, a sedate, orderly labyrinth of trees, fountains, colonnades, and pavilions.

After wandering for a while they made their first wary approaches to the fashionable. The women would barely deign to look at them, and the few men they were able to attract were clearly only interested in Pica as a kind of novelty. A fat, painted man in high-heeled shoes followed them at a distance before finally veering into their path. He blinked at Pica through an eyeglass.

– Did we not meet in Venice? A year or so ago, I believe.

Flood took Pica's arm to draw her away, but she broke from his grasp.

– Do you know the Duchess of Beaufort?

– The Duchess, is it? the painted man said. My dear child, I can be a duchess for you, if you like. But yes, she and I have a passing acquaintance. In fact, I believe she is here today, holding court in the Temple of Chocolate. Do you see the Moorish-looking turrets, peeking up over the grove of orange trees?

Flood thanked him brusquely, and as he and Pica were turning away he called after them,

– It was delicious running into you again. If you need anyone else, I'll be here.

The Duchess was tiny, a doll child disguised as a woman. The tips of her shoes swung just above the Persian carpet. Her stubby fingers struggled with the huge china serving boat.

– It was so delightful of you to call, she said, pouring Pica another saucerful of chocolate. And you've come from so far away, too. Goodness, the world is too large to bear thinking on. My father went to India ten years ago. I was a baby then. I don't remember him. He caught a brain fever and died there. I like to think of him resting under a banyan tree. I don't know what a banyan tree looks like, but it sounds like a restful sort of tree, don't you think?

– It does, miss, Pica said.

– There's just Mama and me now, and she stays in bed all day. She's gotten quite fat now, the silly dear. She won't see anyone.

She giggled, her pagoda of powdered hair wobbling.

– Well, almost no one. My brother's gone, too. His name is George. Such a loving, thoughtful son and brother. How we wept when he went away to that island in the Caribbean – I can't recall the name just now, St. Somebody-or-other. . . . He writes us six letters a year. Sometimes we get them all at once, though, if there was a hurricane. Or pirates. Sometimes we don't get any letters for a long time. He's getting on swimmingly in his business, he says, which has something to do with the blacks. He sent me one for my last birthday.

– One what, miss?

— A black. For a manservant. Mama gave the fellow our name. Because he's so lovely, with his skin like chocolate, and so strong. *Beau. Fort.* You see?

She reached up a tiny hand and tugged at the bell pull above her sofa.

— He's just outside. I'll fetch him. You'll see.

In the white mask of her face her watchful eyes danced.

— More chocolate?

The serving boat hovered ominously over Flood's knees.

— No thank you, he said. Has your family always lived here? In England, I mean?

She giggled again.

— Of course, silly. Mama and I were both born just across the street. Did you think we were from Asiatic Tartary?

— No, miss. We've been searching for someone with the same name . . .

— Oh, yes. I know. When your family is as old as ours, people steal your name for all sorts of things. There's a wig-maker . . .

— Yes, we've heard of him, Flood said.

— And a fortune teller and a boxer . . .

— A fortune teller, Pica said, leaning forward.

The Duchess pouted into her cup.

— I haven't been to see her, of course, she said. Mama won't let me. Although Mama does have her odd notions, too. She says when she dies she wants to be buried under a tree, like Father. A palm tree. Beaufort's managed to grow one here, the clever fellow.

φ

Back out in the gardens, the swampy heat was now as suffocating as anything they had endured on their ocean crossing. They were drawn into the dusky cool of the serpentine grove, a tree-lined path that turned back on itself in a figure eight. Statues of goddesses lined the pathway and drew Pica onward, until she came out opposite the Temple of Chocolate again, and found that Flood was no longer with her.

She retraced her steps and found him standing in the centre of the grove. He stared blankly at her, seemingly without recognition.

– Only if one, he muttered, stops moving . . .

Pica insisted that they return to the ship, where he went straight to the press room.

That night, when Snow came to take her on another nocturnal excursion, Pica pulled the blanket over her head and lay in her bunk, listening to the young woman's footsteps die away. Then she realized that there was no sound from below. She got up and crept down the hatchway stairs. Her father was sitting at his work table, threading a needle. A pot of glue bubbled on the water-bath nearby. For a while she watched him, and when he spoke suddenly, she jumped.

– What's the matter, Pica. Can't sleep?

She climbed the rest of the way down and joined him at the work table.

– I didn't hear the press, she said. I came to see . . .

– If I was finished?

She kept silent, not sure in what sense he meant it.

He set the threaded needle aside and turned to look at her.

– Almost.

He nodded towards the sewing frame on his work table, in which sat a small, coverless volume she had not noticed until now.

– The type is still liquid, he said, but it isn't producing any more new formes. I thought it was time to bind what I had. Whatever that may be.

He took up the needle and thread and bent again to his work. Pica pulled up another chair, sat beside her father and watched him complete the sewing and then the rest of the binding. With the plough he cut the unruly fore-edge smooth. Tiny motes of paper shavings swirled into the candlelight and after a moment Flood raised his head, turned away and sneezed.

– That happens every time, he said.

He pasted the dyed, stiffened sealskin cover to the end-papers of Trincomalee parchment, rounded the back and worked the leather along the French groove, moulded the head and tail pieces. As always when he worked at these final stages of a book, he whispered soft words of encouragement to the inanimate materials he was urging into shape.

Pica watched and listened, and then asked,

– What was that you were talking about today, in the garden?

He looked up at her, frowning.

– Talking about . . .

– *Only if one stops moving*, you said.

– Oh. Yes. I was thinking about a book I once made. For your grandfather. It was about two young lovers, searching for one another. As long as both of them kept moving their story could never end. The Count was not impressed, so I gave it to your mother to keep. I suppose it's lost now.

At last on the table sat a thick, compact volume, slightly narrower than ordinary pocket-size, bound in soft, dark green leather. The rhythm of the work had lulled her, and when her father spoke next she stretched as if waking.

– We'll leave it under the pressing boards overnight, he said, leaning back in his chair and rubbing his eyes. Let the binding take.

He picked up the book to place it under the pressing boards, turned it over in his hands for a moment and then held it out to her.

– My father used to say, *Make a beautiful thing, but remember, it is not only the material object we strive for. The work is not finished until the book passes into the hands of a reader.*

Pica took the book from him. The cover seemed to breathe under her hand like the hide of a living thing.

– It's so warm, she said.

– The paste, Flood nodded. It will cool.

She was about to open the book, then set it back down on the table.

– All the work you've done. Shouldn't you keep . . . ?

– This one is unlike any other I've printed. It was made, somehow, out of all that has happened to us. What we have been, and will be. Even things hidden, and lost. That means it is your book, too. And maybe more yours than mine.

– How could it be? It belongs to you.

– I was thinking, he said, of the story you told me, not so long ago. About your life in Venice.

– I didn't tell it right, she said with an embarrassed shrug. Not the way I wanted to. I couldn't find the words to say it all.

– You were trying to tell everything. Everything that mattered to you, that was you. Do you remember what Samuel Kirshner said, about the books that come to be when someone dreams them?

– Yes.

– Perhaps this will become such a book, for you. When you enter its pages, I can't say for certain what you'll find. But no doubt it will enchant you, set you puzzles, even lead you astray. Wherever the book takes you, Pica, remember the way that led there, and you'll know the way to go on.

He placed the book between the heavy wooden pressing boards and tied them together with twine. She was tired now, and cold, and so she rose to leave. On the steps she halted to watch him tidying up, methodically cleaning and putting away his scattered tools, as if this work day had been like any other. She felt she should say something more, let him know that this, too, mattered to her.

– Father . . .

– Yes?

Once again, she could not find the words.

– Good night.

φ

The next morning, when Pica went down to the press room, he was not there. The book sat on the work table in the pale light from the hatch, a real book, ordinary and unknown.

Her father had gone up into the city, Turini told her at breakfast, to find his old shop.

She stepped out onto the quarterdeck, driven by a vague feeling of alarm. Up to now they had gone everywhere together. Standing at the taffrail she scanned the roofs and steeples, sharpening out of grey obscurity as the sky lightened.

He would be fine out there. He had lived here. This was his city.

She went back down to the press room, sat at the work table and stared for a long time at the book her father had made, before finally picking it up and opening it at random, somewhere near the middle. Fearing a desert of blank paper she was relieved to see rows of small, close-spaced print. She did not try to read at first, but flipped with her thumb through several pages, then shut the book again, held it in her hand, hefted it, felt the reassuring weight of a real book.

Everything that mattered, her father had said. Everything she was a part of. Things hidden and lost.

She opened the book again, this time at the beginning. Several pages, she could not tell how many, slipped between her thumb and the inside front cover. Try as she might, she could not reach the very first page, if there was one. The first few leaves, impossibly thin, evaded her blunt fingers.

She began to read at the first page she could reach, found a table of contents. A listing of numbered chapters, but in no apparent order.

XC. The briefest of chapters, nevertheless containing a very long kiss.

VII. In which a choice of evils lies before the reader.

LV. Storm, shipwreck, earthquake, and a preliminary note on what followed.

XXXVII. Containing little or nothing.

IX. How they were going to cut off the Princess's head, and how they did not cut it off.

DC. Containing a multitude of things the reader may not have expected to find in it.

MCDLV. A chapter which would best follow the concluding chapter of the narrative, and which has thus been placed here to prevent its exclusion from the book.

She suddenly understood that she might search for these chapters but never find them. In such a book they could remain ever out of reach, tantalizing and perfect. She thought of how she approached other books. On the shelf or just opened, a book was all possibility, a wondrous box of paper that could contain anything.

CCLXV. A chapter within a chapter within a chapter within a chapter within a chapter . . .

Repeated to the bottom of the page, and onto the next. She turned another page, and then another and another.

. . . within a chapter within a chapter within a chapter . . .

She felt a surge of panic and shut the book. A dizzying fear had come over her that in the few moments she had been reading time had raced on past her in the real world: days, months, years . . . Footsteps clumping across the planks overhead told her that the others were still aboard, getting ready for the day.

She would join them, but not yet. Not yet.

She opened the book again and riffled through, stopping here and there at random.

A minute description of someone's right ear, of the surprising contents of an iron chest buried in a sandbank beside the Orinoco River, of rain dripping from flower petals in a forest at night . . .

She found the table of contents much further on, as if the thin leaves of paper were growing out of the covers, the book like a tree.

Pages in other languages, pages of numbers and calculations, of zeros and ones. Paper dolls that could be scissored out and dressed in the clothes on adjacent pages. A tide and weather almanac for the year 2092.

She skipped from place to place. Was there any order to all of this?

Reams of baffling hieroglyphics. A description of the contents of another infinite book. A roster of forgotten lovers. A primer on how to read hieroglyphics . . .

Her question was answered by a voice speaking out of her memory. *You could ask the same thing of the universe.*

She looked up. The girl, Miza, was standing in the doorway watching her.

– We're going now, she said.

Pica closed her eyes, distracted by the giddy thought that she was still reading. For some reason she thought of the Abbé, digging ancient manuscripts from holes in wet clay walls. She opened her eyes, tucked the book into her apron pocket.

– Let's go, then.

Gently she closed the book on itself, almost certain she could hear, like the scratching of insects, its pages still turning.

φ

Flood was not sure why he had stayed away. He thought it might be the dreams that had begun to haunt the brief sleep he collapsed into in the small hours of the morning. Dreams in which he was living and working in the shop again. And in the dream someone would come to tell him that Pica was gone. The messenger was never someone he knew, and the reason was always different. Angry with him, she had gone back to Venice. She had found her mother but they could not wait for him to finish his work. In one dream she had married, and when he hurried outside he was just in time to see the wedding coach, absurdly huge, rolling away into the morning light.

In his years in the cell he had learned to trust his dreams. They had rooted him, he understood later, in a ground of sanity far beneath his printing of an imaginary book. And now he sensed that something was in danger of being lost should he revisit the place of his youth. But if he did not go, he would never know what it was.

He went along Cloth Fair, under the shadow of old St. Bartholomew's, a ridge of grey stone in the luminous morning fog. The ancient Norman church had fallen into ruin long before he was born, its porches and side-chapels invaded by commerce, its cloisters become stables. A blacksmith had his forge in the north transept: the hours of his childhood were told not by bells or hymns but by the steady ring of the hammer on the anvil. He had wandered here as a boy, led by vague dreams of adventure, amid lace-makers and tailors whose shop doors were still flanked by grimacing devils and mournful, crumbling saints. Never stopping to consider what it meant that his forebears had chosen to settle here, up against a church named for the saint whose feast day had been stained with their blood.

The entrance to Lady Chapel Court was narrower than he remembered, a gullet of wet stone. The square itself was deserted save for a ginger cat washing itself on a doorstep. The rusted old pump still stood crookedly over its weathered trough in the middle of the square.

They used to play here, with the children of the other Huguenot merchants clustered around the church. Blind man's buff. Fox and geese. He remembered a Christmas morning, Meg at the window, waking him with her breathless whisper, *Nicholas, look.* The snow that had fallen the night before was gone, leaving the dark cobbles bare except where someone had walked, pressing and hardening the snow underfoot so that it had not melted with the rest. A wandering track of white foot-prints crossed the square, circling the pump twice, turning back on itself so that the path, if there was one, was obscured by its own convolutions. Someone had passed through the court the night before, the veil of Christmas. Years later it occurred to him that the wayward tracks had probably been made by a drunken reveller weaving home. But that morning, the kind of white winter day when the world seems magical, unreal, he and Meg read another message in the unhurried meandering of those footprints. There were others like them.

Past the pump, his feet remembered their way down the sloping cobbles to the doorway of what had once been Flood and Son, Printers. The old sign with its painted book no longer hung over the lintel.. The windows were shuttered.

As he was about to knock, the door opened suddenly and a thin, sallow woman appeared with a wash basin full of dirty water in her arms. She caught sight of him and stared with wide, frightened eyes.

– May I speak to you a moment, ma'am?

She continued to stare and said nothing. He took in her dry, cracked lips, the goiter under her chin.

– I used to live here, Flood said. When it was a printing shop.

The woman nodded her head slowly.

– I've been away a long time, Flood said, and I just came to see if the house was vacant. For rent.

The woman's eyes went wider. She clutched the wash basin as if to protect it from him.

– The landlord sent you?

– No, I'm here on my own business. I just wanted to know . . .

– He's not here.

– Who?

– He won't be back till after dark. You can come in and look for yourself. He's not here.

Flood was about to protest, but the thought of seeing the shop again drew him forward. He ducked in through the door and waited in the sudden dark for the woman to take the lead. She tossed the contents of the basin onto the cobbles, shut the door, and stood beside him, her wide eyes still fixed on him, her mouth gaping.

The front room, which had been the print shop, looked much smaller and darker. Shirts and stockings hung from sagging lines along the walls. The air was close, and rank with the earthy smell of old potatoes. There was a small deal table near the window, heaped with unwashed crockery over which fat flies crawled.

– I do keep things tidy, the woman said. I've been feeling poorly this fortnight, you see. You can tell him that.

Flood nodded, glancing around for some evidence of the room he held in his memory. He found it at last in the hooks from which the laundry lines had been strung. His father had hung the damp, freshly printed sheets the same way, on wires tied to those hooks. His gaze travelled upward to the ceiling timbers and found the holes where the press had been bolted in place.

– We didn't make those, the woman said quickly. They were there before us.

He nodded and climbed the steep, narrow staircase to the upper floor, stopping halfway to knead a sliver of pain out of his bad leg. Looking back, he saw the woman watching him from the bottom of the stairs.

The doors to the two bedrooms were both slightly ajar. He stepped into the one that had been his and Meg's. Something tattered, a curtain or blanket, had been hung over the window, and he crossed the dark room with his hands outstretched to brush it aside. The light struck him like a blow and when he could see again he looked through the warped glass down into the square and saw her.

She was spinning, her red cloak bright against the snow. He scraped a nail against the frost to see her better, saw her fall into the drifted snow laughing, her arms outstretched.

He tried the latch and found it had been painted shut. When he looked again she was sitting, looking up at the window and calling to him. He saw her lips move and knew what she was saying, although he could not hear it.

Nicholas. Come outside.

He touched his fingertips to the warped pane, felt the sun's heat in the glass. She was gone. The court was dusty and bare.

A whisper of a voice spoke behind him.

– Is that you . . . ?

He turned. In one corner of the room stood a narrow bed he had not noticed in the dark. On it, covered in a heap of rags, lay the skeleton of a man or woman, he could not tell. Long white hair growing out of a yellow skull. The eyes in their deep sockets clouded, unseeing.

He backed slowly out of the room, left the house without speaking again to the woman downstairs.

For the rest of the morning he wandered, letting his feet take him where they would while his thoughts chased round and round the blank at their centre. Finally he was brought up short by a wall and looked around to see that he was at the blind end of a lane he did not recognize. There was no one about to ask, and the houses were grand but cold and unwelcoming. Had he strayed north, or south?

After an indeterminate number of turns and windings he came out unexpectedly into the clamour of Fleet Street. As he stopped to rest his throbbing leg and gain his bearings, the street began to waver before his eyes. He tried to work out how many hours it had been since he had eaten and remembered that at dawn, before Pica woke, he had wolfed down some bread. Perhaps he could eat at the coffee house the coachman had recommended, although he could not remember its name now. He held out his hands, alarmed at how badly they were shaking. A memory came to him that made him smile, Irena's white hand at the breakfast table that last morning, the tips of her fingers touching his for an instant, a secret message among the porcelain and silver.

Then his head seemed to swoop upward into the air, the street fell away from him and he found himself kneeling, gazing at drops of blood blossoming on the pavement.

– Nasty spill, sir.

Someone clutching his arm.

– I'm fine.

He climbed shakily to his feet and faced his helper, a pock-marked boy in a straw hat and grimy apron.

– Bit of a scrape.

Flood held up his hand, saw the gash below the thumb, the welling blood.

– So you'll be all right, then, sir?

A tall wicker basket stood nearby, covered in a white cloth napkin under which Flood glimpsed golden-brown rolls, the dark sheen of ale bottles stippled with droplets of condensation.

– Could I –

He patted his pockets, forgetting where he had put his purse of coins.

– Would you be able to sell me something?

– Sorry, sir, the boy said, eyeing him now with distrust. These are already paid for by a gentleman up the street. I'm on the way now to deliver them.

With a grunt he shouldered the basket, then seemed to hesitate. He plucked the napkin from the basket and handed it to Flood.

– Here. For your hand. 'Day, sir.

Numbly, Flood took the napkin and watched the boy stagger away under his load. He held the warm, starched cloth up to his face to inhale the steamy aroma of fresh-baked bread. He folded the napkin lengthwise twice, wrapped it around his hand and knotted it. A spasm of pain shot up his arm.

He had to get back to the ship before something worse happened. But instead of moving on he stood in the street, letting the unending stream of passersby flow around him.

Something Irena had once told him flitted moth-like through his thoughts. What was it? He stared about him in the street as if the answer lay there.

Here the buildings move, she had said, *and the people stand still.* She was speaking of her father's castle, of the system that, in changing ceaselessly, never changed anything that mattered.

All at once he thought of something he had seen yesterday, a fleeting image noted in passing that had only now, in the dark corridors of his mind, encountered the memory of her words. He knew now where he might find her, but still he stood, waiting, tugging at the thread connecting image and words to see if it would hold, or break and leave him stranded.

He was almost spent. It would be best to return to the ship while he was still able to make the journey. He could find Pica, bring her with him in case he lost his way again. But if the thread leading him out of the labyrinth was a lie, the answer to the wrong riddle . . .

He had to find out for himself, without raising the girl's hopes. If he was wrong it was better for her not to know.

φ

Pica stood in a great open square, a place without a name, surrounded by a milling crowd of strangers. She had bought an orange from a fruit vendor but had not yet peeled it. If she could just find the river, she was certain some familiar landmark along its banks would orient her. She had already asked three people how to get to Blackfriars Stairs and had received three different answers. That told her one thing for certain: she was a long way from the river.

In the morning she had accompanied the Turinis to Covent Garden and then struck out on her own. She had a vague idea of where to look for her father's print shop, but after losing herself among the winding lanes around St. Paul's she simply wandered. When she rested, she would take the book out of her apron and turn it over in her hands, tempted but unwilling to brave two labyrinths at the same time.

Near her, someone started to sing, in a high, sweet, perfect voice that soared above the noise of the crowd.

> Quoth I, "Such sweet lips were for kissing decreed."
> Cried she, "Very fine, very pretty indeed."
> I kissed her and pressed her still more to obtain,
> Till she sprang from my arms and flew over the plain.

The song pealed like a bell through the hot, dusty air. She looked around but could not find the singer through the foot and horse traffic that passed on all sides of her.

> Like Daphne she strove my embrace to elude;
> Like Phoebus, I quickened my pace and pursued.

Pica looked up. The slightest of breezes swept dust in swirls from the pavement. Around her, heads began lifting to the sky in expectation of heavenly relief.

> What followed, ye lovers, must never be said,
> But 'twas all very fine, very pretty indeed.

As the last line ended, a shadow persisting at the edge of her vision made her turn. Amphitrite Snow stood nearby, dressed in the straw bonnet and frock of a servant.

– Put black skin in a slave's clothes, Snow said, replying to Pica's look of surprise, and no one looks twice. It's been useful, especially today.

– You've been following me.

– You should be thankful, Snow nodded. You're lost, aren't you?

Pica fought back tears.

– We should go back to the *Bee*, Snow said.

– I haven't found my father.

– Perhaps he's returned to the ship on his own.

She took Pica's arm and glanced around nervously.

– What is it?

She had gone downriver to Wapping, she told Pica as she tugged her along, to the taverns where newly arrived sailors drank away the wait for their next outbound berth.

– All the talk, Snow said, was of the huge warship they had passed in the estuary.

A gleaming white legend, riding placidly at anchor. As to how long it had been there or why it had come, there were many speculations, but she had kept her own thought to herself: if the Commander was offering such a temptation to his former masters in the Admiralty, it could only mean he knew that his quarry was close at hand.

φ

A freshly-painted sign swung above the door.

The Indian & Conundrum.
All welcome.

Flood ducked through the low entryway and entered a room full of trestle tables at which men sat, noisily manhandling newspapers or huddled together in close conference. At the back a huge silver urn stood burbling and steaming on a squat four-legged stove, a turtle in black armour.

He sat at an empty table and one of the boys running up and down the aisles brought him a pot of coffee and a cup. A burly red-faced man left his stool by the urn and sat down heavily beside Flood.

– The name's Henday, sir. This is my coffee house. Your first visit, I believe.

– I don't know, Flood said. I was on my way . . . somewhere. I can't remember.

– By good fortune, the man said with a toothless grin, your steps have directed you to the one establishment where uncertainty is a virtue. The actors frequent Bedford's, the politicians conspire at Will's, the doctors compare cures and corpses at Child's. Here we cater not so much to occupations, however, as to preoccupations. Phantoms of unreason, obsessions, mysterious perturbations of the spirit. First cup is always gratis.

– I just need a moment. To gather my thoughts.

– I understand, sir. We all have such days. Don't hesitate to shout if you feel the need to talk.

Henday heaved himself from the bench and lumbered off. Flood took a gulp of coffee, grimacing as the bitter liquid burned its way down inside him. It would have made more sense to eat something. This vacancy in his thoughts was simply the result of an empty stomach. He looked up to see that Henday had returned and was leaning forward to whisper in his ear.

– Pardon my intrusion, but I thought I should point out that tall fellow, over in the corner there, with his Roman nose in the *Royal Magazine*. A lord of the Admiralty, upon my honour. Strides in here once a week and goes on about that newfangled luncheon snack that's all the rage in the gambling houses. Beef and mustard and what-you-will between two slices of bread. Can be eaten while standing at the gaming table, or in bed between bouts with the mistress. His Lordship claims he invented the thing and that it should be named after him.

Henday straightened and rubbed his hands.

– So as you see, everyone in here has a story. Myself, I once roamed the wild north lands of America, for the Hudson's Bay Company.

– Did you? Flood said, distracted by his own thoughts, pacing around the rim of a great blank. He had lost the thread he was following.

Henday sighed, sat again on the bench, shifting his bulk so that the flimsy table creaked ominously.

– At sunset one day my Cree guide shot a buffalo. The great beast rolled down into a hollow, and we followed. As we were butchering it I looked up to see figures against the sky. At first I thought they were people. My blood ran cold and then I saw that they were wolves. A grey senate of wolves, around the rim of the hollow, watching us.

Henday's voice trailed off. He shrugged and slapped the table with an open palm.

– Ah, well. I can see that you're tired. I am sure we will compare wolves another day.

Flood's gaze returned to the turtle–shaped stove. Like the one he and his father used to melt down their worn-out type.

– I'm a printer, he said.

– Coincidences welcome, too, Henday said, brightening. This house was formerly a bookbinder's. Before him, if I remember rightly, a short-lived topical newspaper was published here. And before that it was home to a writer of satires and homilies. Remarkable, isn't it? All trades dabbling in ink.

– Until now, I suppose.

– There are those who say my coffee is thick and black enough to dip a quill in. But many of my customers live by the printed word. Once in a while even the esteemed Mr. Samuel Johnson deigns to visit.

– I've never heard of him.

– A dictionary-maker, sir, who has undertaken a labour of Hercules that would've turned any other man's wits. We've seen him in here a time or two, let me tell you, while he toils on that endless book of his.

– Endless . . .

– A dictionary, sir, of our native tongue. Every word of it that is, pinned, defined, and exampled by quotes from the immortal Shakespeare, among others. Soon those of us who struggle with the unsayable will have a new weapon.

He tapped the table in front of Flood.

– And I'm willing to wager you are here for the sake of that struggle.

Flood remembered Pica sweeping type off the work table in one of her rare fits of temper. *I can't learn this. Why should I?*

– I'm looking for lodgings, for my daughter and myself. I've been away a long time, and I'm hoping to set up shop again.

– Alas, my friend, I can be of no help with something that

practical. Business is brisk, and I haven't any room to spare. But come to think on it, why not go see Mr. Johnson? They say he employs squads of clerks and copyists and such people to help him compile his book. Perhaps he has work for you, or can introduce you to someone who does. Gough Square, off Fleet Street. Near the Cheshire Cheese. Do you know it?

— I know it, Flood said, rising. Thank you.

Once Flood was back in the street Henday's black brew struck home. He staggered forward, heart galloping, as the rooftops and chimney-stacks rose and toppled like waves. A coach thundered past, showering him in dust. He stumbled backward, coughing.

A horse whinnied in his ear.

— Thought it was you, sir, the coachman said, leaning down.

Flood fell against the door, felt the window glass shudder in its frame. He was still without the thread, but he had another now. It would have to do.

φ

At Blackfriars Stairs, Pica and Snow were waiting for a wherry to take them back downriver when the coachman drove up on the quay and called to them. They hurried over.

— It's your father, the coachman said to Pica. You'd best climb in and let me explain on the way.

She and Snow seated themselves and the coach lurched forward into the streets. Pica stuck her head out the window and was about to speak but stopped herself, remembering that it was better to let the coachman gallop unchecked.

— Took him to Gough Square, the coachman shouted. To see a Mr. Johnson. Employment prospect, I believe. So I wait for him in the street. After a while there's a great hullabaloo. People running this way and that, like a grand spectacle's just been announced. I climb down from the coach just as they're carrying your father off.

– Carrying him off?

– I only know what they told me. Mr. Johnson not at home, landlady says, but expected soon. Lets your father in to wait. A few minutes later there's a scream that brings half the parish running. Landlady comes flying out of the house, blubbering and shrieking. *Madman, a madman.* Neighbours rush in, find him on the third floor. Standing in an empty room making these unaccountable motions at the thin air. Doesn't seem to see them. Doesn't reply. They jump him, knock him senseless, carry him out of the house. Tall, thin fellow, all in black, suddenly appears and takes charge of things. So off they go, your father, the man in black, and the mob.

– Where?

– I forgot you're not from here, little miss, the coachman said. They took him to the madmen's hospital, of course. To Bedlam.

φ

They rode out along the London Wall to the desolate expanse of Moorfields, passing lone, cheerless houses, the camps of gypsies, smoking hills of rubbish. In the southwest a dark anvil of cloud had risen, towering up behind the turrets and spires. The air bristled like a dog's hackles and a strong, hot wind began to blow, driving straw and dust before it along the empty road.

– Here we are, ladies, the coachman said, drawing up amid a herd of carriages and sedan chairs.

The article on London in the encyclopedia had mentioned Bedlam, but she had not imagined it like this. A great, dark palace. She and Snow climbed out of the coach, skirted the drivers and porters playing dice on the pavement, passed between the lofty iron gates. Ahead of them on the long gravel path ambled a party of sightseers, the men arm in arm and the women two steps behind, whispering together and breaking into little gusts of laughter. Pica and Snow hurried to catch up with them and followed close, slipping through the narrow portal in the door out of the turnkey's line of sight.

Looking back to ensure they had not been seen, Pica collided with two taffeta hoop-petticoats. The women looked back, identified the source of the disturbance, and turned away. One of the men with them glanced at Pica, then at Snow.

– Bringing the slave, he murmured to his companions. Not good for discipline.

Pica muttered a *pardon me* and darted around the women.

In front of her was a naked man. He stood in a shallow tub of water, gazing down at his own body, heedless of her startled stare. Beyond him stretched a long, high-ceilinged hall lined with doors. Vague figures moved in and out of shafts of light falling through narrow barred windows high in the walls.

A keeper stepped forward, his office made clear by the ring of keys on his belt and the iron-tipped staff he banged twice on the stone floor beside the naked man's tub.

– Here was a doctor, the keeper announced in a stage bellow. He fell into a melancholic humour and developed a moral theory of the elements. Now he believes he will escape the fires of hell by immersing his feet in cold water. Go ahead, you may address him.

A red-faced man stepped forward and circled the tub, tilting his head inquisitively. The doctor's head lifted slowly from the contemplation of his own flesh. He smiled and held out his hand.

– Go on, sir, the keeper nodded to the red-faced man. You can be assured he will do you no hurt.

The red-faced man grinned at his friends and gave his hand to the doctor, who pressed it warmly between both of his.

– He's blessing you, sir, the keeper said.

– He looks damned familiar, you know, the red-faced man said, extricating his hand. I may have consulted him once. What's the poor wretch's name, keeper?

– We don't use names here, sir. If you're looking for someone in particular you have to go by trade, or type of mania, or edifying lesson inculcated by sight of the particular unfortunate. For example, in number seven here, we keep the Evils Attendant Upon Excessive Button-making.

The keeper tilted his staff at a cell door and as if on cue a face appeared in the barred window. The women uttered little shrieks and then began to titter.

– There will be a time, a soft voice said, when the feathered tribe holds not sole dominion over the skies.

– Speak up, please, someone in the crowd demanded.

– When I soar with my army of eagles, the voice went on, to do battle, for all humanity, with the pitiless stars.

– Bravo, the red-faced man said.

They moved away from the cell, the keeper leading them to a shallow, roped-off pit, where a manacled wildman crawled on all fours, his face shrouded in a mane of clotted grey hair.

– Our resident magistrate, the keeper announced. Proudest man in London. Sable and ermine, coat of arms.

The man in the pit ceased prowling to sniff at a wet brown stain on the earth floor.

– Only daughter ran off with a lowly schoolmaster, the keeper went on. Now her once-noble father dabbles in his own shite.

– She must have been in love, one of the taffeta women said.

– Indeed, ma'am. One madness often brings on another.

– Will he speak to us, keeper?

– Do you hear that, Your Honour? the keeper shouted into the pit. Some gentlefolk to converse with you.

– We wish to inquire about the cause of your misfortunes, the woman called down.

– She *went*, the magistrate growled up at them, tossing his head from side to side like a chained bear. She went. And she went. She went. She went. Then she went.

The red-faced man leaned over the pit.

– And then what did she do, m'lord?

The magistrate's shriek rent the air and set off an echoing chorus up and down the gallery.

– SHE WENT.

Pica and Snow followed the tour down the long gallery, staying on the fringe of the group while the other sightseers peered through cell windows and into cages. Most of the inmates who had the freedom of the gallery paid no attention to the visitors. Some stood motionless or shuffled slowly about, their lips moving silently, their eyes staring into vacancy. Others were busy scrawling obscure diagrams in charcoal on the walls. One young man they passed, sitting against the wall with his knees drawn up, fixed Pica with blue, arresting eyes, reminding her of Djinn. She tried to imagine where the compositor was now, what he was doing, but her thoughts could not pass beyond these dark walls

At the end of the long gallery the keeper stopped and tapped his iron-tipped staff against the floor.

– Second and third floors are up these stairs, ladies and gentlemen. There we keep the female inmates and the most dangerous lunatics. Not for the faint of heart.

– What about that gallery, keeper? the red-faced young man asked, pointing to a corridor to one side of the stairs.

– That's for the new arrivals, sir. Can't show you those until the doctors have decided just where they fit in, as part of the tableau. It's all about arrangement, you see. That's why we save the best for last.

He flourished his staff and the sightseeing party crowded after him up the stairs. Pica and Snow hung back until the others had all rounded the curve of the staircase, then they slipped down the side gallery. An attendant with a barrow and a broom stood lazily sweeping old straw out of an empty cell. When they passed him he did not even look up. In the cell opposite him two attendants were struggling with a man in the throes of a violent seizure. At the end of the gallery another keeper sat dozing in a chair, his hat over his eyes.

Pica found her father in an open cell heaped with straw, the wooden walls covered with gouged words and scribblings. Snow waited just outside the door to keep watch.

He was lying on his side, his back against the wall, in a torn shirt and breeches. Against the far wall of the narrow cell another man sat with his arms around his knees, the fingers of his hands locked together, his head and arms shaken continually with tremors.

– Father, Pica whispered.

The other man looked up when Pica entered, gaped at her with frightened eyes. She turned and knelt beside Flood. He gave no sign of having noticed her presence.

– He doesn't say anything, the other man muttered, waving a palsied hand at Flood. I don't think he should be here. I don't want him here.

– I will take him away, Pica said.

– Yes. Please.

She stepped back out into the gallery. Snow handed her the cloak from the back of the dozing keeper's chair.

– My boots, too, she whispered, tugging them off. See if they'll fit him.

When she re-entered the cell the man with the palsy stamped his foot, raising a cloud of dust and chaff.

– Wake up. You're going.

Flood raised his head and looked up at Pica, frowning.

– You brought the press last time.

– That was somewhere else. A long time ago.

He sat up, leaned back against the wall and looked up at her.

– Don't let yourself get caught.

She held out her hand.

– Please, Father, get up now. They said we could leave.

Flood closed his eyes, shook his head.

– We can't. He's here.

– Who is, Father?

– Him, the man with the palsy said, pointing a shaking finger at the tall, black-robed figure standing in the hallway watching them.

– I've been speaking with the doctors, the Abbé de Saint-Foix said, nodding to Snow as he stepped past her into the cell. He bowed curtly towards Pica. They are unanimous, he said, that it would be best for your father to be surrendered to my care.

– I think it's a good idea, the man with the palsy said.

Pica backed away from the Abbé and crouched beside Flood. Snow drew one of the pistols halfway out of her apron pocket.

– I would keep that hidden, *Captain* Amphitrite Snow, the Abbé said, frowning. Unless you truly *do* wish to be taken and hanged.

– How did you find us? Snow growled.

– After we parted in Alexandria, I tried to imagine what Pica and her father would do next. Where they might go to find the Countess. Evidently we had the same thought, that she might come to London, her longed-for City of the New.

– My mother is not here, Pica said.

– I did not come looking for *her*, the Abbé said. The time we spent together in the pasha's employ was far too brief, and there is yet some unfinished business between us. I believe, mademoiselle, it should be clear what I want.

– Us, Pica said.

The Abbé smiled.

– I am not your grandfather, the Abbé said. Nor is this the pasha's domain. I will settle for the press, the ink, the paper. And whatever you were given by the metallurgist. Very little, really, wouldn't you agree, in exchange for your father's freedom. And your own.

– Nothing, Flood said. They turned to him in surprise. His eyes were open and fixed on the Abbé. Isn't that it, Abbé

Ezequiel? You once told me every book has a book of nothing concealed in it. Isn't that what you're really looking for?

He made an effort to rise and fell back against the wall. Pica took his arm, helped him to his feet.

— A book, he went on, that will return you to the paradise of your father's library.

— You're not as far gone as I had thought, the Abbé said, his voice setting each word down like a cold jewel on velvet. That is good. I am sure you would rather not spend the rest of your life in a place like this.

— Of course he wouldn't, said the palsied man.

— Let us say you are right, the Abbé shrugged, about what I'm looking for. I would have thought, then, that you would be eager to show me what you've accomplished since we last met. After all, are we not really after the same thing, you and I? If one could print an infinite number of pages there would have to be, amid all those words, an infinite amount of nothing. Is that not so?

— I haven't any answers for you, Flood said. Take what you will and make of it what you can.

The Abbé sighed.

— You *have* come to your senses. And thus we need not tarry much longer in this terrible place. If I may, though, let me suggest what you should do in order to guarantee your new-found liberty. When you leave here, return to your ship and, as soon as the tide permits, head downriver. My associates will meet you past Southend-on-Sea, and transfer the printing equipment to their vessel.

— And you? Snow asked with a dangerous grin. I hope you'll be there with your *associates*.

– Be assured you will see me again, the Abbé said, moving towards the door, and I will hold you to the bargain we have made.

– We will hold you to it as well, Snow said. You have my word.

The Abbé stepped up to her and raised his hand. She stiffened but made no other movement as he tucked a loose curl of hair back under her straw bonnet.

– Your word, Captain Snow, is of little consequence to me.

– Well then, the palsied man said brightly. You'll be going now.

Outside, the air had turned green and electric. The coachman's horses snorted and tossed their heads.

– Pleasure to see you again, sir, the coachman said, doffing his hat to Flood and glancing back at the gates. I take it we need to use haste.

At Covent Garden, Snow left them in the coach and waded into the crowd to find the Turinis. By this time the sky had closed over and the first fat drops of rain were pattering on the awnings of the market stalls. People began running for shelter, and those who couldn't find any were lifting baskets and newspapers over their heads. Pica turned from the window to look at her father, who had been drifting in and out of awareness since they left Bedlam. He lay back against the seat, his eyes closed.

Snow returned with Turini, Darka, and Miza. Lolo had just gone off with his hard-earned money to buy himself the toy he had seen in a shop window the day they arrived.

The rain was falling in earnest now, sweeping across the square in slashing gusts. Turini stowed his collapsible scaffold on the back of the coach and was about to set off in search of Lolo when the boy appeared, dashing through the rain with his hand tucked under his coat. When he reached them they all climbed into the hackney coach, dripping. Pica shouted to the coachman to take them to the nearest landing place.

– Savoy Stairs it is, miss.

The coach started off and she settled back, glancing across at her father to see that he was still sleeping quietly, despite the noise Lolo and his sister were making as they quarrelled over his prize. Turini growled at them. They left off arguing and took turns blowing on the whirligig so that the loop of card-paper spun on the end of its curiously contrived wheel. Pica saw now that there were tiny paper figures affixed to either side of the loop.

The rain roared on the coach roof. She leaned closer.

On one side a rider on horseback. On the other side another rider, galloping upside down and in the opposite direction from the first. When Lolo spun the wheel, she could see that the riders were in fact both travelling in the same direction. Pursuing one another.

– May I see that?

Reluctantly, Lolo surrendered the toy to Pica. She set it spinning and saw that she had been right. Tracing the twisting path of the riders she saw that they galloped on the same side of the paper ribbon. Or was it that the ribbon really only had one side?

Pica slid the window open, stuck her head out into the rain and shouted to the coachman. The coach slithered to a halt on the muddy pavement. She leaned towards Lolo and held up the whirligig.

– Can you show me where you got this?

The boy looked up at his father, who nodded.

– Cabinet of Wonders, Lolo said.

Pica glanced at Flood, who was stirring restlessly in his sleep.

– We'll get him to the ship, Snow said, swinging open the door.

Tucking the whirligig into her breast pocket, Pica climbed out of the coach after Lolo. She let him take the lead back along the street to Covent Garden. Pelted by the driving rain they dashed across its flooded, empty expanse and down the slope of a narrow, winding alley. Lolo soon outpaced her and she called to him to wait, but the water pouring from the spouts of the eaves drowned out her voice.

She ran, slashing through puddles and slipping in her thin shoes, under an arcade and around the curve of a lane of shops, where at last she saw the sign she had barely noticed that first day, the name painted in green and black above a deep-set narrow door.

Lolo stood tugging at the brass door handle.

– They must be closed now, Pica said. We'll have to come back another time.

She took hold of the handle and gave it a last tug to make her point. The door cracked open.

It seemed to her at first as if they had stepped inside a giant pocketwatch. Wherever she looked something was in motion, bobbing, spinning, whirring away with a life of its own. In an alcove to one side a tin mouse crawled through a maze of whirring gears and ticking hammers. In another niche an Arabian xebec rode a sea monster's back over waves fashioned of revolving tin cylinders. A hooded spectre rose from a trapdoor in the floor, and sank again. Mechanical birds sang and twittered from perches overhead.

Down the long narrow room life-sized automata swivelled and bowed and danced. A Cossack gnashing his wooden teeth and brandishing a sabre. A woodcutter and a milkmaid leaning towards each other and then away again, with each approach almost but not quite embracing. An Indian woman and child in buckskin stepping out of a dark pine forest, startling her, their painted eyes seeming to watch her as she passed.

In the centre of the room, in a great glass-sided case, stood a palace of ivory spires. Minuscule guardsmen paced the jewelled battlements. Around the walls fountains sprayed tiny jets of water over revolving statues of nymphs and nereids. A hedge maze spread in green whorls on either side of a broad marble thoroughfare. As Pica watched, her hands pressed against the glass, a gold carriage pulled by a team of six miniature white horses appeared, whirring out through the seashell gates, circled around and disappeared inside again. Pica's wandering gaze finally came to rest on a wooden scaffolding on the palace lawn, a mounting for a toy-sized telescope into which little bending tin figures of a man, a woman, and a child were taking turns peering.

Through the double panes of distorting glass she caught sight of Lolo, blowing on his coveted whirligig, about to disappear behind a clock case. She called his name in a furtive whisper and went after him, following the puddles left by his shoes.

Further on, the shop broke up into smaller rooms and compartments on different levels, so that she found herself going up and down short flights of stairs and having to turn back and retrace her steps as she pursued the boy. She shivered in her wet clothes and kept on, aware that she was heading generally away from the front entrance.

At last she caught up with Lolo, in a dark nook cluttered with wooden limbs hanging from the ceiling, empty metal housings stacked like discarded armour, bits and pieces of oily machinery piled on shelves. Unlike the rest of the shop, nothing here moved or made a sound.

Among these unfinished and set-aside wonders she found Lolo and saw that he had found Madame Beaufort.

The automaton sat in a velvet-curtained booth that resembled a travelling puppeteer's stage, her name painted in spidery gold letters across the front panel. A pane of dusty glass with a window cut in it for coins separated her from prying hands, so that Pica could look both at the fortune teller's porcelain features and her own reflection. The drunken Englishman in Canton had been right: despite Madame Beaufort's Persian costume, there was a resemblance. The wavy auburn hair. The pale green eyes. She wondered if, when she reached the age the automaton was meant to portray, she would look out at the world with this glassy stare, the same for everyone, seeing nothing.

With a waxen hand Madame Beaufort drew Lolo's penny across the rough wooden counter towards her, until it disappeared in the folds of her dark green satin cloak. The automaton's eyelids slid shut, its jaw rose and fell soundlessly. A bell chimed somewhere inside, the eyes clicked open, and the hand reappeared, holding a tiny paper scroll bound with red ribbon.

– There you are, Pica said.

The boy unrolled the stiff paper. Slowly he read the inscription to himself, then solemnly tucked the scroll into his vest pocket.

– We have to go now, Pica said. Before someone catches us here.

Lolo dug in a pocket, took out a second penny and thrust it at Pica.

– My fortune? No, Lolo, Madame Beaufort has nothing to tell me.

In the glass pane of the booth she caught a reflected movement behind her, turned and glimpsed, through a hanging garden of limbs, the most life-like creation yet. Another Madame Beaufort, but an older and more convincing one. She was seated at a table under a narrow glazed window, bent over a watchmaker's vise that held a sphere of dull metal the size of a child's fist. Unlike the other Madame Beaufort, this automaton was clothed not in a gaudy costume but in a pale blue dress and apron. Strands of faded russet hair had slipped from under the lace cap, and as Pica watched, a hand rose to brush them back behind an ear. This was accomplished, but still a finger strayed among the strands of hair, twining them slowly round itself. It was then that Pica realized her mistake. Machines did not forget themselves like that.

With a pair of tweezers the woman plucked a small flat disk out of the top of the metal sphere and set it on the stage of a microscope. Peering through the aperture she scraped at the edge of the disk with a tiny hooked tool, the tendons in her thin hand pulsing. When she had finished she picked up the disk again with the tweezers, blew on it and inserted it gently back into the top of the sphere. She freed the sphere from the vise, twisted it in her hands and set it on the table. The sphere buzzed for a moment, gave three unevenly spaced clicks, and went silent.

The woman sighed, lifted her spectacles and rubbed her eyes.

– The shop is closed, she said. But you must be soaked. You can stay a while and dry off.

Pica shrank back, then took Lolo's hand and stepped forward.

– The door was open, she said.

The woman turned slowly and searched her out through the intervening watchworks.

– You found your brother, she finally said, taking off her spectacles and rising stiffly from her chair. Good. I heard you calling him.

– He's not my brother, ma'am.

– Be that as it may, he shouldn't be unattended. Things in this shop move unexpectedly. Some are dangerous. He was here alone just now . . .

Pica held up the paper whirligig.

– Yes, and bought this, the woman said, moving closer to take the toy from her. Is there something wrong with it?

She spun the wheel.

– No, ma'am, Pica said. It's very clever. But I don't really understand. How a piece of paper can have only one side.

– I know, the woman said with the trace of a smile. I never understood it either.

As she handed Lolo the whirligig, it slipped from her fingers and spun to the floor.

– We heard about you, Pica said as Lolo dived after his prize. In Canton.

– Canton? You've travelled a long way to get here.

– We have a ship. My father used to live in London.

Her throat tightened and she turned away. The Cabinet of

Wonders seemed to have shrunk, closed in around her, so that she had to struggle to breathe. She put her hand to her chest and felt, under her bodice, the quoin key jab against her breast-bone. She turned back and saw that the woman was sitting again at the table, her hands twined together in her lap.

– What did you hear about me in Canton?

– That you answer questions.

Pica nodded towards the fortune teller.

– That she does, I mean.

The living Madame Beaufort was gazing at her with such motionless intensity that for a moment Pica thought the world had stopped. The look in the woman's eyes was the same she had glimpsed in her father's when she found him, frozen in time, at the top of the hatchway stairs.

– Everything in this room is a question, the woman said, not taking her eyes off Pica.

Lolo had left Pica's side and stood nearby on tiptoe, batting at a painted wooden torso hanging from the ceiling.

Not trusting herself to speak, Pica looked at the fortune teller in her glass cage, at the limbs hanging from chains, swinging where Lolo had passed and disturbed them. She glimpsed, through a thicket of gears and levers and pendulums, the far-off ivory palace. At last her gaze came to rest on the metal sphere in the vise.

– That is a special kind of clock, the woman said. I've never gotten it working properly. It's supposed to tell time by turning, like the earth.

Lolo had strayed farther away, this time in the direction of the front of the shop.

– I have to go, Pica said. My father . . .

She stopped, tugged the quoin out by its frayed ribbon, slipped it over her head and hung it from the curled forefinger of one of the hanging arms.

She went after Lolo and found him near the door, where she stopped for a moment and looked back the way she had come. The woman could not be seen.

φ

At Savoy Stairs, Pica found a wherry to take her and the boy back to the *Bee*, although they had to share it with another passenger, a young woman in a mud-spattered grey cloak, marked with a livid scar down one side of her face. After a moment, Pica realized it was the woman they had passed the other day, in the tunnel on the way to Covent Garden. She leaped nimbly aboard as the boatman was already casting off. When Pica asked to be taken to the custom-house dock, the young woman said that would be fine for her as well.

Pica stood near the stern of the boat and gazed back the way they had come, even after the jutting wall of Blackfriars Stairs was obscured by the swarming river traffic. The world had grown larger, emptier. The rain had drawn off and the clouds were scudding away, their edges reddening in the sunset. From the river, the city was an exquisite crystal, washed clean of its grime and its memory, pitiless and perfect.

When they pulled up at the custom house, Pica paid the boatman, helped Lolo out and hurried with him along the quay to the ship, glancing back to see the young woman with the scar following them at a steady, determined pace. She walked faster, whispering to Lolo to do the same. By the time they reached the gangplank they were running.

Snow met them on the quarterdeck and told Pica that Flood was in the great cabin and the Turinis were tending to him.

– Someone's behind me, Pica said breathlessly, as the scarred woman stepped onto the gangplank.

Snow raised a hand in salute.

– Lucy Teach, she said. In ahead of the pack.

Pica followed the direction of Snow's nod and saw two more women in dark ankle-length cloaks, hurrying along the quay from the opposite direction.

– Cat Nutley. Abena Khedjou.

– You knew all the time, Pica said. You were waiting . . .

– For you to finish here.

There was a thump of boots on the port ladder, and the close-cropped head of another young woman appeared over the side.

– Crook-Fingered Jane, Snow said, nodding, then turned to Pica. That's the lot then.

All four women were aboard the ship now, huddled together near the mainmast and gazing around inquisitively at the timbers and ropework. Two of them knelt on either side of the gangplank and looked up at Snow as if awaiting her order to draw it in. Lolo had already gone into the great cabin, and Pica was turning away to follow when Snow spoke again.

– Are we ready to cast off, then?

– Yes, Pica said, looking back once more at the river.

She ducked into the great cabin. Flood was stretched out on the banquette, his shirt open to the waist. Darka sat beside him, holding his wrist. Turini and the twins stood nearby, watching.

Darka looked up at her husband and drew a hand across her forehead. He mouthed words to her and she nodded.

— She says he has a fever, the carpenter said. It is not bad, but we must watch him.

Pica crossed to the banquette and knelt beside her father. Darka rose from Flood's side and was stepping noiselessly across the room when suddenly she halted, staring at the doorway. Pica turned, and at first she thought one of Snow's shipmates had come to speak with them. Then the cloaked woman in the doorway pulled back her hood and stepped into the candlelight.

— I followed you, the woman said, holding up the quoin key on its ribbon. There's something I would like to give you. Again.

Pica climbed to her feet and stood beside the banquette. She saw that Turini and his family had shrunk into a corner of the room. Darka's hand was over her mouth. The woman from the Cabinet of Wonders stepped closer and set the quoin key on the chart table. She spoke Pica's name softly, like a question. Pica stood without moving, unable to look at the woman's eyes, but she saw the pallor of her slender neck, the fragile shadow of the pulse beating there. Then she crossed the space between them, stepped forward into the damp rainy scent of the woman's cloak, into her arms. She felt the woman's uncertain embrace grow stronger as she surrendered to it, felt a trembling hand stroke her hair. Near her heart another heart beating.

φ

The night Flood was caught leaping into her bed, she was already gone from the castle. Taken by her father's men across the river and up into the mountains to his hunting *salash,* where she was watched day and night. The Count came to see her only once. She asked about

Flood and was told he had fled the castle the night she was taken away. That was the last time she saw her father.

When spring came his men took her down the Danube on a barge, brought her at last to the ship, where she was locked in a cabin without windows.

All that she could glimpse of the world beyond the walls of the cabin was through a crack along the seam between two timbers: a thin sliver of sea and cloud. The voyage was stormy and rough. She understood, overhearing the curses and complaints of the sailors, that they were making little headway. Days went by during which her only sight of others was the hand that slid her meals through a narrow slot in the bottom of the door. For the life growing within her she ate every-thing, though she was often sick afterward and threw it all back up.

It was when she first tried to escape that she discov-ered the Abbé was her jailer. Late one night she found and pried loose a panel in her cabin that opened into a narrow tunnel. After crawling through a cramped, lightless space alive with rats, she came up through the floor of the great cabin and found the Abbé sitting calmly at the captain's table as if waiting for her.

Your father planned to have you shut up in a convent, he said. *I persuaded him otherwise. Rest assured that you and your child will be well cared for.*

Although he tried to conceal it with his words, she saw that he was agitated, at war with himself, and she had a sudden hope that he might be persuaded to let her go. But when she pleaded for her liberty she saw his eyes grow cold with satisfaction.

The Count had given him the ship's plans, he told her. He knew its secrets better than anyone. For the first time since she had been taken from the castle she gave in to despair and wept.

Quebec, he said as he escorted her back to her cabin, *may remind you of your father's island, a fortress perched on a rock. But in my home you shall find all the comforts you lack here.*

She did not see him again for what seemed like weeks, and when he finally came to visit her, she understood that he had stayed away deliberately, had left her to the rough care of the sailors so that he would appear as her only benefactor. He expected humility, gratitude, and she gave him cold silence. She also noticed the dark crescents under his eyes, how much paler he was than usual. The voyage was not going well for him either.

He asked her how things were with her burden.

The time is drawing close, he said when she had given him no answer. *You will see me again.*

One morning she woke to the cry of gulls. From the steadiness of the deck beneath her she knew that they had anchored somewhere, but all that her secret window showed her was its usual vista: grey sky and dark waves. That night her water broke and she screamed for someone to help her. After that she was seized and cast away by waves of pain and came back to find faces over her, hands on her body. The frightened old woman who assisted at the birth would not speak, even when Irena pleaded with her eyes for any word at all to bring her some comfort.

Then the agony was gone, vanished as if it had never been, and she saw through tears a blood-streaked little body squirming in the midwife's arms. A girl. At the first tiny cry she struggled out of her delirium, knowing she would be given only a moment. She reached for the quoin key she kept on a chain around her neck.

And a name. *Small Pica, or philosophy.* A good name for the heroine of a novel. She did not guess that in the place her newborn child would live, the word already named something.

– At the Ospedale, Pica said, I collected things that had stories. I thought everything had a story, except me.

The hush of night had fallen on the river. Irena and Pica sat together in the great cabin, watching over Flood as he wrestled with the angel of fever. Darka had brought more candles as the evening waned and the cabin darkened around them. Snow and her crew were readying the ship for departure, and from all parts of the ship came the sliding of chains and the flap and rustle of unfolding sailcloth. The scent of the smoke from London's many fires grew sharper in the cooling air.

Irena told her story in a whisper and Pica listened, spellbound. Once Flood surprised them by speaking.

– You'll go with me then.

He was looking at Irena.

– Nicholas . . .

– We'll go to London, he said. Your father won't find us there.

She bathed his forehead with a wet cloth and he closed his eyes again and slept.

Please understand, the Abbé said when he took the baby, *this is no more to my liking than to yours. But for now, it must be.*

For a long time afterward she wished only for death. Then in the distant call of a seabird, shrill and wavering but strong, she heard that tiny cry again, and she knew that she had to live.

One night there came a terrifying storm that seemed to hurtle the ship into another world. She heard the splintering of wood and a shudder throughout the ship, the hoarse shouts of the sailors, the Abbé's among them, shrill with desperation.

In the calm that came with morning, the ship limped into a port where the only sound was that of a church bell. As the ship yawed on its anchor chains she was able to piece together, through her sliver of a window, a picture of a quiet, tidy, red-brick town that she found out much later was New York. At the sight of a child playing with a dog she knew that this was not where the Abbé had intended to bring her.

He was not there when they bound her and led her under cover of night into a black mail coach. She wondered if the journey had killed him, and the thought left her only with even less hope. She was transported miles over terrible roads, until at dawn the mail coach pulled up by the mossy ruin of a watermill. She was allowed to drink from the stream, and then her hands were bound and she was placed in a canoe and for days travelled upriver with three silent, leather-faced woodsmen who brought her at last to a colony of religious dissenters in the forest. She was lifted from the canoe, her legs cramped and useless after the long ride. The people would not speak to her. They asked no questions of the men in the canoe, and as soon as she could walk again they put her to work in the fields.

For a long time she scarcely gave a thought to running away. Where would she run to? And worse, she began to believe the things she was told again and again, night and day, about why she was there. How she had to pay for her sins. And so, though they soon relaxed their watchfulness over her, a year passed before the day she made her escape. The thought came to her suddenly, while working in the tomato patch. She simply set her hoe down on a furrow and walked into the forest.

She walked on and on, running now and then at the thought of the colony's vicious watchdogs, the iron bodice she still wore cutting into her flesh. That evening she waded across a stream and almost froze to death during the night in her drenched clothes. She wandered for another day and night in the woods, starving and feverish.

They came out of the forest silently, like people in a dream. A woman and a child, dressed in deerskins. The woman had a knife. She spoke to Irena in their language and a word of her father's came back to her: *savages*. There was nothing left in her to scream. She stumbled backwards and fell, crashing through dead leaves, into the dark. They bundled her in blankets beside a fire. They fed her thin strips of meat, a kind of porridge made of corn. When she was able to walk, they brought her from their camp in the forest to a Dutch settlement.

Irena ceased speaking and gazed into the distance.

– I was with them for days, she finally said, but I never found out their names.

The candle flames fluttered and black shadows lapped at the corners of the cabin. To Pica, Irena seemed the still centre of a dancing web of light.

– I made my way to New York, she went on, and found work as a seamstress. When I had saved enough to buy materials, I began to make clockwork toys and curiosities. The colonists loved them. Such things are scarce in that part of the world.

– Then you came to London, said Pica.

– Yes. I thought about a book your father showed me once. I decided to return to the beginning of a story, his story, and wait there.

φ

The candle near him shed a yellow parchment light. He gazed at the flame, bending and folding in the night air.

– Irena.

– I'm here, Nicholas.

– I don't hear the clock.

Something else he had to tell her. He could not remember. So much had vanished, the world rolled up like the two ends of a yellowed scroll, so that there was only the gently rocking bed making its nocturnal rounds through the castle, the dim wavering half-light, Irena's hand on his. There had only ever been this. Only ever would be.

She spoke again and he struggled to hold on to the words. His body felt weightless, as though it had burned to ash and left only a lingering shape of smoke.

– We're on the ship, she said. Do you remember?

– I've finished the book, he said. But I don't know if the Count will be pleased.

– My father is dead, Nicholas.

For a moment he was lost and then everything returned, clear and sharp. The castle's walls and floors fell away from him, scattering like a house of cards.

– Your father, he said, thought he wanted a mirror of the world, of everything. But he really wanted the world to mirror him.

– He wished to own books, Irena said. Not read them.

All that had happened since rushed like a wave into his thoughts. Pica . . .

– I must go, Nicholas, Irena said. It is late. Rest now, and we will talk again soon.

– The girl, he said. I tried to teach her the craft. I thought she needed something. For when I was gone.

– She told me about your lessons, Irena said. She says you're a good teacher.

He closed his eyes. Her voice was already small and far away, receding with the rest of the world. Everything a father does, he thought, becomes a lesson. Even this.

The night wind had swept the smoke away, and in the cold moonlight the river lay outstretched like a pallid arm. The mortal stillness of the air told Pica that dawn was not far off. The world itself seemed to be brooding on her mother's story. She glanced up into the mainmast rigging, where Snow's crew was already perched, setting new ropes and tackle. The tide would be nearing the ebb now. She shivered and pulled her cloak about her shoulders. Soon they would be casting off, and she would meet the Abbé again. After all he had taken from them already, he would have her father's work, too.

She heard a sound behind her and turned to see her mother stepping out onto the deck, her face pale with exhaustion.

– How is he? Pica asked.

– He's sleeping quietly now. He spoke about you.

Snow joined them at the top of the gangplank, carrying one of the lanterns they had brought from Canton. Irena stood looking out at the black wall of the city, and then turned to Pica.

– The Abbé can't be trusted, she said. Remember that.

Snow lit the lantern and handed it to Irena, who took it with a nod.

– You have a place here, Irena said, touching Pica's hand. Take care.

She turned and descended the gangplank. Pica watched her hurry along the deserted quay until her cloak was swallowed up in shadows and only the light of the Chinese lantern could be seen, swaying and bobbing in the dark. Finally, when she must have rounded the corner of a lane Pica could not see in the blackness, the light winked out.

– I didn't tell her about the *Acheron*, Pica said to Snow, who was peering upward to survey the progress of the refitting.

– Good, Snow said. Leave that worry to me.

Pica returned to the great cabin to sit with her father while he slept. She took the book from her pocket and held it in her hands, weariness tugging at her like an undertow.

She sat up suddenly. The book lay unopened in her lap. She felt she had only slept a moment, but the candles were out, and pale, cold dawn-light illuminated the cabin.

Her father was not on the banquette. His blanket had been placed over her shoulders.

She descended to the press room and, as she had expected, she found him there, slumped at the work table with his journal open before him. While she had slept he had put away his binding tools, tidied up the clutter on the work table, and then sat down to make an entry in his journal. The paper was untouched, but the quill was in his hand, the ink on its tip gone dry.

She set the book on the table and knelt beside him, saw that his eyes were open, unseeing. She placed a hand on his arm.

– Father . . .

After a while she stood and looked around the silent cabin. The chase of gooseflesh type still sat on the carriage of the press, and a sheet of fresh paper had been fixed to the tympan.

Hearing sounds above her, she stirred at last and climbed back up on deck. The Turinis stood together near the gangplank, donning their hats and cloaks for the journey to Covent Garden. The children, still yawning and rubbing the sleep from their eyes, noticed her first and called her name. Numbly she joined the family at the gangplank, and told them that her father was dead.

They followed her back to the press room, and Snow joined them. Pica stood by while Turini picked her father up in his arms and laid him out on the cot he had so often collapsed onto after a long night's work. Then the carpenter went up on deck, and after a while they heard the sound of his hammer. Darka and the children bowed their heads, Miza glancing up timidly as if waiting for her to join them. Then she understood. It was for her to say what would happen now. Instead she turned to Amphitrite Snow.

– We can take him with us, Snow said. If you wish.

– No, Pica said with sudden certainty. London is where he wanted to be.

Snow's crew came down soon after, and carried the body up on deck, placing it in the rough casket Turini had hastily nailed together out of his scaffold. When the carpenter had nailed shut the lid, the women lifted the casket and carried it down the gangplank. They set their burden on the wet stones of the quay, where Pica stood with the Turinis, then hurried back up the gangplank to their posts on deck. Vaguely it came to her that they were eager to be off. There was no time for mourning in their world. The *Acheron* remained to be dealt with. And the Abbé.

She said farewell to the Turinis and followed the women up the gangplank. Snow looked up from the helm and frowned at her.

– I thought you would be staying behind too.

Pica shook her head. Everything that had belonged to her father was on this ship. She had to be the one to give it away.

As Turini was starting off in search of a cart, Pica had a sudden thought and called to him from the rail.

– There's a man in Covent Garden, she said. Monsieur Martin, the playing-card maker. He knew my father. He will help you. Then find my mother, please, and tell her.

φ

As the sun rose, the *Bee* sailed downriver with the tide, past the low meadows where cattle grazed, the salt marshes loud with hosts of raucous gulls. In the estuary a sheet of wet morning fog swept in off the grey sand flats.

The crew had left Pica to herself in the press room. She sat for a long time at the work table, her hand on her father's book. When she became aware of the crying of the gulls she rose at last, to finish setting things in order. She polished Ludwig, hung him back on his hook, and then turned to the press. The surface of the gooseflesh type was blank, still, but when she touched a fingertip to it a dull wave radiated outward. If the type would not solidify, she would have to give the chase to the Abbé as it was. She unclipped the paper from the tympan and hung it on the drying wire. Unlocking the chase, she lifted it carefully and set it down carefully on the work table, under the light from the hatch.

She stood looking at the press for a while, empty now of type and paper, silent. It would have to be taken apart, she realized, in order to be brought out on deck. The Abbé and the Commander's men would crowd in here with hammers and wrenches, and she would have to stand there, and let them take everything.

Everything but the book. She would not let them have that.

As she was polishing the ancient timbers, the scarred woman, Lucy Teach, appeared in the press room.

– We're nearing Southend-on-Sea, she said quietly. Snow would like to see you.

As she followed Lucy Teach up the hatchway stairs Pica felt a shudder pass through the ship and heard the sound of the boilers firing up. It occurred to her now that Snow and her crew had been sailing without help from the *Bee's* steam-driven winches and pulleys.

Pica found Snow on the quarterdeck, unpacking the chest that contained the fireworks Djinn had bought in Canton. Picking up one of the compositor's bamboo rockets, Pica turned it over in her hands and thought of Djinn. During their travels, his belief that everything would end in sadness had always comforted her. She had only needed to look at his boyish face to know that he was wrong. Now she was alone, with no one to tell her what the future would be.

She was about to ask Snow what the fireworks were for, when she heard the rumble of rolling barrels and looked up to see Lucy Teach and the other women hauling the ink casks up from below. They stood the casks in a circle around the mainmast and roped them together. All at once Pica knew what they had planned. She turned to Snow, who was busy at the helm console, lowering the longboat over the side.

– You're going to burn the ship.

Snow smiled and shook her head.

– You are a slow learner, little girl.

– What about the Abbé?

– Oh, I am hoping he will be there for this, too.

The women stowed blankets, rations, tinder, and a lantern between the thwarts of the longboat, and at Pica's request, Ludwig the automaton was also placed aboard. At least he could be saved, she thought, from what was to come. When the women had finished provisioning the boat they stood about the quarterdeck, tensed and expectant, gazing into the fog that drifted across the bows.

– If there's anything else you'd like to save, Snow whispered, you'd best be ready to fetch it.

Pica held her breath and stood with the rest of the crew, listening and looking out into grey obscurity. At first they heard only the creaking of the *Acheron*'s towers of canvas, the thud of her bows against the waves, and then finally out of the wet mist the great hull materialized like a white wall sliding across their path. An instant later there was a flash, and a booming like thunder. A volley of spinning chain shot screamed through the air, buffeting the *Bee*'s hull and tearing through her ropework fore and aft. Shattered tackle rained onto the gangways as the *Bee* staggered through smoke across the *Acheron*'s mountainous wake.

On Snow's lead they had all dropped to the planks, awaiting a second volley that did not come. Snow scrambled to her feet to see the *Acheron* in a long starboard turn that took her back out of sight into the fog.

– He's lamed us, she said, working furiously at the helm. Now he'll circle, closing in, then try to board us.

She turned and pointed at Pica.

– You get in the longboat. We'll fire the ship and join you.

– There's something I need, Pica said. In the press room.

Before Snow could reply she ducked into the hatchway and hurried down the stairs. She glanced at the chase of gooseflesh type on the work table. The metal had not yet solidified, and there was no more time to wait.

The book was not on the work table where she had left it. As she stood staring at the place where it had been, wondering if someone had taken it, she heard a panel slide open in the bulkhead behind her. Even before she turned, she knew who would be standing before her.

– You and your mother have been parted again, the Abbé said.

He stood with her father's book in his hands, his face so haggard and drained of colour she was not certain at first if it was really him.

– I sincerely hope you will not have to wait so long this time for a reunion, he said.

Pica felt tears sting her eyes, forced herself to speak.

– Why won't you leave us alone?

He lurched forward into the light from the overhead hatch, laid a hand on the frame of the press. As he moved she saw the dark sheen of blood on the black folds of his cassock.

– There is something of your mother's fire in you, he nodded. It is a pity we have not been travelling companions all these years. In time I might have moulded you into something more than a pale shadow of her. But to the matter at hand. If you'll kindly recall, I am here because of the agreement we made.

– My father is dead.

– Yes, I know. That is unfortunate. But you are still here, his apprentice. Your freedom, I believe, was part of the transaction.

The Abbé gazed at the dark green leatherbound volume.

– I must admit I did not expect to find this, a finished creation. A wonder, isn't it? Your father, rest to his soul, surpassed even my grandest imaginings. The marvellous binding, the ink. And the paper. The luminous, gossamer subtlety of its weave. I have never seen such paper . . .

– You can have the press, she said, staring at the book. The ink and the paper. And then . . .

The Abbé looked up at her and smiled.

– And then will I go away? He turned the book in his hand. Perhaps, but I must know how this was accomplished. Where it came from. And as your father is sadly no longer with us, I will have to rely on you for answers. When this business with the *Acheron* and Captain Snow is finished, I would be most pleased if you would accompany me home to Quebec, where we can study these matters without the world interrupting us.

– You were taking my mother there, Pica said. Why didn't you?

– You desire answers, too, of course. Very well. During the

storm I was seized by the apoplexy that has plagued me since childhood. For seven months I lay like a graven image, unable even to tell my servants to remove the clock from my room. Seven months. Eighteen million one hundred and forty-four thousand seconds. By the time I recovered, her trail was lost. You may not believe it, but I did intend the two of you should meet again.

He stepped closer, clutching the book more tightly to his breast.

– You have what you wanted, she said, looking away. When the Abbé did not reply she turned back and saw that he was clinging to the press, his head bowed, his breath coming in gasps.

– That first volley was only meant to cripple you, he whispered, slowly raising his head. Unluckily it appears to have done worse damage to me. The Commander is certain of his prize, you see, so he is taking his time, savouring every moment. His oracular nose has sniffed victory in the air, as surely as, he has informed me, my native land will soon belong to King George. Help me now, and perhaps he can be persuaded to let the women live. At least long enough for there to be some hope of a miracle, like the one that saved you from the Commander the last time, off Alexandria.

There was a shout from up on deck. Amphitrite Snow calling her name. Time was running out. Either the *Bee* would go up in flames, or they would be taken and she would become the property of the Abbé.

– There, she said, stabbing a finger at the chase. That's where you can find out everything.

Grimacing, the Abbé hauled himself upright. He staggered to the work table, leaned against it and bent close to the blank forme of type.

– What is this . . . ?

He flicked a finger at the smooth, mirror-like surface. Wavelets rippled inward to the centre and outward again, like water in a basin that has been roughly set down. As the waves subsided letters began to leap up and vanish instantaneously, as if an invisible shower of rain were pattering against the metal from below.

– So this is what the ingenious Samuel Kirshner gave you.

– The formes appeared, she said, one after another, and my father printed them.

The Abbé looked up at her, his thin features seeming to sharpen as understanding dawned.

– You found your own well of stories, as indeed I should have guessed you would. When I visited you at the Ospedale, I felt that we were somehow akin.

He rolled up the sleeve of his cassock, hesitated a moment, then thrust his arm into the liquid metal. He withdrew it slowly, intently studying his hand, his fingers, as if amazed that they had returned intact. Suddenly he bent forward, his face contorting with pain.

– You will doubtless take comfort, he gasped, to learn that I may not live to return home. Do you know, mademoiselle, my only regret would be to have spent so little time with your father's creation. And with you.

– I have been to a place, she said slowly, where you can read forever. Where nothing changes, except what you want to change.

The Abbé's brows knit together. He studied her for a long time and then gazed down at the rippling pool of metal.

– You went, he whispered, into the type.

In the cold light Pica saw beads of sweat gleaming on the

Abbé's forehead. His bloodless face seemed to age as she watched, his gaunt form sagging in his cassock as if he were struggling under a tremendous weight. Slowly he sank down into the chair at the work table.

— It's as if time doesn't exist, she went on, for anyone except you. Nothing else moves. You have the whole world to yourself.

— Of course, he finally said, his hands sliding along the sides of the chase. Of course. Without time the world bends itself to the shape of one's desire.

— My father told me about you, she said. About the library where you hid as a boy. In the well, the whole world is that library.

The Abbé continued to stare into the shifting metal, as if he had not heard her, or was oblivious now to everything but his own thoughts. From without came the crack of the warship's guns opening up in clockwork succession and a moment later Pica was tossed to the planks as a violent shudder rocked the *Bee*. Dazed, she picked herself up and saw that the Abbé, who had fallen against the work table, had his eyes raised to the oily black smoke now pouring through the overhead hatch. His hands found the edges of the table, gripped it like someone about to be swept away by a torrent.

— The Commander, he said, is not a patient man. It would seem he has forgotten about me.

She saw that the book had slipped from his grasp and slid across the table, closer to her. Before she could move, his shaking hands found it again.

— I've waited too long.

He rose, seemingly possessed again of strength and will, pulled the chair out from the work table, and set one foot on the seat.

Pica took a step towards him.

– The book wasn't part of our bargain, she said, her voice trembling.

He seemed to hesitate a moment and then turned to her and slipped the book into the pocket of his cassock. In his eyes for an instant flashed the familiar knife-gleam of cold wit.

– I pray you will forgive a last *bon mot*, he said, but either way, it would seem that I am out of time.

Laboriously he hauled himself up onto the chair, oblivious to Pica now as she backed towards the hatchway, then lunged up the stairs. Halfway she stopped and stood still, listening. In a brief flaw of stillness she heard the tick of the ship's timbers, the slap of the waves. From the press room, a sound she had never heard before. Like water furiously boiling.

She turned and hurried back down the stairs. The Abbé was gone. A column of raised letters was sinking into the seething matrix in the chase, glowing white-hot so that the heated air in the press room rippled like water.

She leaned over the chase and read the words vanishing into the metal.

> And when I look, behold,
> A hand is sent unto me; and, lo, a roll of a book is
> therein; and opened before me.
> And it is written within and without:
> And there is found therein lamentations,
> And mourning, and woe.

As she read, the type disappeared completely and then suddenly rose again, even more agitated, with some sorts almost leaping from the matrix. She wondered if it had been a message meant for her. How long had he been in the well? A moment of her time could be countless centuries for him.

The words she had just read were broken now into a seethe of letters that she tried to make sense of, until she realized that the type was being pushed outward by something within, forming an image in relief. A face, distorted by the torment of the metal, rising and then sinking away again so quickly that she wondered if she had really seen it.

She lifted the chase gently from the table, not knowing for certain what she intended. Perhaps he had been trying to get out, and the metal was too hot, or he had gotten lost on the way, as she had, in the place where there was only darkness.

The metal was darkening now, waves of heat rising into her face as she carried the chase towards the stairs. She was about to set foot on the first step when the *Acheron* fired again. The ship reeled from the blow and she was thrown backward, the iron frame wrenched from her hands. As she fell she saw the chase wheel end over end through space and strike a crossbeam. The pieces of type burst forth, showering onto the planks with a crash like falling water. Even as the scattered sorts came to rest, lifeless and inert, the sound of their fall seemed to carry on, diminishing slowly, blending in with the slap of waves against the hull. As if whatever living force was bound within the metal had trickled away through the seams of the ship to mingle with the ocean.

She climbed to her feet and stood for a moment, dazed. The sound of cannonfire, of the wounded ship's groans, receded into distant murmurs and she seemed to be alone in the world, utterly alone, as if it was not the Abbé but she who had descended again into the well. What was he now? A shoal of broken-up type. Hastily, she crouched amid the spill of letters, plucked a single sort from the planks and raced up the hatchway.

On deck, a few of the wooden casks had been broached so that the gangways were now awash in black ink. Off their port quarter, the *Acheron* was ranging up again out of the mist.

– At last, Amphitrite Snow said, hauling Pica by the arm across the deck, and then suddenly stopping to look at her. What happened to you?

– I . . . I couldn't get the book.

– Never mind. Your father wouldn't have wanted you to lose your life over it.

The *Acheron* had still a wide seaway to cross, but from her forward guns another impatient volley boomed out and exploded into spray just off the *Bee*'s stern. Snow helped Pica climb down into the longboat, then clambered back up over the heaving side, disappeared for a moment and then handed down Djinn's kite, folded up and bound with its string.

– If you don't reach land on your own, send this up on fire and pray someone sees it.

Pica caught the kite, set it beside her, and stared up at Snow.

– You're not coming.

– You've read all the books, Snow called down to her. Don't you know how stories like mine have to end?

The longboat dropped with a drumroll of sliding chains, struck the waves and rode the surge of the *Bee*'s wash. Then the chains were released, a swell caught the longboat, and the ship's hull slid away from her like an opening door.

The candles have long since guttered out. Beyond the shattered walls a fine rain is just drawing off. It will be sweeping away eastward now, the colonel thinks, hurrying across the sodden, abandoned fields. As he should have been, hours ago. A sullen lassitude comes over him at the thought of climbing back on his horse and riding to another day of pointless bombardment, of the same haggard faces around the map table, of endless inconclusive debate over what to do about the English.

He takes another sip of the tea she brewed to warm them. It has gone cold.

And then? he asks, unable to resist, his voice hoarse from long silence. Despite what Captain Snow said, I doubt that was the end.

The young woman had risen now and then during the telling, to light a candle or simply to stretch limbs chilled with long sitting. Now, with a charred stick of wood she is stirring the coals in the brazier that has kept off the sharp edge of the night wind.

It isn't the end, she says. But it is a good place to stop, for now.

Bougainville eases back in his chair. His horse, which he had tied up for the night just inside the entrance, whinnies impatiently and knocks a hoof against a fallen board. A suggestion he chooses to ignore.

May I attempt an ending, then? After all, this is a book I would very much like to read, too. The longboat, I imagine, drifted away. The girl saw the smoke of the first unseen flames darkening the Bee's sails as she came at the Acheron. Then all at once the little ship was blazing, flames hurtling to the skies. She watched helplessly, straining for any sight of figures leaping over the side.

The young woman leaves off tending the fire and sits down across from the colonel.

The smoke blinded her, she says, nodding and closing her eyes. The girl shouted for Snow but got no answer. Then there was a great roar, and suddenly through the fog and smoke she saw the Acheron's hull burning. Bursting apart. Shards of her aft timbers spinning in slow, winking arcs, falling into the sea.

She huddled in the boat with the automaton for a day, drifting on the waves. When evening came she was still alone on the water, so she sent the kite up on fire. That night she was found and rescued by La Constance, a naval transport out of Calais. Bound for Quebec with men and supplies.

The young woman opens her eyes.

The girl arrived here four years ago, just before the war began. With nothing. Knowing no one. She was taken to the convent first, to be looked after by the nuns, but that did not go well.

She disliked their cloistered life, no doubt.

On the contrary. She wanted to stay with them, at least for a while. She liked them. Their life. They were more worried about an early frost ruining their beans and cabbages than about the threat of invasion. But they did not know what to make of her.

I am not surprised.

For a time she lived in the streets, but then the snow started to fall. Finally she found the Abbé's house, deserted, and camped there like a gypsy for the winter.

I don't know the place, the colonel says. Is it near the town?

Not far. When the war began, soldiers came to live there. She had to leave, again. When she first appeared on the bookseller's doorstep he didn't want to hire a girl, but she convinced him she could keep track of things better than he had. She fixed up the broken old press he kept under a sheet in the back room.

She looks down at the heap of wooden fragments on the floor, and the colonel realizes what she was doing when he first entered the shop. Trying to assemble the pieces of a puzzle.

You became a printer, he says.

I tried. Much to the bookseller's amusement. He told me not to waste my time.

Where is he now?

Not long after war was declared he went home to Paris. I sent a letter with him. He promised he would find someone to take it across the channel to London and deliver it.

Even at the best of times, the colonel says, letters miscarry. Perhaps when the siege ends . . .

Yes. Perhaps then the war will be over.

The stillness outside is broken by the crowing of a rooster. A sound, the colonel thinks, like a half-hearted challenge to the day, to bring something other than yet more bombs, more waiting. The young woman has sat down again and her gaze has come to rest on the broken remnants of the press.

So, the colonel says with a smile, the Commander of the Acheron predicted Quebec would be lost, did he?

He hears his own voice ring hollow. The mocking words echoing with the bleak certainty he cannot conceal. When she looks up he sees that she has heard it, too.

He wasn't always right, she says. That I'm here at all is proof of that.

Yes. But even if Wolfe sails away this winter, someone else will come next spring at the head of another armada of ships crammed with men and guns. The Commander was really the most typical of Englishmen. When they have their minds set on something, even a handful of escaped slaves, they pursue it to the death, theirs or someone else's makes little difference.

He rises stiffly from his chair, brushes plaster dust from the shoulders of his coat.

If the English hadn't destroyed your press, he said, you would have gone on printing, I suppose. For the conquerors.

They would have asked me to print their proclamations, you mean. Their warnings and reward placards. And then, some day, their books.

Your father was obviously a rare craftsman, he says. We need such people in this part of the world.

She stands and looks out at the ruin of the shop, its vague shapes and shadows taking on harsh edges now in the morning light. She seems taller to him now, unburdened of the night and of her story.

Things can be taken away so quickly, she says. Lost almost before they are found. I thought if I could create something, out of what I've learned . . . But now I think this trade isn't the way, for me.

So, he says quietly, what will you do?

She bends and sifts through the heaped remains of the press.

When the siege ends I will try to get to London, first of all. And then, I don't know.

The colonel buckles on his swordbelt.

Indeed, mademoiselle. Perhaps, when the war is over, I will search for a different way as well. I would very much like to see some of the places you've visited. China. Terra Australis. Uncharted places.

I hope you will, Colonel.

And who knows, perhaps we will meet again somewhere. On the other side of the world.

I would like that.

When she hears the clop of his horse's hooves fading away down the street, she returns to the wreckage of the press. She digs through the jumble of its shattered timbers, finding here and there a few broken shards of Ludwig. An ear. A bit of gold trim from his coat. She lifts the tympan and finds beneath it the head and trunk of the automaton. Miraculously, most of Ludwig is intact. Perhaps he can be repaired, in London, at the Cabinet of Wonders. She sets him aside and continues her search, finally unearthing a tray of type. The sorts, shifted in their compartments, have piled in corners like hillocks of leaden rubble.

She picks through the sorts, searching for accidental exiles in the wrong compartments, returning those that have strayed to their proper places. Her fingers are clumsy with cold, but as she works they warm, and soon she is moving almost at reading speed, barely noting each letter as it passes through her hands. When she is satisfied that all is in order she sweeps the brick dust from her unscathed work table and sets the typecase there.

Before she closes the battered lid, by habit she digs into the pocket of her leather work apron, in search of stray type. She fishes out a *single sort. A blank slug, the last piece of the metallurgist's type. She turns it over in her fingers, examining its absolute, unreadable surface. Gently she shuts the lid of the typecase and closes her fingers around the blank sort. Magpie, she whispers, and smiles. This one bit of metal, infinity in her pocket, she will keep when she leaves here, the beginning of a new collection.*

For the star of the sea and the wise one

ACKNOWLEDGEMENTS

This story is a work of fiction. The characters, including the historical figures, have been imagined.

Many books helped write this one. The art of printing was illuminated by Robert Bringhurst's *The Elements of Typographic Style* (Hartley & Marks, 1996); Elizabeth Eisenstein's *The Printing Press as an Agent of Change* (Cambridge University Press, 1979); and Kristina Johannsen's *Cabinets of Wonder: Nicholas Flood and the Magic of Technology* (Porphyry Press, 1968). The China of this novel was inspired by Cao Xueqin's *The Dream of the Red Chamber* and Wu Ching-Tzu's *The Scholars*. Details of eighteenth-century Canton and the porcelain trade have been adapted from *Chinese Export Porcelain*, by Jean Mudge (Associated University Presses, 1981). Luciano Canfora's *The Vanished Library* (University of California Press, 1989. Trans. Martin Ryle) and E.M. Forster's *Alexandria: A History and Guide* provided threads into that city's labyrinths. The midwife's fairytale on page 115 was adapted from a story in Italo Calvino's *Italian Folktales*. (Pantheon, 1980. Trans. George Martin). The excerpt on pages 128-29 is from *The Adventures of Eovaii*, by Eliza Haywood. The song on page 314 is by Thomas Arne.

The description of the *alam* owes much to "The Book of Sand," a short story by Jorge Luis Borges. The novel that he never wrote was also a great inspiration.

An early version of "The Cage of Mirrors" was included in *Threshold: An Anthology of Contemporary Writing from Alberta*, edited by Srdja Pavlovic (University of Alberta Press, 1999). A version of the "Gardener's Tale" appeared in *Descant* 105, Summer 1999.

Many thanks to Richard Harrison and Peter Oliva for their generous advice and encouragement, and to Aritha van Herk, the ideal reader. A special thank you to Ellen Seligman for her invaluable contributions to this book.

I am grateful to the crew of Pages Books in Calgary, for book talk and lore, and to the crew of NeWest Press for helpful suggestions. Thanks to George Bowering, Peter Ehlers, Jon Kertzer, Pamela McCallum, and Richard Wall; to Maria Batalla, Peter Buck, Anita Chong, Sharon Friedman, Carolyn Ives, Yukiko Kagami, Alberto Manguel, Ibrahim Sumrain, Ralph Vicinanza, and Thomas Wharton Sr.

Thank you, David Arthur, for the hour spent in your wondrous library. And finally, to Sharon Avery, descendant of pirates, boundless gratitude.

A NOTE ON THE TYPE

This book is set using Bembo. The first of the Old Faces is a copy of a roman cut by Francesco Griffo for the Venetian Printer Aldus Manutius. It was first used in Cardinal Bembo's *De Aetna*, 1495, hence the name of the contemporary version. Although a type cut in the fifteenth century for a Venetian printer, it is usually grouped with the Old Faces. Stanley Morison has shown that it was the model followed by Garamond and thus the forerunner of the standard European type of the next two centuries.